AF527668

SAVAGE BLUE

Vikram Balagopal is the author of the award-winning graphic novel *Simian*. Following his training at the New York Film Academy (New York), he has worked in India with various film-makers, and his screenplay was chosen for Mira Nair's Maisha Screenwriter's lab. He is a published poet, illustrator and cartoonist in magazines. His first book, *Simian* (Parts 1 and 2), was published in 2014. He lives in New Delhi.

SAVAGE BLUE

VIKRAM BALAGOPAL

HarperCollins *Publishers* India

First published in India in 2016 by
HarperCollins *Publishers* India

Building 10, Tower A, 4th Floor, DLF Cyber City, Phase II,
Gurugram Haryana – 122002, India
www.harpercollins.co.in

Copyright © Vikram Balagopal 2016
Illustrations and dingbats copyright © Vikram Balagopal 2016

P-ISBN: 978-93-5264-005-8
E-ISBN: 978-93-5264-006-5

2 4 6 8 10 9 7 5 3 1

Vikram Balagopal asserts the moral right
to be identified as the author of this work.

The views and opinions expressed in this book
are the author's own and the facts are as reported by him,
and the publishers are not in any way liable for the same.

This is a work of fiction. Names, characters, places, and incidents are
products of the author's imagination or are used fictitiously and are
not to be considered as real. Any resemblance to actual events, locales,
organizations, or persons, living or dead, is entirely coincidiental.

All rights reserved. No part of this publication may be reproduced,
stored in a retrieval system, or transmitted, in any form or by any means,
electronic, mechanical, photocopying, recording or otherwise,
without the prior permission of the publishers.

Typeset in 11/14 Minion Pro by
R. Ajith Kumar

Printed and bound at
MicroPrints India, New Delhi

For my niece, Anushka

My grandmother, mother and sister
for their love and support

1

IT IS MY RIGHT to make the wrong choice. To take the selfish path and destroy this happiness.

He stood there, on that root as thick as a sturdy oak, and all he could do was bark after passing thoughts like a mutt. Fuck love! Love is a pop-song you tap your foot to for three minutes and then the music stops. The music stopped when she left him there.

A warm scent of maple rose up in the air. The decaying faces of animals and birds gawked at him from under the still water. Fine hair-like tendrils lining the bottom of the roots swung in the breeze, dripping with ooze. The field of giant roots stretched about him in every direction. And atop the twisted mound in the centre, cast against the purple sky like an innocuous stump of broccoli, sat that damn tree. He watched the two distant figures make their ascent and could not contain himself any longer. Shyam let go and the call burst out of him, ringing out her name.

'Akila!'

2

IN AN OLD COLONIAL cottage a ward lies still in the cool Nilgiri night. It has whitewashed walls, dark teak floors and rows of vacant cots. Lifeless as graves, they sit flat and grey in the glow from the lamp post outside. The hazy amber cast of the night-light at the top of the stairs falls through the doorway. All is quiet on the first floor, with slumbering figures in just two of the beds. One by the door. Another by the window in the far corner.

The far one stirs and twists to a melody of twangs from the cot-springs, and the round face of a nine-year-old boy peeks out from among the folds. The close-cropped hair mussed like a carpet trodden upon, and those large piercing eyes, which float above a scattering of chickenpox boils.

There is a shallow hum and a form slides in through the doorway, along the floor. The beds bar the boy's view of it until it slips out of the light. Then it creeps around the foot of the other patient's cot to exit through the crack in the bathroom door. The boy has no time to ponder, for the thing returns and escapes into the corridor. He sits up, his eyes trained on the lighted doorway. Again it comes, hissing and sniffing, and slinks into the bathroom.

The cot by the door shows movement and the boy bites his lip with dread as the sleeper groggily sits up. The thing returns and waits by the foot of the cot. The boy freezes, his mouth agape, volleying from the creature to the imperilled patient. And he sees that the figure is asleep again. But the thing remains still for an entire minute and then two, becoming one with the shadows, before sliding into the corridor once more. Two seconds later, the patient sits bolt upright and a head fringed with a bobby-cut leans into the amber light to look outside.

Then she notices the boy in the distant corner and beckons him closer with a stern flick of the hand. He refuses and slips back under the blanket. But she is adamant, waving emphatically, and the boy finally gives in. He is too excited to ignore the mystery that has him up. He abandons his slippers and tiptoes across the cold floor. The girl flashes a palm for him to halt and flips under the covers. Caught in no man's land, the boy desperately hops onto the nearest cot. He catches a hint of the thing at the doorway and, pushing down flat, clutches the metal frame to dampen the springs. The hissing sounds so close. He cannot understand why he would move closer to the unknown. And yet, when the girl motions him to approach, he obeys like one entranced. He steps cot to cot, not considering the lament of the springs, and the girl orders him to get down. At the emergence of the thing at the bathroom door, he prostrates himself in a flash, enduring the blanket's stubble against his cheek. He recognizes her then as one of his seniors. Her startling eyes are not on him. A dark grey cat with ugly yellow and orange flecks stops between the beds. The crescent apertures of its eyes regard him a moment, and then the girl. They vanish with an eye roll, and with a flick of its tail the cat struts into the corridor.

With a sigh, the boy deflates and swings his legs over to make his way back to his cot. The girl shushes him and he is instructed to observe. She waits in an easy pose in her pink pyjamas littered with smiling bunnies, propping up her attentive chin. The cat returns with a hissing kitten dangling from its jaws. The girl follows them to the bathroom door and opens it wider to get a look inside. She peers back at the boy still seated on the cot, and comes back and tugs him by his wrist. The cat comes out just then and, without so much as a glance in their direction, carries on with its chore. 'What's your name?' the girl asks in a whisper.

'Shyam,' the boy hiccups.

'I don't remember you, what standard are you in?'

'Fourth.'

'Oh!' she says, a little disappointed.

'You're in the fifth, aren't you?'

She nods impatiently because he should know that already.

'What's your name?'

She eyes him suspiciously.

'I told you mine.'

'So?'

He is stumped by her response.

'It's Akila.'

'What?'

'My name, it's Akila.'

Why does that name sound familiar? Just like her face. A fourth kitten is transported into the bathroom. Akila enters after the cat and tugs at Shyam's sleeve to follow. Then it hits him.

'You're Akila Raina, you're the principal's daughter, aren't you?' She gives him a sullen pout streaked with annoyance and tugs him into the bathroom after her.

A faint light streams in through the large windows in the individual stalls. At the row's end a window sits open to the night air. On seeing the cat hop out over the sill, they rush to it. The sill is chest-high for them and they peer over it, watching the cat glide down a narrow wooden staircase badly in need of repair. They exchange chickenpox-marred smiles, their shoulders nudging one another with glee. In the pre-dawn glow, the cat cuts across the garden into the shadows at the tree line and they can barely make out the kitten being deposited in a pit there. Shyam feels the girl's pox-blistered hand take his and he catches a flash of her eyes, the colour of sun-baked granite. Neither of them notice the cat coming up onto the landing. Only when it hops between them is the spell undone, and they hurry, blushing all the way to the door to wait for the next kitten.

'What's her name?' Akila wonders.

'I've heard the nurses call her Mush.' Shyam shrugs hesitantly.

'Mush!' the young girl tries out the name.

Mush saunters in with the fifth kitten and the children follow at a respectable distance. It pops out the window and they go to watch it make the trip through the garden again. Instead, they are surprised to find Mush waiting on the landing outside, scrupulously cleaning its paws. It licks the kitten's head, inspects it for two seconds, gives it another lick, and looks up at the ogling faces. The tongue curls, licking its snout, a feminine voice comes out. 'I think you two should follow me. It's dangerous to stay here any longer.'

The children stare back at her stupidly.

'If you're coming, come now. But don't say I didn't warn you,' Mush adds, with a solemn wag of her tail. Then, she picks up the kitten and slides gracefully down the weatherworn steps. Shyam turns to Akila to tell her he may be coming down with a high fever, but she is already halfway over the windowsill.

'What are you doing?'

'Didn't you hear Mush? It's dangerous. Something's about to happen.'

'You heard the cat too?'

Huffing impatiently, she hauls the shorter boy by his pyjama collar. 'I'm coming, I'm coming,' he groans, and follows Akila onto the landing. The wooden steps creak under their combined fifty kilos, as they chase after Mush's nervous tail flicking among the saplings, to a pit holding the other kittens.

'What is going to happen?' Akila asks, trembling with a cocktail of excitement, fear and adrenalin.

An ear-splitting crack tears through the dawn. There is a crash some distance away, large enough to scatter great chunks of dirt and debris, prompting Mush to admit, 'What I was afraid of.' Though no one is listening at this point. Another crash follows, and then another, the last of which feels too close for comfort. 'Pick up my kittens and follow me. We have to get to a safe place!' The two children gawk at her and then at the dust plumes rising from the persistent impacts.

In an unexpected moment of hush, a faint whistle slices through, and the earth quakes in a vortex of flying dirt and debris, swallowing the small hospital. The children are sent flailing to the ground. The little boy brushes the soil from his face. He feels Akila's fingers claw into his shoulder and he looks up. Amidst the hospital wreckage there lies a colossal stonehand, its petrified fingers hooked in agony.

—And then?

—That's where it always stops. I've had this dream before. I've told you, I've had this dream before.

—Really?

—Yes. I know I've told you. It's not something you'd keep from your psychologist.

—Okay, but have you had it frequently?

—No. The last time was … you know, it was a while ago. I mean, it must have been eight months.

—Okay. And the time before that?

—What the – I don't keep track of when and where it occurs. It's infrequent, but when it does happen, it goes on every night for a few days. I don't know why. I used to have it a lot when I was seventeen, eighteen, nineteen. Yeah, and not everyday, but it used to come every once in a while. And then it stopped. It's come every couple of years after that.

—Is there some stress in your life right now, to have brought it on?

—(Laughing) There's always stress in my life.

—I don't mean work, but in your personal life. Anything you want to talk about?

—I wouldn't say my personal life is stressful…

—Okay, so something did happen.

—Well, it's kind of 'happening'.

—Why don't you catch me up on what's 'happened' so far?

—How much time do I have left today?

—Another half hour.

—Good. So, we went out.

—Tell me about that.

—How can I put this – yup, it was the worst date of my life and I don't think I'm far off the mark if I add that it was probably just as bad for her.

'AKILA, YOU look … stunning.'

'Stunning's a good word.'

She stood beaming before Shyam, a little awkwardly it seemed, and yet enchanting with her flowing black hair curling about her bare shoulders. The dress teased with a glimpse of athletic cleavage and hung no lower than mid-thigh. A satin collar wrapped tightly around her slender neck. A large, exotic flower sat in her hair above her right ear and she drew him in with a flash of her sun-baked granite eyes.

Flowers had always unnerved Shyam, since the time he had presented a girl with a handful of red lettuce. So he avoided commenting on the blossom all night, with its blood-red feathery stamen.

After a while, he led Akila up a narrow flight of stairs into the restaurant. They had picked it at random, having strolled along either side of GK-1's N-Block Market, and without a reservation they were relegated to seats at the bar.

The waiter pulled back the raised barstools and Shyam helped Akila mount her seat. Then he stepped up the foot-bar to hop onto his with some flair. The brass rod gave way and he tumbled backwards, sending his barstool clanging enthusiastically on the black stone floor. Amused diners interrupted their meals and observed him over their poised forks, as he floundered on the floor attempting to prop up the heavy seat, managing at last with the help of the smirking waiter.

—Well, you know – she had emailed me.

—Who?

—Akila.

—Wait, is this the same Akila from the dream?

—Yeah, didn't I mention that?

—No.

—Oh.

—When did she email you?

—We hadn't been in touch since school. So when she emailed me around a month ago it was totally out of the blue. We're not friends on any of the social sites, I don't even know how she got my email, but there it was.

To: ShyamB.in3d@shyamb.com
From: Akila.RRRaina@Akila.com
Woooooh!!

Shyam!!! Guess who! This is Akila Raina from school! So what's new with you??? X-D

Akila

—Were you two close in school?
—We hardly spoke.
—But from the email, it sounds like she thinks of you as a friend.
—I have no idea ... frankly, I thought I'd just see where it was going.

To: Akila.RRRaina@Akila.com
From: ShyamB.in3d@shyamb.com
Hey Akila,

It's been years! I'm a freelance 3D modeller based in Delhi. Not much else to report really. What about you?

Take care.

Shyam

To: ShyamB.in3d@shyamb.com
From: Akila.RRRaina@Akila.com
Wooooh!!!

Sounds exciting!!! But I meant the more meaty stuff like relationship status, silly! Ne ways, I'll be in Delhi in a month's time and I'd love to meet up!!!

(What does 'take care' mean anyway? =P)

Akila xox

To: Akila.RRRaina@Akila.com
From: ShyamB.in3d@shyamb.com
Hey Akila,

That's great! I look forward to seeing you then.

As for relationships, I'm not in one right now. My work keeps me too busy to socialize. You could say I'm in a relationship with my work, haha. It's not like I'm lonely or anything, I'm waiting for the right time, when my work settles down and I can relax a little. On the plus side, work's going well :-)

Take it easy.
Shyam

To: ShyamB.in3d@shyamb.com
From: Akila.RRRaina@Akila.com
Woooooh!!!

Booooorrrringgg!!! I can't believe you're staying holed up in your office all day, everyday!!! Work blahblahblah!!! Live a little!!! I'll show you how to have fun when I get there!!!! I'm single too!!! Broke up with a guy a week back!! We had been going out for four years, but I realized that he didn't really know me. He thought I was this 'perfect perfectly perfect' girl and so does everybody else. And I can't find anyone to talk to about all the bullshit! That's why I'm glad I'm getting to come to Delhi for a while. I just want to get away from this entire scene where I feel like I'm pretending to be something I'm not, you know?

(Seriously? Take it easy? You are cordially invited to enter this millennium, Mr Shyam!)

Akila xox

—And the emails got longer from there.

—That is good, isn't it?
—It was...

SHYAM WATCHED the lime wedge sink to the bottom of his lager with a trail of bubbles. Akila sipped her pink cocktail, smacked her lips and daintily downed the entire glass. He watched her slide it over the bar and their eyes met for a lingering moment of awkwardness as her drink was poured from the mixer.

'Would you like a taste?' She inched the cocktail glass towards him with a finger on its foot. He shrugged and nodded and smiled all at once and reached for it, knocking its frosty pink contents all over her lap.

—How well did you know each other in school?
—We didn't. We were never close in school. She was a year senior and after the 'incident' in the hospital, I'd only seen her around, and sometimes she'd discreetly wave to me, but nothing more. I was always so intimidated and shy (chuckling), that I'd blush and hurry on. She was after all the principal's daughter, that's like the school princess. I had always assumed that was why she did not have any friends. And ... since she was a year older, there weren't many situations for us to ... mingle.

WORK, OR the manner in which Shyam worked, had perverted his routine into something an astronaut might follow, where the position of the sun did not matter. He worked late into the night till anywhere around 5 a.m. and woke up past noon around 12.30. He could not recall how his routine had desynchronized to this degree, but all he knew was that it did not seem to be moving any further along, dashing his hopes that eventually his routine might right itself through a solstice, welcoming him back to the real world.

His phone rang shrilly five inches from his ear. It was 7.30 a.m. 'Hello,' he heard the voice say, and his heart skipped a beat. Eighteen years since he had last heard it outside of his dreams, and though it had matured, with that distinctive bite to every 'T' and the melody to the vowels, he knew at once that it was her.

'Hello,' he said, and held his breath.

'Hi.'

'Yes?' It was his phone-manner to always inquire even when he knew who it was, and it got on the nerves of more than a few people.

'It's Akila Raina. Remember, I said I'd be coming to Delhi?'

'Oh, hey, yeah, hi, Akila, how've you been?' he said, affecting enthusiasm to counter his grogginess.

There was a moment of hesitation from her side and then she said, 'Hey', singing it as girls do sometimes. 'Guess what, I'm in Delhi! Why don't we meet up?'

'Yeah!'

He slapped his forehead for yelping like a schoolboy.

'I want to take you out to dinner, Thursday night. Are you a free man, Mr Shyam?'

He sat up in bed, his eyelids weighing a ton while he tried to figure out what the hell was happening. Am I still in the 'dream'? He had dreamt of her just the other night and now here she was, eighteen years older, but here she was.

'Yeah, yeah, sure. Thursday, that's good for me.'

'Great, I'll give you a call Thursday morning and we'll figure out the details.'

'Yeah, but–' The line clicked and the call disconnected as he trailed off, muttering, 'What the–?'

AKILA TOOK a sip of her blue cocktail, her eyes twinkling unsteadily like a distant flame. 'So tell me about what you do.'

'It's not very exciting,' he replied glumly.

She laughed out loud. 'Oh, come on. What is it that you do all day, Mr Shyam?'

'I make 3D models of things, anything really, but it's usually architectural. I've even done blood cells for a medical company–'

'Do you work for some firm?'

'No, I'm a freelancer. I work for whoever hires me for a particular project.'

'What does that mean in this case?'

'I work at home.'

'Oh, that must be fun! You can sit in your underwear and watch porn while you work,' she remarked, louder than necessary.

Shyam sneaked a timid glance around the restaurant. Her intoxication hadn't gone unnoticed. He lowered his voice in an effort to counter her exclamations. 'Not entirely. For many jobs, yes, but for some I have to go and work at their office with my comp until the assignment is done.'

'What?' she snapped. 'Why are you whispering?'

—The hospital featured in your dream, was it the same as the one you had in school?
—Yes, pretty much.
—Even the cat?
—Yup, same ugly cat.
—Is this dream based on an actual event?
—What do you mean? The giant hand falling from the sky?
—No, did you in fact get chickenpox when you were there?
—Yeah, in my first year. I was nine.

—See, so there is some truth.
—Yeah, it is kind of based on a freaky incident…
—Oh?
—I guess that's why I never questioned the dream, when I had it earlier, because of what happened. I figured this was my brain's way of trying to make sense of what had happened.
—What exactly did happen?
—I'm sure I've told you.
—No, no, if you keep all the juicy stuff to yourself, how can I help?
—No? I haven't mentioned it?
—I have to admit, you've mentioned the dream before, but you never shared its significance. That it's based on something that really happened to you. Tell me about it.
—Well, I guess the first half of the dream is pretty much as it happened.
—Why were you two kept alone in the same ward?
—In boarding school there are seasons of illnesses when a chunk of the school catches the bug in a wave. With chickenpox, the first week is fever, where you're stuck sleeping day and night. Once you're over that, you've pretty much recovered, except for the itchy chickenpox boils all over your body. And soon, what we had was a ward full of nine to eleven-year-old boys who were 'otherwise fine', instructed to stay in bed all day. It was great fun. We had to stay quiet for most of the time, but we'd still whisper loudly across the room.

There was no TV, and in the evenings the fun really started. An ancient speaker hanging on the wall at one end of the ward would stutter alive at 6 p.m., and we'd have an hour of old Hindi and English songs. I was nine, I didn't know what old or new music was. Who knew music can grow old? And they were fun rockin' numbers, the likes of Chuck Berry, Jerry

Lee Lewis and Neal Sedaka. We'd hop up on our beds playing air-guitar with combs, mouthing the words and twisting our bodies. The heavy footsteps of Nurse Decker coming up the wooden staircase had us diving under the covers, making our beds bounce loudly, lying there thinking we'd fooled her. Of course, she knew what we were up to. Little boys never change, and she'd been there for decades.

The only other distraction was reading and the selection of books was limited, to say the least. We had to rotate them among ourselves when we were done because they said anything we touched had to be burnt to kill the chickenpox virus. And pretty soon we were done with all the books. I was thrice befuddled by Lorna Doone, and I've never attempted it since.

Then, rather abruptly, kids' parents began showing up and taking them home. The first day, two were gone, then one, and I grew excited at the prospect of going home. I had my toothbrush, toothpaste, soapbox and mug packed and the next day three more boys left. The day after, the rest were gone, leaving me sitting on my cot with my drawstring toilet bag on my lap, looking up that garden path for my parents to turn the corner. They would bring the love and broad smiles that a nine- year-old boy two months away from home hungers to see. Sweeter than the milkiest chocolate bar or softest oven-fresh cake.

I spent that night alone in the ward, eyes burning with thick tears and curled into a ball under the blankets, all because the note from school to my parents had got lost in the mail. And it was the same for the next two days.

By then all the girls with chickenpox had also been picked up, leaving only poor old Akila, the principal's daughter, behind. The nurses decided that it would be easier for them if the only two children left with chickenpox were kept in a single ward. And so this rosy-cheeked ten-year-old Kashmiri girl with her heart-shaped face dragged her feet heavily into the room and regarded me, a dark little Malayali boy sitting at the far corner, over a suppressed bottom-lip.

She tossed her toilet bag and mug onto the cot by the door, which just happened to be the one furthest from me, and with a strained sigh to mask a sob, she rushed into the bathroom, shutting the door behind her.

ONE NEW *message.* He touched the flashing icon to open it.

> *HELP MEE!!!!!!*
> ***sent at 10.53 p.m.***

Shyam had sent it to himself a moment ago. There was nothing else to do, with Akila leaning over the counter, staring into the drink she was lazily stirring with a cherry. The previous messages in his inbox read:

> *It's been more than five minutes already and she is still just sitting there!!!!!*
> ***sent at 10.48 p.m.***

> *She is just sitting there!! I have stopped drinking for the night! May never drink again! The bartender and manager are staying away from us!!!*
> ***sent at 10.44 p.m.***

> *She has finally shut up and she is sitting quietly. A little too still and quiet. Will observe the subject. I don't know what she*

is capable of. Dating is stressful!!!
sent at 10.41 p.m.

Hey Shyam!!!!!! Almost there ... another five minutes tops! Delhi Traffic!!!!! Looking forward to tonite!!!!!! Wooooh!!!! – Akila
sent at 8.17 p.m.

HE CHECKED her message one last time to be sure.

N-Block Market, Greater Kailash 1,
7.30 p.m. Can't wait!!!!! Yay!!!!!
sent at 1.23 p.m.

The full-length mirror had not seen much use in the two years since he had bought it. For a good three minutes, Shyam turned this way and that, checking his bum and the thrust of his stomach. Travelling up to his face, he confronted equal parts of both parents gazing back at him. His hair was perfectly set with a neat side parting, but no matter how much he tried, he could not smooth down the protesting tuft towards the back. He felt for his phone and wallet in his pockets. Check. His shoes looked clean. His breath – he popped a wince-inducing mint-flavoured lozenge into his mouth. What else? This was as good as it got for him. He nodded his satisfaction, clicked his heels and made for the door.

He held it open, poised with his finger on the light switch, racking his brain for anything he might have forgotten.

'Akila must not be disappointed' was the mission brief. He counted the cash in his wallet. It may not be enough.

He went to his desk drawer and took the last few notes he kept aside for emergencies. Just in case. And then it hit him.

He checked his watch and ran to his bedside table, pulling out the drawers and pushing aside the phone chargers, business cards and takeaway menus. It lay to one side, the sealed box of condoms. But for the odd fling, it had been years since he'd had a chance to use them. They were not his usual variety and he could not recollect when he had purchased them.

At the door, he patted the three he had slipped into his back pocket, wondering why he had bought ribbed. Double the pleasure, double the fun.

THE MANAGER handed the leather-bound folder to his bartender, keeping a safe distance from them. Akila had not shifted from her assumed position. The cherry stirred a full glass. The folder was discreetly slid to Shyam, and before he could open it to attend to the bill, the bartender was at the far end wiping a glass to calm his nerves. Shyam's eyes dropped down the short list and gulped at the total. There had to be some mistake. All they had were some drinks and snacks, not even dinner. No, there was no mistake in the sum. He nervously pulled out his wallet, and bit his lip when he saw that with every note accounted for, he was still a thousand rupees short.

He smiled jovially at the bartender. He cc-ed the smile to the manager and leaned close to Akila. Sustaining the god-awful smile, he whispered to her, 'Akila, could I borrow–'. Then all of a sudden he sat straight up, his face glowing with revelation. He reached into the traitorous wallet and brandished his credit card like a divine talisman. He reserved it for online payments, and with it hidden behind his metro card, it had slipped his mind completely. Replacing the cash with the card he sat back, the burden of further humiliation lifted. She could have at least offered to go dutch. The bartender returned with the card and Shyam graciously accepted it. 'Where do I sign?'

'Your card doesn't work, sir.' Any sympathy the bartender had for him had evaporated.

'Oh.' Shyam handed over all the cash, along with the card, urging, 'Charge the card whatever is left over, after the cash.'

'You don't understand. Your card does not work. Not at all.'

'What?'

'It has expired,' the man announced funereally, a finger thrust at the embossed digits. Shyam stared in horror, masked by calm confusion. 'I see. Will you give me a minute, please?' The bartender returned to the far end of the bar and watched him grimly with folded arms. The manager assumed his post by the entrance. Shyam leaned close to Akila again. 'Akila, could I borrow some money?'

THEY MADE their way to the small park bisecting the market. It was quiet at this time of the night. Cars were still parked along the street and a couple loitered at the corner cigarette-wallah. Akila appeared sullen as they sauntered across the street to the park's iron turnstile. Her lithe strides wiped the awful night from Shyam's mind and all he saw was the hint of sadness behind her stoic gaze.

The trees in the park chittered with a cool breeze, breaking the stillness. He wanted to see her again, but he knew that would never happen. Not after the catastrophe that was tonight, and worst of all she would never forget that he was there to witness it and play a part too. He felt compelled to hug her then, and forgetting all form, he took her into his arms and embraced her. He felt her hug him back. Her fingers clawed into him and she pushed her face into the curve of his neck. A brief flutter of wind had her glance past his shoulder at the trees behind.

'The wind usually picks up in Delhi before it rains,' he remarked, rejuvenated.

'It won't rain tonight.'

'I have a taxi waiting for me, I can drop you where you need to go.'

'Don't worry, I've got a way to get back home.'

He took in her pretty face, smooth and defined in the moonlight, those warm granite eyes boring into him.

'It was great,' he lied. 'It was a ...' He stopped himself from saying 'disaster', even in jest. 'It was great,' he said beaming, with irony in his brows.

'It was...'

'Goodnight, Akila.'

'Goodnight, Shyam.'

He leaned in to kiss her cheek and she pushed up, and their lips caught each other on a corner. They lingered for a moment and then withdrew. She returned the smile, though again he sensed the sadness. She turned and pushed past the turnstile into the darkness draping the park. A gust of dusty wind had him covering his face. He thought, it will definitely rain tonight.

—And I got home feeling like shit and it was not her fault. It was not. I'm twenty-nine. What the fuck have I done to earn my place in this world?

—You're doing what everybody does. You're working – living your life.

—I want more. I want to do something. And more than that, I want to have done something. Do you know what I mean? Even if all that is left is an Ozymandias ruin, I want to have struck this planet with a brand and left my mark. I don't want to be stuck in my room for the rest of my stupid little life or even do what every other bugger does – work, cum on tits and crap!

—What kind of life do you want?

—The kind I can proudly display and tell everyone about.

The kind that feels wasted if it isn't displayed. I want to live a Facebook life.

BILLOWS OF dust churn in the twilight air. A giant stone hand lies amidst the ruins of the old hospital cottage. The children stare at it in equal parts wonder and horror. 'You're wasting time. It's dangerous,' Mush appeals to them. She meows grumpily and picks a kitten up in her jaws. Shyam and Akila carry a wriggling kitten in each hand and follow the ugly cat into the thick coniferous woods sparkling with quivering morning dew, as impacts resonate in the distance.

—That same night I had 'the dream' again.

—That was to be expected, considering the night you had. Although I would have expected the meeting to perhaps have acted as a catalyst for closure to the adolescent fantasy. And then perhaps the dream would have stopped altogether.

—Well, it didn't. It got longer and now there's more to it.

—Is there anything at all you haven't told me about what really happened? After you two watched the cat carry out the kittens, did you go back to sleep?

—There is one thing. It's odd, but when I think back to my chickenpox episode, I remember playing air guitar on the cots, and the night with Akila and the cat, but what never turns up is the incident that marked the rest of my schooldays with the occasional whisper and curious stare. I think the teachers decided to keep it a secret, but these things have a way of popping their ugly heads out from time to time as some distorted rumour. And then they are forgotten for some time again.

—Do you remember what happened?

—My memory is clear all the way until that moment I was with

Akila at the bathroom window, watching Mush take the kitten through the garden. From that point, it is either blank or void, completely, as though there is nothing I can even reach for.

—What is the next thing you remember?

—Waking up in the hospital bed on a drip, surrounded by teachers and policemen.

—Policemen? What happened?

—Apparently, we had been missing from the hospital for three days, and there had been a massive search conducted on the roads and through the woods. They had no clue where we were. We were discovered unconscious in a clearing, deep in the forest. I couldn't remember what had happened so the general consensus was that we had gotten disorientated playing in the woods and lost consciousness after more than two days without food. They didn't give me any details. I was nine. I was sent to a psychologist in Ooty everyday until they were satisfied and then sent home for the chickenpox, though they let me stay home until the semester was over and through the holidays, and I had to return to school only four months later. I get this strong taste in my mouth of bitter gourd just thinking about it.

—What is it?

—I remember them pumping something out of my stomach into a pan. That's the taste. When they pulled the tube out I saw the pan was full of water as though I had drowned.

—And what happened to Akila?

—The same thing, I suppose. I saw her around after that but like I said, we never became friends.

—Did you have a crush on her?

—I suppose I did. But—

—We don't have much time left. Tell me about this extended dream.

THE GRASS is crisp and wet with dew under their naked feet. The kittens have settled down and no longer hiss as the children hurry uphill. Mush is a blur of feet, leading them up the winding path and every couple of minutes she pauses for a sound that does not belong, or a stretch of silence amidst the explosions. Her ears prick up and her flashing eyes pierce the emerald shadows of moss and fern, through a veil of drizzling dew from a shockwave.

The children stumble over slippery rocks and help each other up, the shockwaves mere pulses amidst the raging heartbeats thundering in their ears. They arrive at a sheer rock face capped by a large boulder ten feet above. Mush climbs halfway up and stands at the edge, looking back across the valley. The kitten in her mouth grows restless. Shyam turns and gasps at the sight. Akila backs against the rock wall, unwilling to believe her eyes. The whole expanse of rolling hills before them is marked with craters. Familiar buildings are gouged with great blocks of stone heads and limbs. Her eyes flood with tears and she turns her face up to the sky, screaming. A block of stone hurtles towards them, striking the tree line above the capped boulder. The hill shudders at the impact and Akila cries out, 'Where is the sun?' As though its rays would wake her from this nightmare.

Mush hops down and places the kitten in a deep cavity between the rocks. 'Here,' she tells the children. 'Drop them in here.' Akila kneels by the hole and places the kittens into a foot-deep chamber that will keep them from wandering out. With the kittens safely stowed away, Mush turns to the two children. 'Come now, follow me!' She regards them and then the small opening where her kittens mewl sensing her presence, and back at the frightened faces of the little boy and girl in her care. A nimble spring and she is racing through the brush with the children following hand in hand.

They wind their way down and around the hill into an unfamiliar valley on the far side. The thickets beat their tear-smeared faces as they rush out into the clearing along the valley. Mush follows a narrow stream with the children growing breathless after their dash downhill. They begin to slow and then stop, crumpling to the ground with burning lungs and gashed feet. Mush returns and urges them on. 'We're almost there. Please get up. Just a little more.'

'Where are you taking us?'

'Some place safe for you.'

'What place can be safe from this?' cries Akila, her arms spread to encompass the apocalyptic scene.

'Please trust me, child. Now on your feet, time is running out!'

The children exchange an exhausted look but nod, helping each other up. The earth shatters ahead, flinging them back onto the ground with dirt raining upon them. A fragment of a colossal torso rocks into stillness with the sound of grinding stone. Mush rolls onto her feet, shouting, 'Hurry now!' She rushes headlong up the stream, hopping inside the hollow torso and exiting through it. Akila grabs Shyam's hand and they follow. The stone trunk pitches with their weight and they hesitate before leaping into the forest beyond.

The dawn light filters through the dense brush. Solitary bands of lustrous light catch the dancing water particles above the bubbling stream. The rocks become larger and covered in moss and they help each other up and over. Mush hops onto the next boulder and waits impatiently. Her head twists about to scrutinize the obscure forest. 'Just a little more.'

They no longer have the strength to say, 'You keep saying

that.' The impacts besiege them like artillery bombardment and their minds can do nothing but focus on the next step. Until finally, beyond an enormous boulder, they arrive at a shallow pool. The water is pristine, presenting a bed of polished cobble. It leads to a tunnel of reeds forming a dark cavern. Mush tensely watches the children pant out their exertion. 'You can rest soon. We just have to enter the tunnel.'

'Are you sure we'll be safe there?' asks Akila.

'I am.'

'Then why didn't we bring your kittens here as well?' Akila takes Shyam's hand protectively.

'They're safe in that hole. If the rest of us could have fit in there, we would have stayed.'

'Why did we go there at all, instead of coming straight here with the kittens?'

Mush tilts her head, seemingly confused. 'I was in a panic, I didn't think it through. Now please, children, carry me across the water and we'll be safe.'

Akila is not convinced and begins to argue. 'I still–' but she is silenced by Shyam squeezing her hand. He picks up the cat and they slide down the side of the boulder. The cobbles are slick in the water and every step must be taken with care. Mush's tail wags with agitation as they wade closer to the sinister tunnel. The water feels colder when they enter the reed archway. The air pricks their skin with an uneasy chill. Their breathing and the troubled water echo in the passage. They come through it into a dimly lit domed space around the base of a large tree.

'You heard my call,' a deep rumbling voice declares from the shadows.

'The world is crumbling. Only because the world is crumbling,' Mush calls out.

'But you came.'

'Only because–'

There comes a groan like crushed gravel.

Akila's fingers dig into Shyam's hand. A shape stirs among the shadows and comes towards them. It stands like a man but moves along the uneven floor with a hypnotic grace. In the razor thin strips of light Shyam can see the roots wrapping its body. The head has no face, only a mouth. It is not built like a man, but a weak imitation only successful when obscured in the shade. It approaches them without a word and swings its right arm. Something glints in an arc. And silence falls. For the first time in what feels like forever, Shyam can hear no explosions around him. Shrouded in the abrupt tranquillity, he watches Akila's head drop backward and hang from her neck, almost completely severed.

—It's a fascinating glimpse into your subconscious.

—I know that!

—What do you think it means?

—You're the psychologist and you're asking me?

—It's your head, Shyam. No matter how much you tell me about yourself, there is no one who can understand you better than yourself.

—Then what's the point of coming to you?

—That's up to you. If you think I'm not helping you in any way, you are free not to come here anymore.

—Okay, okay, I'm kidding. But there's more to what happened that night.

—How recent was this? The past couple of days?

—Yeah, and I was sitting up in bed, when there was a knock–

—Shyam, I'm afraid our time's up for today.

—But—

—I look forward to our session next week. You can tell me then.

—But I—
—I'm sorry, my next client is already waiting outside.
—Oh, all right.
—Goodbye, Shyam.
—Thanks. Bye...

3

'AKILA!'

Shyam waved his arms frantically to get her attention. At the base of the mound, he saw the two figures stop. And he was off, scurrying up and down and under the huge tangled roots, using his arms to push off or pull his body up and over. The roots were coated with crusty lichen, alternating between rough patches and soft fuzz. He switched roots to keep his path aligned and went up and under another, and down all the way to the water surface, the route not quite dipping below. The lichen was damp and he felt his feet skidding to the sides. Up a few feet and suddenly right down into the water, and the only hope he had was to leap recklessly. A tube of root rose out of the water, close enough for him to make it without getting a toe wet, and he clambered up the twisting path. He hopped over one, cutting through, and when he emerged at the top level again, he shook his head with relief. Another root lay across his path and he vaulted over it but found no footing on the other side. He got a hard bump on his rear and slid down with both legs precariously to one side, trying to steady himself with his hands grating like cheese over the surface. The end of the slide dipped into the water. He prepared for it and twisted his body, thrusting his feet ahead of him. He coiled his muscles for the right moment and an instant before the water came up, he pushed down on the balls of his feet with all his might and sprang towards a hump of root. The evasion passed him through a curtain of tendrils. It slimed past his face and he lost all sense of orientation.

The landing was awkward and he clung on, his arms throbbing with the adrenalin. His feet were in the water, halfway up to his shins. It was all he could do to keep from falling in entirely. He crept to his feet and started up the meandering root to the top, made all the harder by the slime on his legs. He was approaching the base of the mound, leading up to the tree. He could not see Akila anymore. A strip of lichen slid under his foot and he fell to the side. He saw a root he might reach, if he could just push off with a foot. He managed the push, but it was not enough.

He knew the instant before that he was a fraction short, and the impact to the side of his face and chest left no prospect of holding on. He was not aware of his body doing cartwheels in the air before he hit the water. He bobbed in and out of consciousness, the sky flashing crimson and then ginger and a dull turquoise, and returned to the dense tangle of roots with patches of lavender hue for sky. He knew what had happened, even as his cognizance teetered on the edge, with the fluid filling his nostrils, mouth and ears. And then he was terrified because he did not know what was going to happen.

HIS MIND reeled through an inky blackness, a field of stars surrounding him like a school of sardines, their brightness dimming and lighting up with an intensity that burnt his eyes as they shot past in white streaks.

AND THERE he was again in his bedroom, after that terrible dream with Akila's head hanging off her neck. The sheets and pillow were damp with sweat.

Shyam sat hunched over, holding his head, a strangled murmur expressing his alarm. The ceiling fan stirred the thick air and it was a blessing against his skin. He felt awake, and right then it felt like the most important thing in the world. Stay awake. There were three knocks on the window. The damn pigeons would sit on the sill outside and coo, or beat the glass at all hours. But they had never knocked before.

The canvas blinds at the window glowed somberly in the light from the streetlamp. He was three floors up and his only other suspect was a squirrel. Probably the one that chewed holes in the underwear he hung out to dry. 'Shoo,' he coughed from the bed, scratching his groin. Another three knocks sounded. 'Shoo, damn you, shoo!'

'No, I'm not shooing, so you better open up and let me in.'

'What the–?'

Shyam hopped to the window and jerked the blinds aside. Akila beamed at him through the glass, her elbows on the sill, streetlamp blazing behind her like a lopsided halo. 'So are you going to let me in?' He unlocked the window and swung it open. 'You know, if someone saw you climbing a ladder up my building in the middle of the night, you'd get into deep shit.'

Her feet were bare and her hair was manic as she shoved her way past. 'Don't worry about it,' she mumbled and encircled his head in her arms. She thrust her mouth against his. It hurt like hell but he hugged her back, pulling her body in with a ferocity he had never let loose before. One hand clutched the back of her head and the other travelled around her back and lifted her. Her legs wrapped around him and he eased her onto the mattress, his pelvis grinding hers as they lived off each other's breath. They were lost in the dry thrusts, grasping at buttocks and licking down necks, her chest pressed against his. He deftly undid her buckle and stole his hand into her panties. She dragged down his shorts and stroked his erection in a frenzy. He tugged at her jeans and got one leg free. Her panties were pushed to the side and she guided him inside her. The bed shuddered as they thrust, mouth to mouth, rolling over in wet passion, sucking the essence out of the other's skin. Kicking off the quilt with legs stretched out in the grasp of ecstasy. Dripping with his sweat and hers, his heart near bursting, Shyam suddenly broke free of the spell and pulled out, just as he came over and over on her stomach. Breathless, he leaned into her and let their sopping wet bodies cling to each other. Until they recovered from the storm and became aware of the fan and the streetlight, and the world again.

DROWNING. So helpless and afraid. He was not alone.

AKILA WAS on his bed in her crumpled kurta. Her legs were folded Indian style and she beamed at him once more. 'Seriously, that was a crazy thing to do,' he was saying, leaning against the wall by the open window. 'Seriously, I had to do it,' she retorted.

He had slipped on his shorts but she stayed as she was.

'Well, I don't hear any sirens, I guess, so … what is this?' he asked.

She said, 'I just had to see you.'

'You have my number.'

'There's a lot to say.'

'Phones are good for that.'

'This has to be done face-to-face, for you to believe me.'

He hesitated. 'Does this have to do with what happened in the school hospital?'

She leaned on her hands, hopeful. 'You remember?'

Shyam tried to read her face but all he registered was flashes of cleavage, so apparent in her kurta with its buttons undone. He slid down to the floor and sat against the wall. He looked up at her and admitted, 'I don't. I just keep having wacky dreams about it, about us.'

'Oh? What kind of dreams?'

'That doesn't matter. What did you want to say about it?'

'No, tell me about your dreams.'

'They're really out there.'

'Good.'

'What do you mean?'

'You don't know how much it means to me to see you again.'

He eyed her sceptically, hungry again for her but confused. 'Really?'

'You don't understand, do you? And then to embarrass myself as I did at the restaurant tonight!'

'Hey, it wasn't that bad. I embarrassed myself too.'

'You were great!'

'Now I know there's something fishy going on. What is this about?'

'You won't believe me.'

'You won't know until you try.'

'Okay.' She wiped her right eye and sat up straight. 'Shyam, I'm dead ... or something like it.'

A FLASH of stars whirled past. The cold touched every sense.

AKILA EXPECTED the grin.

'Don't tell me you're part of a zombie cult,' Shyam chuckled, trying on the joke. She lay on her stomach at the corner of the bed. Searching his eyes, she pressed on. 'Tell me about this dream.'

'It's just a dream.'

'Then why does it matter? Tell me about it.'

He blushed in the dim light and from her smirk he thought she could tell.

He told her, 'We were in the hospital, one night we saw the cat taking her kittens to the bathroom, we followed, and saw her taking them out the window.'

'And?'

He shifted uneasily. 'You'll think I'm nuts.'

'Believe it or not, I'm hoping you are, a little.'

'Why?'

'So you'll believe me.'

'I'm sure I'm more than a little nuts. After all, I just had a girl climb up to my window and I let her in without any sweet talk. And I let her fuck me.'

Akila laughed, a little self-consciously. 'Go on. What happened after that?'

'Wait a minute,' he said, 'you were there too, what do you remember?'

'I'm not the one having "wacky dreams" about it.'

'Okay, you win. This is the dream, so bear that in mind when you're judging my sanity.'

'Oh, it's going to be a while before the question of your sanity even arises.'

'Haha, very funny. All right, so, then the cat turns to us and starts talking. She asks us to get out of the hospital fast, and we do, and right then a giant stone-hand falls from the sky. We've barely escaped, and the cat asks us to follow her if we want to stay alive. All the time stuff is falling from the sky and there are massive explosions everywhere. We run and run through the forest, stash the kittens and then run some more. The cat takes us to this eerie tree. Where – yup, that's about it.'

She studied him for a while. Then, in a sombre tone, she probed, 'There's more, isn't there?'

He shrugged and resumed, 'So we're at the tree and a creature comes to us, and ... basically cuts your head off.'

'You remember all this?'

'Considering I had the dream for the first time, well the extended unrated cut at least, barely ten minutes ago, it's hard to forget.'

She considered his reply. 'What do you remember from school after that?'

'You mean, of the incident?'

'The incident?' She paused. 'Yes, yes, the incident. What do you remember?'

'They found us in a clearing. We had been missing for three days. Apparently we'd gone wandering in the forest and gotten lost.'

'And what do you think happened to me?'

'I think we were in the hospital together after that, weren't we? Recovering, and then, well, nothing happened. We went back to school and that was it.'

'What if I told you I didn't come out of the forest alive? They didn't find "us", they found you. I died and my body was never found.'

'Wow! You're morbid, man.'

'That's what really happened.'

'Who are you trying to kid? You're sitting right in front of me. We just tore my bed apart.'

'Yeah, that's a little harder to explain.' She gazed out the window with a grin, saying, 'You let me in ... take a look out the window and tell me what you see.'

Shyam frowned with mock reluctance. 'Is it necessary?'

'Please, it'll help. At least, I hope so.'

He rose to his feet and peered out at the intense street lamp. A narrow lane ran by the building. Across it, in an empty lot, stood a creature seventy-five feet tall, staring cynically at the light.

Shyam gripped the sill tightly as his eyes tracked down the velvet neck, the spotted slim body with the folded wings, the long furry tail lost in the shadows. It was a true chimera in monstrous proportions, with the short, pointed head of a fox crowned by those distinctive bat-like ears and great big eyes, wearing the markings of a king cheetah from the uneven spots and the tear marks to the three stripes running along its spine, down the tail. Akila lay on her side, watching the back of his neck. She said, 'When you heard me at your window and let me in, your brain told you that I climbed a ladder. What do you see out there?'

Shyam did not respond.

'What is the label in your mind, closest to what you're seeing?'

'I have no idea,' he sighed.

'Good. And just like that,' she snapped her fingers, 'this reality of yours has been shattered by the appearance of something that couldn't possibly exist. Because, frankly, it doesn't belong to "this" world. And neither do I. I haven't since I died.'

SHYAM'S EYES burst open and his head pitched wildly. He was floating a few feet below the surface of the water at the base of the roots.

All around him creatures as varied as mice, snakes, bees, sparrows, weasels, foxes, crows and dragonflies were suspended in various states of decomposition. Mouths agape, necks locked back.

He could not move a finger. The fluid burnt his throat like acid reflux and his eyes rolled back into the visions.

'IT DOESN'T make any sense.'

'Think back to school, after "the incident". Your mind has obscured so much because it was afraid to confront the truth. But there are details that can reveal it. The veil will come undone with a little yank.'

'What are you talking about?'

'You live in a world that only makes sense because it is your brain's job to have it make sense to you. It can alter perception, change details, and you will be completely convinced because that is your reality. You believe the speedometer in your car because you trust it. You believe this reality because you trust your brain. And, in truth, neither of them is infallible.'

'Is there a point to this?'

'I'm dead. Accept that.'

'I can't believe that you're dead. We just fucked, Akila.'

'You're seeing me now, so how can I be dead and here, right? You're looking at a Fenek. What does your brain tell you about its existence? If I belong here because you see me, does the Fenek outside belong here as well?'

'How can you be dead? How can it be possible?' He turned away from the monster in his backyard and lowered himself to the floor. 'I remember you in school even after what happened.'

'How *do* you remember me?'

'I'd see you once in a while.'

'That's right, you could perceive me when I'd splash through.'

'I saw you with your friends.'

'You saw me, there were some children nearby, and your brain made the assumption that they were my friends. How did it account for me still wearing the pyjamas I was in the night I died?'

Shyam scoffed. 'You weren't wearing pyjamas! That would have been crazy!'

'I was, the first few times you saw me. But it didn't make sense to your brain either so it "decided" to ignore that fact entirely and filled in the missing blank with what made sense, me wearing the school uniform, just as my "friends" were.'

'You're fucking with me.'

'I need you to understand. I need you to accept this.'

'Why?'

She slid off the bed onto her hands and knees, and crawled to him until her face was five inches from his. 'Because I don't want to be alone anymore.'

'Why me?'

Her eyes welled up with tears. 'I don't know. I honestly don't know.' His thumb caressed her face and wiped the tear creasing the soft cheek. He said, 'You're real. I can touch you. At the restaurant, they could see and hear you. You drank more than any illusion could.'

'I'm really here. I'm real. The closer I am to you, the more "real" I get.'

'Then what are you saying? Maybe it's just because I was woken up, maybe I'm not awake, I don't know, but I'm trying to make sense of this,' he cried, cupping her cheeks in his hands and gazing into the warm granite pools. She replied, 'You're my anchor to this world. I need you, to exist.'

A TEN-YEAR-OLD Akila in pink pyjamas, streaked with dirt and blood, ambles along the tangle of giant roots. Her sobs shake her body as she stumbles barefoot along the lichen. Her hands and feet are bruised. Around her neck a narrow scar shows the bright red flesh. She smears the snot and tears in an attempt to wipe them off, her eyes darting about this alien world in trepidation.

She climbs over a root obstructing her path. Her foot slips and she catches herself, leaning precariously over a yawning gap. Her sorry chickenpox-stricken reflection in the water below brings her to tears again, muttering in a wobbling voice, 'Papa ... Papa...'

She sees something in the water. A monkey with its fur burnt away and the skin a deep maroon. The wide-eyed pupils are milky. The contracted lips bare the teeth in a horrid grimace. She rights herself inch by inch and pushes off with her arms. She looks around her at the expanse of roots and the forest at the periphery. She is alone. She is tired. She does not know what is happening. She scrambles onto a root and shields her eyes as the terror chills her bones. She is lost in a place where she does not belong. 'Papa!' she screams, over and over.

'I DON'T know why I'm doing this.'

'Trust me, Shyam.'

'Trust you?'

'You let me in your window in the middle of the night and fucked me, didn't you?'

'What does that have to do with anything?'

She laughed. 'Now just shut the hell up and get on Macoco's head.' Shyam was on the windowsill with her holding on from behind. Outside his apartment, the Fenek's fox-like head with its massive pointed ears waited patiently.

'Don't push me,' he stuttered.

'I'm not, but you need to take that first step, or we'll be here all night!'

'Just let me take my time. I don't want to fall to my death, if I can help it.'

'Sheesh! You still think he isn't real, don't you?'

'No,' he replied, without much conviction.

With a firm grip on his shirt and the waistband of his shorts, Akila leaned her head out the window. 'Macoco, buddy, you're going to have to come a bit closer. Let him touch you or the big baby won't budge.'

The head moved a few inches closer to the wall. Shyam gingerly touched the snout with his toes and gave a start when he felt the velvet skin, almost falling out, and then back in, with Akila holding him steady. 'You're pretty strong,' he remarked sheepishly.

'Yeah, get on his nose.' Shyam crossed onto it, with Akila directing him. 'Great, that's good. Don't worry, he's watching your balance. Now grab his ears and turn around and start making your way backwards. That's right, slow and – watch it! You almost stepped on his eye. Don't worry, stay calm, breathe, and start moving back again. That's right. Now get down on all fours and start going backwards down his neck. Take your time. When you get to his shoulder, stop and wait for me. You'll be able to sit there. Great, now relax. Breathe. I'm coming down.'

Akila nimbly moved onto the head and slid down the neck with a guiding arm trailing. She bumped into Shyam and turned around to sit facing forward. He recovered from the jolt and asked, rather worried, 'Where are you taking me?'

A playful grin tagged her face. 'I'm in the mood for some ice cream. Do you know a place?'

A BIRD'S-EYE view reveals a pit of serpents petrified in their knotted coils. And amidst the grey and green mass is a small blemish, a pink dot buoyant amidst the despair. Stooped, with hands splayed at her sides, Akila stares into the distance at the fluid mirage. Her hair sticks to her face and her large eyes are bloodshot and sunken. She swallows drily and comes out of the daze. The amethyst sky turns boysenberry as the sun begins its descent. She squints at the nearest treeline with its brooding canopies and unfriendly shadows. She knows she cannot remain here on the roots another night. Her stomach bubbles and burns her insides with hunger but all she craves is sleep.

When she arrives there she realizes the trees are far larger than she had expected. The thick trunks bend and twist like dancers, reaching out long curling branches. A wobbling hoot breaks the silence, rising in pitch, and stops just as abruptly. Akila cannot be certain if it is an animal or a bird, or some strange creature that has never crossed her imagination. It feels good to walk on firm ground again and not balance her way along. However, the novelty soon wears off on her bare, bruised feet. Her wounds burn. She needs to find a river or a stream at the earliest. All the time, the sun is getting lower, gathering the claustrophobic shadows about her.

The stream is wide and filled with fish in its brisk current over the rocks. High hanging branches cross over but there is enough light trickling through for her to appreciate the little sanctuary she has found in this alien world. It is not very alien, she reflects, as she rests on the bank with a stomach full of cool, clear water. True, the sky may be purple during the day but the trees are still trees and green, the water tastes like water, the fish look like fish and the colourful birds high up in the branches resemble macaws and hornbills. She knows she is stranded here. Her father will be searching but he cannot find her on another world. If there is a way to get here, she thinks, there must be a way to get back.

She finds a pool further down the stream, lined with rocks and a modest waterfall capping either end to segregate it. The current is calm and there is easy access to the water from the skirting rocks. They open up at one point onto a brief pebbled shore. She prudently surveys its depths for anything dangerous and finds it uninhabited, with only a few fish flitting about. Akila gauges how much time she might have left before nightfall and judges that she can comfortably have a wash. Having carefully laid her clothes out to air, she slips into the water, withholding a shrill squeal of delight. She finds a seat with the water at her chest and rests her eyes, just feeling the affable current wash away the grime and clean her wounds. She recoils at a flurry of gentle pinches over her torso, her heart fluttering in a panic. It is only some small fish nibbling at the dirt and dead skin. Others join in at her legs. They don't seem to be hurting her, so she relaxes, letting them nibble the bruises at her thighs and feet.

After a few minutes she opens her eyes and lets them wander over the branches with their drooping creepers and vines. Birds scrutinizing this furless stranger. The leaves shivering in the breeze. The odd animal call echoing through the jungle. She feels she can survive here for as long as it takes, though she may only be ten, which she can do nothing about. Tonight she will sleep in the trees. If she can get some fruits before that, all the better. One thing at a time, that is what her father always said. Have a plan and follow it. The fish have stopped nibbling now. She teases aloud, 'Have you had enough of me already?'

There is a slight movement in her peripheral vision. She turns to the rocks lining the pool. A slimy black hand, large, with four thick fingers, hangs onto a rock three feet away. Beneath the undulating surface of the pool, it is hard to miss the enormous black shape to her side. She waits, perfectly still. She moves slowly, trying to find a secure foothold. Before she can be certain of it, she sees the exposed hand flex and she kicks down with both feet. Her wet body slides up the rock in a flash. A hole opens up in the water beside her and a great black head, flat and wide, bursts through. She gets her feet out of the way, over the rock, just in time as those massive jaws slap shut. A spray of water swipes her back from the intensity of it. Akila clambers backwards while the creature pushes its head, glistening with slime, over the rock with an arm gripping the crevices.

At a safe distance, she gets onto her feet. The creature watches her with its button-like eyes.

'Get away!' she screeches and hurls a large stone at it, striking the side of the broad mouth. The creature snaps its jaws and crossly slides back into the water. It is a massive salamander, she realizes. Its fifteen-foot body slinks along the bottom into a hidden crevice under a big rock beneath the waterfall.

Akila creeps towards her clothes on the rocks. Her toes slip and her foot slides, sending her reeling into the water with a shriek. Thrashing about submerged, her feet cannot find the walls. Her body plunges out of the water for air and she feels the sudden chill hit her. In that instant before submerging, she sees the pink sky unhindered, and the snow-capped peaks. She goes under the surface again and comes out in the pond, her feet kicking painfully at rocks that were not there a moment ago. She scurries out of the pool, grabbing her clothes on the way. She hides in the bushes some feet away, clutching her pyjamas to her trembling body, wondering what sort of nightmare has her captive.

A PINK drop of melted ice cream ran down the side of the waffle cone. His tongue caught it before it touched his hand, and he said, 'It was just a dream.' He hated getting sticky fingers. Rajpath rolled out before him like a landing strip with the solemn domes of the Rashtrapati Bhavan peering through the Delhi haze far ahead. He had always wanted to have ice cream on top of India Gate, and though the top was carpeted in bird shit, it was still worth it. 'Do you remember any other dream that vividly?' Akila asked, perched beside him with a scoop of chocolate ice cream on her cone. Shyam looked past his bare feet at the hundred-foot fall.

'No.'

'Because it's not just a dream, it's a memory. We were together when it happened, holding hands, even as that blade cut out my life. Shyam, I'm not talking about heaven or hell or the afterlife. I'm talking about different physical planes existing in the same time and space. Thirteen in all, excluding this one, all ruled by a being that has no name. I call it the Sentinel.

These worlds exist on an unstable foundation, and it says that I am the key.'

'How?'

'I am the sacrifice. I was ten when I stopped the worlds from crumbling. Every three years, the ritual is repeated to keep these worlds stable. I am the Beli. I am the sacrifice.' She wore an ironic grin as she said it.

'How did the worlds exist until they found you?'

'There was another Beli. There is always a sacrifice in place. But after many offerings, it no longer has the strength necessary. Eighteen years ago, that Beli was spent and there was a call for another. Lucky me, huh?' Her tongue licked around the shrinking chocolate ball with long swiping turns to maintain the hemisphere.

'So have you been coming here all this time?' he asked, trying to make sense of the jigsaw, piece by piece.

'No, not all this time. This has never happened before, a sacrifice being able to come back to Earth. At first, I didn't understand it. It's not supposed to happen. There was some fundamental glitch. On random trips to other worlds I found myself climbing out of a water body on Earth.'

'How are you travelling back and forth?'

'That's not the point. Whenever I found myself on Earth, I was always in the water body closest to you.'

'What?'

She popped the remaining tip of the cone into her mouth.

'Somehow, something between us has shattered the Sentinel's fabricated boundaries of time and space, and allows me to cross over to this plane, but gravitated to your vicinity.'

'And the Fenek?'

Behind them, the hulking figure of Macoco, the Fenek, sat perched like a prehistoric bird of prey.

'Wait, you'll see,' she smirked.

A POLYPHONY of screeches and howls, caws and soft melodies. Akila lies curled in a ball in the nest she has made of long grass and leaves, high up in the nook of a tree. She has been awake since the night dissolved into the first shades of light and the bird and animal calls roused her tired soul. It is morning and she is still here in this strange world. A band of golden light dances across her face. She languidly watches her breath ruffle the loose threads on her sleeve.

AKILA STANDS ready on top of the waterfall flowing into the salamander pond, where it is too shallow to house any giants. There cannot be too many around like the black salamander that attacked her. She undoes her pyjama top, the bunnies still smiling under the layer of dirt, and flaps it in the air to knock away pieces. She has a plan for the day. Wash her top and leave it to dry, while she wanders the jungle to find some food. With her stomach filled, she will put on the clean shirt and wash the pyjama bottom before heading off to set up some suitable shelter. 'One thing at a time,' she imitates her father's voice with a rueful smile.

Squatting at the water's edge, she unfurls the shirt, letting the bubbling current churn it like a washing-machine. A thick cloud of dust spreads out. Dirt and small insects fall away. Only the blood streaks remain. When she scrubs at them with her small thumbs, they don't come off. She holds it spread out under the surface, admiring her effort for the most part. She does not notice the long, thin tail in the water disappear behind the fabric. A gaping mouth launches itself at her through the shirt. Three inches of razor-sharp fangs cut through the cloth at a squealing Akila. It lunges again and again, held back only by the tautness of the fabric held stretched. She whips it out of the water by a sleeve, shrieking and waving the shirt in the air. She slaps it on a rock, lets go and hops away, squealing like a maniac. The wriggling under the shirt subsides. She stays focused on the curled shape. There is some movement, followed by a shallow splash, and something like a short snake shoots up the current and out of sight.

AKILA STANDS ready at the bottom of the waterfall emptying from the salamander pool, armed with a wooden staff and her soiled shirt. Her reluctance to stray too far from what she knows piques her because she will have to explore the surrounding area soon if she is to survive and find a way back to her world. A troop of little golden-furred monkeys have gathered in the trees above her, unimpressed by the stranger's antics. The stream is only knee deep here, with fish lazily fighting the current at the base of the waterfall, waiting for the bits and scraps it brings.

Akila does her preliminary check with the stick, prodding the gaps between rocks and the narrow crevices. She startles the fish but nothing else. She dips the shirt into the water and scrubs it again. The blood is stubbornly clinging on, no matter how hard she works at it. She slaps it twice against the rock but still nothing. Then there is a tug on it. She picks up the staff with her free hand and holds it ready as a spear to jab at the danger. Another tug, this time harder. It's not letting go and the shirt is obscuring the culprit. She cautiously moves it aside with the end of her staff and uncovers two fish flashing their red bellies and pulling back on the sleeve.

They are only five inches so she is not worried they can pose a threat, but they may tear her pyjama. She pokes at them with the staff. It is tough for her tiny body to pull and prod at the same time. More fish join in and a pair attacks the staff, holding on with their teeth. She shakes it out of the water as they flap wildly, their silver backs gleaming in the sun. Hungry and irate, she whacks her sleeve with it and sprays water all over herself and the rocks. The shirt comes free. She does a cursory examination for any damage. Besides some minor holes, there are no rips and the seams are fine.

The splashing subsides and the stream resumes an air of tranquillity. However, twenty of the red bellies are gathered at the rocks, inches from her feet. Suddenly they don't seem so harmless. She takes two steps back from the water's edge, wondering what would happen to her if she fell in and they attacked all at once. Her simian spectators in the branches have multiplied. A male leans forward and hoots a gruff encouragement. Then reclines and watches. Further down the stream, where the water becomes a mass of writhing eels, Akila shakes her head in surrender and turns back.

At the salamander pool, she watches the creature's enormous silhouette hover beneath the surface. She concludes that it keeps the water clear of predators, and this one cannot sneak up on her. Better the devil you know. The wide jaws snap, swallowing a fish into the black hole with little commotion. Further along the body, something wriggles and twitches within. The fish is being digested alive.

HALF-EATEN YELLOW fruit with juicy white flesh are scattered over the jungle floor. A fruit falls, marking a white streak down Akila's bare shoulder. She wipes it off and studies the white goo on her palm. She has never been so consumed by hunger in her life. It feels like her gut is digesting her insides in retribution. A tentative lick and she winces in anticipatory disgust. But it is not disgusting at all. It is quite delicious, and she slurps what is left off her fingers.

Her eager face stares round-eyed at the yellow packages of yumminess enticing her. With a run-up she climbs the sloping trunk, springing up branches until she finds one with the fruit in easy reach. She bites into the first and gags immediately. The yellow skin is rubbery and bitter; the aftertaste is intense, compelling her to scrape at her tongue to remove the tang. She examines the next one thoroughly. She runs a nail along the seam that bisects the outer shell and tries to tear it open. It comes away in little strips rather than as a whole. She recalls eating mangosteens once on the highway. They had to carefully twist along the seam and undo it without damaging the innards. She tries that and it requires a little pressure, but then the fruit splits neatly in half, presenting its creamy goodness to her. With her lower teeth, she scoops out the white filling and smears it across her chin. Her eyes squeeze closed in the sheer ecstasy of eating something delightful at the height of hunger.

In a matter of seconds she has gorged on everything within reach. She then proceeds to knock more down with her staff and collects them with a smile wide across her face. A blue spider crawls up her elbow and she starts with a shriek, slapping at her bare arms and chest. When there is no sign of it, she gathers up the fruit again and heads towards the stream. Her smile remains, though not half as wide.

THE SHIRT has been lying in the sun all morning. It feels dry to the touch and she picks it up, uncovering a long, bright red and green frog with a black stub of a tail. It flashes its silvery eyes at her, turns around and hops down the waterfall.

With her pyjama bottom washed and in the sun, she stores the fruit in a groove in the rocks, covering it with leaves. The next step in her plan involves preparing a shelter and she sets off to where she had found her trusty staff.

She returns carrying some fallen branches and sticks and drops them by the pool. The leaves covering the fruit are strewn about, and the groove is empty. She scowls up at the monkeys watching her with their sleepy eyes. She knew they were up to no good.

She scales the tree she had spent the night in and ties some branches together to make a small platform in the wide nook. It takes three tries but finally it feels firm and she's impressed by her own resourcefulness. But there is no teacher to grade it, no father to ruffle her hair with pride. Her body still itches from the chickenpox and she feels like screaming at the absurdity and sheer loneliness of her situation. She sits, hugging her naked legs to her chest, her face buried in her knees. Conscious not to scratch, she rubs her palms gently over the boils, tasting her tears as she quietly weeps.

Then a deep rumble clutches her heart with archetypal fear and she freezes on her flimsy platform. Twigs crack and bushes rustle as something large and heavy moves along the ground. The rumble descends into an eerie silence as the movement halts. For an entire minute there is not a single living sound in the vicinity. Akila knows she must not move. In the intense silence she can discern a slow rhythmic sound like a hand sliding on silk. It is long and deep, and occasionally its pitch rises and she realizes it is the creature sniffing the air.

Suddenly her tree quakes from a mighty jolt. She locks onto the rickety platform and keeps dead centre to stay out of sight. The tree trembles, confronted with a savagery she does not want to face. The violence stops after a few seconds, and then there is the guttural rumble again. Twigs snap and then nothing. Another minute and the birds are singing again and the monkeys chattering. Sliding over the platform on her stomach, she peers over the edge. It is a scene of chilling destruction at the base of the tree, with the ground dug up and the bushes ripped out and tossed in every direction. As high up as twelve feet from the ground, the tree's bark is scarred by claws, showing the light brown wood underneath. There must be some escape from this place, and she vows she will do whatever it takes to find it.

HE SCREAMS, but there are only bubbles. They hang in the liquid and one near his eye rotates with a pearlescent sheen. The space beyond expands into nothingness. He has never known such solitude. Where have all the stars gone?

'WHAT WAS it like there, alone?'

Shyam was seated on the wooden floor of his apartment with his back against the wall, next to Akila, their legs extended and feet splayed before them. She smiled but he knew it was a mask. She said haltingly, 'It was – well I'm here, aren't I, so I guess it wasn't so bad.'

'Come on, tell me.'

'What do you want to hear?'

'What was it like?'

She sighed, smiling sadly. 'Imagine an adolescent Robinson Crusoe in another dimension, with no hope of rescue and knowing it. That was the first few years.'

'Was it dangerous?'

'Considering I survived, even as a ten-year-old, it couldn't have been that dangerous.'

'Why won't you tell me?'

'I am telling you.'

'But not seriously.'

'Because there was nothing funny about it. And you have to look back on that sort of shit with a sense of humour or you'd shrink into a tiny little ball.'

He touched her hand. He sensed the burden in her disposition.

'Can I see it?'

'See what?'

'The scar.'

Akila gaped at him for a while. She got up on her knees and leaned forward, clicked the latch on her collar so that it slid along the sweet curve of her neck and fell on the wooden floor with a *patt*. Flipping her hair over, she tilted her head to one side and revealed the deep running scar. He could not help but touch it, and she drew back with a gasp. Their eyes locked, and she saw his filling rapidly with tears until they flowed over and streaked down his cheeks. He covered his face with his hands. 'I'm sorry, I'm so sorry.'

She sat back onto the balls of her feet, her fingers caressing the scar, mumbling, 'No, it's okay. It's just that no one's ever touched it before.'

'I'm so sorry.' He could not stop.

'I'm fine. It didn't hurt when you touched it. I was just surprised.'

'I'm sorry, Akila.' Spit frothed at the corners of his mouth. He rocked back and forth against the wall, apologizing through his sobs. She was shocked by his reaction at first but then she understood. She took him in her arms and held him. 'It's not your fault, Shyam. There's nothing you could have done. You were nine.'

He sobbed into her neck, 'I feel like I'm going mad.'

She cocked her head to the side with a grin. 'That's the least of your worries.'

SHE IS falling. The world is a spinning haze of green and blue, and the sound of gurgling water. That last impact still rings in her ears. No time for pain or even a scream. A flash of long slithering bodies and the water smashes against her face, bursting her lungs as she comes out the other side, struggling for air. She shrieks and beats at the water, kicking and punching, and jumps out of the shallow creek. Dripping in the clinging pyjamas and trembling in the sudden cold, she looks about in shock.

It is a green valley with hills rising on both sides and a stream cutting along it. The sky is a healthy shade of cobalt. Akila knows this place. She whirls about and comes face-to-face with a tethered cow, indifferently chewing cud inches away.

'I'm back,' she hears herself splutter.

She screams and runs up the hill to the red-tiled buildings she can see on top. Wet, teeth chattering, she stands at the gate to the principal's house wondering why her German Shepherd Macoco has not dashed out to greet her. It is an old British bungalow with a circular driveway around the modest garden. Flowering creepers invade the right flank of the façade and manicured hedges line the walls.

She darts up the driveway, the gravel pinching her feet, through the car porch, up the steps, and slams against the front door. She pushes it open and bursts into the living room.

'Papa!' she cries, tears of joy blurring her vision. She knocks over chairs and runs through the elegant dining room and up the staircase, all the time shouting, 'Papa! I'm home, Papa!' There is no one to answer.

She hurries down the steps and rushes out of the house, wiping her tears with her wet sleeve. She holds onto the iron gate, her head spinning with nausea. Some girls a little older than her walk past in their neatly pressed school uniforms. She reaches out to them, whimpering, 'Please help me. My father is the principal. Please take me to him.' She falls to her knees and retches on the road. The girls neither stop nor take any notice of her. 'I'm talking to you!' she screeches and hurls a stone. It strikes one of the girls on the back of her thigh. She jumps with a yelp and scans the area for the perpetrator. 'Now will you listen?' cries Akila. The schoolgirl yells at a passing group of boys, wagging a finger at their crudeness.

Akila no longer has the energy to shout out to them. Her stomach is turning in on itself and her head is pounding. She does not know what is wrong with her, but her body seems to be drawn back to the stream. She shakes her head and screams, 'No!' and vomits again. It hurts so much. Every retch feels like she is trying to cast out her insides. Her throat burns and so do her eyes. She does not understand what is happening. The road tilts and she falls over and then rights herself. There is no more coherent thought. Only pain and burning, and she surrenders, her tears streaming down her soft, full cheeks. She cannot look back. All the energy that is left in her draws her back to the stream in the valley. At the edge of the water her body stops, barely awake, and the last thing she registers is the unsympathetic cow, before her eyes roll back and she flops into the water.

She is slowly floating on her back down a stream. Above

her the sky is purple. Things wriggle in the water underneath her, but she does not care. She had made it home. She really had. It was not a dream, just like this is not. She had felt the cold. The gravel under her feet. The metal doorknob in her hand. And yet, she wonders, did she really go back? Those girls couldn't see her. They couldn't hear her. She shouted and shouted, but no one stopped and said anything. And the vomiting. Her head still spins from the retching. Why did she feel so horrible so suddenly? A rock bumps her head and she stops floating downstream. Still in a daze, she clambers out and tracks the stream back to her tree. She makes it up to the platform and curls up into a ball. She is a ghost, she knows. And she is in hell.

'WHY DID you pick me up now?' he asked her, his mouth an inch from her ear as he rode behind on Macoco, the Fenek, a thousand feet from the starry ground. His hands held onto her sides, the tips of his index fingers intermittently grazing the swell of her breasts.

'Does it matter?'

'Doesn't it?'

'Not to me.'

'So you just decided?'

'I didn't have a choice. I had to meet you.'

His hold on her tightened. 'Is this real?'

She looked back at him and said, 'I hope it is.'

He tipped back, pulling her onto him, wrapping his left arm around her neck and they fiercely kissed. She drew away, touching her lips. 'Not so hard. I don't want my lips to get swollen.'

He pulled her back and pushed his lips onto hers. She turned her body, swinging her legs to one side. One slip and she would fall to a messy end, but she moved with supreme confidence as she twisted to face him until their bodies were aligned and she drew close to his. Macoco's large hearts pulsed warmly with a heavy beat against their inner thighs. The wind invaded their clothes and licked their bodies with cool air. Akila pushed Shyam further backwards and he let her guide them onto Macoco's striped back.

She straddled Shyam so their groins met, grinding against each other through their jeans. She wrapped her arms around his neck, letting him maul her upper lip as he lightly held the back of her head, her long locks stroking their faces and closed eyes. They were following the sensations now and each other's lead. Manoeuvring up and down with her arms on his shoulders, she ground harder against him, her chest smashed against his, their flapping clothes beating their skin into a frenzy. He moved his hands down to her buttocks and helped her move as she swayed to the music of the night, with the spying stars bright and thick about them. Their rhythm rose to a wild passion and the tempo was lost in the approach to the crescendo. They could no longer hold their kiss but breathed hard into each other's mouths, open with the ultimate release. Then calm, with their hearts pounding like the clamour of cymbals, pressing their zippers together painfully hard, their mouths finding the wetness of the other soothing, the roaming tongues relaxing, the warmth of the bodies so natural. And Macoco banked to the left. With it their uncertain worlds tilted and they held on, cuddling faces into comforting necks. Akila tenderly sucked his skin. She said, 'I want to try something.'

IT IS full of stars. Unblinking. One squirms through the black, a faint trail follows and vanishes. Another does the same. And another. And all the stars begin to dart about in serpentine paths and fade away, as new ones twinkle into existence and restart the cycle. A sea of stars worm through his eyes. He can feel himself letting go. Falling. No, he mustn't. He has to stop Akila. He has to wake up. With all his might he lifts eyelids that weigh a ton, and looks out. Stars stretching out into infinity. They're singing to him as they leisurely drift past. They each have a song, sweet low tones winding their way into his mind, caressing his anxiety and loneliness. It is full of stars.

AKILA CARRIES the yellow fruits wrapped in her shirt. The chickenpox boils on her face, chest and back show signs of healing, and some have dried and fallen away already. Those that remain will not last the week. They don't itch as badly as they did at first. In fact, she has not noticed them at all; a few itching boils seem inconsequential compared to the larger issue of survival. To that end, she has upgraded her staff with a sharp shard of obsidian bound in a big clumsy bundle of vines.

She marches down the strip of pebbled shore and dunks her shirt into the salamander pool. She jiggles the dripping fruit and squats a few feet from the water's edge. There are almost a dozen wet and juicy orbs in the shirt. Her mouth drools as she greedily twists them open and scrapes out the creamy white filling with her teeth, moaning at the divine flavour. She hums a spirited tune, shaking her head to the beat as she sets about twisting open the next.

The spectre of the salamander's head emerges from its sunken lair. Its long, dark form slithers under the water, creeping towards the unsuspecting little girl. The slimy black hands dig into the pebbles and drag the immense body forward, its wide head with the tiny button eyes breaking the surface as it inches towards her. Akila licks clean an empty husk. Her mouth and chin are coated with the white juice but she is too involved to care about manners. A few feet from her, the giant amphibian has crawled so half its trunk is out of the water. The mouth yawns open with the blunt snout rising higher than Akila. A deadly gaping hole with a glistening tyrian-purple tongue wobbling in the centre.

Akila carelessly tosses a fruit over her shoulder and the jaws snap it out of the air. A second later they open wide again and catch another flung fruit. After throwing the fourth, Akila focuses on having her fill. The salamander shifts closer. Akila turns, yelling, 'No! That's too close! Move back!' She taps its upper jaw with the end of her stick and the mouth shuts.

'Move back,' she commands, gesturing with a hand. The salamander lunges closer and she raises her staff threateningly. The animal either does not comprehend or does not care. It crawls forward heavily, the arms and legs unused to carrying its body outside the water. Akila wraps the fruit in the shirt flap with a disapproving grunt and prepares to get up. The salamander waits. She confronts the fifteen-foot long river monster, its hulking body slick in the light of day. She screws open a fruit and licks the creamy innards in emphatic ecstasy. The salamander begins to move forward. She holds the fruit away and wraps up the rest, preparing to leave again. The creature stops at the movement, small button eyes observing her. She signals it to move back, but nothing happens. She takes the satchel of fruits away from it, compelling the salamander to withdraw a half-step. 'Good boy!' She tosses a fruit at it and with a flash of movement it disappears.

Although she recognizes the dangers, she also feels she can tame this beast. It approaches her again, and again she moves the bag of fruit away an additional foot, forcing the great beast to yield. She waits for it to retreat further. Then tosses it a fruit and waves her left arm to motion it back all the way. It snaps up the fruit but does not obey. Instead it moves towards her, and with a weary sigh, she takes the fruit and enters the jungle.

The next day, Akila sits in the same spot. She starts eating, chucking the empty shells for the small blue birds waiting at the side. The salamander emerges from the water and yawns its jowls wide. She tosses in three fruits and then discontinues her generosity. The salamander advances and she motions it back. It halts at the gesture, starting towards her again when she stops. She calmly makes her exit with the fruit.

It is the same routine the next two days and each time she gives the salamander one less fruit, and as soon as it moves towards her, she gets up and leaves.

The next day she is there again. The large jaws gape open for the expected treat while Akila disregards it and continues eating. The salamander shifts towards her with an irate rasp, prompting her to pick up the fruit and leave. She hides among the trees and watches its reaction. The great black head looks slowly to either side and then despondently reverses into the water.

The following day Akila unwraps the fruit and starts eating. The salamander appears out of the water, keeping a respectful distance from her. It opens its jaws. Akila pretends not to notice and ignores the creature for some minutes. Then she idly tosses a fruit its way. There is that hair-triggered snap catching it and the jaws open for more. She does not offer any. The jaws wait without betraying any hint of impatience. At last she provides another that vanishes with a snap so sudden she can feel the suction from where she sits. Her mind made up, she places the covered fruit to one side and gestures to the creature to withdraw. To her surprise, it scuttles backwards and slides into the pool. She repeats the practice for the next three days, increasing the fruits by then to three.

ONE MORNING, as she conducts the routine, and the salamander is keeping its distance after the third fruit, Akila picks up a fourth. Her strategy is silly and only guided by instinct, but it has worked so well and she wants to push it even further. She is aware that it is among her biggest faults, the stubborn determination to push things that extra step, and sometimes she falls, badly. Nervously rolling the fruit in her clammy palms, she steps forward, knowing perfectly well that what she is about to do may, and probably will, ruin everything she has achieved so far with the creature. It contradicts the ground rules she has been trying to establish.

She takes another step towards it and holds out her arm, presenting the butter-yellow fruit in her elfin hand. She could be sucked into those jaws and vanish in an instant. Show no fear, she instructs herself. Don't be startled if it moves. The jaws tentatively split open two feet from her. She lightly tosses the fruit in and the snout snaps shut, leaving no time to react, but only stay rooted to the spot. The salamander lies there waiting. Now to achieve her real aim. To touch it. To prove to herself that she, a little girl, has tamed this monster, just as she will tame the wilderness and survive against the odds. She leans forward gradually. Her arm extends and fingers reach out. She stretches within a foot of the slime-coated snout and the creature sharply recoils. With a thrash of its tail, it rushes backwards into the pond.

Akila picks up her bag of fruit and spear and hustles into the shadow-ridden jungle. She has grown used to it now. The birdcalls and the monkey hoots no longer bother her and are now just part of the ambience. She strolls through the jungle, so deep in her thoughts and the taste of the fruit, that she does not notice the sudden absence of noise. True, she has not managed to touch the salamander but she has tamed it with her fruits. She did it her way. She smirks at the thought. It is not so bad in this jungle really. She will have to find some way to fish and then, of course, to cook the fish. Can she eat it raw, she wonders. After all, the birds and animals eat the fish raw, so why not her? But then, chewing on the raw flesh is such an unappealing thought; she will have to cook them somehow to make them palatable. She has to catch them first. As delicious as the fruit is, she is beginning to tire of having it day after day. And her stomach has been complaining lately. Maybe she needs to start hunting birds.

She stops, searching for them in the high branches while scooping out the fruit filling. Where are they? Why has it gone so quiet? Mid-thought she drops the fruit and spins around with her spear, attentive. The freakishly large head of a scaly lizard towers three feet above her. Red and black stripes cover the length of its body and short curving horns jacket its muscle-bound shoulders. The head angles to one side, the crimson eyes with jagged waves of yellow reading her reactions. The long dessin-blue tongue flicks at her scent in the air. A crackling moan swells from deep within the lizard's chest. She turns to flee but her left foot is caught, sending her face first onto the mushy jungle floor. She screams at the pain shooting through her leg from the chisel-like teeth tightly gripping her ankle. Its head rises, lifting her clear off the ground, swinging her flailing body. Hanging upside down, she can see only the lizard's pale neck and chest, and strikes out with all her strength, piercing her spear into the wattle at its throat. Its muzzle tightens and she screeches in anguish.

Then the pressure on her ankle releases, letting her fall and roll on to her feet. Its shoulder trembles and the horns emit a deafening rattle as it yanks its head about. The torn skin at her joint burns but she strikes her attacker again, the obsidian point penetrating the lizard's eye. It rears its monstrous head, hissing madly amid the rattling, breaking her staff in two. Without wasting a moment to panic, she runs in the opposite direction, gripping the broken stick like a baton. She can hear the thing tumbling about in agony, and then the thunder of trampled bushes and soil in pursuit of her. Trying to outrun it is hopeless. She scampers up a tree, jumping from branch to branch. She balances along a narrow limb to the end and looks down. The lizard collides with the tree, shaking it violently. The head glowers up at her, blood pouring out one eye with the wooden staff still protruding from the ghastly wound. Then with a lunge it begins to climb the tree trunk with its formidable talons digging into the wood, effortlessly pulling the enormous weight.

With each step up the tree quivers and Akila holds onto her branch in mortal fear of the thing that is charging up at her, crashing through thin branches like they are twigs. It reaches her branch and punches out at her with the deadly claws. She hurls the broken staff at the rattling beast and jumps wildly for a branch on the next tree. She hits it hard but her hands hold on. She scrambles up in time to hear the branch she was on fracture and smash against the one below with an explosion of leaves and splinters. The cascade of crashing branches hits the ground with the creature in the thick of it, mewling in panic. Akila holds on, listening. She can't see what is happening below through the branches. It has fallen silent. She grits her teeth, listening for any sound. The thickets rustle as the lizard squirms. Akila crawls along the branch to the tree trunk, looking down to its base. The bloody head of the lizard glares back at her, its blue tongue menacingly flicking the air. She hunts about her for some way to escape. The tree shudders as the lizard ascends. She goes around the trunk to cross over to the other limb and proceeds along it until it gets too thin for her to go any further. There are no trees on this side. She has reached the end of the treeline, marking the periphery of the field of roots. The pool of strange water it soaks in lies below.

There is a flash of red and black on the lower branch followed by a sudden stillness. The leaves are too thick to see past but they signal movement behind them. A blue tongue flicks out at her. Akila screams, 'Papa!' She hops up and holds onto the branch above, then swings her body forward with all her might, letting go with eyes closed tight. She drops beyond the branches, and opens her eyes just before hitting the water with a smack.

She struggles out of the water, spluttering, her eyes blurry and lungs working severely in her chest. Her ears clear to the air filled with the echoes of wailing winds. Tiny soft flakes drift from above. She can feel them falling on her bare shoulders and face. Then she realizes she has lost her shirt back in the jungle, with the fruit. She holds out a hand and catches a delicate fleck as it dances in the air and settles on her wet skin. She rubs it with her fingertips and it smears black on her palm. Black snow. From one strange land with strange creatures into another, she muses. The ground hiccups with a jolt, sending her sprawling backwards onto the thick layer of light-grey snow, streaking her fair skin with dark smudges. She stands, trying to rub it off, but only smudges it further. Glancing up, she does a double take and goes breathless at the sight before her. The ominous landscape is pillared with black plumes rising from volcanoes of all shapes, and among them great stone giants kneel with their faces to the skies, their mouths wide open and distorted. This is not a world of black snow, she knows now, but ash and wailing titans.

'CHEERS,' THEY chimed together and glasses clinked. Akila was about to sip her Sangria but Shyam interrupted, 'Not like that. We need to maintain eye-contact when we do this, or it's seven years of bad sex.'

'Oh, we wouldn't want that now, would we,' she smirked, and held her glass to his for the second take. They looked intently into each other's eyes and called out, 'Cheers.'

'It's a lovely view from here,' she remarked, looking out upon a night-clad Delhi from Shyam's rooftop. His apartment building sat on the edge of the Mehrauli archaeological park with a dark sheet of treetops extending for a bit to the sparkling lights of the city shimmering in the hazy distance. 'It's quiet here,' he said, 'that's what matters to me. I've been to apartments where we couldn't hear ourselves over the racket of passing traffic.'

'Poor Mr Shyam, couldn't talk with his fancy friends over the lousy traffic noise. However did you survive?'

They laughed, though it hit Shyam hard that she did have a point. While he suffered a little traffic noise, she was alone in the wild or whatever that other dimension was like. She had to fight everyday for her survival and his biggest complaints had been his broadband being constantly disconnected or the pizza arriving cold with stale bread. To him, living in India was anyway a daily exercise of questioning the logic of the universe. At every traffic light or 'gaon' you were reminded of abject poverty, and that question with no answer: why do I deserve to be where I am and they where they are? He worked for what he had but he knew they worked too, much harder than he did.

He always had an escape from feeling undeserving of his place in existence – he could distract himself with books or music or movies or video games. But now, here was Akila, a girl trapped all alone in another dimension. Who had her head cut off as a sacrifice when she was only ten and had to endure that gruesome ritual in a cosmic cycle of torture once every three years. There was no reason for anything. Just like there was no reason he could think of for why it had to be her rather than him. They had stood there in that dark cavern, under the tree, side by side, hand in hand. Was it just the luck of the draw?

'What's that dark tower over there?' Akila pointed into the night, visibly appreciative of the Sangria's charms.

Shyam studied the grim silhouette of the familiar landmark. 'It's the Qutab Minar,' he stated. 'It was built around a thousand years ago. Impressive phallic symbolism, don't you think?' She nudged him, sporting a grin he was sure the wine had invited.

'Isn't that the point of a building?'

'You mean, to penetrate the sky?' They giggled together.

'They were building a bigger one right next to it, in fact. But they didn't get past the base for some reason.'

'They couldn't get it up?'

She tried to hold a straight face but failed miserably, breaking out in tittering laughter. She held up her glass. 'What is this wine? French? I like it!'

'This, my dear, is from the bosom of your motherland, well, around the hip really. From the rolling hills of Maharashtra.'

'Maharashtra, you say? Mmmm. Has that hippy flavour to it.'

'Now that's the mark of a true connoisseur.'

They clinked their glasses together and raised them with the cry, 'Hippy!'

They sipped through their chuckles and then subsided into a drawn out silence where they sat admiring the sparkling scenery. Akila reached beside their marble bench and poured herself another large glass.

'There's something I've wanted to ask you,' she said.

'Shoot,' he said.

'There was a period of three years when I couldn't splash through to Earth.'

'First, about this thing you keep saying – that you splash through, I've been too embarrassed to ask so far because you say it like it's something I ought to know. But – what the hell does it mean?'

'Splash through?' She grinned. 'You know that I travel back and forth through water … and I make a splash coming and going, so "splash through". Brilliant, I know.' She shrugged modestly, then threw her hands up in the air. 'But don't ask me how it works because I don't know. Something to do with surface tension?' She stuck out her lip. 'I just know that it works. But that's not what I was coming to...'

'You were saying you couldn't "splash through" to Earth.'

'That's right – for three years. There was something barring my passage and at the end of that time, suddenly I could travel to Earth again. I never could figure out what had happened during that time. It's never happened before or since and I've run it through my head a bunch of times, and I'm thinking that maybe it had to do with a change in you, or your life.'

'Let's see. When was this?'

'It would have been when you were ...' She performed a quick mental calculation, 'About seventeen-ish?'

'Seventeen-ish? That's a while ago.'

'Yup. When you were seventeen-ish, into eighteen, nineteen and maybe a bit into twenty-ish? Yeah, I think so.'

Shyam flexed his back. 'That was an odd time in my life.'

'Odd? How?'

'Just odd, I suppose.'

'Tell me.'

'That's around the time I started experimenting with weed.'

'*You* did weed?'

'And hash and bhaang. Then harder and much harder stuff.'

'Sounds like you went all out.'

'Almost...'

'Why don't you like talking about it? I bet you have a bunch of "high tales". Must have been a fun time.'

Shyam hesitated. 'Not really, not at all ... I was having issues with my family and I wasn't doing very well ... So I dug myself in deeper and deeper until at some point I realized I wasn't experimenting shit, I was hooked on the stuff.'

'This went on for three whole years?'

'All through the three years of architecture school. You lose track of time when you're "comfortably numb".' He sighed. 'Do you think that had something to do with it?'

'I really don't know. Just like I still don't have an explanation for why I can travel through water, or why I can cross over to you now. Maybe,' she hypothesized, 'at that time ... because you were doped up ... the connection to you couldn't be made? Who knows? It's not like there's someone I can ask these things.' She took a sip to punctuate her thoughts. 'But it is fascinating in a way ... because consciousness is thought to have a link to the quantum realm. Everything in Quantum Physics needs to take our consciousness into account. And since narcotics affect your neurons on a molecular level, maybe they acted as a barrier. I've never looked into that aspect of things. But I've been reading up on anything and everything, trying to make sense of my situation as much as I could, and here's the thing I soon realized.' She wiped the corner of her mouth. 'It's a fun crazy universe out there, my friend.'

A VAST cloud in the darkness. It is thick all about. A sweeping flash of light, so bright and pure, and then it is no more. And it comes again. Pulsating in the cloud like a ragged lighthouse warning ships of danger. The cloud seems to never end, the light always hanging within it, flashing amidst the gloom in a persistent beat.

THE SKY flashes bright with a blazing hand of lightning and the dark clouds of dust and ash churn scornfully above her. The pool she has climbed out of is barely larger than a puddle, some black water filling a small fissure in the ground. Leaving a trail of black footprints, Akila climbs a heap of boulders to get a lay of the land. She is careful not to disturb the giant nearest to her, only five hundred feet away, kneeling as the ash rains about him, his fingers dug into the earth in agony or despair. The air feels thick and a chilly wind makes her hug her wet body for warmth. She can feel the chickenpox boils against her arms and it feels like she's dying. She wants to surrender. The wound around her ankle burns like a cinder anklet. She pulls her pants down an inch to touch the wound with some wetness but it does no good. She cannot stay here, whatever kind of place this is.

She limps down the mound and stumbles onto her hands and knees when the ground jerks for an instant. She tries to get up, but the ground shakes again, and she stumbles sideways onto her back, smearing her body and half her face black. Once more the ground rumbles but she pushes herself upright and makes for the puddle. Every two seconds the ground does a jolt. She has no choice but to get back the same way she came, even if that means she will wake up in the water filled with corpses. What if she dies there like them? She shudders at the thought but it vanishes in a split second.

Less than a kilometre away, past some dips and shallow hills, a mirage sways through the rising vapours, of a form as tall as a mountain charging towards her. Every footfall is an eruption of debris and dust. There is no thought, only instinct, and her body reacts. She dashes forward, no longer minding the bruises or the wound at her ankle. All that matters is making it to that dingy water ten feet away.

The hill before her explodes with a leg kicking through. The noise is deafening. The ground quakes as the colossal frame comes crashing to its knees and lunges forward with an arm reaching out at her. She dives as the torrent of ash rushes past and feels the thrill of hitting the water. She thrusts out of the surface, clinging onto the thin roots and reeds at the bank. She wipes the water from her eyes and looks around. It is gloomy with a thick rolling mist, but there are no volcanoes or titans. She panics for a few seconds when she realizes her feet are caught under water. The roots in her grip tear away and she falls. With hardly a breath in her lungs, she plunges her shoulders down and blindly pulls at the reeds tangled at her feet. Something small and slimy brushes her stomach.

Frantically kicking and tugging at the hardy reeds, she breaks free and bursts through the surface, greedily sucking in the air.

She crawls up the one-and-a-half foot embankment, collapses on her stomach, her legs hanging over the edge and her water-logged pyjama bottoms pulled down to her knees. She simply does not care. The grass smells wonderful and it is soft against her cheek. She rests, her eyes half-closed and feet in the water. She does not know where she is, not that it really matters. Something lands on the grass four inches from her face and she barks a shrill scream. Staring round-eyed into the frowning face of a frog, she tries to get up, but her legs are caught in her pants. The frog sits there idly wiping its slimy red face with a webbed foot. More than anything, the sputtering scream has relieved her tension and now she feels a little foolish.

Holding eye contact with the frog, she pulls up her pants and stays on her stomach, breathing heavily. After a couple of minutes of calm, the frog ribbits and hops into the pond.

Akila sits up on the mushy ground and surveys the place for the first time. The mist is thick and flows like syrup. The few feet about her that her eyes can pierce give the impression of a marsh. A sort of swampland with a network of narrow grassy pathways connected and intersecting among pools of still water, disturbed occasionally by a frog breaking the surface. Their ribbits seem to fashion a chant to some casual primeval rhythm. So calming is its effect that all the tightness releases from Akila's joints. She speculates whether she is back in her world, the one she calls Earth. But where? Is it in Ooty or some other country entirely?

Already she thinks she can feel the intense nausea that gripped her so utterly the last time. She waits, anticipating the dreadful wave. She can't stay, so why bother remaining here? But, maybe, she can somehow get a word to her father. That is what matters. She can't be the first person this has happened to. If there have been others, maybe there is a way they've figured out to save people like her. She stands up on the squishy ground, her limbs still unsteady from the adrenalin. The eerie haze drifts about her and the only way is through it.

The frog croaks rise in tempo, so dense that they become a humming sheet of sound. A patch of fog ahead of her glows dimly. It moves closer, getting brighter, though not blinding. Akila prepares to leap into the water.

The glow emerges from the mist in the shape of a majestic Irish elk standing more than six feet tall, with antlers a dozen feet across. Its translucent body spellbinds Akila with its ethereal beauty. She does not see the glowing shapes of three Hokkaido wolves weaving through its legs till they pose before her. A ring of light surrounds her in a gathering of animals and birds of all shapes and sizes, species long extinct. These are forest spirits, Akila senses at once. She approaches the deer, no longer afraid in her heart, and reaches out to touch its neck. It lets her dainty fingers caress the thick fur. The frogs grow hushed and a heavy curtain of silence descends upon them. The deer bows its head so she can reach its face.

She feels something wet on her ankle, but she does not jump. One of the wolves is licking the wound and there is no more burning. The stag tilts its head against her touch, nuzzling into her palm. The profound sense of joy at being reunited after an immeasurable span of time cascades over her like a blessing. It is cathartic and yet like something she should have been doing all her life. A gathering of human and forest spirits. The chickenpox boils shrivel and drop away without a blemish. She does not notice because she is too busy smiling.

'THESE WORLDS you've been to, are they different dimensions or universes laid one on top of the other?' This was Shyam's fourth glass of Sangria. Akila was ahead by a glass, and it showed.

'No, it's the same universe,' she caught herself slurring.

'How do you know that?'

Straightening her back, she tried to focus. 'Because, other than this planet, everything else, the stars I mean, appear to be the same.'

'So?'

'So ... if the worlds were in fact in different universes, I would have expected there to be at least some variations, if not a total shift.'

'Why would there be variations? It's just the worlds that would be different.'

'Different universes allow for different causalities, however minute, that would result in more and more variations, according to Chaos theory.'

'I've heard of Chaos theory,' he said, raising his hand like the teacher's pet.

'There might be some hope for you, yet.' She winked. 'Now, if you were to take the theory into consideration, theoretically, from the beginning, in a manner of speaking, of this, or any, universe until this point ... over the course of, let's say 14 billion years, which is our current understanding,' she said, straining to keep a handle on the dismantled thoughts rolling out of her mouth, 'everything we know and don't yet know, would have been completely different.'

Shyam squirmed in an effort to keep up.

'Let's take the creation of the moon as an example,' she said, gesturing vaguely at the sky. 'It was the collision of another body with Earth approximately 4.3 billion years ago that created the satellite we call the moon, and it has happened only once. The odds against it happening at all are so tremendous, and yet it happened.'

'I think I'm getting it.'

'Now, if it, this collision, hadn't happened and this other body passed by without incident, there would be no moon. And if there wasn't a satellite of our very own to protect us from countless asteroids over the past 4 billion years–'

'Life would probably not exist,' he blurted eagerly.

'Good.'

'And who knows, maybe life was a result of a combination of forces, *including* the tidal force caused by the moon.'

'Maybe.' She licked her lips, impatiently tucking a lock of hair behind her ear. 'Don't interrupt. Now, coming back to the point you asked about, these alternate worlds exist in the same universal plane. So they, and I assume, we, exist in a sort of "bubble" in *this* universe.'

Shyam was obediently listening now, which gave her the chance to set off on the subject of her fascination with Quantum Mechanics. With a rushed sip of Sangria to moisten her mouth, she elaborated on the principles of quantum entanglement and quantum supposition, marvelling at their mind-bending revelations and how they might relate to the 'bubble'.

'Quantum mechanics is fucking amazing like that,' she added finally, 'it is not to be confused with classical mechanics in physics. Things like gravity. Quantum mechanics is beyond this. And it is the non-locality of quantum mechanics in space-time that got me thinking.' After another five minutes, dense with ideas, she underlined the lecture with a philosophical shrug. 'But there will always be mysteries.'

'And you're trying to figure them out,' he offered.

'Yes, I'm trying, always … but maybe some mystery is built into the very fabric of the universe, with its vast depths of the unknown.'

'What do you mean?'

'Space is not the final frontier, Shyam. It is only the beginning.'

Akila's eyes twinkled with excitement so infectious, it ran through him as a shudder.

'I'm glad you've gotten all that off your chest,' he chortled, 'because I didn't understand a thing.' He clinked her glass and downed the wine. She sipped hers as Shyam reached for the bottle. She was glad he hadn't challenged her. For though she was in her element when it came to theoretical physics, she had realized as soon as she began that her mind was muddled with the Sangria. She had wanted to impress him so much with what she had taught herself. Not only had she survived her many trials, she had nourished her mind.

It had been such a rush to charge through those ideas like a blind horse, though she could not recall if she had made much sense or just talked out of her ass. Either way, Shyam seemed impressed. Mostly with the terms she threw about no doubt. I'm not just good in bed, she thought, I have a mind that can bound over yours effortlessly, even drunk. I'm not a victim, not anymore.

But all he could think about were the dimples above her buttocks beneath that shapeless kurta bottom. Nibbling on those goose-fleshed curves. The small of her back rising through the cleft along her spine, up those elegant shoulders to the back of her neck, feeling her pushing back against his hungry body. The universe is a weird place, but it has somehow, for some reason, brought us together, he thought.

And he felt that heat in every fibre of his being, pulling him to her, as he tried to sit calmly beside her, sipping his now insipid Sangria.

THE PINK pyjama top with the cheerful rabbits hangs unfurled high up in the trees like the banner of a race of loonies. Akila keeps a wary eye out for the lizard. She does not know how long she has been away. The jungle is not as comfortable as it was before. It is a dangerous place, she repeats over and over in her head. Don't forget that. Don't ever get so comfortable again that you forget it. The monkeys have taken all the fruit she dropped, and toyed with her shirt. That is annoying, but considering what she has just been through, she does not begrudge them taking advantage of an opportunity. All she wants to do right now is to eat and scrub the black smears from her body in the pond. She recovers the shirt and tosses it down. It has animal stink all over it.

On the large flat rock she calls the Mez, perched beside the waterfall draining from the salamander pond, she basks naked in a patch of evening sun filtering through the foliage. Her body is free of chickenpox boils. Her pyjama top and bottom lie spread out over the rocks. Beside her is a fresh spear with a shard of obsidian bound neatly at the end. The last one served her well enough for her to craft another right away, in preparation for the lizard's return. A few of the yellow fruit she has come to call jamblis bob on the surface of the pool, occasionally vanishing into the giant black salamander daintily snorting them from below.

A gentle breeze rustles along the water. Akila lets it flow over her, playing her long bangs over her eyes and face. She is not in any pain. Except for the scar around her neck, her other wounds – the gashed ankle and the bruises covering her body – are all healed. The forest spirits in the swamp world were thorough. But she could not stay there. How she longed to. They instilled a sublime comfort in her body and nerves but there was no food or place to take shelter. The salamander stops five feet from her with its massive flat head just breaking the surface. Lying with her arms spread on either side and her head cocked, she scrutinizes the small button eyes.

'Are you trying to talk to me?' The salamander does not react to her words. 'Maybe you aren't but I think those forest spirits were, I could feel it. What were they trying to say? I felt like I should have understood.' She shakes her head. 'I don't know what I'm saying,' then with a grunt, 'and now I'm back here. Not exactly where I want to be.' She talks to the salamander as the sun slips behind the trees.

THE MORNING sun shimmers across the surface of the stream filled with red-bellies. Their backs glint like silver coins as they fight the current, grabbing anything brought by the waterfall that is worth eating. She has named the waterfall draining her pond, Machu, and the waterfall feeding it, Picchu. Akila stands on the Mez above Machu falls, looking down at the fish and chewing on the fruit that had once charmed her with its sweet creamy innards. But no more. The past few bowel movements having been rather unpleasant; her body is leaner than it had been when she first arrived, and she is feeling worse off for it.

She checks the edge of her spearhead. It is sharp enough. Taking the last bite out of a jambli, she tosses the remainder from a large leaf into the salamander pool. 'You don't think I can do it, do you?' The black head sucks down a fruit in reply.

'I'm going to start calling you Kala. That's your name from now on, okay?' Another jambli is sucked down. 'Good, now stay here, Kala. Akila is going fishing.'

She hops down the rocks and climbs down the rest to the stream below. The spear cuts cleanly through the water, but she misses her mark. She holds onto the end so she does not have to wade in to retrieve it. She tries again and again, missing every time. On her fifth attempt, she aims carefully and throws it as hard as she can. It slips out of her hand and there is a loud crack. The spear recoils from the impact and Akila can already see the damage through the pristine water. The obsidian blade has snapped in half. Thankfully, the staff is within reach and she gets hold of the end. A fish comes out with it, its jagged teeth dug into the wood. A smack against the ground makes it let go, flopping towards the sound of water.

It is so unexpected that for a few seconds Akila does not know what to do about it. Coming to her senses, she swipes the fish away from the edge of the stream with the flat side of the glassy obsidian and runs the broken end into its side. It continues to wriggle against the blade embedded in its body, blood seeping into the dirt. Akila pushes down harder with the spear. She feels the obsidian grind against the soil and her eyes fill with tears as she watches the fish open and close its mouth in its final moments of life. The tail flicks as it gasps for water one last time and then lies limp on the ground. Akila stares at it long and hard. The bright red of its belly and the silver back seem to have lost their raging glory. What lies at the end of her spear now is just a shadow of what it had been a moment before.

But this is for her survival, she reminds herself. She steps on the fish, jerks out the spear and plunges it back into the water near some red-bellies. A couple of them gnaw at the stick and she swings it out a little too fast. They are knocked off by her eagerness. Slower, she tells herself.

By now the fish have begun to gather closer. Their aggression chills her to the bone and she tries not to recall her nightmare of falling in, with those saw-like mouths ripping off pieces of her as she thrashes in the water. Just the thought of it makes her angry rather than afraid, and hones her patience. She thrusts the spear in and waits for two or three to latch on. Then tugs at the stick and notices how they fight harder by tugging back, making their teeth sink in deeper. Then swiftly, with delicate grace, the staff is swung up and over the edge of the rocks and tapped on the ground. She has managed to get three more.

The red-bellies flop around, snapping their jaws with loud clicks. With the butt of the spear, she whacks each on the head as hard as she can. She certainly does not want to see one half-alive with its head crushed in. Consumed by hunger, she does not mind killing them. But those eyes; she can't bear to see them goggling up at her as they fight for life.

That's me, she thinks. I'm the lizard and these fish are me. Am I a monster? She takes them in her palms. All the energy they had coursing through them as they fought the current and snapped at her stick, it is all gone. They are just this now, cold pieces of meat crusted with soil and blood.

She had been a good student in class not long ago. The principal's daughter does not really have a choice. But she has no clue how to start a fire. She hits two stones together, rubs together two sticks, rubs a stick on a stone, throws a stone against a rock, hurls the sticks into the stream, and the end result is a small pile of broken sticks with four dead fish piled upon it. And sore fingers.

'I thought man made fire,' she shouts at Kala, who watches her with trepidation from the safety of the pool. 'If Mowgli figured out how to make it and set Sher Khan's tail on fire, I can too.' With a suppressed bottom-lip, she glowers at the four fish lying there uselessly, and picks up her spear with a huff, shouting to Kala, 'He didn't even go to school!' Then marches off into the jungle as Kala slinks under the surface.

What the birds and insects haven't carried away, Akila places in the shallow hole she has scooped out with her hand. She shakes her head at the waste and her eyes tear up again. What is she going to do? She can't even make fire. Stupid Mowgli could make fire. How is she going to survive? Her last bowel movement was gut-wrenching and she is not looking forward to the next. Something, anything, other than fruit. A cooed howl diverts her gaze to the branches above.

Akila crawls along the branch on her stomach. At the far end sits a large nest with three blue-freckled eggs, each the size of her fist. And a wonderfully electric-blue plumed male bird is perched on one side, tilting its head, trying to comprehend the danger. The bird is the size of a small chicken and Akila is not worried about it. But she is concerned about the forty-foot fall below her. The bird clicks and caws, spreading its wings to flash silver feathers in her eyes. She looks away and crawls closer. In its final attempt to ward her away, the bird hovers, pulling at her hair and clawing at her arms. However, despite its attempts, she arrives at the nest, prompting the bird to withdraw to a higher branch and watch helplessly. She grabs an egg and it bursts in her hand. The clear liquid and the bleeding yolk drape her hand and forearm. She grits her teeth through the shock and picks another, far more gingerly, and crawls backwards. The tree bark is harsh against her thighs, stomach and the inside of her arms but when she is on the ground again, there is that intoxication of triumph coursing through her.

With a swagger, she examines her prize. It is delicate and

expertly crafted like a ceramic form and she can't wait to eat its contents. Happy memories of the scent of fresh omelettes and fried eggs, and the burst of flavours drown her mouth with anticipation. Why has she not thought to eat eggs until now? She has always loved them, and they are easy enough to get. A coo draws her gaze up to the nest where the plumed male sits on a higher branch, watching the plain-looking female frantically examine the ruined eggs upon her return, all the while cooing and howling in distress.

Shielding it with a palm over her breast-pocket, Akila slips from the scene of the crime like the lowly egg-snatcher she has become. She is too hungry to let her conscience come in the way of a meal. It is only one egg, and upon inspection, it appears even smaller than before. But no matter, for in her mind she can already taste the yolk.

She sits cross-legged on the Mez with her right hand still crusted by the destroyed egg and the dirt stuck to it. She daintily taps the top of the egg with her nail, cracking the seamless wonder, and picks away the small pieces to make an opening. The top of the clear egg-white shows and without wasting a moment, she sucks it down like a shot. She waits to savour the treat, but it is not delicious at all. It is gooey and tasteless and repulsive around her tongue. She leans over and spits into the Machu falls, trying to banish all traces of the awful thing.

'I need fire, Kala. Where can I get fire? I know you love the yellow jambli. I do too, and the red jambli isn't too bad, but I'm sick of it. I need to eat fish and eggs or I'll keep getting weaker. I just know it. I need to find a place where there's fire so I can bring it back to …' She stops talking as an idea takes shape. Why not go to the other worlds and get it? Maybe she'll even find a better world to live in, although she is reluctant to abandon Kala.

'Don't worry, if I do decide to stay, I'll keep visiting you with fresh jambli. Okay? But I need to go, boy, you understand, right? I won't abandon you, you're my only friend, Kala. But you need to stay here. I'll be back soon. I promise. Take care of our pond.'

She washes her hands and stands with her spear ready at her side. She prepares to leap into the pool, takes a moment to spit, coming to terms with the haunting aftertaste. Her body shakes with dread. She waves to Kala. 'I'll be back to see you, I promise.'

The freezing cold chokes the breath out of her. She fights the rapids but the chill has drained her strength and it takes the greatest effort to lift an arm and grab onto the thick ice sheet lining the shore. With both hands aching to the bone, she strains to heave her body out, but there is no stimulus left in her. Clenching her teeth, she wrenches with all her might, her face already glazed with a layer of fine crystals. Her legs weigh so much that she can barely lift them. They begin to go numb. Shrieking at the top of her lungs, she drags herself and rolls her hips over the ice. She rolls again until she hits the snow bank on the shore. She takes in quick jerky breaths and gets onto her hands and knees. She stands up and slips on the ice, stumbling into the deep snow bank.

She has never seen snow up close before, let alone touched it. Her first impression is not ideal. All around her loom towering mountains of rock draped in the white powder. There is no fire here. And she definitely cannot survive for much longer. There is only one thing left to do. She faces the gushing river, a lovely glacial hue that she would have appreciated far more in thick clothing or on picture postcards. But now all it transmits to her is the biting cold she must somehow convince her body to re-enter. Her body yells in every trembling limb that it is madness, and if she can remember how, in that disabling cold, she would have wept. She has learnt in a hurry that she no longer has anyone to console her. To clean her wounds, or help her up. It is up to her and her alone. Blockading her mind from the apprehension, she barely manages to toss her numb body into the water.

Her head plunges out of the water, and she is crouching on her hands and knees in the shallows. Her limbs are still numb and her body shudders, despite the heat. Asserting her way to the shore, she lingers, letting the heat draw out the evil chill.

'Ah!' She revels in the revitalizing of her senses. Her fingers are no longer aching stubs and her teeth have stopped chattering hysterically. On her feet again, she lets her chest draw in and exhale at leisure. When the ice locking her eyelids closed slides down in tears, she opens them to determine where she is.

It is a parched wasteland, flat and fading away into the distance below an emerald sky. She turns about to investigate how water could exist in such a place. A set of jaws, lined with two-inch teeth, lunges out at her. In a split second she falls back on the cracked ground and rolls onto her feet in the harsh glare of the sun. A seven-foot-long crocodile glumly draws itself back into the tepid green water. It is no more than a stagnant pond lying in the shadow of a careless mound of boulders. The pond enters further amidst the narrow gullies in the rocks. Though the water is green, she can clearly see three crocodiles, all around the same size, suspended under the surface with only their keen-eyed long faces above. There are some fish darting about, but not many. Akila goes around the mound to take a look at the other side, but it is more of the same. Flat and drab. If this whole world is a wasteland, there is no point in staying. The sun-baked ground burns her feet and she hurries back into the shade. The crocodiles stir with welcoming smiles as she dives in.

Standing up in the knee-high pool, from the metallic taste alone she can tell which world this is. She takes a step back into the water. The ground rumbles with volcanoes spitting fire and ash and a wailing giant kneels in the distance.

Her first impulse is to turn and escape back into the water but she does not when she realizes this could be her source of fire. Her spear was lost in the icy rapids and she needs a stick for her plan to work. Five hundred feet away she spots the charred skeleton of a small tree. It is her only hope. She stays alert for any rabid giants charging at her. With the coast clear, she sprints to the tree and rips off a two-foot stump. The heat sucks out the water from her clothes and skin. Moving quickly to keep the soles of her feet from burning, she cuts across to a glowing hole in the black rock. A torrent of magma flows three feet beneath her. The red heat scorches her skin. It has to be done quickly. She dips the stick and brings it out with a glowing ball dripping from the end.

She runs back across the sharp lava rocks to the pool and skids to a halt. How can she not have thought this through? She has to jump into water to get back, so how was she planning to transport fire? She hurls the stick away and slaps her head with both hands like a grieving widow. She stops only when her arms grow tired. All that she has been through is for nothing and she has to return to that damn jungle, empty-handed. She feels like a complete failure for she knows that without fire she has no chance of survival. She observes a wailing giant through the heat haze for some minutes, her mind absent of thought. Then she turns back to the rippling water.

It is cold. She gulps for air as she goes under. Her feet can't touch the bottom and the water is still, with no current to draw her to the shallows. She knows how to swim but the dead bees and insects floating about her trigger panic. The water stings her eyes. She must be in the field of roots. She is going to die like those animals, frozen in their agony, to rot away. Beating and kicking, she gulps volumes of the cold bitter water. She breaks the surface, thrashing her arms wildly, searching for something to grab on to and climb. Her knuckles knock against a hard surface. She yelps in pain and grabs on regardless. She pulls her body to it, gathering dead insects along the surface. Her other hand takes hold as well, her muscle memory finds a foothold and she steps up and rises out.

She is at the school swimming pool behind the gymnasium. She remembers freezing in the unheated pool, finding it fun only because of the novelty of swimming in school and standing with her friends wrapped in their towels afterwards, giggling together in the embarrassment of appearing in their swimsuits in front of the boys. Now it hosts floating leaves and drowning bees and alarmed water-boatmen bugs taking their turn. She snaps out of her nostalgia. This time she must find her father. From the pool she can take a slightly longer detour by his office in case he is not at home like the last time.

She scales the gate of the pool compound and hastens along the tarmac road, her naked feet stinging but she does not care. She can't care or she will run out of time again, and that is something she is not willing to let happen. She is not going to waste this opportunity crying. She will find her father and tell him everything.

As she runs, she recalls how no one could see or hear her the last time. So how will she talk to him? She turns in to the path leading up to the grand clock tower sprouting from the shoulders of the 150-year-old main building with its gothic arches and carved lattices. She bounds up the steps into the lobby and turns to his office door on the ground floor at the left. She turns the knob mid-run and bursts in. A pudgy dark man with black-rimmed spectacles and a pencil-thin moustache looks up from the mahogany table. He gawks at the door and shouts out, 'Miss Iyer, the wind just blew the door open. Could you please close it for me, I need to finish what I'm writing here.' An adjacent door clicks open and a middle-aged woman with jet-black hair in a red sari and cream cardigan rolls in. Astounded, Akila steps aside to let the woman pass. Miss Iyer looks outside and then at the door. The wind has never blown it open before, she muses. But there is too much work left unfinished on her desk to ponder this mystery. Akila waits at the top step of the porch, the image of this strange man at her father's desk having totally thrown off any plan or sense she had. The placard on the desk had read Dr P.V. Rajan, followed by a nonsensical stream of credentials.

A brief twinge in the stomach startles her out of her spell. Like a bolt, she is off to her house. As she clips down the steps past the hedges, onto the winding lane, she makes a mental list of essentials to pick up. Running along the driveway to her house, it no longer feels like home. She knows it can't be hers anymore if her father is no longer the principal. Has he left the school for good? Does he think she is dead?

Tears course down her full cheeks as she scrambles through the house, pushing aside chairs and knocking over vases. In the kitchen, she rummages through the cupboards like a looter. Her stomach spasms and she cringes on the floor, tumbling crockery clanging loudly about her. She recovers and collects all the matchbooks she can get into a jute bag kept rolled up on the bottom shelf. She throws in some knives and biscuits and salt and sugar. It makes sense to take all she can.

The bag has grown pretty heavy now and with the nausea

on the verge of overwhelming her senses, she suddenly realizes she needs some books on how to make fire and all the other stuff one needs to know, to survive. The school library is back the other way, behind the school administration building. She does not think she can make it, but she knows she has to try or she might die. She is sure this is what dying must feel like.

With the bag flung over her shoulder, she runs back on to the driveway and along the winding lane up to the school building. Her body is on the verge of collapsing, and it feels like her stomach has risen to her mouth. Her stomach throws up something into the back of her throat and it burns her nostrils and eyes. Where are you, Papa? she screams in her head. She knows nobody can hear or see her but she was taught to be silent during class time.

She goes huffing into the art building, down the staircase and into the library. She can't stand it anymore. All she can think about is the acid burning her insides and the compulsion to spill her guts on the floor. Her eyes fill with tears from the agony and the desperation. She grabs a handful of the books nearest to her sitting in the returned stack and starts out back up the steps again.

Coming out of the building her toe catches on a stone but she manages to recover. With her first steps there is the sound of something ripping behind her and a heavy clattering. She turns and almost tears her hair out at the sight of everything she had packed lying strewn along the past ten feet. One of the knives must have cut through the bag. She can't bear the pain and nausea anymore. Her brain wants to burst free of the confines of her skull. She frantically grabs the things closest to her – a box of matches, two knives and a book. Her hands can't hold anymore.

She races to the hedged-in swimming pool by the sports

grounds that are teeming with boys and girls in black shorts and coloured shirts. Here her pain and discomfort ease considerably, but the recent memory of them compels her to the swimming pool. She tosses the loose items over the gate and clambers over. On the other side she collects her things, her eyes wet with tears, her body achingly tired and her soul sapped. Hugging her prizes to her chest with the knives in her hand warily pointed outward, she launches herself sideways into the bleak, chlorinated water.

THE WIND was soft and inviting against his face. Macoco sailed above the city with his bat-like wings unfurled, catching the air and hovering for a bit. They were surrounded by stars against an inky-blue night sky, without a cloud to be seen. Above them the ivory moon floated like a peering eye, and the Earth below seemed distant, the city and streets sparkling like a tangle of jewels upon the floor. Akila sat facing Shyam, riding side-saddle on Macoco's shoulders, her eyes hidden by her squinting brows. But he knew she had meant what she said. After spending a series of nights with her, he had grown to trust her implicitly. Though he was not sure whether he trusted his own sense of reality anymore. Why was he so lucky, to be here right now with a beautiful girl grinning impishly at him?

She took off her hairband and slipped it on her wrist. Her long curls waved gracefully in the wind. She quickly pulled off her spaghetti top and slid the slacks down her athletic legs. They watched the clothes flutter in the air and glide away. Akila sat there for a moment, a mermaid upon a rock, tying her hair back up, letting Shyam admire her body bathed in the moon's satin glow. Then she snapped her fingers at him and he hurriedly undressed, flinging the shirt and shorts over the side. He was already erect and waiting.

She slid across Macoco's back, skimming the smooth velvet skin, laid one thigh over Shyam's and raised the other to do the same. Then she lowered herself onto his shaft. Their insides burnt, joined in wet passion. Shyam waited, his hands yearning to grasp her buttocks and thrust but there was a plan to follow. They had discussed it step-by-step and he had feared there would be no spontaneity after the dissertation. But here, aloft the world, among the winking stars, he felt the tremors of hunger coursing through his limbs. She wrapped her arms about his neck and her thighs slipped around him. Their bodies pressed against each other with every breath and they could feel the other's heart beat just as rapidly as their own. She kissed him gingerly with a lick on his upperlip and breathed, 'Now.' He pushed his foot down and let their tangled bodies slide over and fall away into nothing. They accounted for the lack of traction by using their hold on each other. She used her arms and thighs to move her body and he helped with his hands as they pirouetted through space, feeling the air tearing at them. Their mouths parted as she drew away a little to look deep into his eyes, moving up and down, and grinding against his pelvis in frantic circular motions to get him fully inside. The air groped roughly at their limbs and faces, flowing over their bodies in a lustful rush, flicking at their nether regions and genitals, escalating the sensation beyond belief. They closed their eyes, just letting it pour over them as their bodies slapped harder and harder, their fingers dug deeper into flesh, the pitch of the rushing air screaming in their ears.

Shyam's eyes sprang open when he was about to burst and saw the streetlights and cars charging towards them. His eyes met Akila's dampened grin and they held each other tightly, letting the warm fluids explode in a succession of intense spasms. Their mouths met and Shyam hugged her close, relishing the sensation of her breasts crushed against his heaving chest. He became aware of a force pushing against them from below and suddenly they were lying on a pulsating surface. Akila ground herself against him and he nibbled on her bottom lip, his thumb delicately rubbing her nipple. They rolled apart on Macoco's back, holding hands, trying to reclaim their breaths, watching the stars course above.

IT IS difficult to make out the red and black stripes, but there is no doubt that the dead lizard is the same one that tried to kill her. Just looking at it makes her ankle twitch with a wound it no longer bears. But the predator had at some point met its match and now lies prone, delicate white stems tipped with fine feathery bulbs rising out of its skin, all along its length. From the caved-in stomach sprouts a small garden of the bulbs and from its eyes grow two thick twisted furry stems. It is beautiful, lying there in the splinters of sun through the leaves.

She does not ordinarily venture so far from her pond or so close to the field of roots. It is visible through the edge of the treeline just a few feet ahead. She wanted to further explore this world and find more varieties of fruit, having grown tired of the red and yellow jambli day in and out. Of late she has found more dead animals with these fluffy growths, even a nest with eggs blanketed in it.

Her hair is a ruffled mess and she blows a lock off her face to take a better look. If not for them being carcasses, she would have admired the natural beauty of the arrangements, like miniature exotic gardens. She assumes that this is what happens to the dead of this world. Perhaps they are consumed in this manner.

She keeps her distance from it as she paces around, studying the tendrils growing out from within the body with the skin surviving as a shell. A loud horn like a large animal's call resonates in the air. There is no mistaking where it comes from, for a red plume of smoke cuts a wavering line into the purple sky above the tree at the heart of the field of roots.

She goes to the treeline to investigate this new phenomenon. What can it mean? She watches for a minute but nothing happens. Maybe it is no concern of hers. So she shrugs and turns away, then does a double take. She squints back at the dreaded tree. Some movement had caught her eye but she has lost it. A trick of the eye or the shadow of a bird or some poor animal lost among the roots? There it is again, certain specks travelling in her direction. What are they?

She leans the spear against a tree and uses both her hands like binoculars. She focuses her gaze on the moving specks through narrow slits. They are approaching with great speed and dexterity over the roots, like a pack of wild dogs on the hunt. It takes her a while to notice that the five swift shapes are heading straight for her. She collects her spear and rushes along the treeline to get out of the way of whatever those things are. The first lesson you learn when dealing with animals is to avoid danger whenever you possibly can. It saves you valuable energy and keeps you from getting wounded, which may as well be a death sentence in the jungle.

Three hundred feet later, she stops to take account, panting heavily. Hugging the roots and sliding along with no discernible gait, they have altered their course for her. They are scarily near now. She has to make a run for it into the jungle. There is not a single place that sticks out in her mind as a good spot to stand her ground. She starts sprinting towards her pond. Maybe she can hide. But her heart is gripped with the knowledge that whatever they are, they are fast. She has no choice but to escape into another world. She nods to herself with the decision firm as she races through the thick foliage.

The jungle has grown deathly quiet and the sound of her rushing through the leaves resonates loudly in the hush. She stops and listens for the creatures. There is not even distant birdsong. The silence clings with an ominous feeling of something horrible gathering about her, and that indelible sensation of being surrounded fills her with terror. She starts running again, determined not to look back, no matter what. Just get to the water and dive in. She can tell from the familiar trees and harmony of flowing water that the pond is close. There is a muffled rustle above her. Quickly glancing up, she dives to the side to avoid a falling object. It lands on the ground with an anticlimactic *plat*. Akila kicks back some feet from it and halts when she sees the shape and colour. It looks like a baby golden-furred monkey. It must have slipped and fallen. She can't leave it here for those creatures after her. She crawls to it and picks it up, cradling it in her hand as she prepares to run.

Then she shrieks and hurls the thing away. It is the top half of an adult monkey, eyes rolled back and the limp lower jaw hanging to the side. Her hand and arm are covered in its blood, still warm. She stands there, petrified with horror. She can feel something watching her from above. No sound indicates its presence but the prickling hair on the back of her neck and the compulsion to turn and look are unmistakable. She fights the impulse hard, but she has to see. Hugging her spear close to her body, she rolls her eyes up.

In the low-hanging branches and twisted trunks above her,

three insects hang inverted. They are each a little larger than a man and the one closest to her is suspended no more than seven feet away. Its face is bathed with blood. Her gasp triggers multiple sets of clicking patterns. They are unmistakably insects. Those large, dome-like pale-green eyes with cold black dots for pupils are fixed on her, and she is certain there is no escape. In her peripheral vision she can sense something moving without a sound, followed by more clicking. She had seen five in the field of roots, so the other two must be around here somewhere. If those jaws can snap a monkey in two with no effort, what will they do to her? Her grip on the spear tightens and her palms burn from the friction. She quickly whips it to her waist, ready to strike out. At least once before she goes down.

'Put down the weapon, Akila,' the bloody-faced one speaks. They are the first words addressed to her in weeks and she almost does not comprehend, blubbering, 'What?'

'Put down your weapon.' It is not a human voice, but one formed with clicks and eerily machine-like.

She gapes at this bizarre face speaking to her.

'Put it down,' it repeats, 'and come with these insectoids. Come to me.'

She understands now. 'You are not one of them.'

'I am not.'

'How are you speaking then?'

'Through them.'

'How?'

'Wait, you'll see. It is vital that you accompany them to the tree.'

'The tree?'

'The tree at the centre of what you call the field of roots.'

'How do you know what I call it?'

'You are only a Beli. I don't answer to a Beli. You are in my realm.'

'What are you talking about? What is a Beli? This is some mistake. I don't belong here. Please let me go home.'

An insectoid appears from the bushes, its short antennae shuffling in front of her face. 'Then come and we will see,' it tells her. She takes a step, hesitating. 'You won't let me go home, will you?'

'It is tiresome to converse through these inane creatures. They are consumed by hunger, an insatiable hunger, and to talk through them I must command their consciousness. I must share that hunger. Come to me so we can speak in person.'

'Are you that ... thing that cut my neck?'

'Yes.'

'Are you going to cut my neck again?'

'Yes,' it says plainly.

'Is this heaven? Are you God?'

The insectoids fall silent for a while.

'Come to me, and I will tell you all.'

'Come to you so you can hurt me again?'

'That is your purpose, Akila.'

'What?'

'You are the Beli.'

'Beli? What is that?'

'The Beli fortifies the foundations. You are the Beli.'

'What does that mean?'

'You are the sacrifice.'

'Will you keep cutting me?' she asks, touching the scar that marks her throat.

'Every three revolutions around the sun I will shed your blood or these worlds will crumble.'

'What are you talking about?'

'None of that is your concern. Your role is of the Beli, you are the sacrifice.'

Akila steps back.

'It hasn't been three years,' she appeals, shaking her head, 'only a few days.'

'Enough time for the filth you brought with you to infect the being.'

'What filth? I didn't bring anything. You brought me here. You put me in this place. I didn't bring anything!'

'You were infected at the time of the initiation. It shouldn't have mattered, but somehow it has permeated the fabric of the being. Now that you are cured, you must be sacrificed again, and your unpolluted blood shared to wash away this accursed contagion.'

'Chickenpox? You're saying you caught my chickenpox?'

'You've already seen what it can do. Everything is dying because of the pox. And whatever you have touched, directly or indirectly, dies even sooner. You saw the lizard that attacked you. You killed it.'

'With my spear. I killed it with my spear.'

'You are a child and you poked it with a stick. You think that is enough to kill such a creature? The pox eats at the jungle as we speak, killing everything slowly from within, and then it consumes them. Your blood has cursed this being and now I must revive it. Before it is too late.'

'Why are you talking to me?'

The insectoids fall silent.

'You don't need to talk to me,' she says, eyeing them. 'You could have taken me away with these monsters. So why haven't you?'

The insectoid inches towards her with its clicking rising to a frantic pitch, and then it stops, clicking and all. Five pairs of small black points focus intensely on her.

'You need me to come willingly. You can't force me, can you?' She caresses the scar. 'I am the sacrifice because it is my sacrifice to make, not yours. Am I right?'

The insectoid speaks, its clicks as sharp as crackling corn, 'The first time, the initiation, it has to be made cleanly. The Beli must offer to be present.'

The insectoid above her continues, 'I have underestimated you. You are not as little as you look.'

'Oh, I am,' she retorts, 'but I will grow bigger.'

Another insectoid emerges beside her, its long face and the large eyes studying her reactions. 'And I will watch you closely.'

'Smart. Smart, little human,' the one before her mocks. 'You must be smart enough to realize that if this jungle and this world are infected and die, then so will you soon after.'

Not if I have a way out to another world, she thinks. 'There is nothing you can say that will convince me to let you kill me.'

'You will come to me.'

'So you can kill me again in another "three revolutions"? No, thank you!' she barks, with a petulant shake of the head. Her father would have slapped her if he ever caught her speaking to anyone with such disrespect. But suddenly finding herself with leverage over these monsters, after being lost and alone all this time; she can hardly help herself. If the chickenpox is really so dangerous to the living things in this world, maybe it will kill the creature talking through these insectoids. After all, it seems pretty worried about it.

'Will you really let all living beings in this world perish because of your selfishness?' the bloody-faced insectoid clicks.

'Don't call me selfish – you're the selfish one. I was never given a choice to come here. You kidnapped me. And now you're cribbing because your world has caught my chickenpox? Why should I care? This isn't my world,' she yells and thrusts the spear point into the nearest insectoid's face. She dashes away through the bushes. All she has to do is get to the pond and dive in to escape. But she has to make it to the water. The insectoids are fast. She has seen them in action and she knows her short legs are no match for them. Hopefully her spearing has surprised her pursuers enough to disorient them and buy her some time. That is all she needs right now. Just a few seconds so she can reach the water, and then she's free. Wherever she goes, she will know that the creature that stole her is dead. And she planted the seed of its destruction. The raging adrenalin pumps her blood harder and focuses her mind.

A viscous white fluid leaks from the gash made by the spear. The insectoid tilts its head, examining the discarded spear's metal blade with its debossed kitchenware brand. The clicking between them is sparse and crisp. The wounded insectoid drops the spear and the five slide into the shadows.

Dashing through the whipping underbrush with her arms shielding her face, she can tell she is heading in the right direction from the familiar trees along the way. She bursts into the clearing at the salamander pond, squinting at the light, elated that she has made it and her escape is imminent.

Suddenly her eyes fall upon Kala's black head resting on the shore. A white twisted stem some inches long hangs from the rim of its button eye. Akila jerks to a halt, almost snapping her ankle. She drops to her knees on the pebbles, before her beast lying there, half out of the water like a beached sea-monster in its death throes. Its mouth opens and closes with wheezing breaths, exposing the infection of the white thread-like fur around the edges. She can't bear to see her friend suffering;

her only friend in this savage world. The gentle monster that befriended her.

She bursts into tears, sobbing and slobbering as she tries not to cover her face. She wants to see him, these last few moments of his life. She can hear clicking, the sound surrounding her. She wipes her face and looks about for the five insectoids, though she can only see one. The one that she knows wants to be seen. It stands on the rock crowning Picchu falls above the pond. The monkey's blood still covers its face. It speaks calmly. 'Every living thing. Did you think your pet would be immune?'

'Don't hurt him. He doesn't hurt anybody. Please let him be okay.'

'You're the one who brought the pox to this world. You're the one who can cure this world. I'm not doing anything to your pet, Akila, you are.'

'He's not my pet, he's my friend.'

'Good.'

She snarls at the insectoid but does not get any reaction.

'Why are you angry with me?' it asks patronizingly. 'You can stop this, you can save it. You know what you have to do. It is what you were brought here to do in the first place, so why complain and resist? You are the Beli, you are the sacrifice. You are meant to do this. You can save this creature and the life on this world. The sacrifice is not death, Akila. You will see your "friend" again, very soon.'

'I can save him?'

'Yes. But you must act now.'

'Are you sure I won't die?'

'The pox meddled, so things were not as they should be. You can't die in this realm as long as you're the Beli. The Beli sustains it, so to make you pervious to death would be illogical.'

'Then why isn't there another Beli here? If a Beli cannot die and this world needs a Beli to sustain it, where is the one that came before me?'

'Very good. I'll tell you, once you come to me and this matter is behind us.'

Powerless, Akila watches Kala gasp. She wipes away her tears and stands up. An insectoid waits beside her with its back bowed for her to climb on. They race through bushes, up tree trunks and through branches with such rapidity that Akila can hardly believe she ever thought she could outrun them. The field of roots flows by below them in a grey-green blur of twisting and winding tubular arteries, and she finds herself on firm ground again, before the tree on top of the mound. She draws back the windswept hair from her face and reads the scene about her.

The insectoids have arranged themselves on either side of her and she is standing again at the centre of the field of roots, where she had awoken for the first time into this nightmare. Thirteen small-holes gathered in no obvious pattern mark the ground by her with its strange leathery texture. She turns, longing for the jungle, the damp soil, the docile rocks. Now it is just a hazy line skirting the ghastly field. She does not sense the presence moving up behind her. It waits, as still as the tree. The hair on the back of her neck stands, and she spins around. A sharp edge catches the sun as it slits left to right and Akila's head flops off her neck. Her body crumples to the ground. The blood drains into the thirteen holes, gurgling vulgarly on the fresh sacrifice.

THE MARBLE bench on the roof sat vacant but for the two wine glasses, the white wine showing no sign of fatigue. A hand reached up over the edge, felt its way to the nearest glass stem and dextrously manoeuvred it down, out of sight. Akila lay supine, on a patchwork quilt Shyam's mother had given him, on the damp floor of the roof. She had her head propped up on a fluffy cumber-cushion, her eyes resting as she sipped the wine. She moaned as some spilled outside her mouth and she propped up on her elbows to wipe her chin. She placed the glass on the floor, just within reach so they would not accidentally knock it over. Licking her lips, she watched Shyam's head stirring under her skirt between her splayed knees. She pursed her lips slyly, reclined her head on the pillow, and slowly drew the skirt off his head. He looked up at her inquiringly, the area around his mouth wet with his saliva and her juices, as he asked, 'What's up?'

'No, nothing, just watching.'

Gleaming a smirk back at her, he resumed the business with his tongue and lips on her. She reached for the glass again and took a lazy sip. Gently rolling the dry wine over her tongue, she let the tingles wash down her throat and chest to blend with those rising from Shyam's tender attention. Something moved amidst the potted plants flanking them. It shot by before Akila could see what it was. The glass on the bench moved, scraping along the marble. She looked up at the whiskered face of a grey tomcat peering down at her. A small bell dangled on its collar. 'Oh, shit,' she said, rescuing the glass from the bench and putting it on the floor beside her. Shyam looked about anxiously. 'What is it?'

'It's a cat.'

They both looked up at the cat perched on the edge of the marble bench. 'That's just the building cat. We adopted him when he was a kitten, don't mind him.'

'I don't mind him. I'm just not too keen on cats, and I do mind him sitting above my face and watching us.'

Shyam assumed she was joking, only a second before realizing she probably was not. He wiped his wet cheeks against her thighs and kneeled before the cat. He waved his hand, hissing, 'Okay, get away, Sikander. Can't you see I'm busy?'

Sikander watched his antics with keen interest. He then sniffed the air and his gaze wandered down between Akila's open legs. 'No, don't look down there. Look up at me.' He guided Sikander's focus back to him. 'She's mine. So you don't get to look down there. Can't you see I'm busy, man?' The cat mewled. It suddenly turned and hissed at a bright light, and disappeared into the shadows. A beam rested on the empty bench. Shyam fell forward, his shoulders pushing down Akila's knees, his cheek pressed on her damp pubic mound. The inquisitive beam stayed on the bench and then shot off to the side, following the rustling among the potted plants as the cat tried to make his escape.

'Paagal billi,' a voice whined from the door to the roof, and a stout man barely five feet tall trudged over to one of the large rubber water-tanks. Shyam crawled up a few inches, sliding Akila's top up her stomach with the bridge of his nose. She flicked his ear, making him wince. 'What?' he mouthed silently. She mouthed back, 'Who is that?'

'The building's security guard,' he whispered, barely loud enough to hear himself. The guard pulled a screeching ladder across the roof to the tank and took a peek over, opening the lid. Shyam pulled Akila's top over the swell of her right breast, exposing the alert nipple to his breath. He nudged it playfully with the tip of his nose. She flicked his ear again. He lightly bit the swell of her breast, and she pinched his earlobe. The guard reset a valve at the tank's base and grumbled back to the roof entrance, sighing as he made his exit. They let go of each other and chuckled, Akila adding another flick in retaliation. Shyam lay between her legs with his head on her chest, his lips brushing her breast as she ran her fingers through his hair. In these past few days together, he felt like they had never let go of each other's hand. They never had, he thought, even on a Quantum level, according to Akila. And that feeling of oneness with someone – not sameness or togetherness, but being two halves that form one, tangibly incomplete apart – that was a novel emotion to him, and he did not want to let go of it. He would not, no matter what he had to do. 'Will he be back?' she asked, not really interested, her finger winding a curl of his hair. He shrugged and took the aroused nipple between his lips.

THE COLLAR and shoulders of her pyjama top are still damp with blood. Akila trudges through the jungle in a daze, her arms hanging limply by her sides. Again she had woken up alone under that strange tree and made her way over the roots. She is awake. She can see and hear and feel the dead leaves squishing under her bare feet. But she can't believe she is back. Part of her had wanted to die and leave this place forever. It would have been so much easier. It would have all been over in a flash. Wherever death takes her is sure to be better than this place. If this is truly the afterlife, she wishes she had been reborn as something else. A dragonfly or a horse. Or maybe even nothingness would be more suitable than this.

But she has three more years of living in this jungle before having to go through that again. This cheers her up for a minute before she is reminded that she is trapped here, solely to be sacrificed over and over again. An oblation to this insanity.

The Treeman that had spoken to her had not kept his word about giving her an explanation. At the thought of Kala her face transforms with the joy.

He would be okay now. At least she has saved him. She makes a detour and gathers some of his favourite yellow jambli in her shirt flap. She hesitates for a moment, wondering if it's okay to eat them, if everything is infected with her dangerous chickenpox. No, the Treeman had said that this sacrifice with her clean blood would be the cure. And on her way back, she had passed the lizard's carcass, which is now only a collection of skin and bones. The white fluff and tendrils have vanished without a trace. It had been horrible to see that white thing growing from Kala's eye. She hopes he will be able to see properly again.

She counts nine jamblis and hurries to the pond, occasionally skipping with glee and losing a fruit in her frolic. She does not care, there are more where they came from. Having almost lost him once, she realizes just how important Kala is to her. She craves that feeling of being protected again. Of not worrying every second whether something is trying to eat her even if, as the Beli, she cannot die.

She can hear some shuffling at the pond and she is thrilled that Kala has his strength back. She elbows through the bush, and beaming, stares at a wolverine gnawing at Kala's face. Aghast, she drops the fruit and the wolverine whips about at the sound in a flash of gnashing teeth and claws.

Akila dashes back into the jungle to retrieve her spear. She finds it at the spot where she had stabbed the insectoid in the eye. The blade is crusted with a white substance, but she'll have to worry about that later. She returns to the pond to rescue Kala from some scary-looking dog taking advantage of his weakness during his recovery. She leaps out of the bushes, spear ready, but the animal has gone. Not before managing to do some serious damage to Kala's snout, though. The raw flesh beneath is exposed. She knows it does not matter anyway. He is not moving, not even struggling anymore to breathe. Her friend is dead and he's already being eaten by whatever can get to him. She does not know how long she was gone but it has been long enough for the carcass to start reeking. The white growth from his eye is gone but what good does that do him now?

She gently nudges the fruit she had dropped on the ground with her big toe. He loved them. He had probably never tasted them before she came. And somehow they had become friends. In this savage world he had accepted her. To her, an alien in this alien world, a monster had felt her kindness and returned some. Where can she find that again now?

She sits on the Mez, where she had sat on so many occasions and fed him as she talked endlessly about her father and friends, and even about her mother who had passed away when she was a baby. She shoos away a couple of birds that start pecking at his eyes. She decides she will not let him be eaten, not her friend.

'Kala,' she keeps repeating tenderly, sitting with her legs folded and head cocked to one side, wearing a sad, wistful smile. The bush rustles as a wet snout pokes through and she hollers and beats a rock with the spear, driving the intruder away. But she is not prepared for how bad the smell can get and in another two hours, as the sun begins to set, Kala's body is bloated and riddled with streams of ants and beetles and flies. It is a battle she has lost and she shakes her head at the realization that she is not capable of doing even this. The Treeman lied to her. He had said Kala would live. That was the only reason she had agreed, and he did not keep that promise. Was it a promise? Whatever it was, he lied to her.

There have been animals shuffling through the underbrush

beyond the bushes and she can tell they will not keep away for long, no matter what a little girl with a spear supposes. She goes to her tree, resigned to the fact that that is all she is – a little girl with a spear in this wild, wicked place. Does she belong here? Does she deserve to survive? She is tired and that is some comfort as she climbs up the tree trunk to her platform. She gets to it and shrieks uncontrollably. The golden-furred monkeys cuddled together on it shriek back at her. She is in no mood to deal with them. She whacks the platform with her spear and the monkeys scatter up the tree with sharp complaints. She beats her frustration and anger out upon the trunk, shrieking all the while. When the spell subsides, she is exhausted. She crawls onto the platform and curls into a foetal ball.

The jungle night is marked by the regular symphony of insects. Beneath their calls, as sleep slowly overwhelms her, she can hear the hustle of creatures below, attacking poor Kala's corpse.

The next morning the birds are chirping and the little golden-furred monkeys are hopping from tree to tree. Akila squats on the Mez and scrapes the crusted white gob off her spear-blade with a stone.

Kala's hulking frame has vanished overnight but for some scraps. A clean humerus lies on the pebbles, and some feet away there is the pelvis with a femur and some vertebra still attached. She can feel tears coming on and quickly dunks her face in the water. Later, she takes the few vestiges of her friend and buries them at the base of the jambli tree. He would have lived under it if he could. She picks up a jambli and twists it open as she walks away.

A shaggy brown animal scurries away with the bones, having dug them out as soon as her back is turned. She flings the jambli after it, screaming, 'I saved you, I saved you all and you can't even leave him for me?'

There is no one left to listen to her ramblings now. The Mez feels like it is no longer firmly planted. Her stomach growls with hunger but she is in no mood to go fishing. Then she sees a couple of red-bellies in her pond and hops to her feet and takes aim. Kala would never have tolerated their presence, and neither will she. Her first jab catches one, while the other attacks the staff. She hauls them both out in one swoop and lands them on the pebbles, flopping and kicking up a fuss. 'I'll show you, if you think you can come into Kala's pond,' she mumbles, going around picking up sticks. 'I'm going to have you for breakfast!'

Akila hates to admit it but the two interlopers are delicious. She sits hunched on the Mez, basking in the sun, letting her pyjamas dry on the rocks nearby. She could not get all the blood off this time, but it will have to do. The loneliness hangs over her in a shroud of gloom. Chance had brought Akila and Kala together, and it has taken Kala away. How can she take control of this all-powerful demon called chance and bend it to her will? Anger and depression take turns assaulting her. She gets dressed and stares at her reflection in the water. She wants to go back home. She wedges the spear among the rocks and prepares herself at the edge of the water. She opens her arms wide and closes her eyes. She stands poised in the sun, swaying with the breeze like a scarecrow, then lets herself fall flat onto the surface with a smack.

When she hikes out of the stream, she knows where she is with her first glance at the sky. Only Earth is blue. At least chance did not kick her around this time and she is here on her first try, but now what? She scurries up the slope from the stream, snaking through the valley in the Nilgiris she loves so much, listing items to collect. She comes up beside the church at the junction and touches the old artillery gun kept there. She had spent hours fiddling with the clutches and gears along with her friends as they discussed boys and other things that did not matter. The principal's house is right there and the view of the sunken horse-riding grounds had let her keep an eye on her father when he headed back home after his evening rounds with his trusty bay stallion, Jules.

There are children walking past, some her classmates, none looking in her direction. One girl suddenly looks her way and runs forward but a friend calls her back, reminding her of the last time they played at the gun and got scolded by the principal.

She has forgotten all about the list. There is only sadness and self-pity in its place. Suddenly she freezes mid- thought, her gaze following a boy chatting with his friends. She has no doubt it is Shyam. How did he escape? Then he looks at her and their eyes meet. He is not looking through or past her, she has no doubt about it. He is clearly looking at her. Rather stupidly, some impulse in her makes her raise a hand and wave, her mouth doing the impossible and smiling. To her utter shock, he smiles shyly and waves back before returning his attention to his buddies.

What just happened? She waves at the other kids, smiling broadly, like a mad person at a passing parade but nobody responds. And yet Shyam did. Why didn't he come and talk to her? Why didn't he ask her why she is still in her dirty pyjamas? And what was that flush of elation when she saw him? But now it has passed and she knows there is not enough time to make it into her house for more matches or supplies. Next time, she'll have to run to the girls' dorms and steal some underwear and clothes along with more matches. She rushes to the stream shouting to no one, 'Shoes! Why do I keep forgetting to add shoes to the list?'

She tears the surface of the water and splashes about trying to gain some foothold, but she's either too short to touch the bottom or the bottom is deeper than she would like it to be. Her eyes are burning and she gags on the salinity. She flips a clump of hair out of her eyes and evaluates the flat, endless blue in all directions. A small island more than a kilometre away is the only blip marking the clean horizon. It is too far to swim and she is certain she can't make it. What terrifies her is the smacking realization that she can't dive into another world without someplace to dive from and hit the surface. The island is her only hope.

She floats lifelessly on the surface, resting from the exertion, her heart beating manically in her chest as she massages her right thigh, which is beginning to cramp. To avoid drowning and make it to the island, she'll have to slow down and pace herself. There is a tingling in her cramped leg, and then in the other, and then a deep vibration resonates in the water. Her legs shift marginally with a wisp of a current drawing her to the side. There is something moving down there.

What if the water is infested with sharks? And what was that? Did something just swim past her leg? She wants to swim but the island hangs in the distance beyond the languid tides like a mocking mirage. She dunks her head in the water and peers into the unfathomable depths. There is a dark shifting form the size of a hill, perhaps fifty feet beneath her pencil legs, but even that is difficult to judge. It blends so well with the background that it could be twice that distance and even larger than her estimation for all she knows. The shards of light dancing on the huge domed body do not reveal much detail. Maybe it will just pass by and leave her unnoticed.

She takes another breath and continues watching it sail past. The tapering second half, now below her, splits and spreads wide and she realizes they are tentacles. They stay open like an umbrella and odd patterns begin to form and flow over the body, like static amidst the dancing light. Smaller creatures, a fraction of its size, emerge out of the opening like a black stream of weird tadpoles. They shoot about the large tentacles in an agitated swirl. The patterns on the dominant body grow brightly coloured and a flash of white runs along it before going dark. Another flash of white that dissolves into a static of sparking spots and then the creature changes its colours seamlessly from green at one end to orange at the other.

She is mesmerized by the show and gawks at the colossal octopus in wonder. The little ones swarm about, reeling at incredible velocities. Then they too begin to show patterns on their skin as they swim in a school, sparkling with alternate shades of green and black and white. They swim in a spiral that arcs under the host and then swoops up. Their tails spread into tentacles and they jet upwards, sweeping and winding towards the surface. Akila frantically tries to escape by swimming towards the island, but she knows evading the octopi or making it to the island from this distance are both against the odds.

The water about her erupts with froth and hundreds of tentacles as the octopi collide with the surface. She has no idea what they are trying to do. A tentacle grabs her leg and plunges her downward with such force and speed, she has no time to prepare herself. About her the water is seething with tentacles and bulbous heads and huge eyes amidst flashing colours ranging across the spectrum. She tries to pull against the tentacle but another one wraps around her waist. The octopus holding her twists and turns in the water between the others that soon begin to chase after her. One of the pursuers catches up and binds a tentacle around her arm and tugs her free from her captor. Her lungs are beginning to scream as her breath runs out. She kicks the one at her leg in the bulb-head as hard as she can. Hard enough to make the creature go floppy and leak something blue into the water. In the blink of an eye its body is overcome by the others. The one holding her arm lets go to join in the partaking.

Her body twists about with the churning of the frenzied octopi, but she keeps kicking and propels herself up with her arms. Light. It seems so remote. She kicks and kicks but she does not feel she's getting any closer. Her chest aches like an empty can crumpling. She keeps her arms close to her sides and paddles hard with her legs. She surges up through the water, unaware of the octopi that have turned their attentions back to her. As they tear towards her, she punches out of the surface, breaking the hold of the sea with enough power to project her body out past her knees. The air fills her lungs and she feels alive again with hope. The water about her foams as she falls on her side.

She splashes hard and instantly her body relaxes. It is fresh water and she swallows it in massive gulps to wash away the sour flavour of the endless sea. She recognizes the rocks on the bed of her pond. She's home at last. A tail disappears into Kala's cave under the sheltering rock with a red-belly swaying near the side.

More of those damn red-bellies are trying to invade Kala's pond, and Akila is hungry. She is not going to let them desecrate his lair. She climbs out, plucks her spear from the rocks, hops out of her pyjama bottom and dives back in. While Kala was alive, though she considered him a friend, she never dared come so close to his domain and truly test that trust. Descending to the jutting rock, she pushes the staff into the cave opening. The fish is not in sight anymore, probably hiding in there.

She turns the spear around and pokes the blade in to drive out the fish. There is only the feel of metal scraping stone. If it had been a handful of the red-bellies, she would have preferred doing her fishing from the banks, but she can handle herself against two even underwater. Although it's a whole different matter entering the dark confines of a cave.

She returns to the surface for air, unsure how to proceed. She knows she can wait and get them at her leisure, but after the day she's just had, she wants to mark her territory with the pointy end of her spear. She'll have to draw them out with bait and at the moment she does not have anything that might serve that purpose, except for her hand. It will hurt but she is eager to kill those pesky fish, even if it costs her a little blood. On second thought, why take the risk? She gets her pyjama bottom and ties it around her hand.

Taking a long draught of air, she dives deep into the pool, one hand wrapped in pink cloth with smiling bunnies and the other armed with a glinting stainless-steel spearhead. She takes her place above the opening and juts her hand inside. There is nothing biting yet. She starts poking around, and still getting nothing, she shifts to dig in more of her arm.

The pain flashes a memory of her hand getting jammed in a car door. She calls out in agony and the water rushes down her throat. Her hand is still being crushed as she kicks off the rock to the surface. There is something attached and it is pulling and jerking wildly, and she can't shake it off. She swims over to the pebbled bank and flops on her back with the spear ready to cut up the fish. On the hand she holds up to the sun is no flailing fish, but a black salamander a foot in length. Its stomach bulges abnormally large and the little thing is twisting and flopping with a vengeance. Akila manages to pull her fingers free. It stubbornly clings to the cloth, whipping its tail as its whole body sways in the air.

It takes a few seconds for Akila to react. She slowly sets it down on the pebbles and watches it tug at the cloth. Kala was a girl? Why didn't she notice that? Well, how could she have known? But this one is so small in comparison, nothing like the hulk Kala was. Your mother is gone now, she thinks. How will you survive without her? The bulging belly answers the question. It must have eaten that red-belly.

Akila's eyes well up. Kala did not leave her alone. It is her responsibility now to take care of Kala's baby. A thought brings her up, onto her knees. The little salamander tugs the cloth off her hand. What if there are more young ones in the cave? She wades deeper into the pond but something nags at her. She glances back at the salamander attacking the knotted pyjama bottom, so tiny and helpless in this jungle. He could be swooped away by a bird or monkey, or that wolverine that had torn pieces off Kala's jaw. She hurries to the salamander and picks it up by its slimy tail to keep it from biting her. She improvises the pyjama bottom into a makeshift sack and grips the salamander's lower jaw before entering the water with it. Back at the cave entrance, she goes below the protruding rock and peers into the dark recess. The narrow mouth opens into a larger chamber. She slips in and gropes blindly with her free hand while the cloth bag in the other jolts about. As far as she can tell, there are no other young ones. She retreats out the cave when her hand brushes against something spherical and light. An egg?

She goes up for air and returns as soon as she can. She finds it again and ascertains that it could definitely be an egg. Thrilled by her success, she reaches around for more and finds three others. Cradling them to her chest she rises to the surface, giddy with relief. She kneels by the cloth bag with the captive baby salamander to one side and carefully arranges the eggs in a neat row, one at a time. They are eggs but something is definitely not right with them. They seem unusually light and the shell is perforated with tiny holes spread over one side. She has seen something similar recently. It was on the dead lizard after the white infestation had disappeared. Where the white straight tendrils had stood in the skin, there had remained tiny holes to mark their absence.

She sets down the first egg and picks up the second. Only the top half comes away in her fingers. The bottom sits in the pebbles like a case holding the delicate fragments of what might once have grown into a salamander as enormous as Kala. She picks up the other eggs with more care and learns they're all empty except for the dainty skeletal remains. There is no way to tell how far along they were from hatching when the infection got hold of them. The infection she had brought and plagued this world with.

How could she have known?

It was the fault of the Treeman, but a part of her knows it was she who killed Kala and her young ones. All but for the restless little one wrapped in her pyjama bottoms. She can't keep him in there indefinitely and she can't let him run around either. He is bound to get eaten, sooner rather than later. She taps the cloth and a mouth snaps at the fabric. Warily, she grabs the back of the head and gets a grip on the squirming body. It is slippery and she turns her hand until it is firmly over the belly. She unties the opening and a black head emerges, snapping at the air.

'Come on, boy, relax. You're going to be fine. I won't hurt you.' She gets a few snaps in reply. 'I have no idea how you survived.' Snap. 'You're a real fighter, aren't you? What should I call you?' The salamander watches her vigilantly with his miniature button eyes. 'Fighter?' Snap. 'Biter is more like it.' The salamander snaps and wriggles in her hold. 'I'll call you Kala. That was your mother's name.' She goes quiet then and even the jungle seems hushed about them.

'I'm sorry about your mother dying. I wish you had time to know her. She was wonderful. My mother died when I was very young too. So we're both the same really. I'll take care of you and you have to take care of me. Okay? I had my papa to take care of me. I'll be your papa because you already had a mama. I'm your Papa Akila, but you can call me just Akila.'

The black face watches her impassively.

'What am I going to call you? How about Kala Junior, huh? Do you like that? No, you're not really Kala, are you?' In the light, the skin has a dark brown sheen beneath. 'You're not black, so Kala wouldn't be right. You are brown, you look like Coke. Yeah, I'll call you Coke, no, Coca, Coco, no, Cola. Cola, I like that. I'll call you Cola.' She brings the salamander close and greets him. 'Hello, Cola.' Cola nearly gets her nose with a vicious snap.

LEANING AGAINST the fridge, Shyam let his eyes follow her winking buttocks. It was his T-shirt she wore every night and when he would wake up the next morning to find her gone like last night's dream, the T-shirt alone would be spread out on her side of the bed. He'd pull it to his face and draw deeply on her scent and his body would tingle and his penis harden at the thought of her skin and her wetness. She stood at the kitchen sink, busy washing the pans and setting them aside to dry. Was this fair? Somewhere, in another world or dimension or universe, she had a home in the jungle. She struggled all by herself day after day for her very survival, and then she crossed over at sunset. She escaped to spend some time with him. She did not deserve to be trapped in such a life.

He realized what luxuries they must be to her – the fridge he was leaning on, the lamp above their heads, the taps splashing the dishes, the AC in his bedroom. And it upset him how little he appreciated them, while she would have to again withdraw to the wild. What could he do for her? This was his life and that was hers. They met every night but could their lives not intertwine rather than kiss for brief moments? Was there no way to make their lives one thread so he did not feel this torturous pity for her? He did not want to pity someone he admired, and yet, when he caught her lingering in the shower, enjoying its warm spray over her body, holding her face in the jet of the AC with the ringlets in her hair bouncing with joy, spreading out her limbs, letting her body relax on the mattress with a deep sigh, he had to fight back the urge to burst into tears.

'What have you got in the fridge?'

'Shit.' He swung the fridge door open with a slap on his forehead.

'You forgot, didn't you?'

'I'll get them tomorrow, I promise. Shit! I can't believe I forgot.'

'You're so predictable.'

'What are we going to do for dinner then?'

She pointed her nose at a plastic packet in the corner.

'What's this?'

'I picked up some stuff.'

It made him flush and almost run out of breath that she had

made this effort, for him. He went up and wrapped his arms around her with crushing affection.

'Hey, I can't see,' she protested with a laugh. 'Who knew you'd be a hugger.'

'I can't help it.'

'Well, leave me alone for a few minutes so I can get a couple of dishes done.'

'No.' He released his hold and let his hands wander down to her smooth thighs.

'Not now, you pervert.'

'Try and stop me.'

His fingers snuck under the shirt and floated over her buttocks, up her lower back.

'What're you making?'

'Well, I'm trying to make a mushroom sabji with onions and something on the side with beans.'

'Anything I can do?'

'Actually, yes. Get the mushrooms and beans out of the packet into two bowls so I can wash them.'

He snipped the ends of the bean-pods while she tended to the mushrooms simmering on the fire. Akila placed a cover over the pan and snuck up behind Shyam. She slipped her wet hands under his shirt and tickled his lower back. He yelped and turned to face her with a surprised laugh. 'What the – I almost cut my finger off.' Laughing still and shaking his head fondly, he went back to cutting the beans. She thrust her hand into his shorts and pinched his bum.

'How do you like a taste of your own medicine?'

'Chodo, pervert, chodo,' he screeched in a falsetto.

'Mmm, being a pervert is fun.'

Shyam carefully laid the knife aside and pulled her closer, softly setting his mouth against hers. His piercing gaze was so intense it startled her for a moment, but then she understood, and hugged him back. They were a cast of two.

IF ONLY she could stay here. Akila basks on the supple grass, her long hair spread about her head. Feathery clouds drift above, hanging in the avocado yellow sky by some magic she can't yet understand. The air is cool but not chilly and she has let her pyjama top lie open to suck in the tender warmth of the sun.

Something shifts under the cloth at her side. A small black tail quickly withdraws from the light. Akila rolls over, onto her side, propping herself up on an elbow. She uncovers baby Cola lying curled up in the grass and shields him from the sun with the open flap of her top. His slimy skin is not made for direct sunlight. 'It's beautiful here, isn't it? What do you think, Cola?' she asks the salamander. He shifts his head to one side. 'Yes, you're right, I can't stay here. I won't survive a week. There's nothing to eat and I don't think I'd like to sit in the sun day in and day out.'

She sits up, plopping Cola in her lap, and hunches over, chin in hands. All about her are nothing but the green backs of rolling hills. There is not a tree in sight. Nor a bird or an animal in all the time she's been here. There it is again, that strange sound carried in the wind. It starts as a deep rumble rising, and falls in pitch in a pleasing refrain. Back in her jungle she would have thought it was a distant animal call or even birdsong echoing through the trees. But here, there is nothing. Only the hills and valleys.

A few hundred feet down the slope flows the wide marshy brook through which she entered this world. Then another voice enrolls in the song, enriching the tune. And another, faint in comparison, and a fourth, fainter still. Soon the air is vibrant with an intoxicating symphony of coordinated harmonies so close to voices, either animal or bird, that Akila cannot believe it is just the wind. Some part of her gives her a hint and she knows then that it must be true. If it is, then the rules in this world are truly different. But that fact does not scare her, not in the least. It consoles her. For now she understands why this world is among the rest, the secret it holds. Akila rests Cola on her shoulder and breezily saunters down the slope as the voices sway in pitch. She will come back here, she tells herself. She will lie on the hill just as she did today. If what she thinks is in fact the truth, then she is safe here. She comes to the brook, takes a deep breath as she collects Cola in her hand and dives into the water. She leaves behind the world with the singing hills.

At first she can't believe her eyes, though they are still blurry from the cold mountain lake she has splashed through. A pod of sperm-whales is swimming through the turquoise sky. Maybe she's not awake. She can believe worlds populated with stone giants and forest spirits and hills that sing, but not flying whales.

Even as that thought forms in her mind, she identifies small specks gliding in formation. They swerve in the air and dive by a mountain peak a kilometre away. They dart about with such ease and expertise, it is enthralling to watch. The specks transform into a pod of dolphins as they near, flitting about, nudging each other with their snub noses and showing off. They swoop down and head straight for her at breakneck pace. A scream tears out of her as they swoosh past, barely inches away, without so much as a graze.

The pod does a circuit above the lake and, coming down low enough to skim the water, they swerve in zigzags, with a daring couple diving below the surface and then bursting out. They come up to Akila and surround her with their sleek bodies magically suspended in the air, their amiable faces studying every inch of her, excitedly circling about to examine this novel creature from all sides. Their eyes exude a playful intelligence. The largest of them barks three times and dashes away and the others follow with yelps and a string of chortles.

But one remains behind, smaller than the others, circling her with untiring wonder. Cola lifts his flat head out from under her collar and stares at this oddity with his tiny eyes. Akila reaches out to touch the dolphin and it draws back. Then it reconsiders, and slowly pulls in towards her fingers. Now Akila is not so sure this is a good idea. It can probably snip off her digits with a bite, but she keeps her hand out nevertheless. The tip of her finger grazes the smooth skin and in a flash it whips its tail and zooms away to join the others two hundred feet above.

Her father had once taken her to Ladakh, in her homeland of Kashmir. The grey, barren hills about her remind her of the stark landscapes from that trip. She had found it monotonous but it was lovely to have her father all to herself for once, and not share him with seven hundred other students. He had his well-preserved Canon FTQL hanging from his neck and, time and again, he would pose her on a rock or beside a robed monk and she would eagerly oblige, bathed in his glorious attention.

Here she is now, in this magical world with flying whales filling the skies and there is no camera to pose for. How she wishes she could tell him all that she has seen, not that he would believe her, of course. She can hardly believe it herself. Even after having touched the dolphin, she doesn't understand how any of this can be possible. Her feet are getting numb and she wades out of the freezing water, her eyes glued to the spectacle above of a massive humpback rolling through the atmosphere with abundant grace.

A black shape descends behind her. It makes a furtive approach, with careful flicks of its tail tracing a rascally line along the water. The orca is twenty feet long and well equipped at this game. Akila does not sense a thing as it veers its head to the side and rolls its body to catch her midriff in its cheery jaws. Then a grey bullet comes out of nowhere and knocks the orca square on its exposed belly. It crashes into the shallows with a growling splash, whipping its tail in a frenzy, sending a shaken Akila scurrying backwards up the shore. Above the thrashing orca hovers the small grey dolphin Akila had greeted, glowering at the distressed killer whale with child-like bravado. In moments the ruckus is past, and the black and white beast ascends with the vengeful rage of a kill denied.

Akila is certain she is next in line. Its tail gently beckons the air, as the body coils for the strike. The gap between dolphin and orca is extinct with a lash of the tail, teeth sinking into the back of the evading dolphin. A spray of blood strikes Akila's face. She screams and sprints into the water as flesh batters flesh and loud, high-pitched wails ring out. She desperately wants to get back home. She throws herself headlong into the lake.

Breathless, she climbs out of her pool in the jungle, the blood washed from her face but the tremor still running through her. Her mind is a mess of gnashing teeth, blurred black shapes and flippered tails. Cola has sensed they are back and struggles to climb off her shoulder. She helps him down and he happily slips into the comfort of home. Akila is glad she is back, though she begins to wonder if it is more than a coincidence that she has arrived where she wanted to go.

'IT'S BEEN a while.'

'Yeah.'

'You cancelled your last two sessions because you were unwell. What happened?'

Shyam shifted uneasily on the stiff leather seat. For years now, he had been coming to this small room with the overfed bookcase, the carpeted floor, the writing desk at the window framing the top branches of a neem tree swaying outside. In the middle sat the short-haired, pretty, middle- aged woman with a flourish of grey slack across her forehead and large-rimmed spectacles. The wall behind her displayed a constellation of framed certificates from reputed Indian and American universities, ranging from Chicago to Punjab. And in all this time he had never held anything back.

'Nothing much.'

'But you cancelled your sessions.'

'Oh, yeah, I was sick.'

'With what?'

'I had a bad stomach.'

'Both times?' she asked, her suspicion aroused. He saw it in the way she folded her arms.

'No, I was … I actually wasn't sick.'

'Then why did you cancel?'

'Are you upset or something?'

'No, I'm not upset, Shyam. I'm just wondering why you lied about the reason for cancelling your sessions.'

'There was stuff happening.'

'I would have guessed that. What was this "stuff"?'

'It was two sessions I missed, it's not a big deal. I'll pay you for them, if it's such a huge thing.'

'That won't be necessary. You called me more than twenty-four hours prior to the session and I was able to fill the slot with another client, so that's not why I'm asking. I'm harking on about it because you've never missed a session in all the years you've been coming here.'

'Yes, I have.'

'A couple of times for work, I'm sure, but not in the past two years at least.'

'Okay, listen, I was about to tell you in our last session but the time ran out.'

'I remember.'

'Do you really? It was three weeks ago.'

'I kept a note of it. Since you've brought it up, what were you about to tell me at that time?'

'A lot has happened since then.'

The psychologist glanced at her watch and pushed her glasses up the bridge of her nose as she returned her focus to Shyam, waiting for him to begin.

'What I was about to tell you was, I saw that girl Akila again later that night.'

'That's the girl you have the dream about.'

'Yeah, so anyway, she ... "popped" in to see me in the middle of the night, at my place. And we had sex.' He paused to allow for her reaction.

'And?' She had a good poker-face.

'We did a lot of talking. Her situation is a bit freaky.'

'Freaky?'

'Yeah, she can, um, she's stuck somewhere and she can only spend limited time with me. Turns out she's been thinking a lot about me over the years. When we had sex, it was like dynamite. I was giddy for a few seconds afterwards. That's never happened to me before. We've been getting together at night ever since.'

'How are you two getting along? I remember your first date didn't go very well.'

'It's – we've been getting along great. We've been having sex every night.'

'I didn't ask about the sex, I asked how the two of you were getting along.'

'What's the word? That's it – we've been getting along "swimmingly". Of course, she has a lot of issues, but who doesn't?' The woman sitting across from him pursed her lips at his comment, refusing the bait. 'What sort of issues does she have?'

'I suppose feelings of abandonment and loneliness for much of her life. Apparently, what I remembered of her from school, after the "incident", was completely off.'

'What do you mean "off"?'

'She was in a bad way and it turns out only I could have helped her, but neither of us realized it. It was just a bad situation.'

'Her trying to deal with what happened during the incident?'

'Yeah, exactly. And she's been living with all that baggage and not spending any time with people.'

'You said she's stuck somewhere. What did you mean?'

'Where she lives and works. She can only spend the night with me and then she has to go back.'

'Is it far?'

'You could say that.'

'You're being very evasive when you talk about Akila. Why is that?'

Shyam shifted uneasily in the seat he had occupied hundreds of times before.

'I'm just so unused to this kind of thing. It's getting very serious for me.'

'Do you want to end it?'

'No, that's the thing. I want to move with it. I want to go forward with what we have.'

'In what way?'

'I want to spend more time with her.'

'How?'

'I'll move to her place.'

'Have you discussed this with her?'

'No, not yet. Probably tonight.'

'You have deep feelings for her, don't you?'

'I've never felt this way about anyone. It's driving me a little – you know, it's frustrating as hell because all I can do is think about her. I can't concentrate on my work, I can't sleep. The situation is so complicated, it's ... I've been thinking about it, a lot, and I think I want to do this.'

'Sounds exciting.'

'I'm fucking shitting my pants. I'm terrified. You don't know.'

'Tell me, then.'

He shook his head, biting his bottom lip. 'It's such a messed-up situation. If only it were different. But then, maybe if it was, we probably would never have met again. That's the crazy thing. It almost feels like, in this relationship, I'm the only one who has a choice to be in it.'

'What do you mean? You're running around what you call this "situation" without telling me what it is and all I can see is how "giddy" you're getting. I can't force you to tell me what it is. You will, when you feel comfortable enough to discuss it. But you're obviously about to make some life-altering decisions here.'

'You're not kidding.'

'See, I don't know what you mean by that, but I'll trust you to judge for yourself what you want to tell me.'

Shyam sat, nervously pressing his knuckles.

'Why won't you tell me? I'm wondering what the reason could be. Are you worried about what I'll think about you? You don't have to worry about that, it's not my place to judge you, Shyam. I want you to know that. You can speak freely with me.'

'I know,' he nodded, 'but let me just sort this out to some degree.'

'That's up to you.'

'I'm going to tell her tonight that I want her to take me back with her. I don't care about leaving my work for good, but after all that she's been through, I can't ... I don't want to have her keep coming to my place and heading back there again. I don't want her to go back alone. I don't want either of us to ever be alone again. I may not be able to come back here, but if it's with her, that's good enough for me. Shit, I'm sounding like some sappy romantic fool, but that's the way I feel and I don't want to let it go. She's so wonderful, she's amazing, she's so smart and beautiful. She's survived so much and now she comes all this way every night to spend some time with me. With me! And I want to see all those places she's talked about. I don't want to live my life in my room anymore. I don't want my life to be a succession of emails every day. I want her to be with me and take me to all these worlds. I want her to fill my life.'

'And what are you offering her?'

Shyam shrugged, at a loss.

'Myself?'

WITH A bunch of paperbacks under one arm and some clothes under the other, Akila strides down the slope towards the stream. This has been her second successful trip back to school without any unwanted stops in other worlds. True, there were a few times in between when she went around in circles from one world to another without ever getting to Earth, arriving back in her pond instead. The only explanation she has is a lack of focus on her part. It is not enough to just think about where she wants to go, but to really want to go there. More than want, she has to force some need for it into her bones.

At the edge of the stream she sets everything down and, with the grunt of a satisfied shopper, gazes upon her accolades. She can't wait any longer. She's been living in these tattered pyjamas long enough. From on top of the books, Cola watches her tear herself free and hurl them to the side without a second look at the faded smiling bunnies. She slips on a fresh pair of panties, feeling odd after so many weeks of 'freedom'. Then a pair of black sports-shorts and a sweatshirt with the school's crest blazoned on the chest with the underlying dictum 'Never Surrender'. Her skin feels lovely against the fabric. No chafing, no draughts from rips. She feels like a girl again, and not some jungle wildling. Setting Cola around her neck in his customary lock, she gathers up the rest of the gear and dives in with a contented heart, realizing only a moment before hitting the water that she has forgotten to focus on her destination.

She curses herself, flailing about, disorientated, water gushing down her throat, her chest burning. Then she freezes, lets her limbs relax and unclenches her fists. The clothes she has brought open out under water, and the *Nancy Drew*'s and *Hardy Boys* fall away. They don't matter, she tells herself. What is important is to stay calm and think. There is no getting the taste of brine out of her mouth, and her eyes burn. That's not important, she screams inside her head. You idiot! You fool! You're so stupid! You're so stupid! All you had to do was focus and you wouldn't be here. Stupid! Stupid! She unclenches her fists again and forces herself to slow her breathing and calm down.

She opens her eyes to the billowing blue expanse of the

water-world she dreads with its tentacled monsters infesting the deep. Unhurriedly, she turns in place, taking in the horizon until the island comes into view. Don't look down. It is not going to help you to see what is coming because you can't out-swim it. Try to reach the island. She checks her neck for Cola. He's still there like a metal link on her skin. She's sure the salt can't be good for him. What would she have done if she had lost him? She can't bear to think about that and starts swimming towards the island with slow deliberate strokes. It is a few hundred feet away, though to her it feels like a couple of kilometres.

Halfway there, the sweatshirt feels like it is shrinking, making it harder for her to pull her strokes. She may pull Cola loose if she takes it off now. She pushes on, trudging ever closer with lobbing water appearing to negate every gain. She does not wish to look down. What is that? Is there something touching her leg? It feels slimy and slides up her legs with every few kicks. Her heart pounds faster and harder, her breaths get shorter and her arms feel like lead trying to move in a sea of syrup. Something rough touches her toes and she jumps. What is that? Her eyes are burning and she closes them, her senses assaulted from all sides.

The swell suddenly picks her up and she can feel the current underneath pull her legs out from under her. There it is again, that rough surface skimming her foot. The sea churns, tossing and twisting her about. With the water gurgling in her ears, she hears the frazzled sounds of crashing currents as though she were trapped in a seashell. The tide draws her backwards and she fights it with all her strength. And then she is standing. There is sand between her toes. She opens her eyes and stares at the line of trees beyond the white sandy beach. She has made it. A wave shoves her forward, almost knocking her off balance. She rushes out of the ocean, thick locks of her long hair sticking to her tuckered face as she struggles out of the shrunken wet sweatshirt. The beach wobbles; no, it is her legs. She collapses on the soft warm sand, regurgitating salt water from her lurching insides.

She has been sitting in the shade of the coconut trees for a while, looking out over the waves. Only a hundred yards away, a dark shape surfaces, its shape and true size indiscernible. She spits out the taste of the sea for the hundredth time, wipes her nose and gets up with Cola in her palm. Setting him on her shoulder, she starts into the trees. Though it is a small island, there must be something on it she can eat. Perhaps a bird's nest to loot or some fruit, besides the coconuts? It has occurred to her to splash through and head back home; however, there is the chance she may wind up somewhere else, where food may be harder or impossible to come by.

The craggy slope rises under thick brush and levels out before a monolithic oblong rock. There aren't any birds she can spot. There are a few lizards and some ancient-looking tortoises grazing dreamily. Their lethargic chomping reminds her of her grandfather smiling without his teeth to amuse her. She can't bear to kill a single one. Skirting around the large rock, she comes across a puddle under its leaning side. It is wonderfully clear and inviting. She drops onto all fours and laps at it, then dunks her face in and gorges herself on the delicious water. It has a slightly bitter tinge, but she is not bothered. All that matters is that it is not brine. Cola slides off her neck and dashes through the water with a wag of his tail. Akila lies there for a while, letting the sea breeze wash over her wet face, staring at the listless clouds against the pale hazel expanse. She squints up the rock-face looming over her. She could swear she just saw something big, bigger than the lizards and the tortoises she has seen so far, peering at her. She could not make out its features backlit against the bright sky and it moved away from the edge far too rapidly. She taps the water and Cola comes to her. With his slimy body on her shoulder once more, she gulps another handful and resumes moving around the rock, keeping her eyes trained on the summit.

There is no sign of the creature and she is soon on the other side of the island, where the view is exquisite. It is sparkling blue on all sides, and a lip of land reaches out, covered with lush greenery. A slope runs down into a crater-like depression. It is hard to tell beneath the shrubbery, but the bottom of the crater basin could be at or below sea-level. She starts down the craggy slope, aware of Cola's tightening grip. She can't explain the urge that is driving her further down to explore.

Through the peering trees along the rim, the thick brush filters most of the light and the only sound is the wind in the trees and the distant rustle of rolling waves. Coming through the enormous arrow-head leaves, she steps into a shallow pool at the base. There does not seem to be anything worth seeing. She hears a movement and spins about. There is nothing there, only a trail of small ripples along the water, running into the thickets. A moving shadow that could be a branch swaying in the breeze. She should not have come down here. And then she sees it, seemingly dwarfed by the coconut trees swaying above. The epicentre of her nightmares. The tree. There is no question, it is the same as the source of the field of roots.

She shakes her head because this is not water at her feet. To her left floats a rotting lizard, its tail hanging on by an exposed ligament. Move backwards slowly, she tells herself. Is this a coincidence? Or is there one like it in every world? Don't wake it. Can it be woken? Can it hurt her? She does not know. Just get away, far away from here. She backs up, watching the shadow-infested tree that stands as still as a rock. There is movement underneath it. A dark shape creeps around the trunk, a smear of light dancing on its large green eye with the pin-prick iris focused coldly upon her. She knows she can't outrun the insectoid but her thoughts are frozen by fear and her instincts tell her to flee. Run like crazy.

The leaves whip her face and she punches through, dashing up the slope. She does not have far to go and stands on the rocky rim of the depression, blinded by the sparkling blue ahead. There are no sounds of anything in pursuit but she knows they are there. She scrambles down to the beach. The long insectoid face leers at her from above. She races across the blazing sand, looking back over her shoulder. The insectoid is still at the rocks, watching her as it recedes up the slope. The next wave rushes at her calves, sweeping her off her feet.

She spits out the sandy water, trying to get back up. The sand at her hands and feet is so loose she can barely get any leverage. Her knees sink in. She scrambles to her feet and glances back towards the beach. But there is no beach. Or rather, there is no island; there is only beach. She blinks the coarse granules out of her eyes and searches again. Sand, great heaps – no – hills of it, rising about her. There is no sea, no trees, no insectoids, nothing. Only sand. She is standing in a rapidly drying pond, the mud sucking in her feet. She can't think straight. What just happened?

This world is new to her. One with new dangers she is not ready to face yet. She needs to get back home and rest. Concentrate this time. Think of your pond in the jungle, that is your destination. But the pool at her feet is already dry, the dark patch quickly fading. Her skin is being baked alive. She can't move yet. Then she recalls her father's counsel: 'one thing at a time.' She scurries fifty feet up the scalding dune, every step sinking and sliding, and reaches the summit, exhausted.

This is a desert world. A sea of sand. Blazing, sinuous backs crowding the horizon. No tree, no shade in sight. The sun is slapping her skin raw and all she has on is Cola and the small black shorts, and they are not near enough protection. What she would give to have back her trusty pyjamas. Why aren't her feet burning like the rest of her? She looks down at them, hidden in the sand.

She lies buried in the desert with her shorts sheltering her head, Cola curled up on the side of her face. There is not much else to do. As far as she can tell, there is nothing else alive and no streams she can drink from, let alone splash through. What was the pond out of which she had climbed? It had to have come from somewhere. At the rate at which it had dried up, it must have formed just a short while before her arrival. Maybe it had rained. Here? Maybe it will rain again, she hopes, hungrily eyeing the clouds lining the copper sky. Wishing for rain. All she needs is a puddle. Please, she thinks, gritting her teeth in desperation.

It rains. It develops into a torrent, washing the sand off her back, and then her, off the top of the dune. Cola clutches her neck, almost choking her, as she slides down the slope on a sheet of water, her hands trying to grab mud. She punches into it elbow deep, and it holds firm. The raindrops are heavy on her back. They are no longer soothing like the initial downpour but so hard she can barely keep her eyes open. Every time she opens her mouth, she almost drowns. She holds on, waiting for the rain to pass, and prepares to dive into the collecting pool below. But she should have known it would not be so simple. The quicksand sucks in her body. Her legs sink into the thick mush and she can feel the rest of her being pulled in. She screams at the roaring sky for it to stop. She does not want to die like this. All she can think is that the day began so well and then, one after the other things, went belly-up for her. What is this curse? Can she never have her way? Will she never do more than just survive? Is this her punishment for thinking she can outsmart her prison? For taking it for granted?

She reaches up the slope with her free arm, twisting and turning onto her stomach, freeing one leg from the sticky goop and then the other. She can't tell whether she is still crying. It is all a drowning blur. Cola's tightening grip urges her on. With her legs free she lies flat, spreading out her limbs. The sheet of water begins to slide her down again. She is depending on it. She steers her body to face the brown pool collecting below and readies herself as she picks up speed. Then, with a jerk she bucks off the surface just a few inches, enough to send her tumbling into the beaten brown muck with a single thought resounding in her head: 'home!'

PURANA QILA lay shrouded in smoky shadows like a lounging beast past its prime. Shyam's eyes roved the murky landscape studded with dirty lights and he felt a tug at the bottom of his stomach. Macoco lay asleep in the amphitheatre below, while Akila sat with him atop Hall No. 6 in Pragati Maidan. The circumcized pyramid squatted there, with its flat top the perfect stage, towering over the city he would be leaving soon. They had spent nights on the rooftops of many of Delhi's landmarks, making love or having a drink. He could feel her hand in his, sticky and wet with sweat. He loved her, and sensing her concern for him only made him love her all the more. And it reassured him that he was making the right decision. Behind them sat two large suitcases.

* * *

THEY ROLLED over the folded rows of clothes concealing the bed by the yawning suitcase, hands hungrily pushing under waistbands and lips connected with a relentless current. Their pants were hurled to the side and she climbed on top, sinking onto him halfway, rising and dipping as he thrust up to meet her. She patted his chest to slow down and let her take the reins. She moved her hips in a circle with only his tip inside her and then sank all the way down, grinding her pelvis against his. Holding his hands on either side of his head, she leaned forward, breathing deep and hard into his ear. He heard her say, 'Are you sure you want to go?'

'Yeah,' he breathed.

'You can go later, it doesn't have to be now.'

'I know.'

'Then why now?'

'Because I can't wait,' he told her.

* * *

THEY STROLLED around the roof of Hall No. 6, taking in the view on all sides, his arm around her waist. He was homesick and he hadn't even left yet. He hated this city, but it had been his home for a decade, and now he knew where to get the best kathi rolls and pani puris and paranthas and seekh kebabs. And which metro lines had the prettiest girls at what time, the best stalls in Sarojini Nagar, the best markets, the best bars for music, the best and worst routes, the places to avoid and the places he'd always planned to visit but never made the effort to see. He knew he could postpone the trip and see those places, have one last tandoori raan and spicy brain-curry with sheermal or a bottle of cold elaichi milk in Connaught Place. Rummage through a sea of second-hand books at Daryaganj or spend a lazy afternoon sprawled on the grass in Lodhi Garden. But he could share only a fraction of this with her. Every hour of daylight, he hated the sun for sneering at him, for holding her prisoner. For holding him a prisoner from her. No more.

* * *

SHYAM AND Akila strode along the Mehrauli-Gurgaon Road, nudging shoulders and touching arms, to the Qutab Minar metro station. She asked, 'What if we can't come back?'

'Back to this world?'

She nodded emphatically and told him, 'The only reason I've been able to come here is because you're here. There's a bridge between us, binding those worlds to this world. But if you come with me, that bridge is gone. We won't be able to come back at all.'

An autorickshaw pulled up alongside and an unshaven face peered out at them. 'Where to?'

'We're catching the metro, we don't need an auto.'

'Arey, where to, bhai? Give a guy a break.'

'Haus Khaz Village.'

'150.'

'Are you kidding?'

'What?'

'We're not tourists here, "bhai", you can't cheat us. We'll get in if you go by the meter.'

'Okay, meter.'

Shyam waited for Akila to enter first. The driver mumbled, 'Meter plus 50.'

'What the–' Shyam nudged Akila to step out. 'Come on, we'll just catch the metro as planned. These guys are such crooks!'

'Arey, what's the problem?' the driver brayed.

Shyam led Akila towards the station, answering, 'Thank you, but the metro will suit us just fine.'

THEY WERE on the balcony of a restaurant on the second floor, their chairs close together, their feet dangling out of the railing into the cool night air as they looked out at the Haus Khaz park. The music and chatter behind them was loud and they sat shoulder to shoulder, elbows intertwined. Shyam sipped his beer and said, 'We've already gone over this, Akila, from every angle. I told you, I don't care. If I'm stuck there, I'm stuck there with you.' He held her hand and brought it to his lips. 'My greatest nightmare is that one morning you'll leave and for whatever reason never come back to me. You're there all alone and I'm left here without you. We never see each other again. In ten years' time, I may even start believing it was all a dream. And I can't have that, I won't. My life became the fading dream once I woke up to you, Akila.'

She sipped the white wine without tasting it, fighting the urge to cry. Why was fate such an abusive guardian to her? Why could joy never come unaccompanied by some misery? She loved him. Her father's love was so long ago, she could not tell if what remained in her memory was a reproduction or something of her own conjuring. But she could feel Shyam's love for her. She had bathed in it for these past weeks, watched him become hers so easily. She loved him too, she did, and it ripped at her heart that it was he who had proposed coming to the other realm.

HER HAIR is held up in bands, in wet bunches of dirty wild locks. She has in a blue kameez reaching to her knees, yellow jambli gathered in the front flap. A belt is strung about her waist, with a couple of small pouches and a knife. She is perched atop the pallid hill, waiting with an open book. A thousand feet above her, a blue whale rolls in the clouds making its drawling call. She is older and it shows on her features as she admires the leviathan. Her eyes are steadier, her feet in white canvas sneakers draped by the black form of a sleeping Cola.

She slips a purple feather between the pages, closes the book and gazes up at the dolphin hanging in the air five feet in front of her. A distinct curved scar runs along its side. Her face brightens at the sight of him. 'Fin, I've got a new book I like. I thought you'd want me to read it to you.'

The dolphin summersaults in the air with a squeal. He comes close to her and rubs his snout on her neck, touching cheeks. She hugs him, the smooth, soft skin of his long, slender body under her hands, the power and deftness of the ripcord muscles beneath. She can't understand the way he makes her feel. When she returns home after a visit, her body trembles with a yearning deep in the pit of her stomach. She kisses his snout and he says with a gentle timbre, 'Lovely Akila, read to me.'

AKILA LAZES on the Mez after a swim, chipping away at a curled slip of stone, rough-hewn into the shape of a dolphin. She can't help herself. Clothes lie spread out on the rocks to dry. Cola lies beside Akila with his head and arm on the small of her back. The tree-house has grown with an additional two levels, each with a suitcase tied down to the floor. It has taken her a few tries, with the monkeys making off with her clothes, and books and spiders and lizards sneaking in, for her to realize she has to keep them shut and tied down.

Akila scales the tree to the highest level, unties a box and takes out a Walkman. She replaces the cassette in it with another and gets a box of chalk. With the stone carving hanging at her neck as a locket, she sketches a dolphin on the rock-face, humming *'The Summer of '69'*.

WANDERING THROUGH the jungle with her trusty spear, her ears are alert to every sound and her eyes catch every twitching twig. She has the knife belt and a hunger for something furry. She is crouched in one of her usual spots in a hollow below a branch, waiting for something to come along. Sometimes it takes all day and there have been times when she had to leave with nothing.

A fern shudders and then a bush nearby. The snorts inform her it is a small wild pig before she spots its tail raised in the air. Tasty, soft flesh marbled with succulent fat. She waits, her eyes fixed on a patch below her. As the wild pig enters her kill-zone, she pounces with the spear. The blade misses by a hair's breadth and the pig runs bang into her, throwing her off her feet. She rolls up onto her right knee and hurls the spear after the trail of frazzled shrubbery. The spear catches in something, its handle rolls up and sticks in the air, wobbles with a huffed breath and then goes still.

She is thankful the pig did not squeal like the last one. It attracts unwanted attention, and still can, if she is not quick to collect her prize and rush back to the pond. Usually, her first move is to remove the guts, which rot the quickest, toss them to Cola, and then cut off a hefty portion of a hind leg and haunch. Then she seals the rest in a plastic ziplock bag she has lined with salt and buries it, covering the spot with the heaviest rock she can shift.

Akila runs to the downed animal, plucks the spear out of its side and holds down the head with a firm hand. It is still alive with those damn eyes looking up at her, wide with shock. She takes out the short blade she has christened Zorba, and uses it to pierce deep into the front of the neck. She does not know any better way to kill for certain.

'Run,' the hushed voice rasps. 'Run, run, run.' The pig's legs twitch.

Though the sound of Fin speaking runs through her like liquid joy, she can't bear moments like these, the last breaths of an animal dying in her grasp. She has no choice but to kill it to survive, she knows that. But it was so much simpler to drive her choking empathy out of her mind when she could not hear their voices pleading for her to let them go. Often, by the time she carried a kill home, her appetite would have diminished and she would sit on the Mez, staring helplessly at the bloody gash she had made in the animal to cut out its life. The warm blood gushes onto her fingers and the head jerks for that brief moment, and then it is still.

SHE IS falling, she can barely keep her eyes open. The wind is so strong against her face and body, flowing through her. She knows the ground must be close now, she stretches out her arms, keeping her hands balled into fists. Something soft slides by her knuckles. There is a surge of pleasure and pure happiness in her chest as she reaches out and grabs Fin's flipper. She can feel him moving towards her and when he is close enough, she puts her arms around him. 'Now hold on tight, Akila,' he says. She wraps her legs around him. This is not her first time free-falling with Fin. The wind begins to ease as he decreases the velocity of their descent in a gradual curve. She opens her eyes as they swerve mere feet from the rocky ground.

'Did you like it?'

She can't answer or she might burst into tears. She laughs, holding on tight, as Fin slowly spins between the sky and the hills.

THE DIMINUTIVE cots sit in neat rows on either side in the dorm hall. Their covers are taut, tucked under the mattress and nothing is out of place. Akila has an open backpack slung over a shoulder, stockpiling any sanitary pads she can find.

Her third period is taking longer than the two months it took for the second to arrive and that has her a little concerned. She had laid out some large anatomy books on the occasion of her first period and despite formidable words like endometrium and gonadotropic, she has gotten a good grasp of the human menstrual cycle and understands that she should expect it roughly every twenty-eight days. Then is something wrong with her?

She had been so thrilled that first day when she was anxiously inspecting the blood stains on her white panties and crotch and finally realized what it meant for her. Though that thrill has since evaporated as she has become acquainted with how long menstruation can last. And she has to stay attentive for it when the time comes as well. Why did people make such a big deal about this? She does not feel any different as a person, certainly not like a woman, and it is quickly getting to be a hassle. She wonders whether there is a point at which it will become just another aspect of her life. Just something that happens ordinarily like brushing her teeth or going to the toilet. But she dreads to think of what might happen if there comes a time when she doesn't have any pads in hand. Less than six months ago, that was something she had never had to think of, and now here she is with a backpack half-full of sanitary pads. She wishes there were someone she could discuss these matters with.

She thrusts various articles of clothing into her backpack, when something on the wall catches her eye. She's transfixed by it. It is a calendar, nothing special about it, no colour picture, nothing but the numbers in large digits arranged in grids. There are some notations in Tamil she does not comprehend but that has nothing to do with it. She has not thought of her life as days contained in a week in so long but even that is not it. The first five dates have been crossed off and she's staring at the sixth. It is her birthday. It has been more than two years since she was taken. Two whole birthdays she has lost, gone by without so much as a reminder. She turned thirteen today.

AKILA CLUTCHES Zorba tightly, her eyes drawn skyward to the line of red smoke. It is time, again. She glances at the calendar hanging on the rock amidst the cavorting chalk-dolphins. It has been more than a month since she 'borrowed' it. The crossed out dates score out the past. The jungle is quiet again. Absolute silence reigns. Like the last time they had come for her, those insectoids with their cold dead pinprick pupils. 'Fin,' she murmurs as a comfort. She looks up at the lovely amethyst of the sky. Fly me away from here, Fin. Save me. But she has to prepare for them. She's stronger now, no longer the scared schoolgirl but a hunter hewn by the jungle. Her eyes dig into the brooding depths. They're here already. Three still shadows mark their presence amidst the swaying branches. She returns the blade to its sheath and waits. Someday, she swears to herself, I will slaughter the devil's pets. A jagged movement reveals a monstrous limb and ogling large eyes. A long insectoid-face extends out of the shadows.

HE SAT drenched on a rock at the pond-side, still clutching his suitcases as he spat out water and tried to get a look of the place with his blurry vision. Before him stood a massive tree deformed by little huts clinging to its sides like giant mushrooms, connected with rope-ladders and tethers. From the lowest and largest hut extended a suspended path across the stream to the tree behind, where more of the mushroom-roofed structures studded the thick, winding trunk.

It did not feel like they had travelled at all. It took barely a moment to break the surface of the water in Delhi and appear out here in the jungle. And now he felt it. His life as he knew it was gone forever. There was no going back. Where was he? Why had he suggested this? No matter how he tried to blame Akila, he could not. He had convinced her to bring him here. And all for love. To feel that magnetic, undeniable force prescribed by nature between opposite poles. His grip on the suitcase handle was so fierce his knuckles turned white.

A shadow shifted under the surface of the pond. It was sliding towards him, a form as wide as his queen-sized bed had been. It is mesmerizing to watch the rocks on the pond bottom gradually vanish into an abyss that yawned towards him, foot by foot, until his own foot felt the water shift with the advancing mass. With a yelp he hugged his dark green case and pulled his legs out of the water, rolling away just as the giant black head snapped.

'Cola,' he heard Akila shout. Cola? This is Cola, her pet salamander? The one she carried on her trips to other worlds? She had told him of some of their adventures, how Cola would lie curled over her shoulders. He spun about, still clutching the wet suitcase to his chest like a life-saver.

Akila stood on a rock, arms akimbo, demanding, 'What the fuck, Cola? What the fuck!' Her jeans were already spread to dry on a rock and she was in the process of unbuttoning her full-sleeve blouse. With her wet hair glossy in the sun and those gleaming ripcord thighs, Shyam knew again why he had come. To give her something, so she would give him everything he had ever wanted. There was nothing in his old life worth hanging on to. Air conditioners don't warm your heart with their smiles first thing in the morning and refrigerators don't look like goddesses. Akila turned to him with concern written on every line on her face. 'Oh god, Shyam, I can't believe he did that! I never imagined he would.'

Shyam lay back on the rocks and laughed so loud a nearby troop of monkeys began to howl and hoot in chorus. Akila stepped off her rock and bent over him. 'What's wrong?' When his laughter subsided, he replied, 'I'm not worried about Cola right now. I think I've got a bigger problem.'

'What is it?' The distress on Akila's face was almost comical.

'I don't think I've packed enough!'

AKILA PLACED the dark green suitcase on the wooden floor and helped Shyam up the last rungs of the rope ladder. He caught his breath as he looked around. 'This,' she said, 'is the wardrobe.' It was the hut on the highest branch on what she called Tree One, the first tree she had occupied. The walls were lined with jeans, skirts, tops, sweaters, jackets and dresses, all vacuum-sealed in plastic bags and neatly organized. On the floor against the walls, there were plastic storage-boxes, some with shoes and slippers and others with underwear. There was barely enough room for his suitcase. Akila squatted and unzipped his bag. 'So, where do you want to put all your stuff? You haven't brought very much.'

'I don't think I've packed enough.'

AKILA SWAM in the pond. Shyam sat on a rock, hugging his knees to his chest, careful not to let his toes touch the water. 'What, now you're going to be terrified of him?' she snorted. 'He's the one who tried to eat me,' he replied with a shrug.

'You guys have got to get along.'

'I'm a nice guy. I'm easy to get to know. I don't snap my stupidly monstrous jaws at people.'

'He isn't a monster.'

'I didn't call him a monster, I said he has monster jaws.'

'Cola is the sweetest, most loving–'

A deafening, warbling call reverberated through the jungle. She resumed, 'Cola and Macoco are both the sweetest and most loving creatures I know! You, on the other hand…'

'I, on the other hand, am just a tasty morsel to them.'

'Hey, Macoco likes you.'

'So, you admit that Cola doesn't like me.'

'Duh! He tried to eat you.'

'So you admit that he tried to eat me.'

'I'm not denying anything.'

'You could have fooled me.'

'I never said he didn't try to eat you.'

'Then why for fuck's sake are you trying to get me into the water with him?'

'Because he tried to eat you. You guys need to get friendly. This is a small pond and this is where we drink our water, bathe and wash our clothes. You get the idea.'

'I get the idea. I understand what you're saying. But how do I befriend this guy?'

'He trusts me.'

'Because you've known him since he was a tadpole!'

'He wasn't a tadpole. Don't interrupt, let me finish. He trusts me and now he needs to see that I trust you. Then he will grow to trust you too.'

'Okay, great plan, let's do that.'

'Then get in the water.'

'Bad plan. Why don't we display your trust in me on dry land first?'

'Get in the fucking water!'

'I'm sure he's sensing the awesome trust between us with all this screaming,' he said, timidly slipping into the pond.

THEY WERE on the wide, Futon mattress in the sleeping hut, their bodies still moist from the swim when Akila switched on her laptop and sat back in bed. She offered, 'Do you want to watch something?' Shyam went to the round doorway and looked out into the impenetrable night. The only light on this side of the planet, he knew, was sitting on the low bedside table. A battery-powered LED lamp cast a cool glow over the room. A sheet of insect sounds veiled the silence, the absence of another human in this world. It may not be such a bad thing. No traffic noise, engines revving, schoolkids getting into their buses in the morning outside his window, or tweaked Royal Enfields barking through the narrow lane. No paperwallah calling out for old newspapers, no construction work boring into his head, or a party raging in the neighbouring apartment. No unwelcome visitors ringing his doorbell, or aeroplanes screaming past, or firecrackers late into the night. No bells and singing at the nearby Vishnu temple or the wails of the muezzin at 5.30 a.m., or the clamour of a wedding band battling for a tune. He could go on, and as wrought with homesickness as he was, he would have. But he managed to come out of it, mumbling, 'What?'

'Do you want to watch something on the laptop?'

'Like what? What have you got?' He moved closer, but she motioned to the door, saying, 'Could you close that? We might have some unwelcome visitors otherwise.'

He did not like the sound of that. 'Like?'

'Don't worry, I know how to take care of us. You'll get used to it soon and it'll become second nature to you too.'

'Okay, but let's come back to these "visitors".'

'Nothing, just insects and sometimes tree lizards or monkeys, and there are chances you might wake up with a bird sitting on your head. Arrey, Shyam, don't tell me you're worried already?'

'I'm not, I'm not. I just wanted to know.'

'This is my home. I've taken precautions. We're totally safe here.'

He knew perfectly well they weren't 'perfectly' safe, but why start an argument on the first night? He closed the door and slid the thick wooden bolt into place. He felt the draught from the narrow shutter-slits on the walls. Cross-ventilation, he mused. Maybe Akila *had* thought of everything. After all, she'd been here long enough and one thing he was certain of was that she was smarter than he was. He crawled over the bed to her. 'So, what have you got to watch?'

She indicated a row of external hard disks connected to a humming UPS. 'TV shows and movies galore, my love. What are you in the mood for?'

He crinkled his brow as he thought about it, and said, 'To tell you the truth, I'm exhausted. I have a feeling I'll drop off as soon as my head hits the pillow.'

She snorted and said, 'Thought as much, Mr Shyam. You're just a lazy bum, aren't you?'

'I'll fight the good fight tomorrow, mon capitaine.'

Akila crawled to the laptop and lay on her stomach, stroking the trackpad. 'So what are you going to watch?' he asked, sliding over the sheets towards her. 'Just reading a little,' she replied. 'I have tons of ebooks here if you want.' Shyam rested his head in the small of her back. 'Nah, it's cool, I have a lot in my laptop too. I'll take some when I'm done with what I have,' he yawned, 'which will probably be in a hundred years.'

'I bet my collection is bigger than yours.'

'Now see, I was afraid of that.'

'What?'

His voice trailed off as his consciousness rolled away. 'That I hadn't packed enough.'

SHYAM SAT bolt upright in bed. As soon as he realized he was encased in darkness, he began to panic and reached for Akila. He could not find her, she was definitely gone from the bed. Where was she? Had something happened to her? He tried to picture the layout of the room in his mind's eye to remember where the door was. He found it and, after a moment's hesitation, gently slid the wooden latch out of the lock. Then he froze. How was it still locked from the inside? Maybe he was still asleep and this was just a paranoid dream. He'd wake up soon. No, the sensations were too vivid. He could feel every breath, the unevenness of the wooden floor and the draught through the narrow slits. He slid the latch back into place and moved away from it. He found his way to the far corner by the bedside and huddled into a ball. Maybe she'd gone out to the toilet. But what if something had happened to her? What if she was dead? How would he survive here? It was quiet, more quiet than he had ever endured in his life, and it unnerved him. He heard a scratching on the outside of the hut. He squeezed his eyes shut, clenched his fists, and hugged his knees to his chest.

Akila sat forlorn on the edge of the Futon bed, looking at Shyam who lay in the corner in a foetal position. He must have been terrified. The round door to the hut lay open, revealing the twilight sky just breaking into dawn. The first golden rays cut in through the slits in the wall, on to her tired face. Her eyes wandered to her trusty blade, Zorba. Was she ready to use it?

THE SURFACE of the sea stretches restlessly to the razor-cut horizon. The clear hazel sky is creased by a ripple of cirrus clouds. The lapping waves burst into spray with a dolphin and a teenage girl shooting out into the air. Fin rises high above the azure plain of water and rolls twice, exaulting in Akila's laughter. 'It worked!' she screams, holding onto his dorsal fin for dear life. 'I can't believe it worked!'

'Is this where you live, Akila?' came Fin's smooth voice.

'No! But I wanted to show you where others like you live.'

'I don't see them.'

'Don't you remember, Fin? I told you they live under the water.'

'Down there? In all that water?'

'Yes!'

'How?'

'Let's look for them, then you'll see.'

Fin raises his left flipper and swoops down towards the water.

FIN AND Akila hang in the air, a few hundred feet above the small island. Akila lies forward on Fin's body, looking down over the side. 'You see that tree, the strange one that stands alone at the bottom of the crater, in that water?'

'Yes.'

'It's the same as the one on my world, and the one I saw on Earth.'

'I recognize it.'

'You do?'

'Yes. There too, it stands in a pool of water. None of us go near it. We're told terrible stories of what happened to those that did. Even the orcas and great whales keep clear. I'm sure it's the same here too. What is it, Akila?'

'I don't know. But it must mean something that it's there on at least four different worlds.'

'What about the others?' He feels Akila's grip tighten, and asks her, 'What is it?'

'Back in my world, they taught us about heaven and hell, places people go when they die. In heaven people live after death in the clouds.'

'Like in my world.'

'I hope so.'

'And hell?'

'I was taught hell is a terrible place of fire and nothingness. And I have seen it. Where it rains fire and titans crush you if you dare enter.'

'There is such a world?'

She kisses him and wipes her tear-stained cheeks on his soft, rubbery skin. 'Yes, but there are others we can go to.'

'Are there dolphins there too?'

Akila laughs and sits up. 'You've swum with dolphins here, haven't you?'

'Is that a no?'

'Unfortunately.'

'Maybe it's for the best.'

'Why?'

'Too much of a good thing otherwise.'

SHALLOW HILLS roll on forever below them like a petrified green-ocean, an eerie reminder of the sea world they have left behind. Akila knows the hill-songs intimately. Fin dips lower and flies among the shallow hilltops, swimming through the melodies. Closing her eyes, stretching out her arms to the wind and the music caressing her body and soul, she sings as loudly as her little voice can manage, 'The hills are alive, with the sound of music …' She lets the last note fade because she does not remember the rest and with her eyes still closed, she relishes the music of the hills before she has to leave, yet again. But it fades until it feels distant and she feels Fin slowing to a stop. She opens her eyes, urgently asking, 'What happened to the music?'

'There's one in this world as well,' he says haltingly.

The scarred valley below them yawns like a crater ringed with cautious hills. Its basin is flooded and in the centre there is a single tree. The tree of roots, with its hideously unassuming visage. All Akila wants to do is to rush back to the hills and let their music shower over her. She hungers for the peace.

But now that peace is shattered as she is reminded of their mission. They have found the tree.

PAST THE skin of parched, cracked earth and the ocean of sand-dunes, the ground begins to swirl and blister and blossom into bright hues of purple, violet, deep sapphire-blues and shocking aquamarine. Akila is amazed at the lush colours of the shallow pools amidst the salt-flats. She does not know what they are, until she sees in the distance the spine of a ragged hill and the unmistakable broccoli-top of a tree at the summit. As they get closer, she sees the dark pool shimmering with the stern afternoon light on the hilltop. An empty world, she muses, and yet here it is. 'So maybe it's there in every world,' Fin considers softly, as though the tree might hear.

'What is it?'

'You think it isn't just a tree?'

'And I know that's not water either.'

'What is it, if it isn't a tree?"

'Somehow, I have to find out. Maybe it's the key.'

'Key to what?'

Akila freezes for a moment, wondering whether she should confide to him her desire to escape back to Earth, but she does not want anything to upset or push him away. 'To understanding what these worlds are. Why some are empty deserts and others are inundated with water or jungles or snow.'

'Snow?'

'Don't you know what snow is, Fin?'

'Snow? Is that a thing? It sounds like half a word.'

AKILA KNEELS on the rudimentary platform in front of the tied-down suitcase. She discreetly scratches away at the crayon sketching of a dolphin on the suitcase, hiding it from Fin. He has disappeared into the jungle, weaving in and out among the tree trunks and bursting through branches with singular delight. She unties the ropes holding the suitcase fastened to the platform, and rubs the coir over the drawing, disfiguring it beyond recognition. That would have been so embarrassing. She sighs with relief and clicks the case open.

She has been waiting for Fin for a while now, squatting beside Machu falls on the Mez. She has a bound plastic bag stuffed with Vidhi's thick down-feather jacket that she borrowed from her go-to locker in the girls' dorm. It is light pink with odd green triangles spread sparsely over the bloated exterior. There is a small *plop* and Cola's flathead peers up at her with his miniature button eyes. Akila does a mock- frown and shakes her head. 'Not this time, Cola, you know it's too cold for you where we're going.' He does not let up staring at her. 'Okay, okay, I want to be alone with Fin, please, Cola. Come on.' Cola disappears below the surface with only the dome of a bubble remaining in his stead. Akila gets up with the bag tightly in her grip when she hears Fin approaching.

Akila zips up her jacket with the wet plastic packet folded and thrust inside. Her teeth chattering, she draws the hood over her head and tightens the chords until only her eyes, nose and mouth are exposed through the aperture.

'So, Fin, what do you think of snow?' she asks, as they sail above a mountain peak.

'Wonderful at first. Then a bit dreary to be honest.'

Akila laughs uproariously and coughs. 'I can slow down if it's too cold for you,' he tells her.

'Yes, just a little please.' She bites her lip at her weakness. What a baby she is, to cough just because it's a little cold. The ground below flows by with ease. He is magic, she thinks. So warm to her touch. She runs her palm along his skin, hot against her thighs. She does not want this day to end. She will do whatever she has to do to keep them together. Whatever it takes.

She lies forward, her arms and legs wrapped around him, letting her body draw in the searing warmth from his.

'We're alone here too, like the desert world,' she says close to his ear. He does not respond and she can feel his heart quicken against her body, and his voice asks in its sweet even tone, 'Are you sure, Akila?'

She peers down at the dalmatian mountainside with patches

of black rock infecting the white. Against it sits a giant carved of the purest blizzard blue ice. His head is craned up to the sky, following Fin's line of flight with keen interest as he makes a wide arc to circle overhead and study the being. The ice giant stirs, lifting an arm to a ledge on the mountainside, his fingers digging in. Akila expects it to sound like rending Earth or cracking ice but there is no sound at all.

'Fin,' she gasps in alarm. The giant slowly twists his body as his head moves around to keep Fin and Akila in sight. 'Fin,' Akila urges a little louder, her finger stroking the skin by his eye. But he still circles the giant, marvelling at its form. 'Fin, let's leave, please.' Akila kisses the top of his head. She waits for him to respond, and kisses him again. 'Please, Fin.' Fin's calm voice finally answers. 'I just want to see–' The giant rises with astonishing speed and Fin swerves to the side to avoid the head, pitching over the peak with a whole mountain now between them. Akila glances back at the giant scrambling over the mountain, knocking over the rocky crest in a hail of rubble.

She senses something in the pit of her stomach and directs her gaze down to the massive hand shooting up at them. Her scream catches Fin's swerve, up and around, and then downward, flying past the out-stretched icy arm and descending rapidly to the cleft of the valley. They shoot along it, almost dragging in the snow. The mountains on either side shudder with the quaking earth, and avalanches unleash massive frothing clouds of white. Two ice giants scramble after them, clawing and kicking through the ravines. Fin can try to go higher until they are out of reach but there is no time to do so without being snatched out of the sky.

Akila feels his heart race for every drop of vigour it can muster. 'Hold on,' she hears him say, and she clings to him, her love, the sky-swimmer. Then it is all white with the rumble of avalanches from every side as rock clashes with ice. The wind hits her like a wall as something large sweeps past and the thick bed of snow in the valley explodes beneath them from the impact. Then, with a whip of Fin's tail, they burst out of the blinding cloud of powdered snow, higher and higher, and careen away at a blistering pace for the river.

A TOUCHSCREEN MP3 player sat on a solar-powered dock and Gene Pitney's crisp chords sang the soulful *'Something's gotten hold of my heart'* in the misty jungle dawn. Side by side on the Mez, Akila and Shyam moved into bhujangasana in one coordinated movement, and then flowed through the asanas of the surya namaskar.

Over the past few days Shyam had gotten used to her pace and already they moved as one, inhaling and exhaling in unison to a tempo felt more than heard. Cola's dark head lay at the pond's surface, watching them against the blooming sky, as wisps of cloud rolled into neat lines like the dappled reflection of a wet beach.

SHYAM FOUND the whistle ridiculous but Akila had insisted he hang it around his neck in case he got into trouble. He admired the spear she had armed him with, using it to move the brush aside while he nervously made his way through the jungle. He felt the ground squish and realized he was there already. He pushed a branch away from his face and saw the ground littered with yellow jamblis.

'JAMBLI? What the fuck is a jambli?' he asked later, handing her one from the woven basket. 'You need to close the basket, or they'll attract birds and monkeys and there'll be nothing left,' she said gently. He appreciated her patience with him. He fastened the basket cover closed and admired the wickerwork. 'Did you make this?' Akila scooped some of the jambli cream with her teeth and resumed mending a pair of shorts for Shyam. She shrugged in response to his query. 'That's one thing you'll notice here, you have a lot of time on your hands when you're not worrying about doing your job or paying the bills or shopping online. I've got a lot of "how-to" books in one of the trunks in the library. Basket-weaving took just another couple of days to learn; it was something to do. Then when you know how to weave baskets, you weave baskets.' She looked up at him and grinned. 'Beats downloading porn all day.'

'Hey,' Shyam protested, 'I've gone through your video library. You have a porn section too, you know.'

'Unlike you, I never wasted my time masturbating all day.'

'And you have the porn for?'

'Curiosity's sake.'

'Four terabytes is a lot of curiosity.'

She snorted and punted him playfully. He reached into the basket for another jambli. Akila glanced at the one he picked and said, 'Oh, I wouldn't open that one.'

'Why not?' He held it warily at arm's length.

'You see the red spots on its side? You'll find it infested with maggots. They're tiny, so you don't notice them right away. They won't kill you but you'll have a hell of a shit-fest for the next two days.'

'Good to know,' he said, tossing the jambli away.

'No,' Akila said, 'throw it down Machu falls.'

Her frequent nit-picking irked him at times, especially when it made him feel totally inept. He resented that she was well adapted to this place and he was forever relegated to being an outsider. He caught himself before he showed his irritation and asked, 'How come?'

'It's nothing serious, but I try to avoid it. On the one hand, it attracts unwanted attention from animals. And on the other, they end up getting an upset stomach and we'll have to live with the stench.'

'Again, good to know.'

Akila made a knot at the end of the stitch and bit off the tail. She set aside the shorts and moved close to Shyam. 'I'm sorry, Shy, I know it's a lot to get used to, but in no time at all you'll find your way about without me nagging you constantly.'

'You're not nagging.'

She laughed, 'Good, you know your cue.'

He wrapped his arm around her neck and they kissed.

The insectoid's watchful eye caught the light, indicating its presence among the shadows. The black dot at the centre of the orb stayed fixed on the embracing couple.

SHYAM SAT in the highest hut of Tree One, leaning into an open trunk packed with books. It was only one of Akila's library huts, and it was a small space showing signs that it had been her first attempt at construction, with many marks of upgrades since. On the other end of the spectrum, the sleeping hut was a crafted work of art, from the even floorboards to the neat thatch of the roof and the stylistic touches of the wood-panel walls that could be slid open like vertical blinds. The ornate carved headboard of polished wood and a headpiece made of animal horn lent the impression of a royal suite. The quarters of a savage tribal queen.

The trunks in the library were well made and preserved the books from the moisture and insects, keeping them dust-free and in near archival condition. She obviously treasured them and he knew he should too, if he'd learnt anything from past relationships. While the artful assembly of the trunks preserved the books, the state of the hut itself did nothing to keep out the odd arachnid or freaky centipede, often sending Shyam into melee-mode with the hunting spear. Most of the trunks were packed with 'how-to' books, all the way from *How to Camp in the Wild* to *How to Play the Guitar* and *How to Win Friends and Influence People*. She must have picked up any book she could find with 'how to' in the title, Shyam mused. Who could blame her? She had nobody to teach or guide her. He was more fortunate, since he had her to protect and guide him in this world. He opened the window for more light and screeched at another spider.

The next trunk was full of school notebooks, every one of them packed with beautifully rounded, adolescent handwriting. The labels in their distinct sketch-pen strokes read *Adventures in Neela*, *Adventures in Pila*, *Adventures in Saleti* and so on. Probably the scribblings of a child's imagination. He opened to a random page in *Adventures in Firozi* to get a glimpse of what a child trapped among alien worlds might conjure. He placed his finger mid-page and began to read, '... but they were all staring at us. I wanted them to go away and leave us alone. I wanted to scream at them but I didn't want to upset him. All of them just floated there in the same spot. They could see me looking at them, but they just kept staring at us. I want to kill them! I want to cut them up and cook them for dinner. I hate–'

'What are you doing?' Akila's voice rent the silence as she burst into the cramped hut. She snatched the book out of his hands and tossed it into the trunk. She slammed the lid closed and fiddled at the latch, but there was no way to lock it. She swung to face a perplexed Shyam and let loose.

'What do you think you're doing, Shyam?'

He tried to find the words, stammering, 'I don't – I was just – you told me – I was going through the library?' He waited for her to review his case. 'Do these books look like they're part of the library? Do you think you can just–' Shyam braved the consequences of interrupting her. 'I was going through the trunks, one by one, and I opened this one just a minute ago. I was looking through one of the books, just to know what they are.'

'Why did you pick this one up?' she asked, flipping open the lid emphatically and pointing a shaky finger at the label *Adventures in Firozi*. He shrugged. 'I don't know – it was the one on top.'

'Don't lie to me!'

'I was – listen, Akila, I don't know why you're so upset.'

'Why were you reading this book?'

'I saw *Adventures in Pila*, *Adventures in Gulabi*, *Adventures in Santari* and I thought they were something you wrote when you were a kid, that's all. I just wanted to see what they were about.'

Akila calmed down as he spoke.

'What are they?' he asked, timidly.

'You tell me. You read it.'

'I had time to read a couple of lines. I don't understand why you're so upset.'

'What did you read?'

He could not tell if she was being serious. She was.

'Just two lines about you being angry with someone. I don't know who with, or what about, and now you're angry with me. I don't know what's happening.'

Akila kept her eyes on Shyam, but the intensity began to wane. She closed the trunk.

'They're my diaries,' she said softly.

'I didn't know,' he offered quietly.

'I know, I forgot they were up here, though I still make entries from time to time.'

'I wouldn't have read them if I'd known. Everyone has the right to the privacy of their thoughts.'

Akila faced the trunk, her hands caressing the corners. 'I had no one to talk to. Writing a diary was the closest I could get.' She spoke with her back to him. 'Don't open this one, okay?' She went quiet for a few seconds, drawing in long troubled breaths. 'I trust you, so I'm not locking it. But please don't read them.'

'I won't.'

He remained perfectly still, not embracing her as every fibre in his being compelled him to do, but respecting her space, waiting for her to make the first move when she was ready. And she did, after a few minutes at the trunk. She wore a forced smile, now so obvious to him with their intimacy, and hugged him, with a kiss to his chin. Shyam knew that it was best to leave and help her prepare the catch of the day. However, the question was itching a hole in the back of his head, and he blurted out, 'Can I ask one question?' Akila swallowed, and nodded with pursed lips. He might as well now, he thought, and asked, 'What's with the Hindi names of colours? Pila, Saleti, Neela?'

'Oh,' she said and visibly relaxed. 'That's what I named the worlds back when I was a kid. I named them after the colour of their sky. I couldn't think of anything else.' She shrugged. 'If you can think of something better, we'll have an official renaming ceremony.' He held her by her waist, contemplating those deep eyes, the shade of sun-baked granite that sometimes wavered from his. They did not this time.

THE LARVAE pulse and wriggle over her skin. They are finger-long and ivory-white with black beaks. Akila can feel the beaks scraping against her thighs, the plastic smoothness of the bodies sliding over her stomach and under her buttocks. And that pulse. Is it each one or the mass throbbing to some rhythm as a whole? Lying among them chest-deep, her body is covered with a thick, gelatinous slime she can't crawl out of. She can't move. But she remains lucid enough to wonder whether she really does wish to move. Does it matter if she is fed to these larvae? Her grimace is slick with tears and sweat. She looks up at the clay ceiling in surrender. It is smooth and the edges straight, forming the extended hexagonal chamber filled with these crawling things. Shafts of bright light shine through the uneven circular holes in the far wall. The beams flicker briefly. She can't be sure it was not just a tremor of her eyelid, but there it is again. The gobs of jelly slip on her body as she looks on. A flutter of shapes, and an opening in the wall darkens. Something crawls through easily, the sunlight shimmering on its skin in rainbow hues. It waits on the ceiling in perfect stillness, reminding her of something. Then a deep, grating voice penetrates the silence. 'Beli...'

* * *

AKILA UNWRAPS *To Kill a Mockingbird* from the wet plastic cover. She's wearing a school tie too, to show off. Her outfit is nice and dry. She jaunts up the slope, skipping over familiar boulders that mark her path to joy each time, looking up from time to time for Fin, all the while gaping at the whales among the clouds. Only thrice thus far has she seen a blue whale, a really massive one swerving through a cloud. They seemed so much more spirited than their lesser cousins, almost as much as the dolphins. A herd of manatees sail in the distance. She sits on her rock on top of the hill and waits for Fin, with her finger marking the page they had reached the last time. After a while she fiddles in the bag at her feet and brings out the Walkman. She hadn't wanted to 'borrow' it from her classmate Sheena, but she was desperate to get something special for Fin. Bubbling with excitement, she hides it in the bag again and scours the crowded sky.

'Akila.'

She flinches and swings about with a broad smile blooming across her face. Fin hangs in the air in front of her, a sight to which she has become accustomed. She gets up and reaches forward to hug him, but he withdraws with a jerk. It catches her by surprise and she loses her footing, twisting her ankle in the stumble.

'Akila, are you alright? Are you hurt?' Fin asks urgently, coming low.

'Yeah,' she giggles. She puts an arm around him and he helps her up. She shakes her head, giggling at herself, toying with her hair. She hugs him, saying, 'I can't believe I–'

But Fin draws away again. Akila winces, trying not to rest too much weight on the injured ankle. 'What is it, Fin?'

'Akila …' His even voice trails off.

'What's the matter?' she asks, in wide-eyed innocence.

Fin does not speak. He watches her for a while.

'Fin?'

He turns and glances back. Akila looks beyond him at a pod of five large, almost rotund, dolphins. Their intense stares upset her. 'Fin?' she asks again, frightened this time.

'We are too different, Akila.'

'What are you talking about?'

'You are a Beli.'

'So? So what?'

'I'm falling in love with you.'

The statement, spoken so plainly in Fin's sweet voice, strikes her dumb for a moment.

'I'm falling in love with you, and I can't,' he tells her.

'I love you too, Fin.'

'I know you do.'

'Then what's the problem?'

'I can't be in love with you.'

'Why not?' She does not realize she is shouting.

'We can't belong together.'

'I don't understand.'

Fin waits a while, again watching her. She starts to speak. 'Fin–'

'I can't see you anymore.'

'What?'

'It is not accepted.'

'What are you – what's happening, Fin? The last time I came, you didn't say anything about this.'

'I know.'

'What's the problem? Is it them?' she yells, pointing at the dolphins behind him. 'What are they saying? They don't want you to be with me?'

Fin remains quiet.

'What the hell do we care what they want us to do? I love you, Fin, and I know, I know you love me. We'll get out of this world and we can do whatever we want.'

'This is my home, Akila. And you are a Beli. Please, don't make this more difficult for me than it is.'

'Difficult for you? It doesn't seem that difficult from where I'm standing. All you're doing is being a coward.'

'Please, Akila. Try to understand.'

'I understand, Fin! I understand! But that doesn't mean I accept it!'

'It's not that simple.'

'It should be, and frankly it is.'

'It's not.'

'You're just a coward.'

'Yes, I'm a coward,' he says, his voice low.

'Fin, please, let's go.'

'You're a Beli. I'm a dolphin. I belong here with my kind, not exploring other worlds with you.'

'That's not you talking.'

'I should have realized it long ago, then I wouldn't be hurting you this way.'

'You don't have to hurt me.'

'I can't see you anymore.'

Tears stream down Akila's face and she blubbers, 'Please, please, Fin, okay we won't fall in love. Okay, I'm not in love with you anymore. But don't ask me to stay away. Don't tell me I can't see you.' She reaches out to touch his face and he draws away. 'I'm sorry,' she blurts out, 'I'm sorry, I won't touch you either. I promise. I won't touch you, I won't be in love with you, and I won't make you fall in love with me. Let's just go back to what we had in the beginning. That's all I want. Let me come and read to you. Please, Fin.'

'I can't see you ever again.'

'Let me just come and read to you, Fin! I won't do anything! I won't touch you, I won't – I won't do anything else. I just want that…'

Fin does not speak.

'Please,' she screams shrilly at the dolphins hanging there, diminishing her with their apathetic stares.

'Fin?' But he does not respond to her pleas. 'If I go now, I won't come back. Ever! I'll never come back to see you!'

'Akila, it's for the best. We can't see each other anymore.'

'Please, let's just stay friends so I can come and read to you. I need you. You know I need you.'

Inclining his body, Fin slowly moves backwards. 'Fin, let me just hug you then. Let me at least say goodbye properly,' she implores in a trembling pitch.

Fin hesitates, then moves to her. She lunges forward, wrapping her arms around his head, clinging on tightly. 'I won't let you go. You can't make me, Fin, you can't make me. I won't let go.' Despite her protests, Fin slowly lowers her. Her feet touch the rock and she kicks them up, wrapping her legs around him. 'Please, let me come back. I'll just read to you, I swear! I swear! Please! Fin!' He lowers her to the ground. Her back feels the cold rock and she shrieks repeatedly, 'Fin! Fin! Fin!' And when at last her entire back rests against the ground, she drops a kiss near his eye. Her limbs slide off his warm body and smack the rock like lengths of rubber.

Fin nudges her face with his snout one last time, tasting her tears. She just lies there, her glassy eyes staring off into space. Fin retreats a few feet and lingers to make sure she is all right. Three minutes later, she sits up exhausted, as though disoriented from a troubled sleep. She sees the book lying on the rock and callously swipes it with her fingers. It falls noisily among the stones. She gets up, and without another look at Fin, starts down the hill in a daze. A fifteen-year-old taking tiny unsteady steps with dirt in her hair.

When she reaches the foot of the hill, she undoes her tie and lets it fall. She unbuttons her shirt and it slides off her shoulders with a sigh. At the edge of the water she removes her shorts. She kicks them off and steps out of her panties, now standing there, just her bronzed nubile self. She does not look back. She steps towards the water, her feet getting heavier with every step. Her stomach twists and turns and she is about to erupt with grief. Her toe catches on a rock and she falls off balance.

The water bursts into her as a scream tries to escape. She emerges, gulping for air and coughing. Her lungs are burning as she crawls up a muddy shore, spitting out water, weeping and coughing. She collapses onto her side, lifting her eyes to the spectacle. Before her great earthen spires reach thousands of feet into the crimson heavens, and from the holes perforating their sides spew little roving specks, like insects. She has fallen beside a termite mound, she realizes, as her consciousness spirals in and out of itself. One of the specks separates from the mass and comes charging towards her at a terrific speed. It stops some feet away, its frame now towering above her fallen figure. And at once she recognizes the long face and large eyes with the black pinprick dots studying her. Then she knows she should not have entered the water in her condition. For now she is a helpless visitor to the metropolis of insectoids. With that last thought sprinkling the gloom, her eyes roll back and she sleeps.

SHYAM PUSHED through the bush, cradling a lumpy carry-bag to his chest. The pond-side was deserted and his stomach lurched with hunger. 'Gone hunting' was scrawled in chalk on a rock. As per Akila's directions, he poured the jamblis into a pressure cooker. With one red jambli between his teeth and a couple on the ground, he twisted and turned the heavy cover into place. There it was, the foolproof safe to keep the jamblis from monkeys and birds. He sauntered along the edge of the pool, tossing the two jamblis in. Somewhere among the twilight shadows in the water, there lurked a giant salamander called Cola. He was used to the idea now. Whether or not he could share the same space with Cola was another matter.

SHYAM SAT on the Mez, peering out into the jungle. The winding stream reflected the sky, gleaming like a tanzanite path amidst the gloomy shadows. So this was home now. It was beginning to feel like it. He gazed down at their toilet, a lip of rock with a naturally formed seat. Akila had carved out the back to have it form a U, and with it aligned at the edge of the falling water, your lower back was constantly being washed. Could he have thought of that if he had been in her place? She had set up everything perfectly. Living quarters and storage in the trees. The solar panels on top of the huts charged the batteries. There was food and clean water in abundance. A toilet, an equipped kitchen, a giant watchdog, a Fenek for transport. All that had been missing was him and here he was now.

Savouring a mouthful of creamy jambli, he wondered when he would get sick of its deliciousness. Probably as soon as it lost its exotic allure and became commonplace. He studied the pond's surface. The two jamblis he had tossed into the water were gone. It perturbed him that something as large and unwieldy as a gargantuan salamander could move unnoticed, hardly a few feet away. This was his world now, he thought. Where danger lurked behind every tree, and he survived not by his wits, but by association.

He noticed Akila's bare, grungy body standing tall by the pressure cooker, with two dead furry things tied together and hanging from her shoulder. He greeted her with a smile and she beamed in reply. Beneath her forced jocular tone, he sensed a strain of irritation. 'That's not where the pressure cooker goes when you've filled it with jamblis, Mr Shyam.' Wow. Mr Shyam. She really was pissed.

He shot to his feet and shifted the cooker, even as she tried to compensate by saying, 'No, it's not that big a deal. I'm just reminding you, that's all.'

She tossed the kills by the water and with two lithe steps, dove in. The surface barely rippled and she was gone. Forty seconds later, Akila resurfaced and sat at the edge, her toes affectionately rubbing Cola's lip. She scrubbed her arms with her homemade loofah, made from a sundried husk, and caught him staring.

Her eyes were suddenly wretched. She held out her bar of soap. 'Can you help me with my back?' 'Sure,' he stammered, confused by her change of demeanour. He sat behind her as she swept her hair to the front, leaving those marvellously lean, muscular shoulders bare for him. Taking a palmful of water, he worked up a lather, wondering all the while whether he should ask her what the matter was. Sometimes the worst thing you could do when a person had something on their mind was bother them by asking what it was. But he could not help himself. He blurted out, 'What's the matter?'

'Huh?' Her voice bounced like a hiccup.

'It feels like there's something upsetting you.'

'I'm not upset, I'm thankful. No, that's not the right word. Grateful, no, more than that, so much more and full of love.' She fell silent again. He scrubbed her shoulders with the rough sponge and she involuntarily leant forward when he started on her upper back.

'I have to keep telling myself I'm not alone anymore. And I can't believe it yet.' She stood up and he continued to scrub the small of her back down to her hips, over the swell of her buttocks and down the thighs. Soapy all over, she snuggled against him. He smelt her hair and dotingly rubbed his nose and lips against her head. 'What is that,' he asked tenderly, 'do you put jambli juice in your hair?'

'Great conditioner and gets rid of dandruff.'

'Smells good.'

'I know.'

She reached out and stroked his flaccid penis. He played with her nipple. 'Why haven't you shown me anything yet?' he asked.

Her grip on the tip tensed, and she gave him a playful grin with her pursed lips but she gave no reply.

'There are so many worlds out there but you won't take me. Even this one, you haven't taken me anywhere really. What are you afraid of?'

Akila moved onto him, straddling his lap, her hand never pausing. She snorted, smirking down at him. 'I'm not afraid that you're incapable of taking care of yourself here. I know that's what you think, but I just ...' She ran her fingers through his hair and pulled his head to her chest. His hands touched the goosebumps on her buttocks, and he let a finger travel down, between them, to the soft wet curls of flesh, probing gently and caressing the warmth. 'I want you to make this your home.'

'It is now,' he mumbled.

'I know you know that but I want every fibre of your body to feel that instinctively, so if you ever splash through to escape some danger, your body brings you back here and nowhere else.'

He licked the hollow between her breasts, and tenderly nuzzled them. He took a deep breath of her scent and said, 'I'm just tired of being restricted to one place day and night.'

'You're right,' she said, moving forward, rubbing his tip along her wetness.

THEY LAY together, their legs tangled and bodies in a light embrace. Faces pushed together, admiring the haloed moon sailing through the brightly starred night sky. 'It's the right time for you to see it,' she said.

'See what? Now?'

'Yeah, I was waiting for the best way to initiate you into all this craziness.'

'I'm here already. Craziness ahoy.'

'Oh, my dear boy, Macocos and Colas are nothing compared to what awaits you.'

He could feel her tremble against him.

'Wow, you're really excited to show me around, aren't you?'

The moon shimmered on her teary eyes for a moment before she hid them against his neck.

'I've waited so long for this.'

He touched her hair to comfort her. 'I understand. I'm the first person you've had a chance to do this for. I'm excited too.'

He felt her sigh against him, wait and then say, 'Hold on.'

'Hold on? What, now?'

'And don't make a sound. Everything will be alright.'

'Not right now.'

'Remember, don't make a sound.'

'For god's sake, Akila!'

She held him tightly and heaved them over the edge of the rocks. Under the water, Cola's button-eyes gazed up at the moon through the dispersing splash. Akila and Shyam had vanished.

The placid lake surface rippled outward from them. Akila held Shyam, steadying him as he gurgled wide-eyed, spitting out water and beating his arms. She hushed him in her firm embrace, whispering, 'Calm down, we're okay. We're okay, Shyam.' He obeyed but she could still feel the reflexive panic coursing the adrenalin through him.

'Come on, breathe slowly. Deeper, now in and out, there you go. No, don't worry, it's just a little water, that's right, spit it out.' She rubbed a hand along his spine, murmuring softly, 'There, breathe now. Good. Are you feeling better?' He drew in a deep breath and nodded, 'Yeah.' She hushed him again. They were standing chest-deep in the water, his eyes still bulging comically as he swallowed the acidic tinge in his mouth.

The pebbles on the shore were small and comfortable to lie on, cool against their backs like a bed of stars. Akila and Shyam lay hand in hand. Faces skyward, eyes soft and mouths open. Shyam felt the gratitude tumble out of his chest for this privilege that he was not sure he deserved.

The delicate chiming of the water among the pebbles and Akila's quiet breathing could not distract him from the midnight sky, and the two dark forms of humpback whales swaying past the silver moon, singing their night-song with a long, low call and thumping moans. A pod of dolphins came weaving through a pale smear of cloud, knitting through the couple amongst the stars. Three orcas played among themselves, teasing and chasing each other. Then they were all gone, swimming somewhere outside his field of vision. Dark forms in the darkness.

A low rumble raised the hairs on his chest and a shadow devoured the stars. He could barely discern its shape as it entered the radiance, and then the slender form of a massive blue whale swallowed the moon. Cast sharply against the glow, he felt the moonlight leave his body for those moments. Only when its sweeping tail left the light did he let out his breath.

He did not respond to her tug at his hand until the third

time, and when he did, he rolled against her side. Her eyes did all the talking, sad and hungry, and pleading for him not to waste a moment. He slipped himself over her inviting leg. Her scorching insides were wet and he thrust wildly with all his might, disregarding the clattering pebbles about them. Her hand fondled the small of his back to steady him. He slowed his thrusts into meditative breaths, measured strokes filling and emptying. Feeling every fold, undulation and pulse of slippery skin and hearing only the discreet lake and each other's quivering sighs. Shyam felt every drop of love he felt for her coursing through his penis. Deep within her clutching canal, out into the night breeze and back into that welcoming cavern of flesh. Take me in. Take all of me. Take all that I can give. Take all that you want from me. But Akila's eyes were on the sky, watching a pod of dolphins swerve and twist in space. And she was no longer lying on a bed of pebbles but lifted into the air, floating up, higher and higher, to swim among the stars again.

'BELI.' The silhouette of an insectoid clung to the ceiling. The grating voice scratches at her pores. 'I never thought I'd meet a Beli in my lifetime.'

Helpless, trapped in these weird realms so different from her own, cast aside by her love, and now held in this unyielding jelly. Akila screams. The insectoid twitches. 'Kill me! Just kill me!' she shrieks. It watches her convulsions dispassionately. When her throat has gone hoarse and her spirit is spent, she whimpers, head down. It lingers without a word. Though exhausted within and without, she will not show weakness and bow to this thing. 'I'm having a bad day. Just let me go home,' she croaks.

'No.'

'It's not time for the sacrifice yet. You can't take me.'

'Do you think I'm here to take you for the "sacrifice"?'

'You're one of them, aren't you?'

'You've seen my kind on other worlds?'

Flashing her sun-baked granite eyes, she snorts like a peevish schoolchild.

'You've seen my kind on other worlds,' the insectoid repeats, in a more insistent monotone.

Akila rolls her eyes.

'You have. How many?'

Her jaws clench with scorn.

'We are all just prisoners here, you and I.'

She registers the words but conceals her reaction.

'I am the Kier, the ruler of my kind. We are doomed to stay on this barren world, and you're the Beli, kept from your own world to be the sacrifice every three years.'

'Beli.' The word crawls through her sore throat. 'What a stupid word.' She flings a handful of maggots against the wall. Then with a blazing look, she says, 'That's right, I'm the Beli called Akila. Now let me go.'

'Who are you to command me, little human? I am the Kier!'

'I am the Beli! Weren't you listening, ant?'

'True, you are the Beli, but you're also our means to other worlds.'

'Why do you want to leave your world?'

'The old stories tell of a time before this world came to be, when we shared a single world as home with other beings like yourself. Then we were expelled and put here, abandoned to our own devices. Soon we had wiped out every living thing in our wake, because that is our true nature. And when we needed hope most, there came a visitor, bringing our salvation. It called itself Beli.'

She pricks up her ears. 'So?'

'It was a miracle. We knew the Beli had been sent to save us.'

'What did he do?'

'It too was female, like you. She was the first to take us to another world. Generations later, another Beli took us to the next, and we hoped with three worlds to spread ourselves over, we could contain our hunger to expand and consume. But there could be no containment. Our hunger has no bounds. My kind consumed relentlessly, not looking to the future, not conserving, not trying to understand what we were losing. Before long we had stripped these other worlds bare, and needed another. And yet again, a Beli happened upon us in our hour of need. But this time we were stopped.'

'Stopped?'

'Yes.'

'What could possibly stop you if you could destroy three worlds singlehandedly?'

The Kier takes a moment to reflect. 'The creature we have grown to call the Sentinel. The one from the holy tree, the bridge between the worlds.

'What did it do?'

'It stopped us. It compelled us back to this world through some force we could not repel.'

'Magic?'

'We don't understand how or why, but the old stories say that we obeyed its every command. We dived into the waters of these other worlds in our multitudes and were transported here. Thus emptying the worlds we had called home and killed just as wantonly. And to punish us further, the Sentinel takes the best of us every ten years. We don't know to what purpose. Maybe to punish us, it ingests those that deserve to lead us. It deprives us of greatness. It reduces us to mediocrity for what we did to its worlds.'

'I have seen the empty worlds. One is a desert with nothing but sand and the other is worse. Less than nothing. It is a bare planet.'

'That is our nature. We try to fight it. That is why we need you now, and it is fortuitous that you have come to us at this time. Our world is spent. Nothing remains for us on the surface so we dig into the ground, long tunnels that twist and probe the bowels of this planet where we now survive on plants and creatures that live among the rocks. There are regions I know of where some of my kind consume their own wormlings to survive, and even that is not enough. So they war with each other to feed on the vanquished. Look at what we are reduced to. But these others like me that you saw on those worlds, are there many? Are there cities like this? Can they contain this endless hunger?'

'No cities.'

'Then?'

'I've seen only a handful of your kind, and that is enough.'

'How did you see them?'

'They guard your "holy tree". It is your kind that drags me off every single time for the sacrifice.'

'They obey the Sentinel?'

'They are his pets. He talks through them.'

'The best of us reduced to mindless slaves. You must take us out of this world. Our race must survive. You wouldn't condemn an entire species to destruction, would you?'

She slaps the jelly holding her down, snorting, 'You do realize it's harder for me to say yes in this position.'

The insectoid observes her face for a good while. 'True, and then again, we don't need you to trust us. We have you, the first Beli to come to us in twenty-five generations, and we will not risk you deceiving us.'

She shrugs and lifts a wormling to her face. She pinches it in half, muttering, 'Blah, blah, blah.'

'I don't understand the meaning. But I sense your indifference.'

Akila sits bent like an abandoned doll, watching the other larvae devour the one she had cut in two, even as both halves continue to wriggle. One side of her mouth is twisted in a scowling grin. The Kier's antennae wobble in the humid air as it watches her.

THE KIER leads the way, with her riding the back of a beetle built like a tank. They are cresting a narrow path along the spine of a massive mound that slopes into a steep descent on either side. It is the perfect vantage for a panoramic view of the insectoid metropolis. The entire surface of the planet is probably like what she sees before her – a forest of spires the colour and sheen of glazed clay scraping the crimson skies. Their surfaces crawl with insectoids of all colours and shapes.

The mound is the odd one out, pockmarked on one side with hexagonal openings to chambers, like the one she had been kept in, she imagines. Are there other such nurseries for their newborn? No wonder they've run out of living space and are relegated to eating their wormlings. In nature, balance does not last and imbalance always attempts to correct itself in the simplest way. The river flows on the left side of the mound, tantalizingly near, but of no use with her stuck to the beetle's back in the jelly. Her head lolls to the rocking of its swinging steps and the emerald hues cascade off its armoured back in the afternoon sun. She reluctantly admits it is among the most beautiful creatures she has ever seen.

'I don't expect to convince you overnight,' the Kier resumes, without looking back. On the right side of the mound, past the mesmerizing rows of hexagons stretching in precise patterns to the street below, there is a gathering of insectoids keeping very still. Akila notices the contrast to the rest of them bustling about. They are no more than specks, as more join the throng. Are they watching her and her escort, their Kier? Am I really so important to them?

'But look around,' the Kier urges, 'look at them. Only you can save them. Would you really leave them to be crushed by their own numbers?' Akila wants to scream that she just wants to go home. She clenches her hands into fists, and as she does this she feels an edge against the tip of her thumb. Her knife is still in its scabbard at her waist. They don't recognize it as a weapon. If only she could move her hands to get it. But she can. Her hand slides through the layer of jelly coating her body. The time in the direct sunlight has loosened its bond. She reaches her belt and takes a grip of the hilt. Her legs are still stuck to the beetle's shell, but her arms are free to move. This is the only chance she may get before being put back in the chamber and out of the sun again.

But what can she do with this little blade? And where can she escape to? As the Kier continues rambling about Akila being their saviour, her mind works feverishly to formulate a plan of escape, however rudimentary. There is the slope to the left of course, to the river below. She can't tell exactly how high she is, but she is certain it is more than three hundred feet. Supposing she gets out of the jelly, how does she escape from the beetle and the Kier? She knows how fast an insectoid can be and she can't outrun it.

'You are the sacred one, the Beli, the one who is not bound to one world. You are not bound to any world! You were chosen. You are our saviour. You have come in our hour of need to give us salvation.' She goes over the plan one last time – get out of the jelly, get down to the river and splash through. Simple. Keep it simple. Her buttocks slide an inch on the beetle's back. This is her chance. 'Someday soon, you will see the truth. And that day you will say to me that you want to give us this blessing. And you will do so, not only willingly, but wholeheartedly. When you understand your role, when you recognize the opportunity to save an entire race, then you will be bathed in a divine joy and you won't just take us to one world, but from there to another and another. We will be saved.'

It turns to face her and clicks twice in bewilderment. The young girl is squatted at the beetle's tiny head, busily hacking through the soft tissue attaching it to the armoured body. The beetle fumbles and sways at the edge, holding on with its clawed feet. As its last embers of life depart, its grip slackens and the entire body tilts.

Akila is just as horrified as the Kier when she feels the beetle's body lean over the edge of the path. It is going to roll rather than slide down as she had intended. This is bad. With a twist she lunges forward, grabbing hold of the seam of an armour plate higher up on the beetle's back. She closes her eyes as she feels the massive bug keel over and roll. She is not crushed! She opens her eyes.

The Kier is crouched over her, protecting her with its own body, absorbing every impact and roll. And in moments the madness is over. She lies among the beetle's remains with the sound of flowing water deliciously close. Her head still reeling, she approaches the Kier lying sprawled on its back. It has missing and broken limbs, and green oozing from every orifice.

'Please don't leave us, Beli. There is something I can give you,' its quavering voice beseeches. Akila is distracted by a noise from above. A horde has gathered at the top of the mound to investigate. They all see the Beli beside their fallen Kier. 'I will tell you the secret! There is an escape for you,' it squeals. 'A world to which Beli are sent when their duty is done. I planned to tell you once you had served us. Please don't abandon us and I will show you.'

Akila picks the blade from her scabbard and squats by its head. She scratches at the trembling spot of the pupil on its immense eye, hissing, 'I told you, I kept telling you, I was having a bad day. But you wouldn't listen. You didn't care. I'm never coming back here. I'll pray every day that your kind destroys itself because that is your nature and that is what you deserve.'

She gazes up expectantly at the insectoids hurtling downhill. She will soon be out of time. The Kier's disfigured features stir, and it clicks, 'Blah, blah, blah.'

'That's right,' she grins. She shakes her head, chuckling, and replaces Zorba in her scabbard. 'Blah, blah, blah,' the Kier shrieks up at her. Then tipping a wave to the insectoids almost upon them, Akila disappears into the murky canal.

'SO IT'S all water?'

'Yup'

Shyam held onto Akila from behind as they cruised above the rippling sheet of ocean. 'All water,' she said, marking something out with an elegant arm outstretched. 'Except for that.'

Macoco swung about to face the tiny island.

'This is amazing,' Shyam laughed. Akila stroked Macoco's neck and sent him in a gliding descent in easy circles.

'How certain are you that there's no land out there?'

'I've had years to explore these worlds, Shyam,' she replied, a little annoyed, 'and I'm as "certain" as I can be that it's all water. Sure, if this was the middle of the Pacific I would probably say the same thing.' She stuck out her tongue at him.

'WHAT'S THE date today?'

Akila lowered her book with a finger marking the page and leaned over for her tablet. She touched the screen for the date and stated, 'It's 24 March. Why?'

'No reason, just wondering. Kind of lost track of time here.'

'That's the beauty of it, I think.'

'I know. I'm not complaining, Kili.'

AKILA SAT astride him with her wet back to him, flexing and rolling her hips against his. He was only semi-hard in her gripping warmth but it was marvellous, lying there on the soft grass of the singing hills late in the afternoon. Thin serpentine trails of water trickled down her back from her hair, after their recent splash through. Her lithe back did not have a single scar. How is that possible, he asked himself. Surely she must have been injured or attacked by an animal at some point. Sighing dreamily, she leaned back. He moved his book off his stomach just in time as she lay on him, her wonderful wet hair in his face. He held her close gently, breathing in her scent that he had grown to love so quickly.

'What are you thinking about?' she asked, almost to herself.

'What do I do here?'

'What do you mean?'

'You go out hunting for food, and other than gathering fruit and keeping the place clean, what do I do?'

'You do so much.'

'I'm not asking you to console me, Kili, I'm not complaining.'

'Sounds like you are.'

'I'm not, I'm bored.'

'Am I boring?'

'Oh, come on.'

She laughed, playfully slapping his thigh.

'I don't have to work for a living or get food. I love the time we spend together, but–' He broke off.

'What?'

'I want to have *something* to do.'

She sighed. 'Reminds me of my first few months – after I had figured out how to survive, that is.'

'Are you saying that I'm spoilt and ungrateful?'

'No, Shy. All I'm saying is, I had the same problem, trying to figure out how to fill my days.'

'And how did you solve it?'

'I told you already. You're just too lazy to consider it.'

'Told me what?'

'I started teaching myself anything and everything. I started reading. I didn't have the distraction of a social life or endless flowing TV and porn to fill my hours.'

He ruminated for a while. 'Turn around,' he whispered. She did, a bit drowsily, and lay facing him, her hand feeling his erection. 'Ooh, frisky so soon after?'

He held her and softly said, 'No, just lie here with me.'

'What's the matter?'

He kissed her hungrily, then tore his mouth away. He placed his hands under his head and stretched his torso, closing his eyes. He listened to the music of the living hills. She folded her arms over his chest and rested her chin on them. Her sad eyes watched him, and she asked wistfully, 'Are you sick of all this? Are you feeling lonely?'

'No, Akila, that's not it.'

'Do you want to go back?'

'It's the opposite. I don't ever want to go back, don't you see? I'm complete now.' He gazed up at the cream sky. 'Here's the truth, Akila. And it may be ugly.'

'I can take it.'

'It's not about you, it's about me. I hate people. The lying and the hypocrisy. The constant sense of competition and the jealousy – the soul-crushing jealousy – that kept me awake some nights. They sucked out all the joy in my life. Being judged for everything. Feeling like I'm not living my life as much as I should be. Who are they to tell me whether I'm living my life to the fullest? Selfies inundating the net, of people travelling and doing crazy stuff with broad smiles and catchy captions. Ads telling me what a full life should be, and in the end it turns out to be about some energy drink. The fucking with my head, making me feel like my life is worthless. I've always avoided spending time with people because of how awful they make me feel. That's the irony, isn't it? I leave all that behind and come to this paradise. And it's a paradise because of you. Then I begin to feel like I'm wasting my days doing nothing. Shit! What's wrong with me? You still have to show me the worlds, there's so much to look forward to, and I was thinking earlier today, like some jackass, I was thinking, why am I wasting my time doing nothing? How can I get anywhere in life, how can I achieve anything – all that I should have – if I just sit around not building for my future?'

'Shyam.' The relief showed on her face.

'Please, Akila, I'm on a roll here, let me finish. I want to tell you that with you, there is nothing more I aspire for. The purpose of my life is this. It's you. If I had anything to work towards, it is this, here, being here with you. You are the star of my energy-drink ad.'

'You get so sappy sometimes.'

'You bring out the beast in me,' he said, doing an abysmal imitation of Marlon Brando. Akila leaned forward and kissed his chin.

SHE RUNS through the waist-high foliage, among tall, lean trunks striped white and grey in the blue twilight. The tops of the trees are brushed with the last glowing rays of daylight before the sun disappears over the hills. Her breathing matches her rapid pace without being laboured and showing little, if any, signs of exhaustion. With her left hand she hugs Cola to her bare chest and in the other glints her trusty blade, Zorba. Cola is getting a little too big for her to carry around but she will not admit it. 'What?' she huffs at Cola. 'The bug said there is a world where the Belis are sent and I'm just checking out the worlds we haven't been to.'

Her bloody spear lies a kilometre behind them at the edge of a brook, its shaft broken in three. A creature drags itself into the bushes, whimpering between angry wheezes.

Akila hears them behind her, shooting through the bushes, getting into attack formation. Five small flying creatures descend towards her.

'This way,' they beckon, with voices like autumn leaves rustling.

'Yeah, yeah, I'm running this way, you bastards! How much further is it? Just get me to water!'

'This way,' they say in chorus. The hunters are gaining ground and the viridian green sky is quickly darkening. Snarls and claws tear the ground, and the only sign of them is the slithering trail of shivering bushes. Twines and twigs grip her shins and jaws snap at her calves. No further. She does not want to be brought down and attacked en masse by these ravenous beasts. The ground is their domain.

She pats Cola and he holds on tight instantly. With her free hand she latches onto a passing tree trunk. She swings around it, and the arm brandishing Zorba in a hooked arc comes up bloody. A body tumbles through the bushes and lies still. Without wasting a moment, she is on her way again. A hint of a grin is the only sign of gratification that she allows herself on hearing the unsettling squeals and guttural yelps through the sound of tearing flesh.

Damn! They haven't all gone to it. No, that would have been too easy. And these creatures are nothing if not efficient killing machines. She hugs Cola to her neck and pecks his snout. 'I'm sorry, Cola, I'm sorry I brought you here.'

The forest descends into a shroud of cool darkness as the tree trunks become mere shadows in the dusk. The hunters gain on her again and she can feel her legs stiffen with exhaustion, though the rest of her is still charged to go. She hates it when her body disappoints her will. She has felt it before. Soon, moving her legs will seem as impossible as lifting a giant boulder, and then all she will be capable of doing is falling and waiting to be ripped apart. Feeling every tear and shredded joint. 'Here,' the voices beckon.

Ten minutes earlier her muscles would have reacted with lightning agility, but her mind needs a moment to comprehend and then relay instructions to her beleaguered thighs and calves. Before realizing where she is, her legs push her upwards into a leap, over the stream. No, damn it! But it's too late. She rolls through the shrubbery, using what strength she has, to keep Cola safe. She digs her heels into the ground and stops the roll in time to see a furry contour pass above her, just a fleeting shape against the dark sky. Zorba claws at the ground, dangerously close to snapping. It is enough to draw her up into a stumbling sprint for the stream. The bushes on the other side shake violently and dark forms shoot out at her. But she is already diving headlong into the shallow brook.

She is seated with her legs splayed in a V in water up to her chest. Has she splashed through to another stream? Above her there is a clear night sky doused with the Milky Way and the little of what she can make out about her is rock. All she wants to do is stand up and dive back into the water, home to the salamander pool, but she is drained of the will and the energy to even try. With her wobbly joints and swimming head she drags her useless legs out of the water a few feet into an alcove between some boulders. She is too tired to notice that Cola is no longer on her.

Akila wakes up wincing at the scorching pain. She sits up, touching her shins. The phantom pain lingers of them being beaten raw during her chase. She comes out from among the rocks into a crisp breeze. There is a chill in the air and the water is even colder. Her eyes overflow with silent tears as she slides her legs into the crisp bath. The cold soothes her muscles. The burning has stopped. And soon she begins to survey the new world.

All she can see from here is flat rock stained charcoal-grey by the sun, with dark patches of morning dew and nothing but saffron skies. Something does not seem right. She struggles to her feet as it hits her. She has lost him. 'Cola,' she whispers, rushing across the water. She had splashed through at the bottom of a dribbling shelf of rock so he could only be downstream. She freezes in her tracks. Unless she let go of him and he is stranded back in that horrid world of hunters and faeries.

Her hands are at her head, gripping fistfuls of hair and pulling hard. What has she done? He's gone. He can't survive there. He is not meant for that world, she thought. I took him away from his pond. Why?

A glint catches her eye. She retrieves her knife from a few feet away and prepares to return for Cola. 'I'll find you,' she chants aloud, and a screeching cry curdles her blood in response. Her eyes dart to the figure in the sky. It is a winged horror with its long furry tail arched high in the air like a scorpion's. Slack-jawed, Akila follows the descent of this nightmare as it lands beyond the pile of boulders she took refuge among last night. Its movements are surprisingly discreet for something that stands fifty feet tall but it screeches and roars to announce its presence.

Something brushes the back of her leg and Akila jumps with a yelp, slipping on a wet stone. She swings her arms wildly to keep her balance and lands on her bum some feet away. Her heart pounds in her chest and she tastes the bile burning her throat at the realization of what she has done. But it is too late now, even as Cola comes crawling sheepishly out of the water.

She hears the high-pitched call followed by the low rumbling prickling the hair on the back of her neck. Only then does she see its sharp fox head and great bat-like ears emerging from behind the boulders. The velvet sheen of its spotted yellow skin, the custard eyes and the curling top lip. The multiple rows of teeth the size of a man's arm that go back further up the jaw than natural. So every time it opens, the head seems to split in half. The streaked pupils dilate when it sees her and up comes a taloned reptilian hand to grasp the rock shelf.

Akila heaves forward, grips Cola and swings about without glancing back. She can tell all she needs to know from the deafening roar and the thud of crashing boulders. A sudden gust of wind smacks her back. She stumbles, knowing she must not lose her footing now. What Cola and she need is a cavity in the rock they can crawl into and hide. She hurries over the flat expanse, aware that her chances are slim.

Luck appears to have abandoned her for a while. She reaches the plateau's end, where a fall of a couple of thousand feet or more awaits her. The misty jungle extends as a moist green carpet, with the occasional outcrop of flat rock resembling a vast dining hall for the gods that have cursed her. There is nowhere for her to run. She hears the claws tapping behind her and twirls to face what she has no word yet to describe. It prowls towards her with a cat's arrogance.

The tall ears twitch as a shape comes gliding in from the sky. It swoops down on her attacker, to be met by a rabid defence. The engagement is a flurry of snapping jaws and whipping tails. Their gargantuan bodies wrap about one another in a chorus of growls and screeches. The duelling creatures tumble towards her in the melee. She drops to the ground and keeps flat against it, barely avoiding a swiping tail as both beasts roll over the edge.

Akila crawls forward and looks over the edge. Both assailants are clinging onto the steep rock face, thrashing their wings and brawling still. A fist of talons grip the edge three feet from Akila's peeking head. She tucks Cola under her arm and dashes back to the stream. The fight advances to the top once more. She must keep her eyes on the prize and stay out of their way.

But that is easier said than done. She is barely ten feet from the water's edge when one of the creatures comes tumbling towards her. Its membrane wing lies sprawled over the stream, barring her escape route. She must keep moving. The only cover on this rock-top is among the strewn boulders. She scuttles onto the wing flap of the fallen creature and rolls off it into the boulders. The relief is short-lived as both creatures are up and fighting again.

She slips deeper into the crevice and discovers an opening on the other side. She worms her shoulders through the narrow gap and checks. There is certainly no escape this way for there are five smaller females of a greyish hue huddled together in the centre of a circle of five nests. One of the nests, holding three eggs, sits less than ten feet from her. And it is now, during this apocalyptic, earth-shaking duel that an egg decides to come awake and twitch. A pointed end pokes a hole in the shell and pushes, spreading the cracks and the pieces fall away. A slime-covered puppy's head flaunting a large egg tooth inspects the outside world for the first time and fixes its gaze upon her.

Gaping back at it from the hole, Akila realizes the fight is done. She can just about see one of the large males posturing with its great wings unfurled and chest puffed out. It unleashes a reverberating roar to mark its triumph. Hopefully, now that things have settled, Akila can get back to the stream and leave this nightmare behind. However, she does wonder which one is victorious. Do these babies get their original papa back or a new one? She envies them, their cozy nests and safeguarding parents. The newly-hatched infant starts to bawl. Akila frantically shushes it, but it just keeps yowling at her.

The male's sprawling shadow approaches until it encompasses both her and the nest. Then a giant foot slams down on the hatchling to silence it, draping it in mercury ooze. The creature's head snaps on a neighbouring egg as its hatchling thrusts out for the first time. The females howl in grief for the ordeal that has only begun. Two of them try to shield their clutch with their bodies, hissing at the new bull. But the females can't do much against the male's formidable frame.

He proceeds from nest to nest, crushing or devouring the eggs of the previous alpha. The females protest with warbling wails but he pays them no mind. Akila is utterly shaken by the gruesome spectacle. Why does he need to kill them? What harm can these babies do to him, helpless and little as they are? Picking this moment to break out from their eggs to enter the briefest of lives that meets such a horrible end. Their mothers watch helplessly and there is nothing Akila can do either. The devastated nests, the shards of crushed shells and the splattered silvery gore. The stillness of the no-more-living. Is it death if you are never born?

And then she sees it, an egg lying unscathed among the ruins of a nest. The male is busy hobbling to the fifth and final clutch. She can make it to the egg and back through the hole to the stream. She has to try. She has to. With the decision made, she wriggles out of the hole and hurries to the nest with the intact egg. Crouching, she picks it up, checking its integrity with her fingers. Yes, it is unbroken. The air bristles with a shrill call. She squints up at one of the females, glaring at her and rocking from side to side to alert the others. They catch Akila holding the egg and join in the alarm. The male swings his head about and his simmering eyes latch onto the young girl.

Akila curses the first female, 'I'm trying to save your baby, you bitch!'

There is no chance to make it through the hole now. So she improvises and sprints a diagonal path to the stream further down. The male comes swooping out of the air. His claws barely miss her, gnashing on the rocks at the far side. He skids about to face her. She alters her course again to run parallel to the water, a few tantalizing feet from it, waiting for her chance. But there is not long to wait, for the rock soon falls away into a cliff front with a drop of a few thousand feet. The creature rushes her and she is sure she can't make it to the stream. She kisses Cola's nose. Then, embracing both him and the egg to her body, she leaps clean off the rock.

The air rushes past like hissing steam. Her eyes water with the wind, but she grimaces through it. She passes through the wet cloud of the falling stream. That can only mean ... She looks down at a modest lake glittering like a medallion at the base. Splatter into a million pieces on the water surface or survive. No matter what, she prefers not to confront the impact face first. She shrugs her body about in the air, hugging her passengers with all the strength she can muster and curls into a foetal shrimp. A shadow envelops her. The gaping jaws of the male hang above her menacingly. It is diving down after her, its wings stuck close to its body.

Akila shuts her eyes and draws in a deep breath, her chest thumping at the sensation of the air licking her skin as it had once not long ago, but never again. 'Fin,' her heart murmurs. She slowly releases that breath and with it her thoughts and all the turmoil. Leaving behind pure sensation.

SHIELDING HIS eyes from the afternoon sun, Shyam squinted at the faint apparition of the tree atop the mound. It was such an anticlimax that he found it hard to hide his disappointment. 'What?' Akila snapped at him. 'You want to go get a closer look, tourist saab? It will impress the hell out of you, trust me.'

'No, no thanks, I'm fine right here.'

'Sure you are.'

He shrugged and put his arm around her waist. 'Come on, imagine seeing the Eiffel Tower or the temple of Tanjore from a distance.'

'Yeah, well this isn't the Eiffel Tower or the temple of whatever. It is a tree, *the* tree, where the Sentinel resides.' Akila moved around him to hug him from behind, using him like a body-shield between her and her tormentor. They were roughly the same height and she could nibble on his right shoulder through her words.

'What you are looking at, there, is the focal point. Every world has one. The Sentinel uses the tree as the thread that binds them. Whether they are in fact the same tree holding the worlds, one on top of the other, bridging them on a quantum level, hey, who the fuck knows? There sure as hell isn't anyone around to ask.'

Shyam twisted around in her embrace. 'Ooh, teacher, does that mean no one will disturb us if we do a little naughty right here?'

'I didn't say we were alone either.'

'Let the birds and animals watch. Let's teach them a thing or two about being wild, Miss Akila.'

'I wasn't talking about the birds and animals.'

'Salamanders and Feneks? They've seen us do it tons of times.'

'No, I meant the bugs.'

Shyam jumped away, dancing on his toes to look for bugs on the ground. Akila let out a laugh, with no warmth but a strain of disdain. She held him still, speaking in an even, deliberate tone that made him wince. 'The other kind.'

'You mean they can see us here?' His voice cracked. He

drew Akila behind a jambli tree and peeped around it. It was compelling, that unremarkable little tree at the summit of those great tangled roots. They writhed beneath the blazing sun, the mirage of some lurking menace. And standing in sight of it, they were within its grasp. He yearned to return to their pond that instant. He understood now why Akila had been so reluctant to show him the tree. It was a haunting reminder that they resided in the domain of an unknown force.

POLISHED AND defiant, the oblong burgundy egg sits upright in a timid nest of twigs with the shadows of the leaves dancing upon it. Akila sits cross-legged to one side, watching it expectantly. And on the other, Cola's shadowy head floats in a reflected pool of sky, his button eyes focused on the intruder.

The fire brings out the deep shades and creases along the surface of the shell. The jungle is eerily quiet. Akila has only known it to be so still twice before. *'Is it the egg?'* she inscribes in her notebook. Half a dozen reference books of all sorts lie cluttered beside her. A colourful natural history book lies open to a page. The margins are crammed with her doodles of the flying creatures.

'The egg lies three feet from me. I have seen talking insects, flying whales, ice giants, faeries and more. But I don't even have a word for this thing! I've found a fox in the books with the same shape to the head. It is called a Fennec Fox. They're so cute. They live in the desert. But they don't have the cheetah spots and they're tiny.'

Another page begins, *'Why hasn't it hatched yet? Am I doing something wrong? The other eggs were hatching yesterday, so why not mine?'* Further down, it says, *'It's beautiful! I've never seen an egg like it. It is red all over, like a piece of candy.'* She crawls closer to admire the ripples and ridges cork-screwing around the porcelain surface. A dark shape shows, backlit by the flames. She can discern limbs, a head, a tightly curled tail. It stirs. She is seeing through the egg. Her fingers stroke the cool surface, cradling it to her chest to give it warmth. Cola watches, his face barren of emotion.

Akila kneels beside the fire. Little sparks escape into the night air with crackles and pops. She caresses the top of the egg with her thumb, hoping that the fire's heat will hatch it. The heat is almost unbearable on her naked body, close enough to singe the delicate hair on her arms. The egg suddenly shudders and she gasps. The burgundy capsule flips out of her hands. It strikes the side of the tinder with a sickening smack and rolls over, exposing the shattered side leaking the mercury ooze from within.

Akila is rooted to the spot, her fingers clutching her hair at the roots, her eyes wide with shock. What has she done? There it lies, the creature within dead before it can take its first breath. After a while, relief washes over her as the tears dry on her cheeks. What would she have done with a creature like that anyway? Could she have tamed it? Still, it would have been nice, she thinks, shrinking from the heat at last. It would have been lovely to have another companion. She glances over her shoulder at dear Cola coming to the edge of the pool to comfort her. She has to keep reminding herself that she is not all alone as her hand scratches his snout the way he likes it.

'Thank god,' she declares, despondently. Then a call rings out in the distance, a low trilling wail of a night bird. There it is again, and then a series of smacking barks. She realizes that it is not in the distance at all – the sound has a queer quality that makes it bounce off every surface. Cola raises his head to keep her fingers on him as she draws away, turning her attention to the egg again. With a disgruntled bubble, he disappears into the water. He knows why she is smiling. It is no night bird's cry but a warning to every creature within earshot. A monster is born.

'I WANT to show you something,' her voice sang in his ear. Sweat dribbled down his forehead. The salt burnt his eyes. He had followed her advice to wear a T-shirt, shorts and running shoes and he was thankful that he had. Akila did not need anything of course. Although her skin gleamed with sweat, she showed no signs of exhaustion, prancing over rocks and giant reticulated roots of ancient trees with trunks as broad as a bus. Dragonflies a foot in length inspected passers-by. A three-foot long centipede with bright longitudinal dorsal stripes crossed their path, wagging its whiskers, pausing to test the air for danger before carrying on.

Then all at once, Akila signalled Shyam to halt. He was glad to have the break. His T-shirt and shorts were soaked and so were his shoes. A couple of leeches clung on to his calves but he did not bother to remove them. Breathing deeply, with a large drop of sweat gleaming on the end of his nose, he surveyed the thick jungle for any sign of the danger Akila had sensed. All he could see were tree trunks, bushes and vines. Some canary-yellow bugs hovered about a creeping trail of white and mulberry-hued flowers were suspended from the stalky arms of a haggard tree. Birds sang frenetically high up in the trees. Nothing else. Maybe she was being prudent.

A flick of her finger caught his attention and his eyes met hers. He followed her gaze. Again, nothing he could spot that was out of the ordinary. What the hell did she want him to ...

and then he saw it. Not all of it, and he certainly could not make out what he was looking at through the jungle. A small black eye stared back at him from a mass of dark grey. It blinked and with a shift of its body vanished into the wild. 'What was that?' he croaked.

'Not yet,' she mouthed back.

After a few seconds she whispered, 'I've never seen the whole thing up close.'

'Is it an elephant?'

'Thrice as large, and without a trunk or tusks. It's a herbivore but I've seen carcasses of animals as big as bison left trampled in its wake. So best not to spook it.'

'Good. So now how much further?'

She flashed a grin. 'We haven't even reached the base of the hill, you couch-potato.'

'Why couldn't we have just flown to the top on Macoco?'

'Where's the fun in that?'

'Where's the fun in this?'

'Oh wow! Poor baby!'

'That's right, and this baby is about set to shit his pants and bawl his heart out.'

'All right, don't get hysterical. I'll go slower.'

'And make the distance shorter and the climate not so humid and hot.'

'Yes, sir. You whine a lot for a grown man.'

'I'm a Dilliwallah. These are the lungs of a Delhi pollution-survivor, I'll have you know.'

'City boys,' she remarked, showing mock disappointment.

The panoramic view from the top was astounding. They sat quietly for some minutes on a cool rock in the shade of an obliging tree. Shyam could see the field of roots from there, a perfect circle cut out of the jungle, like an inverted crater of roots. The jungle around it was endless, stretching over the shallow hills in the distance.

'What's so special that we trekked up here to see it?'

'This,' she said, with a patronizing wave of her arm. She busied herself opening out the picnic. Shyam assisted, a little miffed.

'Not worth it?' she teased.

'The view is great and all, don't get me wrong, but I've seen it from the air, on Macoco. What's the big deal?'

'There's a world beyond the pond, Shy. Beneath the canopy of the trees. It's hard to be aware of the world around you from the objectivity of a god's point of view on Macoco's back. Walking, you measure that world with every step. This hill is real to you now because you've climbed it. Because you know the world from it.'

Shyam touched her knee to show his sincere appreciation of her gift. Now that he understood, it almost brought him to tears.

'I'm a lazy bum and I need to be dragged out sometimes, out of my cocoon. I'm glad you've figured that out. And I'm glad I have you to do it.'

'Wasn't hard.'

'Yeah.' He stuck out his tongue and drew her close. He carefully shifted the items on the picnic cloth to one side. 'What are you doing?' Akila asked, raising an eyebrow.

'Hush,' he whispered. He turned her away and pulled her down on to her side. She was surprised by his tenderness. He held her from behind and they lay like that for a while, staring out into the world. Their world.

A BUNDLE wrapped in her old pyjama top with the faded rabbits. She had gone back to Earth to retrieve it following her desert-world misadventure, and she has preserved it ever since as a memento that has transformed from something macabre, to a reminder of the warmth from her past life, and now as a means to guard the infant. A furry tail protrudes from it, brushing her abdomen and thighs as she cradles the precious cargo to her chest. It is her fault, after all, that they need to hurry, but she'll reprimand herself for it later. Now she must get Macoco to safety.

A gap in the foliage behind her shows the red plume rising in a nervous line into the clouds. Her foot rips a bush out by the roots without slowing her for a beat as she goes through the plan once more in her head. The pond is as serene as ever when she arrives. For many days now, she has searched for some way to keep Macoco hidden while she is away for the sacrifice. She is haunted by visions of Kala's corpse half-crawled out from the water and imagines a similar fate for this little one. She saved him from the slaughter that befell his siblings and she will save him again. Although the insectoids are always watching from the shadows, she must take this chance, for there is no other choice.

She dives headlong into the pool. Rolling onto her feet in the acrid water, she splutters out any traces of it from her mouth. Her taste buds compel her to vomit but her instincts drive her onward. As tooth-lined jaws clap at the air near her legs, she is already scurrying up a scalding rock. She makes her way through the crags moving higher, and ducks into the shade of a secret grotto. There is barely enough room for her and Macoco but it will do. His tail is still anxiously whipping about.

Under ordinary circumstances she would have smacked his snout, not tolerating his skittishness. She is terrified they will take him away from her. She lays down his wriggling form and as soon as her hand releases his snout, Macoco wails hysterically. He rolls about in the pyjama, frantic to get loose. Then catching sight of Akila he calms down, though his amber eyes still dart about in confusion. He reproaches her with short barks and, in the constricted space, his agitated tail scrubs the walls.

'Please shut up, Macoco, baby, come on,' she hisses desperately. He is as big as a beagle and just as irrepressible. 'I have to go, but I'll be back.' There is no break in Macoco's mewling. 'I'll be back,' she says simply, knowing it will do nothing to console him. With a heavy sigh she rushes out and hears Macoco follow. The scorching rocks under the harsh sun send him whining into the shade. She wants to hurry back and attend to his paws with kisses, but that will have to wait. Gripping his first lost tooth that hangs on a thread around her neck, she wishes as hard as she can that there will be a later. She will not surrender him without a fight.

The soles of her feet have toughened over the years and the climb down is swifter without a struggling toddler to contend with. Splashes. Akila stops rushing as two insectoids shake themselves dry outside the green pool. The crocodiles have withdrawn to the shade to watch the new arrivals with uncharacteristic reticence. Akila strains her ears for any hints of Macoco, reflecting on the acute silence of the wasteland. A faint breeze suddenly sweeps in. She undoes her belt and lays it carefully on the rock. 'I didn't know you could cross worlds like I can,' she remarks, stepping onto the parched earth.

The insectoids stand like grotesque statues in the silence of a dead world. Then the one with a scarred eye speaks. 'I have followed you to many worlds, Beli. I have seen the things that you do.'

'A hell of a bodyguard you are. Do you know how many times I've almost been killed?' She removes the hairband from her wrist and ties her tresses into a ponytail with it. It is fluffy and pink with a cartoon cat dangling from the side, its wobbly eyes in plastic bubbles.

'Your foolishness knows no bounds. That is hardly my concern, Beli. Now come.'

'I can never escape you, can I?'

The insectoid with the scar jumps into the water and vanishes. The one that remains turns to her and says, 'There is no escaping fate.'

'Fate!' She spits the word through dry lips.

'You are the Beli. You are the sacrifice. I am the river. I am the life. We are inseparable.'

THE BONFIRE cast a flickering light on their faces. The darkness of the jungle huddled about them. The moon was a slip of silver in the starry sky. The branches playfully swung above them as Shyam and Akila sat back to back, swaying to the rhythm of the Spanish guitar. They sang along loudly to the acoustic version of *'Hotel California'*.

IN THE rocking shade of coconut trees they mended their clothes. Shyam had his pile and Akila hers. They sewed busily to the soundtrack of the crashing waves around them. A thud on the sand jerked them out of their reverie. A fallen coconut rested three feet from Akila's outstretched leg. Shyam bit the thread and knotted it, suggesting, 'Maybe this isn't the best spot for this.' Akila, wide-eyed and petrified, stuck out her bottom lip in response.

SHYAM SAT by himself at the pond. Akila was out hunting. He fiddled with the DSLR. It was too unwieldy to take selfies and he was not willing to go all the way back up to the hut on Tree Two for the compact. And he was not entirely sure why he had brought this lug. There were no birds in the vicinity. No monkeys. Thank god. They had an unhealthy attachment to Akila. She must have been feeding them all these years.

Cola emerged at the surface of the pond. Shyam leaned over to take some low angle pictures along the water of Cola's large dome head, focused on the little eyes. He got a couple of good shots and that was that. He set the camera aside and leaned out further to stroke Cola's nose like he had seen Akila do. In the blink of an eye Cola snapped at his hand. It took him a moment to register that his hand was intact and he hugged it to his chest. He faced Cola with a dashed frown. 'What the–? Cola, come on!' Cola submerged with a dour plop.

Akila returned in the evening with a small deer with horns running along its neck. 'These guys are tricky,' she said, noting Shyam had chopped vegetables and arranged them on plates. 'What's all this?' she asked, clearing her throat.

'I thought I'd have them ready.'

'Okay.' She was not very convinced. 'Couldn't get any good kaeras? That one looks a bit too green.'

He glanced at the plates, wondering which one the kaeras were again.

'The one that has the purple skin like an eggplant.'

That was not much help. He had peeled them first and could not recall which vegetable had what skin. The plan was for her to recognize his effort and reward him with that addictive grin of hers. Not scrutinize that effort and revise it.

'The little guy you've sliced paper-thin, sitting closest to you.'

He looked down and saw it this time. 'Oh yeah, no, most

of them had gone bad. They had worms.' He shuddered emphatically.

'That's how you know they're good.'

'With worms – good?'

'With worms – good.' She was tired after a long day, although she did appreciate the effort. 'Where did you toss them? Maybe we can salvage a couple.'

'I fed them to Cola.'

'No wonder he looks pleased.'

Damn, thought Shyam. He had intended to punish Cola with rotten stuff for the near dismemberment. Akila munched on a sliced ring of yaddy, saying, 'From now on, let this be a team activity, all right?'

'Okay,' he agreed meekly, trying to hide his disappointment. Making an effort to brighten up, he started, 'You know, I knew a girl once, her place was in C.R. Park. She would invite friends over for a party and she'd never show her face the entire night. We'd be sitting in the living room having drinks and snacks and she'd be stuck in the kitchen with an apron over her stunning party dress. She had some style that one, whenever I saw her, at home or outside, she looked – what's the word – trendy? Or is that a bad word?'

Akila let out a forced laugh. Shyam pressed on, 'I can never get the lingo right. I want to say "hip" but it doesn't feel hip to say hip, if you know what I mean. Yeah, she used to make fun of me. She was a designer.' Akila swiped the leftovers into the pond and Cola sucked them up. Sombre-eyed, she sat skinning the deer. 'Can you get the marinade mix into that bigger bowl?' she requested in an even tone.

'Sure,' he said, hesitating, 'does it bother you when I bring up girls from my past?'

She scoffed, 'Ha, no!'

'Do you want to know about them?'

'Not necessarily.' She peeled the skin over the muscles, skimming where required.

'I want to tell you about them. I want you to know everything.'

'I do.'

'Seriously.'

She stopped flaying and looked him in the eyes. She appeared perfectly composed, though her lips were held firmly as she said, 'Does it look like I'm bothered when you mention them? Listen, you have a past. Duh. I knew that, and it doesn't bother me. I don't need you to make a full disclosure to me. I don't need to know. I'm not worried.'

'Really?'

'You know why?'

'Why?'

'Because I have you now and you're all mine.'

'IS THIS necessary? I thought you liked it long,' Shyam protested. He was sitting for a haircut, but his head kept retreating from the snapping blades.

'Stay still, I don't want to chop an ear off.'

'You need a new slogan, Miss.'

'Stay still and shut up.'

'My mouth getting in the way of your scissors, is it?'

'Better than my scissors getting in the way of your mouth,' she warned with a mock glare. She wore one of his vests tucked into the helm of a pair of denim short-shorts.

'Not much, all right?'

'Just a bit. It looks untidy as it is. Now, shush,' she instructed.

So he sat in silence, loving the touch of her fingers taking measured clumps of hair and catching them in long section clips. She would occasionally tilt his head this way and that, and he gave himself to her hands. This is joy, he thought, not a care in the world, and I'm the most important thing to the person I love. Behind the overhanging fringe, his eyes rested.

SHYAM HANDED her another oddly oblong sandwich. Akila tore a bite's worth off with her thumb and tossed it into the gapping mouth of a crocodile. Lounging in the cool shade of the rocks, they were displaced from the harsh heat of the blazing barren landscape. The horizon vanished into a watery mirage. The crocodiles stuck close to the rocks, waiting for the next tidbit.

'What's your favourite dream?' Shyam asked, out of the blue.

'We run out of things to talk about?'

'Come on, tell me.'

She took a big bite of her sandwich, tossed the rest to the crocodiles and lay back, staring up at the wind scarred rock looming above them. The long flowery dress she had on was dry already and spread out. Shyam had placed his T-shirt under his back.

'I haven't thought about it much,' she said, chewing slowly, taking her time to gather her thoughts. 'Tell me yours in the meantime.'

'Okay. I was home for the holidays. Keep in mind I was fifteen when I had it.'

She nodded for him to go on.

'A passionate fuck with a young Shirley MacLaine on the rocks as waves crash over us.'

'A fuck dream. Nice.'

'A wet dream. I still remember waking up with the intense sensations of cuming, sitting up in bed and wondering at the sticky patch in my shorts.'

'Ew.'

He laughed. 'Yeah, I ran to the bathroom before anyone else was up and tried to scrub it clean.'

'How did you explain the wet shorts?'

'Said I spilt some pee on it and tried to wash it clean.'

'You would rather have your family think you were a bed wetter than that you just had a wet dream?'

He shrugged. 'Fifteen, remember? At that age you don't know which side is up. There's a see-saw in your pants and every pretty girl is a heart-pounding crush.'

'So,' he prodded, after a minute of listening to the wind howling through the rocks.

'My favourite dream,' she said thoughtfully, lingering on the thought with a wistful smile. 'I was a dolphin.'

SHE NEEDS a new backpack. This one still stinks from the last time Macoco peed in it. She's washed it half a dozen times but she still feels icky piling the jambli in. She takes a detour for some of the long blue carikkas. They are great with meat. She'll keep them in a bowl of water overnight and use them for the next day's dish. Most of the meat she catches is consumed by Macoco, and she has begun to depend more on fruits and vegetables for herself. She does not particularly miss it, but when she really craves meat she goes up past Picchu Falls and nets some fish.

Entering the clearing at her pond, she can't get over the calm that has encased the vicinity with the young Fenek's presence. There he is, lazing on his back on the Mez. Akila claps and Macoco starts awake with a yelp. He smells the fruit and immediately his tail begins to wag. He hops about, whooping and emitting mini growls of joy, circling her. He is the size of an adult Dalmatian, bursting with energy.

Akila loves this, being greeted every time she comes home, and as a treat she pours the bag's contents over him. He gets the first fruit in his mouth and sets to tearing off the skin. Tossing the bag aside, Akila stands, arms folded, watching his wagging tail as he ignores the dozen or more fruit lying about him for the one he has in his mouth. There is a snap from the pond.

'I haven't forgotten about you, Cola, my love.' Macoco nips at her hand while she collects some of the jamblis. Akila knows he does not intend to bite her but even then, he needs to know his place. She flicks his ear hard with her fingernail. He mewls and draws away, curling his tail close. He picks up a fruit along his retreat and discreetly peels it, all the while offering Akila a look of dejection.

'That's right, I'm the boss. You don't fucking dare snap at me,' she says, staring him down the whole time, making sure to use a firm tone so that he gets the message.

He avoids her gaze and she commences tossing a third of the jamblis over the rock. The *plops* of them hitting the water are followed by wet *clops* telling her that Cola is taken care of now. Then, taking three in each palm, she hops onto the Mez and lowers herself to the edge. She discards the shells into the stream below, watching large serpentine shapes wrestle for the scraps. A mighty acidic burp announces her satisfaction when she is done. Time to make up with Macoco or he'll pout and lie in a corner all night, whining.

She takes the backpack, dusts it off and sets it aside for the next day. She spots two yellow jamblis lying at the base of the bushes. Patting Macoco on the nose, she wakes him up and turns his head to the fruit. He pulls his head free and turns away, his tail coiling close to his body. 'What're you scared of, Macoco? They're right there.' He never leaves a fruit uneaten and she usually has to fight for her share. He is definitely scared, but of what?

She rolls him onto his stomach and points and issues an order. 'Go, get them.' He attempts to look away, but she holds him firm. 'No, no, Macoco. I want you to go get them.' He looks up at her piteously with his puppy-dog Fenek eyes. 'Now,' she says, her words delivered in an intent monotone, not to be trifled with. Macoco hops down onto the pebbles, takes two steps towards the fruit, and then darts to the left to cower at the base of Picchu Falls. She catches the tip of his tail, eliciting a loud squeal. 'What's wrong with you, you baby? If anyone else heard you, they'd think you were being chopped to pieces. Quiet down, Macoco,' she scolds him as she picks him up. He lies stiff in her arms. She shakes her head with disappointment so he can see it.

Carrying him in a secure grip, she ambles to the fruit. The further she gets from the pond, the more he begins to struggle to return to its security. She stands by the fruit, holding him to her body. Her stomach and sides and arms are covered in scratches, and it burns. She does not like this. This is a majestic creature that flies and hunts at the top of the food chain. No other animals come within thirty yards of him because of the fear the very scent of him evokes. And here he is, terrified of leaving the enclosure of the pond.

Making up her mind to remedy this at once, she enters the jungle with him. She deliberately turns Macoco about in her arms so he does not jump out and can look about without pushing his head into her underarm for refuge. All she does is hold him and walk around for a bit, sometimes stopping and taking the time to let him sniff at a jambli tree or study branches filled with restless butterflies. His body trembles violently against her the whole time. She can feel his little hearts pounding fast and hard. They venture further up the stream where it flows through a mini gorge. Akila positions them right at the edge, slowly peering over. His claws dig into her arms but she holds him there for a few minutes, watching the water froth and fight through the rocks. Within half an hour they are back home.

AKILA WRITES in her diary by the firelight. The moon has risen like a silver disc floating on the deepest sea. She casts the diary aside with the other notebooks in her box when she is done and whistles a tune as she prepares for bed. She lies down, but Macoco has not joined her yet. She goes to the water searching for him. He is not there. He is probably still upset with her for what she did, but it had to be done. She plans to slowly take him out on longer trips to familiarize him with the jungle. He is not in his usual hiding places. 'Macoco,' she calls. He does not reply. But something else does, from the other side of the pond. The low growl of a large predator. Which can only mean one thing. Macoco is not nearby. She will have to go out looking for him tonight once she has killed this pest. Only ten yards from her, the hulking shoulders of a large cat emerge into the moonlight, its fur flowing over coiled sinews. Teeth bared in a grim smile, Akila waits. Feet apart, blade ready.

THEY SAT leaning against different trees, feet touching so their legs joined in a V. Both had long fishing rods propped in their laps, lines dangling in the water in the shade of a great tree with cheery red blossoms littering the ground. They were engrossed in their books. Akila, bare-chested and in her dark-green corduroys, had her earphones in, and Shyam, in his sweat-patched kurta and shorts, listened to the birds. Behind them, Macoco deftly plucked the yellow bushy fruit with his lips so they would not burst. They were at a large lake a half hour's flight from their pond. The placid water reflected the huddled mountains as sharply as a mirror. And then a flower would fall, radiating a series of languid ripples that caressed the mountaintops.

THEY MADE love standing against the tree. Five feet from them, beside the fishing rods, lay the three fish they had caught. Good sized, each a foot long, strung together with twine running through their right gills and out their mouths, with a large knot at the bottom. As the lovers moaned, Macoco watched the fish flap feebly on the grass.

THE SKY was quiet. At their unhurried pace, the ground oozed by below. Shyam sat behind Akila, holding onto her waist with the fish twine held firmly in his right hand. Watching the ground move by endlessly was conducive to thoughts running away in tangents and breaking off into others until you found yourself somewhere totally unexpected. Shyam brought his head over Akila's shoulder to say, 'It is so phallic isn't it, to ride?'

Akila laughed out loud, her usual response to his ramblings, but most of it was lost in the wind. She turned her head a bit as she spoke. 'Why is everything phallic to you?'

'I'm not making anything phallic,' he said shrugging. 'It's just a thought that popped into my head.'

'What is it with guys? You think all women want to become men? You think we are that insecure? Inadequate? Incomplete without a dick hanging between our legs?'

'That's not it at all. I'm talking about a thought I had while riding, about riding. I used to ride back in school, like you did.'

A melancholic smile twisted the corner of her mouth.

'Early in the misty mornings,' he said, 'my head still a bit groggy, on horseback in the riding grounds. I would look down at the horse's neck and head sprouting from between my legs. It was an extension of me as my hips tipped from side to side with the horse's gait. And moving with it, that gait became mine. I was suddenly ten feet tall. Think about it: we are guiding our giant dick around as it leads us through the world. It's so strong and mighty, it'll protect us. The security of its strength becomes our strength. I don't believe the core of our being is at our heart or head; it's in the abdomen. Maybe that's why we embrace that feeling so readily.'

'I'm very satisfied without a dick, thank you. I feel complete just as I am.'

'It's not the penis by itself that I'm referring to but what it represents in us.'

'Maybe what it represents is too much sex, and it's going to your head.'

'I'll shut up,' he said quickly.

SITTING AGAINST the cool rock, Akila holds baby Macoco cozily up to her chest. Her left arm supports his weight and with the other hand she caresses his back. Her voice is low and trembles at the high notes as she sings *'What's new, pussycat'*

with the tenderness of a lullaby. 'And your pussycat ears,' she croons, tugging his ears. 'And your pussycat tail.' She fondles his tail. 'And your pussycat eyes.' She twists her body a little to peek at his sleeping face. An eye opens up to her in annoyance. She tickles the corner of his eye and he lazily snaps at her fingers. 'And your pussycat nose.' She draws the note out, tickling the tip of his nose with a finger. He wags his tail and then, thoroughly embarrassed, hurriedly digs his nose deeper into the warmth of her armpit. Akila kisses his little hand. Cola watches them from the far side of the pool.

AKILA RETURNS from a hunt, a dead moss-deer on her shoulder. It drops down onto the clattering pebbles. This is unusual. Something is not right here. She hops onto the Mez, her bronzed frame magnificent in the afternoon sun. Her lithe five-and-a-half foot frame of ripcord muscle is glazed with sweat. The necklace with Macoco's teeth has more additions in ascending size from left to right. Cola snaps at the water by the rock. 'Not now, Cola. Where's Macoco? Damn it. That fucking Fenek better not have gotten lost.' She paces back and forth, scouring the trees and the sky for some sign of him. 'Macoco,' she yells, cupping her hands around her mouth. She repeats the call. 'Damn it, where do I even start looking? He's getting too big too fast, I can't keep up.'

She hollers his name again, with no response. Monkeys screech in the distance. Then silence. A tree shudders, a cascade of leaves cartwheeling to the ground. Macoco struts out of a bush with a dead deer hanging from his bloody jaws. He sets it down gently by her moss-deer. 'Macoco, behenchod, do you know how worried I was?' she screams at him, waving her arms to make him understand just how upset she is. He is the size of a mule. His velvet skin shimmers as he arrogantly shrugs and poses. She examines his deer. It is a good, clean kill, there is no denying that. She mustn't confuse him with mixed signals, so she nods to show her approval and comes over to hug his neck. He purrs like a kitten at her touch.

'PUT THAT down,' she yelled out. Shyam dropped the knife in a shot and backed away. 'Up here,' her voice called to him from the rock atop Picchu Falls. He backed up further to get a better look.

'What's wrong?' he asked anxiously, trying to understand why she could be hiding.

'I'm going to do something dangerous and I may not come out alive.'

'Then don't do it.'

'I gots'to know,' she replied. Shyam did a double take, wondering if he had heard her correctly. That was their favourite line from *Dirty Harry*. Was it a signal he could not recall? Out of the giggling water rose the teasing rhythm of maracas as Akila approached the edge. Shyam's jaw dropped. The word he later used to describe his condition was 'flabbergasted'. Sensually stirring her hips in an ultramarine blue bikini bottom, she winked at him with a bashful smile, and began to sing in an uninhibited voice. A sweet rendition of '*Blue Moon*'. Not a bird or animal interrupted the entire performance. Even the wind played nice as she gripped Shyam with a flash of sun-baked granite eyes.

Though the old Elvis cover was among his favourite tracks, every word she sang seemed to have a special meaning. And he could not believe it. Finally, he had found someone who loved him enough to let her walls drop and do this. He felt a heat in his hands and the soles of his feet. His eyes burnt from holding back the tears because he wanted to let her finish. He wanted to savour and hold on to every second. This is my love, he thought. When she had trapped the last sweeping beat with the maracas, she grinned at Shyam and did a swan dive off the top. She resurfaced at the rocks and said huskily, 'Happy birthday, Mr President.' He'd completely forgotten, of course. He got down on the rocks, slipped an arm under her shoulders and crushed his mouth on hers. 'The perfect birthday gift,' he whispered.

'Two things I learnt that I thought I'd never have a use for,' she replied with her trademark grin, though her cheeks flushed.

'Perfect,' he said softly, eyes welling up at last. She urged him towards the water, whispering to him, 'Come in. The water's just right.'

IT RAINED heavily and it rained hard. Every drop was a wet prod and standing there on open ground, he felt it head to foot. Puddles flowed into raging streams that gushed over the rim of the plateau into a tranquil landscape veiled in wetness beneath the storm brewing above. At his side Akila stood, a Bernini in the flesh, defiantly tall against heaven's lashes. Her hair hung in matted plaits, face still. Her white cotton kurta was humbled to illusion against her skin and the denim of her jeans clung heavily. Beyond her perched the griffin-like shadow of Macoco, no longer a lethargic pet but a beast to fear.

THE FIRE crackles with life, though nothing remains of their meal. Macoco is the size of a large horse, curled on the pebbles like the pup he had been barely two years ago. Stroking his head that lay on her lap, Akila softly hums a tune. She has thin braids woven into the hair at her temples. Dotingly, she watches the firelight play off Macoco's spots, running her fingers along the bridge of his nose and the curl of his brow. On seeing a tick her fingers pounce before it can hide in his ear. She crushes it between her thumbnails until she hears the satisfying click. He stirs and she brushes his neck, shushing him tenderly, picking up the song a little louder now, running into the refrain, '*Hushabye mountain*'.

His large eye opens and she sees the stars reflected in it. He purrs and bashfully turns his face away from hers. With a chuckle Akila changes her tune to '*What's new, Pussycat*'.

'You make me happy,' a child's voice murmurs, robbing the song from her throat. Her lips quiver with the shock and then the anticipation. Macoco looks about, puzzled by the silence, and then back at Akila. He says sweetly, with a voice as fresh as a virgin brook, 'Sing to me.'

THE SNOW seeped in through the top of his keds. Shyam had always hated winter. Shin-deep in snow with a chilly wind numbing his nose and cheeks was not his idea of fun. The thick down jacket and two layers of thermal pants were not doing the trick and Akila was a good fifty feet ahead of him on the ascent up the slope. 'It better be worth it,' he shouted up to her.

'Blah, blah, blah,' she shouted back, digging her toes in and climbing harder. He shook his head, loving her spirit. She was so positive and easy to get along with and he was lucky, he knew, to have found such a generous person to love. He jogged up the slope, hoping to overtake her without her noticing, but she heard him coming. 'No, don't run!' she warned with an outstretched arm. Shyam halted in his tracks, gaping at something behind her. She turned and saw a long seam drawn across the snow.

'Don't move,' she whispered so low he could hardly hear the words.

'I won't. Is it what I think it is?' He spoke just as quietly.

'If you're thinking it's bad, you're wrong. It's worse.'

'Got a plan?'

After looking around them, she pointed to a small mound six feet to their right. 'That's solid,' she said. 'It's a rock.'

He stared at it.

'When I say two, we jump onto it and you hold onto me.'

He affirmed with a nod.

'One,' she sighed, watching the seam as it began to shift.

'Two.' The two of them jumped and hit the rock and held onto it and each other. The layer of snow where they had been standing slid as a sheet down the slope. The mountain shook as it crumbled into an avalanche and a tornado of white rolled into the stream in the valley below with a thunderous roar echoing amidst the peaks.

'We made it,' she panted with relief. All he could offer was a bowed head.

'Let's get going,' she said, pulling him up by his jacket sleeve. As he struggled to get his footing on the icy rock, something large moved beyond the summit. He jerked his head up to see what it was and gasped theatrically. An ice giant was rising from the valley on the other side. Shyam grabbed at Akila, but his ankle bent as he slipped and he fell backwards. Akila was caught unprepared, watching him for a second as he slid away down the slope.

'Shit,' she barked, and dived forward. Snow smacked her chin and her chest scorched. It would have been smarter to ride down on her back, but it was a bad idea to spin around now. The chances of going into a roll and breaking her neck were too high. 'I'm coming,' she yelled. Shyam saw her and reached out. She was gaining on him, but she would not make it before they hit the stream. That is what terrified her more than anything. He could hit the water and splash through to any world. If he found his way to a world familiar to him, she knew he would have no trouble getting back to their pond.

Their pond. No longer mine alone.

She reached out harder. If he wound up trapped somewhere unfamiliar, the chances against her finding him were astronomical. There were a lot of places that would kill him quickly or slowly. 'Come on, Shyam, just a little more. I've got you.' He could not speak. His stare was like that of an animal about to be put down. He did not even know what to fear and already he was terrified. About to hit the stream, she lunged forward and almost had him. The water sprayed from the impact of the two bodies.

'I'VE GOT the Beli!' The voice rang in his skull. The grip was tight on the back of his neck. 'I've got the Beli!' He felt his limp body being lifted from the water, hanging by his neck. Then another clamp relieved the strain and held him by the right shoulder. He opened his muddy eyelids to thousand-foot high clay spires piercing a bloody sky. Below it a sea of insectoids clicked and squealed. 'The Kier is coming!' A chanting chorus arose. Beckoned by some cryptic signal, every face there turned to a large opening in a mound some two hundred and fifty feet away. A ramp descended from it and out of the darkness came something crawling. A large beetle glinted in the sun with an insectoid rider on its back. The rider had only half a body, which sat in a thick paste. What is this place, Shyam wondered.

'Beli,' the Kier called out, pounding its arms excitedly on the beetle's shell. 'I-have-you!'

AKILA'S HEAD zips along less than ten feet from churning white clouds, hanging magically in the air. She keeps a pen cap between her ink-stained lips, carefully sketching marks on a chart secured across Macoco's shoulders. A black tail wriggles around Akila's neck. Cola lies face down on her back, his little button eyes staring at the ground far below, his slimy arms and legs gripping her torso tightly. Occasionally she pats his tail, struggling for breath. 'Cola, not so tight, you strangling salamander.'

She gazes past Macoco's shoulder at the terrain and then at her map. Not bad, she shrugs to herself. 'Further this way?' Macoco asks sweetly. 'Yes,' she bellows into the wind.

A lake lies before them. Little curtains of ripples skim the surface in the patterns of the wind. Akila holds up the folded map and goes over her calculations. Her hair is tied into three ponytails. She has a little flower nose ring. The map shows the lake's outline. She spreads it out on the ground and checks her bulky digital wristwatch. She holds down a button and the screen becomes a digital compass. She rotates the map to align north and takes a look around at the hills skirting the distant mountains. Then, kneeling with a contented sigh, she makes notes against the landmarks to aid her in the future.

LATER, SHE stands ankle-deep in the shallows, staring in the direction of a little island. This is a beautiful world. It has taken so much away from her. Her father. Her world. But at the same time it provides her with so much. Strolling along the lake, wading lazily through the cool water, she ruminates on her fate. 'Don't go too far,' Macoco calls after her and she gives him a non-committal wave, preoccupied with her thoughts. She can't claim any longer that she is not free. She has read enough to know there is no such thing as true freedom. She may have been brought here against her will but is she not free to go where she pleases and do what she likes? Freer than she would ever have been back in her world. Her world. Doesn't that label suit this world far better? My native world, she thinks, is Earth. Earth, where my father rides his dark bay stallion, Jules. Where he sips his whisky at night and tells her of his school days in Lucknow. Where candy-stores with marshmallows and milk chocolates abound, and her grandmother's roast chicken sits on the dining table with a loaf of white bread on the side. But that is no longer her world. This is where she exists now. A world of lush jungles and monstrous creatures. Where her head is cut off every three years for a purpose she does not yet understand.

But for all that, she is free. Free to travel to any of the many worlds she has discovered. Right here, this water at her feet, if she chooses, can transport her to the realm of ice giants among snow-covered peaks or a world of hills that come alive in song. She can fly freely with Macoco. Live anywhere she pleases, the way she wishes to live.

And yet, there is that human germ of dissatisfaction. What you have can never be as fulfilling as what you cannot have. She wonders how much it rules her thoughts and actions. It is a source of weakness for her, this homesickness for a place she can see whenever she pleases but can never inhabit again. She has been torn from it, every fibre of her being ripped from that plane and planted in this jungle, in a shuffled deck of worlds where she now exists, the joker of the pack. But she does not quite belong here either. Home, but with a bitter taste.

She glances back at Macoco cooling himself in the shallows. This is home. It aches her to think it, but it is true. She has a home, the pond. She has her family, Macoco and Cola. And she has this purpose, which is up to her to change. This purpose she is bridled with. To change it, she needs answers, although the questions seem more elusive. She does not quite know where to begin. What should she be looking for? The insectoid leader had spoken of a place the Beli went to when their time was past. Is that the key? Will finding passage there help free her from the curse of the sacrifice? Will she then be replaced by another Beli? Can she then return to her 'native' world? How many years does she have before she, too, is spent? Is that the only way out of this vicious cycle?

A dark shape catches her eye among the reeds. It has the lines of something crafted by humans. Warily, she goes closer, circling about to get an idea of what it may be. When she is five feet away she realizes what it is, or once was. A boat. A small one, but a boat, not a dugout or a canoe. It is as unexpected a find for Akila as it is for an archaeologist to dig up a mummy under his office floor. The thing itself is a wreck but there can be no mistaking it. Spinning around, her eyes scan the tree line at the periphery of the lake for any sign of a hut or dwelling. Since it would be as old as the boat, it must be covered in creepers.

Then she sees something on the small island. A lump in the shadows under the hood of trees. Macoco takes her to the island to investigate, her heart pounding in her chest. She knows there is no one to find, that she will never experience that in her lifetime. Finding someone who shares her fate. A compatriot in suffering. A companion. She arrives at the hut. One side of it has long since collapsed and nature is on its way to reclaiming it with flowering creepers everywhere. The door is a solid block of wood stuck in place. Akila kicks it open and crawls inside on her hands and knees. It is pitch black. She produces a pen-torch from her fanny pack and the interior is suddenly lit by a spanning circle of light. It smells of rot and dampness, and Akila regrets rushing into this place that could crumble onto her with the slightest nudge. The torchlight shows that nothing remains of anything, really. The ruins of a small cot lie in a pile in one corner, and that is all.

The light catches a texture on the walls. Going closer she finds writing scrawled over every inch of it. It is the same phrase repeated over and over. Holding the torch in her mouth, she copies it into her notebook – 'Ou est tout le monde'. She recognizes it as French, but the meaning eludes her. It is even etched in bold letters across the rotted floorboards. Something metallic winks at the torchlight. A pin holding a stained brown fragment to the wall. Beneath it are the words 'Jacques-Louis Truffaut, 1780' with a series of violent scratches, followed by 'Papa, ou est tout le monde'. Akila carefully plucks the pinned object from the wall and crawls outside with it. Sitting against a tree, she studies its delicate sections. Every touch disintegrates a portion. In the sunlight she can guess now that it had once been circular. On it are three concentric circles of colour, with blue in the centre, then white; the outermost colour has only a sliver showing. Is it a dark brown, possibly a red? She tilts it to look underneath and it crumbles into dust instantly.

At her pond, Akila looks through some recently acquired books. She begins by searching for what the item pinned to the wall could have been. With the colours identified, it is easily done. A tricolour cockade worn on hats during the French Revolution. It matches the date she saw, 1780, although it precedes the revolution by nine years. She deduces it must be Jacques-Louis' birthdate. He could have been anywhere from nine to nineteen when he was brought here.

She closes the book, deep in thought. Whoever he was, he was certainly resourceful and skilled, from making a boat to building a hut.

She gazes around at her little accomplishments. Certainly little compared to his. She dismisses the thought. It's not that hard if one can travel back to Earth and get the tools one needs. She opens the French to English dictionary to do a verbatim translation of the phrase 'Ou est tout le monde'. It is a short three words in English that drives a spike into her soul, leaving her feeling cold and hollowed out. The horror that she had forgotten. Of being stranded and alone.

'Where is everyone?'

SHYAM SAW his captor, a glossy black beetle: nine feet tall with three large horns crowning its head. The beetle the Kier rode was as large as an elephant, slowly crawling through the crowd more than two hundred feet away. The Kier called out, 'Remove that covering so we might see its true form.' Shyam's jacket and pants were peeled away as he was held up in the sun to the jeering spectators. 'This is another,' the Kier cried, squealing manically, 'It is not her!'

His captor twisted him to the left and then the right to allow the leader a better look.

'I had hoped when the time came for the Beli's return, that it would be her again. I had plans for her. The Beli called Akila!'

'The Beli called Akila,' the crowd echoed ominously.

'I suppose she is gone for good, then. No matter! We will use you! At last we will be free!'

A blood-curdling scream pierced the ceremony and the ten-thousand-strong audience stood frozen, staring at Shyam with their large compound eyes. But it was not he who had screamed. The Kier slapped the back of his beetle in a frenzy, shrieking, 'Quickly! Bring him to me!'

Still the beetle that held Shyam stood its ground, defying its leader's command. This was unimaginable to the Kier and every insectoid watching. 'Come here, now! Bring the Beli! Bring the Beli! Bring the Beli!' His voice screeched like a fire siren. But the beetle paid no mind. Shyam hung there by his neck and shoulder, struggling for breath. He felt a spray on his back and the grip slackened. He dropped to the ground gasping, his back covered in a metallic blue ooze. The insectoids gaped at the black beetle in stupefied horror. Something stuck out of its thorax. The object withdrew into the body and plunged through again with another thrust. The shell at the thorax and abdomen gave way and Akila burst out to the collective gasp of the audience. The afternoon sun glimmered off the metallic blue ooze coating her from head to foot as she stood tall like a glazed goddess. 'The Beli called Akila,' the chant began again, now in a hush, over and over like the heartbeat of the swarm.

'Beli,' the Kier shrieked. 'You said we would not have survived by your next visit. Do you remember?'

Akila did not move a muscle. Shyam coughed, trying to collect himself. 'Faster, we gotta get moving,' she whispered through pursed lips.

The chanting rose.

'We still live!' the Kier cried out.

'So do I!' Akila roared. The chanting never faltered. 'The Beli called Akila! The Beli called Akila!'

She helped Shyam onto his feet and they scrambled around the dead black beetle to the muddy river. The chanting subsided as the insectoids broke out of their trance and charged forward.

'We will hunt you, Beli,' the Kier called after her. 'That is our new purpose. To hunt you down! We will meet once more, and you will not escape us again.' Even after Akila and Shyam had splashed through, he cried on, 'The purpose of my kind from this moment on is to destroy you. The Beli called Akila.'

Shyam shook the mud out of his hair in the pond. Akila was already done, squatting on the rocks in contemplation.

'Do you have *any* friends in the other worlds?' he asked her hesitantly.

Her mind swam through some names and she replied, 'No.'

Shyam regretted asking the question. Trying to make amends, he said, 'At least you have Cola and Macoco. And now me.'

THE BOOK is open to a spread of schematics. The margins are filled with notes and sketches. Akila chews on the rubber butt of her pencil. She rolls onto her back and examines the trees about her, nods to herself, and rolls back onto her stomach. There are a series of neat notes on the top left corner of the page. 'Good,' she confirms, and gets onto her haunches with the open book and a clipboard. She backs up until her feet reach the edge of the Mez to get a wider view of the layout of the pond. It is not wide enough. There is a tree beyond the rock that would be the perfect vantage point for her. She backs up a few feet for a run-up to the closest branch, which is a good seven feet away. 'What's the matter with you?' Macoco roars, weaving his way through the bushes. 'You want to kill yourself when you have me around?' Akila moves aside as he comes and plonks himself on the rock, sticking out his shoulder and neck. She climbs up his back, over the ridge of his neck and hops onto the branch. 'Easy as that,' he hisses, annoyed. She sticks out her tongue at him and gets to work sketching the pond and the trees to measurement. Once she has their proportions laid out, she starts sketching, trying out various layouts of huts on both trees, estimating which joint of branches would best suit the weight.

Akila is secured to a tree, at a joint of thick branches. The leaves cheer, beaten by gusts of air as Macoco manoeuvres a narrow log mid-air. Akila guides it into place across the two branches while Macoco hovers, watching. 'Getting rid of these smaller branches would help,' he suggests meekly.

Akila fires a glare back at him. 'I'm not telling you what to do,' he adds, 'it's just a suggestion.' And he drops out of view.

A hardcover novel sits splayed in her left hand with the thumb nestled firmly between its paper thighs. The ancient dust jacket lies ruined to one side. *Tropic of Cancer* it says. 'You cunt, take it, you cunt,' Akila mumbles through her laboured breaths, her body up against the side of the pond, holding the book to that ferocious diligence. Her right shoulder is hunched with the arm reaching in between her body and the rocks. A set of three birds lie bundled on the Mez, beside some reeds and fruit she has gathered. Cola watches her flexing back from the far side of the pond. Macoco peers over the edge of Picchu Falls, his head tilted quizzically.

Akila lounges on her side by the fire on a dark night. Across from her lies Macoco with Cola draped over his belly. Akila reads aloud from a book. It is *Moby Dick*, and she growls in Ahab's voice, '"Aye, Starbuck; aye, my hearties all round; it was Moby Dick that dismasted me; Moby Dick that brought me to this dead stump I stand on now. Aye, aye,' he shouted with a terrific, loud, animal sob, like that of a heart-stricken moose; 'Aye, aye! It was that accursed white whale that razed me; made a poor pegging lubber of me for ever and a day!' Then tossing both arms, with measureless imprecations he shouted: 'Aye, aye! And I'll chase him round Good Hope, and round the Horn, and round the Norway Maelstrom, and round perdition's flames before I give him up.'"

THE SUN slaps her skin. Her shoulders are red already. She searches the sky through every gap in the canopy, her eyes smarting from the effort.

'Macoco!'

She has been shouting for so long, her throat is getting hoarse. The monitor lizard slung over her shoulder was killed hours ago for lunch. She hears a crash. Her finely tuned senses tell her the precise direction and distance. She starts towards the noise and then suddenly skids on her heels as a cloud of red dust rises forty feet away, just beyond the line of trees and thickets. That is not dust. It is blood. Biting her lip with worry, she charges through the bushes into an opening doused in harsh sunlight.

The scene before her is of utter carnage. A candle of giant tapirs have been ripped to pieces and flung about. More than twenty animals, but the true number is hard to guess. Their bodies are disfigured beyond recognition. Bits of flesh and guts drape the branches. And in the centrum stands Macoco, ripping an animal in two in a furious fountain of blood.

'Macoco,' she chokes out, her voice strangled by the sight. Macoco whips his scowl at her, his scarlet-drenched body trembling in the sun. Through the glistening gore she sees his wild and menacing eyes, and at last Akila understands. And now she is truly afraid, for all she can see there is emptiness.

A void with no resident. His lips curl, his teeth polished with death. His voice snaps like a bolt of thunder. 'Don't look at me!'

HE LAUGHED out loud and she smiled at him curiously. He said, 'When I especially hate the person I've become, that's when I call myself a child of divorce.' They were sitting with their backs to the rocks, the pebbles cool under their buttocks. Running the question through her mind before she asked it, she felt she should not, but plunged forward regardless, 'What do you really hate?'

'About myself?'

'No. What do you hate the most?'

He inflated his cheeks as he digested the question. It took him a while to think about it and when he had it, he adjusted his seat to look her in the eyes and said, 'I hate being manipulated.'

She nodded thoughtfully. He took two small pebbles in his hand and rolled them like dice. 'What about you?'

'I hate being lied to,' she said, returning his deep stare.

'Of course,' he said, trailing off, letting the silence swallow what he left unsaid. They sat uneasily, with the air heavy about them.

'Take off that shirt,' she said in the stinging tone she unleashed when something had upset her badly.

'Why?' He glanced at his red T-shirt with the white cartoon outline of an elephant's backside.

'I hate it.'

'What the – what's wrong with it? I've worn it a lot and you've had no complaints before.'

'Well I do now. I hate it. Take it off. I'm going to get rid of that thing.'

'I can put on the one with an elephant's face if that'll help,' he said, making a weak attempt at humour.

'Don't do that,' she said, again in that biting tone that cut him deeper than any curse could.

Shyam stared blankly at her, bewildered by the sudden shift in mood. He said, 'It was a gift from a friend, Akila. I won't throw it away.'

'No,' she barked. Biting down on every word, she yelled, 'I don't give a shit-eating fuck what the hell it is. I just don't like looking at it. Please, take it off.'

Shyam sat up on the rock.

'No. Not until you tell me what's wrong.'

She tossed her book into the bush and yelled, 'Fuck you, give it to me!'

She grabbed his T-shirt. He pulled at her hand to let go, pleading, 'Okay, I'll take it off.' She let go and stood up. 'But I'm not throwing it away,' he said, pulling the shirt over his head.

She caught hold of it and he pulled back with his head still caught inside. She overpowered him easily and got it off, though he held on.

'What is this?' was all he could murmur, stunned by the proceedings.

'Tell me why it's so precious to you,' she yelled.

'Tell me why you want to get rid of it.'

'Fuck you, you piece of shit!' She pulled at the T-shirt, with him still hanging on. He lost his footing and stumbled to his knees. The T-shirt finally tore down the middle and she left him holding the rags. He stared up at her, shaken. 'What the hell, Akila?'

'Fucker,' she muttered beneath her sobs and marched off into the jungle. He struggled to his feet and went after her. He saw a flash of her white dress through the leaves and picked up his pace, but there was no sign of her. He went to the left, calling out her name, and nearly missed her squatting in the adjacent bush in tears, hands thrust through her hair. He came back, retracing his steps and caught sight of her dress vanishing behind some bushes. He chased after her and found a stream. And he knew she was gone.

IT WOULD be far easier to run without the spear, but she doesn't stand a chance unarmed. A mantra repeats in her head. 'Don't kill him. Don't kill him.' Even as she swings around a tree and his bulk comes crashing past, she tastes the blood on her bottom lip from her own furious gnawing on it. Run. It is all she can do. What chance has she got facing him? Thankfully, he is not the size of a full-grown Fenek, though he is big. The size of a minibus.

She can't look back, but she can hear the trail of destruction in his wake. What madness has captured him? No time for that now. She has to stop him, without killing him. She may have to hurt him, she resigns herself to that. That is, if he does not kill her first.

She twists and turns and finds her way to an old hunting hide, a hollow at the base of a tree. She drops the spear in the mud outside and grabs a cluster of mushrooms. Crushing them, she sprays the particles around the hole to hide her scent. A series of tremors mark Macoco's approach. She slips inside the hollow tree and waits. The withered wood rumbles to his steps. What has twisted her loved one into this mindless monster? The tree is knocked over hard and the whole world somersaults about her. Light bursts into the tight enclosure and stillness reigns. She can feel his footsteps moving away from her just as hastily as they had approached.

She is on her side and her right arm hurts like hell. She is sure the shoulder is dislocated and getting out of the hollow is painful business. Biting on a piece of root, she rams her shoulder against a tree. Her eyes roll back as she slumps to the ground, but she recovers. She takes a few seconds to sort herself out, then collects her spear from the mud. Only a splintered breach remains of the tree she had hidden inside. She needs to go back home and regroup her resources for a plan to subdue Macoco. Turning, she finds the path of destruction Macoco has left, leading homeward. 'Cola.' She chokes back a horrified sob. Her muscles tense for action. Visions of mutilated tapirs strewn across the shrubbery assault her mind.

Cola's large flat head floats on the surface of the pond, his long body drooping in the water. The button eyes are fixed at a point in the jungle. The trees shiver, sending leaves pirouetting to the ground in manic displays of yellow and green. He can feel the tremors pass through the water. Like a burst bubble, his head vanishes. He surges to the bottom and turns around, one foot clutching a rock to stay in place. The pond's surface sways in its usual giddy prance of sunlight. With a scream of bubbles Macoco's head plunges through. Cola sinks to the pond's rocky bed, his dark body almost indistinguishable from the slick rocks. Macoco tears out of the water and the force of it swishes the pond about like water in a basin. Taking the chance, Cola makes a dash for the cave. Barely four feet from it, he is wrenched away by the flux and just manages to grab onto the wall as Macoco's head thrusts deeper. Gawking up at the Fenek's insanity, Cola speaks. 'Macoco, please.'

Akila races along the stream, spear at the ready. She can hear Macoco's wild roar and the screams of crashing water.

Rock to rock, five long strides on bare ground and rock again. She has timed it perfectly through instinct alone. She sees Macoco stooping into the pool and drawing up. There is not enough room to alter her plans even if she wants to. Her right foot lands perfectly on the end of the rock at Picchu Falls and she is airborne in a terrific leap. The spear swings in the air as Macoco's head rises. Her body smacks into the back of his head, sending him into a momentary daze. There is enough time for the spear to swing all the way around and come around his neck. Akila latches the spear with ironclad grips trapping his throat. She will not let go. He has killed Cola. She can already feel a yawning abscess in her soul, without any way of expressing it to this rabid beast hugged to her bosom. This wild creature that was once her child, but no more. There is nothing left. She knows she can't let go of him or she will be torn apart before she hits the ground. She must hold on.

His temples are stained with slime. Macoco reaches up for the spear with his arms. Akila twists the spear harder, sending Macoco staggering against the rock wall. His breath is knocked out and he can't breathe. All she has to do is hold on a little longer and he will either have suffocated to death or will crush her against the rocks and break free. She feels alone, again. She tastes the sourness in her lips and realizes she is crying. She loves Cola but she weeps for Macoco as a mother would for her favourite child. The one for whom she had dreamt a glorious future. In her hands she grips the shaft of wood that will choke the life out of him. The life she once rescued. Crushing her face into his neck, she mourns her loss. Through the tears she hums, 'Pussycat, pussycat, I love you, yes, I do.' Macoco reaches up to his throat with both hands, beating his wings violently, but Akila tugs so hard she fears she must have killed him, sending his body crashing against the nearest tree.

Drained of all strength, he tries to get up. She can't do it, she can't kill him. She slides the rod up to his jaw, trying to haul him up, but instead it gives him that breath of air he needs. With a sudden surge of energy, his legs scramble on the rocks and he reaches up to grab her. She tightens the hold against his jaw and twists. His head snaps to the side and his foot misses a step. He falls backwards, with her still hanging on. She crushes her damp eyes shut, hoping beyond hope that it works. And holds her breath.

Akila rolls across a bed of pebbles, the broken halves of her spear in either hand. Coughing up water, she crawls up the bank. She hears movement behind her and spins around, spearhead at the ready, tossing aside the useless half. It is raining and the air is thick with the roar of water. There is a small lake at the base of a towering waterfall. Mists of vapour bathe a bright rainbow and there is no sight of Macoco. He did not make it through. She does not want to cross back. Not yet. She will have to catch him, yet again. And again, try to bring him here, to others of his kind. But she must go back at once. Before he does more harm. Getting up, she ambles to the lake, checking the bruises on her body. A broken spear is no good. She will have to make another as soon as she can. Her mind is already formulating a plan. She knows where to splash through into her world. There is a pond she knows, not far from hers.

The hairs on the back of her neck prickle. She twirls around to face a drenched Macoco, hooting from the back of his throat through bared fangs. Thoroughly exhausted, Akila's body noticeably relaxes and she smiles, speaking through a whimpered sigh, 'It's done, then.' Macoco charges through the shallows, roaring, water frothing and flying about him. She closes her eyes and hops backwards into the water.

She lies floating on the surface of her pond, her hand still grasping the spearhead. The locality of the pond is covered in broken branches and leaves and bloody smears. There is a plop of a bubble breaking the surface beside her face. She does not have to look. She has him back. At last, she sheds a tear for Cola.

DISHES OF food were arranged on the rocks with a bowl of flowers in the centre. There were two places set with plates and cups. Shyam sat hunched, elbows on his knees, chin on his fists, staring at the empty plate like a forlorn castaway. A click of pebbles made him glance up. Akila stepped out into the light a few feet away. He hadn't heard her come through the bushes. She belonged here in this wild place. Would there be a time when he would do as well?

She stood there awkwardly, her hands not quite knowing what to do, fiddling and scratching. She looked at him at last, smiling. It was a scaffolded façade, he knew, behind which hid the guilt or whatever she truly felt over what had happened. She stepped forward and said, 'My lifelong foe, loneliness and I, have long since shaken hands and reconciled ourselves to a marriage. One of convenience at first, but one in which we grew to tolerate and then appreciate the other.' The smile softened, and she waited for his response with a raised eyebrow.

'What the – you hate it if I joke when you're upset with me,' he said through gritted teeth. Suddenly the worry and anguish he felt at her disappearance soured into anger. 'My god, the horrible tone you take when I do it, and here you are doing the same thing to me?'

She was taken aback. He had never raised his voice at her before. 'I didn't realize you were that upset,' she said.

'You left me alone for almost two days. I didn't have a fucking clue where the hell you were!'

'I needed some time to myself.'

'Tell me then that you're going. Where you're going. Don't just disappear. I thought you had – I thought something had happened to you.'

'I'm a Beli, I'll be fine, you don't need to worry about me, Shy.'

He frowned at her use of his nickname at a time like this.

'Fine, you're a Beli! You don't want me to worry about the person I love, fine! Then what about me? I'm not a fucking Beli, so can I worry about my-fucking-self then? What's going to happen to me if you vanish for some reason? What the hell am I going to do if you leave?' He was visibly anguished as he expressed the one fear he had never intended to reveal. But anger opens secret doors when you're looking for only one. And more came tumbling out. 'I have nowhere to go. I don't know what to do, where to go. Shit!'

'I didn't know it was going to be this hard for you.'

'You think this is me complaining about you? Can't you see beyond that? Can't you see what's really bothering me about what happened?'

'I won't go like that anymore.'

'You don't understand, do you? Fuck, the irony of it. The guy who wanted to be left alone can't stand being alone now, and the girl who prayed for company wants some time alone.'

He realized Akila was just waiting for this to end so they could reconcile. He wanted that too. He reined himself in.

'Go, when you need time to yourself. I understand that, but tell me about it first. Can you do that for me? For li'l ol' *moronic* me,' he said, ejecting the word 'moronic' with passion, his rage resurfacing. 'Can you do that fucking much?'

She nodded, eyebrows warily raised. He looked away from her gaze, unable to accept being patronized by her.

'You can't even listen to me when I'm trying to tell you something that means so much to me.'

'It's just the way you start talking when you get like this sometimes.'

'How is that the point of this? I'm angry. Just let me be angry. For once!'

He got up and went out the way that she had entered.

PHOSPHORESCENT STREAKS cascade over a salmon dusk sky swimming in the still pools of her eyes. 'I've lost the sky again,' she whispers. Her naked body is coated with droplets, stars of pink glazing her skin. Hunched shoulders, knees splayed open and the soles of her feet together, arms and hands limp. She sits on the Mez, facing Cola, his button eyes upon her. 'I need to escape, Cola. I need to find some way out of here. This is not life. Love and have it turn on you. Love and be abandoned. Fuck. Marooned in these desolate worlds. I don't belong here. Can't you see that?'

Cola does not move.

'There must be a way. And if there is, I'll find it. If I have to, I'll tear these worlds apart to get out.' Tears run down her cheeks. 'I'll do it. I'll do it. I know I will. I'll do anything to get out. Get out of this horror. This place is not my home. It's keeping me from it. Cola, you of all people should know what I've been through. This is your world. It's not mine. I love you, Cola, but I can't survive this place much longer. I'm not a dog that lives out its life being told where to sleep, eat and shit. Kept on a leash!' She touches the scar around her neck. 'Somehow I'll find the loose thread. And I'll pull, I'll tug until the whole fucking thing unravels because I need what is mine. I must belong to a place and have someone belong to me. If I'm being selfish, then that is what I am. I am selfish! I want to selfishly share my life with someone and have some of theirs. That world where the Belis are sent. That is the key. Somewhere out there, there is a way home. I have to keep searching because there is no one to ask. I have to keep trying because there is no place for me here.'

NIGHTFALL. Akila lies on her side, a finger lazily trailing in the water. Cola floats beside her.

COLA IS a little too big to fit in the backpack. Akila has cut a hole for his tail and his bulk just managed to squeeze in, his head and arms sticking out of the zipper. Akila lugs him onto her back and stands poised for a moment, letting the straps settle in. In front she has another backpack on, stuffed with a jacket and a tracksuit. 'Here we go,' she says, closing her eyes, taking long breaths and clearing her mind until all that remains is a featureless blackness. She sets a pinprick in the black. This pinprick is the unknown world. I am travelling to the unknown world. I am in the unknown world. Her body leans forward and hits the water hard.

The water is sweet. It cools her eyes and scalp. It is shallow and the floor is soft. She stands tentatively, clearing her eyes. Feeling Cola's weight on her back is reassuring. Her first sight of the new world gets her excited. She slaps the water in triumph and goes to the edge. There are trees, if they can be called that, towering hundreds of feet above her, all with thick, straight trunks as broad as a tennis court. They stand in a straight wall, stretching to either side, with thick caps of coniferous foliage on top against the indigo sky. From their trunks spring large branches twisting and weaving among themselves with enormous white flowers. The lotus-shaped bowls of the flowers hold water, and Akila is standing in one at the end of a branch, protruding from the inexplicable woodland. Far below her, before the forest line, is an abyss descending into foggy depths she has no intention of exploring. The fog rises higher the further it gets from the trees, so there is no hope of discerning what lies beyond.

There is no obvious danger so she carefully slips out of the flower onto the large sepals and hops onto the stem. It is solid and she easily makes her way to the main branch. She can't help wondering what she may find here. Not that she knows what to look for. The branch is wide enough, but the fall seems impossibly deep. She moves forward at a deliberate pace. The closer she gets to the thick shadows among the trees with the twisted branches, the more she is certain this is not the path to her freedom. At every flower she passes, she wonders whether it is time to try the next 'unknown' world. How many more can there be? Is there an infinite number? She tells herself that cannot be, or else over the years she would have come across many others.

Counting Earth, this is the fourteenth world she has visited. They've included deserts, waterscapes, jungles and swamps. Waiting at the forest threshold, the hairs on the back of her neck stand on end. She has learnt never to ignore her fine-tuned instincts. There is a taste to dread. It is sour, with the texture of biscuit crumbs sliding down the back of the throat. You want to cough but you don't know what is out there. What you might alert or awaken.

Akila shakes her head, muttering, 'This is a bad idea.' She steps into the shadows to explore what secrets they may hold. Ten steps in and she goes no further. This can't be it. She decides to return to the flower to try another world. If at the end, all the other avenues are extinguished, she will return. If only Macoco were with her. They could have flown above the forest and explored this world in a far shorter time. With that fleeting thought comes the clinging agony of her loss. Reaching over her shoulder, she rubs Cola's head. She is not alone, she reminds herself. And she has a plan. She will find a way home and take Cola along.

Withdrawing from the shadows, she hurries to the nearest flower. A call from within the forest stops her in her tracks. A bleating howl lingers in the air. And then, chatter from the far fog-bank echoes like a school of cooing spirits. Small specks tear out of the fog, a great horde swaying in hypnotic patterns. It approaches the forest in a wave stretching across the murky cloud. She produces a pair of mini binoculars from the backpack on her chest and focuses the lenses. The wavering image at this distance gives a glimpse of a sort of large bird. The closest flower is down a twisting branch that breaks off to the left. It is too much of a risk with so high a fall. 'Fuck you,' she hisses under her breath, her wobbly knees discouraging her from making a dash for the others farther away, before the birds arrive. Grudgingly, she moves back into the shadows, nudging into a groove against the trunk. She could have made it. Damn.

The size of the birds in flight is hard to judge with no point of reference. They are further away than she had estimated. Now it is too late. No. She can make it. She races down the branch and makes for the closest flower. She takes the left, runs along it and jumps past a hairpin curl. She does not time the next hop well and manages to hang on with an arm around an auxiliary bud. There are fifteen kilos of Cola on her back and five more of the backpack on her chest. She can just about manage to hang on despite the extra weight, but she can't overcome it to pull herself up. Hanging on the way she is, there is no way to get rid of the extra load of the backpack in front, either. She swings her body, trying to grasp the stem with her legs and somehow climb over, but the third swing almost has her lose her grip entirely. 'Fuck!' she screams in her head.

The birds are here, landing delicately on the flowers and stems all along the line of trees. Akila is aghast at their freakish appearance. These are no birds. What are they? She dangles perfectly still like a drooping leaf, hoping they are too preoccupied to notice. The creatures are as large as humans with a satin coat of ultramarine blue feathers. Their faces seem human or apish but with beaks curled like a parrot's, only flatter, with the upper mandible less pronounced, serrated at the opening for teeth. They have a pair of pronounced breasts and for legs they have slim human-like arms with hawk-like claws for nails. They appear impractically unbalanced with the large breasts in front and just a fluffy bunch of feathers at the back for the undertail coverts. Their narrow tails are long with a metallic sheen.

Every bird holds a wriggling white worm in its mouth. They dump the worms in the flower and sip the water noisily, a hum of satisfaction filling the air. The branch she is clinging to bounces and a shadow falls over her. She does not move. Does not dare look up. Then there is another bounce on the branch and another as more birds arrive. They don't appear to be moving, so she steals a glimpse. She looks up straight into the leering face of one of the birds only three feet from hers. It backs away and the birds begin to chatter among themselves.

Akila tries to pull herself up but her arms are too tired to do anything more than hang on. And even that is difficult with Cola constantly squirming in her backpack. She can understand why he is nervous. She is feeling conspicuously like a worm herself. There is something so wrong with these creatures. What are they chattering about? Ten minutes go by and Akila's arms are painfully numb. She feels her grip slacken. 'Help me, please,' she cries out. They continue to ignore her. She can no longer hang on. Her arms become rubber and gradually slide over the rough bark, her fingers trying to cling on in vain.

She screams out, sobbing, 'Help me, you fuckers!'

The birds stop and all look down at her writhing form with sullen curiosity. Her scarred arms no longer feel the burden. Her fingers are free. The air beats her hair into her face and through the wet strands she can see the birds still perched on the branches as they fall away into the sky. She spins in the air as she descends. This is no time to cry, she scolds herself. Make a plan. She can't see any water below her through the dirty fog. She pictures her pond. Home. In case she hits water that is where she wants to go. A force knocks the breath out of her and grips her legs tightly. She finds herself hanging upside down from clutching hands. Blue wings flap above. Her backpack shifts and Cola drops out. 'Cola!' she calls out after him. The bird does not deviate from its flight. Akila tries to kick free but the grip is ironclad. She looks back downward for Cola but he is gone. The tears blind her. 'Cola,' her mouth moves, but no sound comes. Cola.

'Your food is safe,' the bird carrying her chortles. 'What?' she barks back. 'Your food, Beli. The black worm-thing.' The arms swing her body to the side and she sees Cola's flat head peering at her from the grasp of another one of the bird creatures. She is then gently set down on a branch and her eyes follow the bird carrying Cola to an isolated branch.

'Why is she taking Cola there? He's not my food! He is my friend! He is not food!'

None of the birds argue, remaining unperturbed on their respective branches, some still with worms in their beaks. A large one at the flower nearest to her speaks to the others in a form of bird speech. They chatter in hushed tones among themselves for a while.

'Please, I'm not a threat. I don't mean you any harm.' The birds twitter with laughter. Akila clenches her fist with burnt pride but she manages to subdue her anger. Anger will only get her killed – that is a lesson she learnt a long time ago. Sadly, it is a habit that never quits, and life makes an addict of us all. She squirms to her knees and clasping her palms together, faces the one at the flower that is obviously the leader. 'Please, help me,' her wavering voice implores. 'I'm only looking for something. A way...'

'Why should we help you?' the bird interrupts.

'You know I'm the Beli,' she says, indicating the bird that saved her. 'She told me that much.' The birds start shrieking, all but the one she is kneeling in front of, and that one has her saviour locked in an arctic glare. The chastised bird does a delicate hop off the branch and glides away.

Perplexed, Akila asks, 'Will you help me?'

The leader leans into the flower and rises with a worm wriggling in its beak. Holding the Beli in its sight, it rips the worm in two. Akila's fear and desperation are written plainly on her features.

'What sort of help?' the bird asks.

The others complain, but the grumbling ends abruptly with a single glance from the leader.

'I'm the Beli,' she shrugs helplessly. 'I'm trapped in these worlds, to be sacrificed time and again.' Her finger touches the scar around her neck and she notices the birds crowding to get a look. 'I want to escape. I want to be free from this torture. All my life I have been a Beli, the sacrifice. No more!'

The birds lean in with their oddly balanced bodies. There is that taste of dread in her mouth again, that something is not as it seems. She ignores it however, continuing earnestly, 'There is a way out for me.'

For the first time, the leader betrays his interest by tilting his head ever so slightly.

'And I believe it is here, in your world,' she says.

'How did you learn this fact?'

Unprepared for the cross-examination, she stutters, 'On one of the other worlds, I was told the Belis are sent somewhere when they can no longer serve as the sacrifice. If I can find my way there, I think I can escape. But I need your help.'

The birds babble loudly at the leader and she snaps, 'Hatt!' Silence falls instantly upon the branches.

'You want our help in finding this "way out" for you,' the leader probes.

'Yes.' Akila warily observes the tilted heads and adds, 'I know it is here, it has to be. Please. I don't think I have a chance of finding it by myself.'

'You're right, it is here.'

Akila feels lightheaded for a second. 'Really?'

'But I will not take you there.'

'What? Why?'

'Because you are not worthy of it.'

'Worthy?'

'Yes.'

'What do you mean, I'm not worthy?'

'If you do not understand that, you're not ready.'

'Worthy?' she spits the question out, searching her mind for some clue.

'It is not a path for anyone. That is why it is so difficult to find. That is why the Belis earn it with their lives of service,' the leader proclaims. 'I cannot take you there. You are not ready.'

Akila can't believe this. She has at last found her path to liberty after so many years of bondage, and this bird feels it has the right to judge her fate?

'Fuck you!' she screams, clawing at the bark, her scorching heart liquefying her insides. In the blink of an eye she crouches, ready to pounce, blade in hand. 'Fuck this bullshit! You will take me there! Or else I'll write my worth to the decimal point in your blood. I alone decide my worth. Not you or any tree! I do!'

A smile unravels on the leader's face as it considers her. 'Perhaps you are worthy after all, Beli.'

'Don't call me Beli! My name is Akila.'

The leader's head bows respectfully. 'I am Arn, the proprietor of my kind. We are the Sawa and this is the forest of Paz.'

Akila holds back the tears of orgasmic relief flooding her senses. It is accomplished. The hand clutching the blade trembles with emotion. Home. Closer than ever.

The leader delivers a clucking call. All the birds rush to the flowers and feed on the worms with relish. There is only one worm to a bird so it does not seem like much of a meal, and yet afterwards they crow with jubilation.

Finally, Arn shakes her feathers into a fine fluff and turns to the girl. 'Follow Astes, Akila. I will come behind you.'

'You're taking me now?'

'Yes,' Arn replies. 'Why? Did you want to wait?'

'No!' she almost shouts. 'I'm ready!'

Again, that bemused smile on Arn's face.

'Good. Let's not waste a moment more of daylight. Astes can carry your things.' Astes joins them and Akila hands over her backpacks. Astes gestures to Zorba, but Akila politely declines. 'I'll carry this, thank you, Astes.'

Astes glances at Arn, who answers, 'Let her keep her little beak.'

'What about Cola?' Akila protests.

'Your black worm?'

'Yes.'

'Your worm will be brought there. Don't worry, you can trust me.'

Akila nods, beaming eagerly like it is her birthday party. Astes leads the way, hopping from branch to branch and entering the forest in barely two seconds. Akila must cover the same distance by following the serpentine route of the branches. 'Aren't we flying there, Arn?' she asks hopefully.

'The path you seek is secret, hidden deep inside the forest. It is impossible to fly there. The forest is our home, you're quite safe with us.' She follows Astes and as they make their entrance Akila shrieks. A pair of folded legs extends from within the fluffy cover of the undertail covert. They are the hind legs of a cat, slim and dainty like the forelegs. Coming up behind her, Arn too stands on four limbs. Akila's jaw drops in amazement. This is all too much for her. Arn has that bemused smile again and it is beginning to irritate Akila. She is no longer a little girl and Arn is treating her like one. But she has to admit she has been behaving like a child with her outbursts and the constant shrieking. And this silly gaping at them is not helping either.

'You aren't birds?'

'What are birds?' Arn asks in reply.

The forest grows dark inside, lit by a few bands of light seaping through. Akila and Arn talk through the trek along the twisting branches travelling ever deeper among the towering trunks. There are no flowers in these gloomy depths. Only mangled arms and giant mushroom patches sprouting from the trees.

'This escape you spoke of,' Arn interjects, 'where are you escaping to?'

'My world. Where I'm originally from. I was a child when I was taken.'

'How is that world different from here?'

'Every one of these worlds is different, you know. Very different.'

'You can travel freely between them then?'

'Yeah.'

'But you still yearn to go back to yours. Why?'

'Why?'

'How many worlds is it that you can travel to as the Beli?'

'This is the fourteenth world.'

'I can see how frustrating it must be, being able to travel among these strange worlds and yet not be able to see your own.'

'I can travel to mine too.'

'I don't understand.'

'I can travel there but I can't stay longer than a few minutes.'

'All these worlds, including your own, and you want to leave them so badly, to risk your life and escape? What is so special about your world?'

'It is my home.'

'Isn't a home where you live?'

'When you are blind to all else but where you are meant to

be, you are far from home. When all you can see is the world around you, you are home.'

Arn contemplates her answer silently.

'I was born there,' Akila adds. 'I am of that world, just like you are of this one and Paz is your home.'

'Tell me about your world then. Your "home".'

They talk for a while and it feels like they have been walking forever, until at last they come out into an enormous circular clearing. All along its periphery the twisting branches reaching inward are filled with flowers converted to nests and they bustle with thousands of Sawa. The noise is deafening, a true cacophony of coos and hoots, with shrill calls echoing from every direction. It is too loud for Akila to hear her own thoughts, but she is astonished by the scale. The nested branches cover the outer walls of the clearing, flowing down hundreds of feet where they gradually fade into a floor of meshed branches. From the centre of the floor rises the thickest tree Akila has seen in Paz yet. A hundred feet below the level at which they stand now, the central tree has a narrow band of branches extending outward on one side, in a meticulous lace pattern. The rest of the tree is bare except for the stubs where branches have been pruned over generations to keep the sleek shape all the way up to the wide feathery canopy that filters light into the open space.

The wide branch Akila is on extends straight out, no more than a hundred feet. It has been primed to hang there with the virility of a massive bird perch. She sees her backpack sitting at the far end with Cola's dark form spilling over onto the wood. Thrilled to see him again, she pushes past Astes and runs forward. Her foot gets caught and she slams hard against the wood. At first she is embarrassed by her clumsiness in front of her newly acquired friends, but then she finds that she can't move her feet. Her left hand is held down. Her right hand shoots to her hip for Zorba, but it gets pinned down swiftly.

'Arn!' she hollers. 'What is this?' She feels a presence saunter over to her.

'What does it feel like, Beli?' Arn asks serenely.

'I thought you were going to help me.'

'Help you?'

'The way home,' Akila sobs aloud, her body held so firmly against the wood that she can hardly breathe.

'You thought I would help a Beli?'

'Arn!' Her scream echoes noisily in the chamber.

'The way home?' Arn's voice is cold.

Her face comes close to Akila's.

'I have never heard of anything like an escape route. And that is the truth, you wriggling worm.'

'Arn!'

'Beli! You accursed thing. Your touch has infected my world with filth.'

'What? I've never been here before!'

'You harbinger of doom! What you see in this humble Reat is what remains of the Sawa, the dominions of Paz. Paz that was once this entire world is now a pitiful forest. Paz, where trees ran from ocean to ocean, where the air was filled with the scent of flowers and bark, where the colours of Sawa were as varied as the rainbow ... where we weren't alone. You speak of being alone. But you have a home to escape to. True loneliness comes with no escape. This is my home. The only home we have. "When all you can see is the world around you, you are home." I'm looking around, into a cloud of dust. Where is my world?'

'I didn't do anything.'

'My world has been chewed up and shit out by the infestation brought by your kind, Beli. You invited them here.

We know, you Beli scum! I'll peel your skin off in thin strips so every day you will feel one millionth of what I feel when the sun shines through this island of trees and I look upon the last of my kind. You want to go home, you carrier of death? You want to escape your prison?'

Arn moves closer so her mouth is an inch from Akila's ear and the girl can feel Arn's breasts pressed against her back. The ruler of the Sawa whispers, 'I can't escape, Beli, because you've made my home into my prison. And you will share that prison with me. Feeling the rending pain within me – on you. I am kind, Beli. You will taste my kindness. Every day, strip by strip. Until there comes a day when your life is pain and nothing else. Your world will be a tear-blurred mess and you will say to me, "Kind Arn, master of the Sawa. You say your home has become ceaseless agony. Then I too am home."' Arn lifts away from Akila's shrunken form, whispering, 'And then I will have kept my promise to you.'

Akila is strung up above the chasm of the Reat, the name the Sawa have given this sacred clearing in the forest. Her limbs are spread wide, her wrists and ankles bound with taut chords tied to branches. She can see only one nest on these branches on the central tree and it is the largest flower Akila has seen yet. It sits over a dozen feet away, seven feet higher than her, so she can't see into it. She has tested the bonds and they are solid, quite literally, with the sap they have poured onto the knots having now hardened. Her limbs have no room to shift and she is held in place securely, utterly helpless to her fate. Arn's head peers over the flower petals above her and holds up Akila's backpack filled with her supplies.

'What is this, Beli?' Arn prods at it.

Akila answers with a flash of her sun-baked granite eyes beneath her brooding brow.

'Well?'

'It's nothing,' Akila spits.

'And that's why you had it strung to your chest?' Arn's voice simmers with irritation. She tears the bag open with her beak and lets the contents spill into the flower.

'What are these fiddlings?'

'I told you, they are nothing. Knick-knacks I have found on my travels.'

'Knick-knacks?'

'Junk.'

It is Arn's turn to glower at her teasing.

'Fiddlings I picked up in other worlds as souvenirs. Nothing more,' Akila assures her.

'Souvenirs?'

'Things to help me remember a place.'

'I understand.' Arn grunts. 'To remember these worlds you have damned, when you escape to your own.'

'I'm not responsible for what's happened to your world, Arn. I wasn't even alive at the time.'

'Are you a Beli?'

Akila knows where this is going. She has no choice but to play along. Arn has a short fuse that she has tested enough already, so she answers, 'Yes, but not voluntarily.'

Arn examines a torch in her hand. The arms are as slender and dainty as a woman's, but the palms have bright red ridges, and the claws are long and curled inward like a hawk's.

'What does it matter whether you were alive or not? There is only one of you, and you have inherited their sins. Your kind brought those pests here, invited them to the home of another. You can travel unhindered through worlds and you feel that gives you the right to do as you please?'

'I didn't do this!'

'Are you telling me you've never hurt someone from another world? Never caused distress?'

'Of course not!'

'Why don't I believe you, Beli? It is in your nature to do evil.'

'And is it in your nature to torture an innocent visitor, Arn? Is this the way of the Sawa?'

'What do you know of the Sawa, Beli?'

'Not much, and what I've seen so far I don't love.'

'Is this a joke to you?'

'I'm the one hanging here, a prisoner for something I didn't do. I think I have the right to joke if I please.'

The corner of Arn's beak twists into that bemused smirk again. She places the shiny objects from Akila's bag alongside the twigs lining her nest.

'Again,' Arn says, 'you feel you have the right to something that hurts others. I am glad my younglings are too little to comprehend what we're discussing.'

'You have children?'

'You can't see their nest from there. They're behind me, in their own.'

'How?'

'How what?'

'Where are your males?'

'Males?'

'The ones you mate with.'

'My mate is here, Uro.'

Akila hears movement in the nest and a head shows up beside Arn's. They look identical, although Uro is slighter. And she too has breasts.

'How? You're both females.'

'Female?'

'You are both the same sex. How can you have children?'

Both Sawa exchange a look, bewildered.

'What is so surprising about us having children?'

'How is that possible? There is always a male and a female. They mate and then the children are born. The males always differ physiologically from the females and they play different roles in a relationship. They are different.'

'All Sawa are born the same. We have no such differences.'

'How do you mate then?'

Uro withdraws and Arn snorts at Akila, 'Are you trying to disturb me by discussing these most private matters? Are you lacking all traces of tact?'

'I'm just trying to understand, Arn. This is unique.'

'This is the way it is. This is normal.'

'Not everywhere.'

'Does that matter? Here it is this way.'

'And which of you lays the eggs?'

'Both mates lay the eggs. We are equal in everything.'

Akila digests this information, briefly forgetting her role as captive. She shakes her head, chuckling to herself at the notion that she should find such a marvellously novel arrangement of nature in a doomed world bent on executing her.

'That is funny, Beli? The Sawa are a joke to you?'

'No,' Akila begins, but Arn interrupts, snarling, 'I'll show you, Beli. That will be the last time you laugh at my expense!'

Arn searches for something in her nest.

'No, Arn, I wasn't–'

Arn returns, carrying Cola in her claws.

'Arn.' Akila's voice wavers, her heart racing, eyes heating with tears.

'This is my joke, Beli. This black worm you hold so dear,' hisses Arn, and with that she rips Cola's right foreleg off at the shoulder. His black fingers flex as Arn chews on it triumphantly.

Akila sags in her bindings, her chest throbbing with her love for Cola. Cola twists in agony in Arn's fist, his mouth snapping at the air. Uro joins Arn and tears off Cola's tail with a savage bite. Arn flings Cola back into the nest and scowls into Akila's bloodshot eyes. 'Are we a joke to you now? Will you laugh at the Sawa ever again?'

Akila is no longer listening.

'Ah, I almost forgot. This is something that will get the appropriate response.' Arn is clearly revelling in her own cleverness.

She comes out of the nest and hops onto the branches from which Akila is suspended. They rattle with the movement. Now she sees how perfectly adapted the four limbs are to these trees as Arn goes around her to the lower branch and they come face to face.

'You know, Beli,' Arn murmurs, 'your worm and you are a rare treat to us. When we chanced upon you, we had just returned from our daily foray. Every Sawa with the strength to fly takes part in the foray. We fly across the dead banks, through the ghosts of extinct forests, to the kingdom of the insects. We know where their young are kept and we feed to our heart's content. They know this, of course. We have been doing it for years. So they move the nursery deeper and deeper into their realm, not realizing that we'd fly to the sun and back for that meal. We eat nothing else so that our hunger will drive us further. To devour more of them. That is our existence. And then we return with one worm alive in our beaks. It is tradition now. We no longer remember what it represents, but we do it. They are not so bad to taste, and yet our hatred has us relishing them as though they were the tender woodworm. Woodworm. When was the last time I had one? I can't even recall, but I'll remember this.'

A hooked claw pierces Akila's chest. Her lips open wide though only a faint sob escapes. The claw cuts to the right, over the ridge of her breast, and runs back in a parallel line until a neat rectangular strip an inch wide has been etched into the flesh. Akila's jaw quivers, her eyes are wide with shock. She asks herself why this is happening. Arn uses both hands for the next step. Akila's shrill scream floods the Reat with her agony. Two claws pinch the end of the strip, and a sharp point runs along the bottom to cut away any resistance. Inch by inch, with the precision of a craftsperson savouring her art, Arn does the peeling. The flap of skin comes away and dangles in the breeze. Arn scrutinizes Akila's unconscious form. A pity she fainted from the pain. Chewing on the skin, Arn contrives plans for the next time. As luscious as the skin is, she must remember to make the strips shorter. For Akila must watch her eating the flesh. Arn can hardly wait.

K-tick. Her eyes snap open, still tasting the sweltering agony of her nerve endings. She had wanted to die. Had she pleaded for death? She can't remember. Night has fallen, and her surroundings are bathed in satin moonlight. Akila eyes the nest warily. Something stirs on the crest of the flower petals and twigs. She can't mistake that head for anything else but Cola. The echoes of her torture fade away with the elation of seeing him alive. She wants to touch his nose and comfort him, but for these damn bindings. Cursing Arn, she grinds her teeth with white-hot hatred.

The trench on her breast is almost healed over already and by the morning there will be no mark to show for the torment. Her Beli perks are perfectly suited for Arn's method of torture. Every day, a piece of her will be carved out, for it is her debt to pay for the sins of the Belis of the past. An object catches the light in Cola's mouth. She realizes it is her blade, Zorba, but there is no way to get to it. Unless Cola can throw it to her. No, that is absurd. He could not manage it. Then again, what's she got to lose? Just the blade and all hope. She waves her palms at Cola and gestures to him to pass the blade. She can see his black form struggling with two limbs lost. She crushes back the tears at the thought of him suffering.

She is a Beli and maybe through some twisted logic, she can understand Arn's hatred of her. However, there is no excuse for what Cola had to endure. He is an innocent.

Cola takes up position on the edge of the nest. In all likelihood, the blade will fall short and she fears Cola will rebuke himself for letting her down. With what he has already had to endure for her sake, she can't bear for him to feel he has failed her in any way. Without a moment's hesitation, Cola whips the blade forward. *Whap*! It catches in the branch above Akila. Three inches to the left and it would have cut her bond and freed her right arm. Quite a throw, Cola. She winks at him.

How can she reach the blade though, with her limbs already stretched to the limit? There is some leeway for barely an inch or two if she tugs with all her might. No, there must be another way. Since she can't get her hand to the knife, perhaps she can get the knife to her. The cords will not yield, but the branch may. Twisting her forearm around the cord, she loops it around her wrist, cutting the distance to only half a foot. She wraps the cord around her wrist again until she has the blade in her hand. In the nick of time, or she is certain she would have been ripped apart if she had to go any further. With one wrist cut free however, she decides that cutting the remaining bonds presents some challenges because there is no way she can bend far enough to free her ankles first. She pauses for a few moments, thinking through the problem at hand. When she has a plan, she frees the other wrist, and lets her body instantly flip backward and hang upside down. She makes certain to fall in an arc so that the branch doesn't get in the way and make a noise. Then straining up, she slices the line holding her right ankle. Dangling freely from the final cord, she reaches up her left leg to her feet. She pulls herself up the cord and grabs a hold of the branch it is attached to before cutting herself free entirely.

Sneaking up the branches, she gets to Arn's nest where the master of the Sawa and her mate, Uro, sit side by side like sleeping doves. There is a smaller flower behind them with four chicks, asleep. All around her, the circular wall of the Reat is occupied with slumbering Sawa. She needs an escape plan with a chance of success.

Cola's dark shape crawls towards her, and the anger wells up deep inside. All reason and plans of escape wither with its storm. There is only wrath. There is only the need to exact terrible vengeance. Her blade feels at home in her grip once more, prepared to do her bidding. Lithe as a jungle cat, she pours into the nest. Arn is closest and opens her eyes at the sensation of the twigs shifting under Akila's weight. A moment later the eyes are drawn at their widest, as a neat dark line blossoms at Arn's throat. Blood gurgles through the slit as she tries to keep herself from keeling over.

Akila holds her trembling body. Then, with Arn's face close, she bares her teeth in a grimace. 'That is for what you did to me, which I can forgive. And this is for what you did to someone I love.' Arn reaches out with a bloody hand to stop her. Akila deflects it as she approaches the sleeping mate. She dips the blade into the side of the neck and Uro quietly slumps over. Akila stands before Arn, wiping the blade on her thigh, and leans over, whispering plainly, 'That I can never forgive.'

Arn gasps tearfully, coughing up mouthfuls of blood. Akila

lies close to Arn's face and stares deep into her eyes. 'If I can't find my way out of this carousel of worlds, I'm making you a promise, Arn. I'll be back. I'll be back to see Paz shit out by the fucking insects, and then it and the Sawa will only exist as a memory.' Akila holds the point of the blade to the side of her temple, hissing savagely, 'In my head.' Arn's tongue swivels in the blood without words. Then her eyes roll back and the yellow lids droop.

Akila goes to the flower's edge and looks for a way out. She has no idea how to find her way back to the flowers at the end of the forest. As far as she knows, they are the only source of water in Paz. There appears to be no way to cross the chasm to the outer wall of the Reat without wings. Is it possible to use the branches in the canopy above? The patchwork is stamped clearly against the moonlit sky. So are the circular silhouettes among the branches. Flowers. That is her way out. They are a couple of hundred feet up the sheer face of the trunk but she has no alternatives. Grabbing her backpack, she gently slips Cola into it and straps it on securely. She races along the branches, arms outstretched for balance, and reaches the trunk. The bark has deep grooves and ridges running in vertical slits with enough foot and hand holds for her to manage the climb. Without wasting a moment, she grabs on and steps up.

The blade handle in her mouth tastes sour with blood and feathers and fifty feet up, her toes begin to complain. More than anything, it is Cola's additional load that is affecting her pace. She takes a breather, regarding the saucer-like shapes against the starlit sky: her portals out of this misery. Fifty feet further and her fingers and thumbs beg to crawl off and die. Her toes are on the verge of becoming useless. They are raw, and the big toe alone is putting up any effort while the others are only getting in the way. The bark is without mercy. With every grip and step up, her nails come loose and squish around. Her arms scream and her shoulders can take no more. Her legs tremble with another eighty feet to go. A splinter wedges between her second and third toe on her right foot. Akila's jaws clamp down on the blade handle. She has already cried out her tears and there is nothing left. Climb. She can think of nothing else but to climb. Thirty feet to go. She is practically there. Her body is in so much pain, it is beyond comprehension and her mind numbs her from it, operating like a basic program, co-ordinating arms and legs, one limb at a time.

She arrives at the bottom-most branches and the grooves get too tight for her fingers. She jabs the blade into the trunk and pulls herself up. She comes out of her daze to wails echoing off the Reat chamber. She pulls the blade out and rams it in higher, pulls up, and scurries clumsily onto the branch. She peers down at what she had feared. They have discovered their leader murdered and they are coming for Akila. Her vision is a blurry mess but she can hear them. Hardly able to stand, with buckling knees and useless arms, she swallows hard. The Sawa are coming. The sides of the tree are crawling with them and the rest are flying up to the canopy – for they see her. There is a flower ahead, but the idea of running is laughable in her condition. Still she makes the attempt, her head spinning, legs barely able to handle each step as she blunders onwards. And suddenly she realizes it is dawn. The flower is lit in the sun's first golden rays, lying open before her. Take me home, she sobs to herself. Take me home. She reaches the flower and almost falls off the branch, nearly missing it. She rights herself as the branches begin to shudder with the oncoming wave. Her legs quake and she falls forward, hoping that will be enough to reach the water, just as a torrent of Sawa storm through the branches from below.

THE DROP hit his cheek and his eye fluttered open. He looked up with a smile for her. The drizzle-soaked branches reminded him. Casting aside the damp quilt, he sat up on the hunting platform they had built together some weeks ago. It had been his first construction project and she had guided him through it. A narrow river flowed a few feet from the tree and at fifteen feet up, it was the perfect vantage point to wait for any quarry that might come for a drink. Shyam lay stretched out on the dripping wood, hating the feeling of his rabid heart trying to bark and bay in his chest. He would not let anyone take him for granted or walk all over him as though his feelings mattered any less. Or as though he had no choice, which he knew was the case – and that is what frustrated him the most. What was he going to do, what *could* he do?

AKILA SAW the pile of discarded jambli husks gathered at the base of a tree, a dozen feet from the one with the hunting hide. She squinted up at the platform, trying to divine how she could make things right again. She knew she did not need him to survive because she had gotten along just fine her entire life, and a night with him gone was not a big deal.

AT THE base of the tree Shyam surveyed the jungle with his spear held ready. When he was certain the coast was clear, he went to the river's edge and splashed his face with water. He sipped a couple of handfuls of it to wash down the hurt in his chest. He took a step into the shallows, scratched his chest, yawned and started peeing into the flow. He turned as he peed, stopping when he caught sight of Akila on the opposite bank.

She was crouched among the roots of a tree, her forked spear poised to strike a fish. Their eyes locked and the sleepless night was plainly written on her face. His yawn faded, but he still had to pee. He turned away from her. It was obvious why she chose to fish at that time of the day, so conspicuously on the opposite side of the river, but he would not give her the satisfaction of acknowledgement.

AKILA SAT at the pond with the food set out on the rocks. Shyam's side had his plate and cup. She waited for a long time, as she had done the past three meals, before she began eating. The lush salad and the roasted spice-rubbed fish could not distract her from her melancholy as she chewed with distaste and swallowed. After years of eating by herself, less than a day without him, and she was already feeling his absence. She tried to convince herself that there was nothing more to it, but she knew it was also that she missed him. To have him sitting opposite her in silence, chewing, was all she wanted.

The bush rattled and she saw Shyam coming out of the jungle towards her. Her cheeks flushed and she tried to gobble down the half-chewed food so they could hug and kiss, and make up. Instead, he went up the rope ladder to the huts. She washed her hands and waited for him, listening to the opening and closing of woven trunks in their wardrobe. He came out with items of clothing draped on his shoulders. She watched him climb down the ladder and depart into the jungle without a single word or look in her direction.

It was a punch to her throat. She held back the sob bobbing there, trying to burst out of her. Maybe she should have said something. But what? Sorry? Would that have been enough? Why did he take so many clothes? Was he that upset with her?

She sat there, food forgotten now, trying to imagine how they would live here if not together. Had she ruined everything?

On the platform, Shyam sat with his back against the tree trunk, watching the lazy flow of the river reflecting the early night sky. The sky was not completely dark yet, even with the sun reaching the other side of the planet. And soon it would be here again, announcing tomorrow. At least sleep was a respite from his despair. He did not want to talk to her even though he knew that would be the only way to solve this.

Why couldn't she understand that this was her home, not his? Now, he was the one trapped in an alien world. Trapped with someone he loved, but who was capable, at times, of anger and a debilitating passive-aggression. Like the strike of a match, her temper would flare without warning, then quickly die out, and they would pretend it had never happened.

He deserved better than this, but what choice did he have? He had already made the ultimate act of commitment by leaving his world with the door back sealed forever. He loved her. He loved her more now than he did when he had made that decision. He loved her despite her temper. He even loved her temper because it was a part of her. But he knew it would only get worse if he did nothing.

He had nowhere to go and he did not want to go anywhere without her. She was the breath of life that suffocated him at times. What he felt for her was how he had always imagined love to be – complete and without inhibition. But when would she understand that he was not Cola, whom she could abandon on a whim? This was the fourth time she had left that way, and it had also been the longest. If you need your space, take it, but don't block me out, he thought. Don't throw me away. As he ran the fights through his head, he worked himself up again, and tried to calm down.

There was a knock on the tree below. He got the spear and slid to the edge to peer over. At the base of the tree a small LED reading lamp shone on a generous plate of food. A peace offering. He did not like being manipulated like this. She knew he had to come down and get the plate, to avoid attracting animals, and she would be there, waiting. He had no alternative but to go down, and he hated being put in such a position. This was the side of her that ate at him the most, the ease with which she would manipulate him sometimes, forgetting that this was a relationship, a partnership. Clenching his jaw, he gathered himself to make his way down, all the while glaring at the plate of succulent food that awaited him.

COLA FLOATS lazily on the surface of the pond, his severed limbs and tail almost fully regrown. Monkeys chatter above him, and a pair of hornbills titter at the hollow of a tree. The sun has begun its descent and the clouds are a soft swirl in the deep purple sky. Akila erupts out of the water and grabs hold of the pond-side. With a groan she hurls her spear wildly into the trunk of a tree and bows her head in defeat. She hides her face between both arms, holding onto the rock, muttering through clenched jaws. 'Again! What the fuck, Cola? Trying so hard to escape to Earth, have I somehow banned myself from it? Every other stinking world lies open to me now but Earth. Kill me! Fucking kill me! What am I supposed to do?' She contemplated the clouds dawdling past. 'For two weeks now, no Earth. I don't know what I'm doing wrong. Am I being punished?' She closes her eyes and exhales, 'Fuck.'

SOMETHING IS amiss. Akila halts mid-stride, every muscle coiled, every sense alert to the slightest hint of danger. Her prey passes her mark but she is not bothered. Her spear is ready to strike in any direction and her eyes search the play of sunlight and shadows for any shape or movement that does not belong. She can only hear the leaves tussling in the easy breeze. Her nose catches something though. A faint scent of maple syrup. She knows it well and has expected it for some days now.

'Beli,' the Sentinel's voice resounds inches from her ear. She turns deliberately to face the insectoid standing a foot behind her. 'Something has come to my attention,' it says.

Akila shrugs off the tenseness in her shoulders and chops the stem of a plant.

'That you have been travelling through all the realms, searching for something.'

Akila hesitates mid-cut while stripping away the leaves. She curses herself for betraying her thoughts and resumes the cleaning until the stem is bare.

'I know what you seek.'

Akila chews on the stem for its sweet juice.

'You have heard of the place where the Beli go once they are spent. You seek passage there, don't you? You seek your escape.'

Akila spits out a tendril of stem irritating the roof of her mouth. A vice-like grip snatches hold of her neck from behind. Her body goes limp though she is fully conscious as she is dragged along the soggy jungle floor. 'I'll show you, Beli, I'll take you there. You want escape? You'll beg me for anything but.'

The insectoid dives into the water with her in its grasp. The darkness is so pitch black she can hardly believe her eyes are open. Her body is dragged out of the sour water over hard, polished rock lined with sharp edges. Then her neck is released and her body freed from the paralysis. She rolls away and uncertainly tries to find her footing in the gloom. Zorba is freed from its scabbard and she is ready to use it.

But the darkness.

It is not mere black, but the stuff of nightmares. The dark we fear. The dark without escape. The unknown dark where you can be certain of nothing. With no point of reference, her head spins; she feels nauseous and sick all over. The only sound is the swishing of the water she has climbed out of and its dribbling from her skin onto the cold floor.

'All right then, show me,' she bellows, her voice echoing through a large chamber. 'You know what I've been looking for. You've brought me here, so it's obviously no escape for me.'

'This is where the Beli are sent when their terms are complete,' the voice clicks, circling about her. 'This is your destiny, after a few more sacrifices.'

'We'll see about that.'

'You're right,' the voice admits. 'You're not seeing the full picture.'

Following a fluttering of illumination, like a tubelight, there is blinding brightness. Akila covers her face from its flash. When her eyes have adjusted to it, she realizes it is the insectoid itself that is glowing. The light casts itself upon large crystalline formations protruding from the grim obsidian floor.

'What is–' Akila begins to ask when there is a flickering of light and another lit insectoid further away, illuminating yet more stalks of crystal. Another flickering, and another, and a final one on the ceiling two hundred feet above. They are inside a subterranean cave. The crystalline formations thrust out of the ground, walls and ceiling in a thick patchwork, and a fine layer of shimmering dust coats everything.

'This place,' the Sentinel's voice speaks through an insectoid, 'is your escape.'

Akila frantically looks about. 'But where are they? What happens to them?'

'They die.'

'And rot away?'

'They are Beli, they don't rot into nothing. They are my garden here.'

Akila examines a crystal closely, wondering, 'How?'

Then she sees something in the rock. A skull, with its lower jaw detached in a distorted scream. Akila backs away into another crystal and turns to find it sprouting out of the chest of a human skeleton and blossoming into a latticework of ever-finer filaments of glass.

'Garden!' Akila cries out. 'This is a graveyard! You bring them here alive?'

'Why does that matter?'

'It matters! Goddammit, it matters more than anything that they come to this place and die alone in the darkness. It matters! It matters!'

'Their purpose is done. Why does it matter how they die?'

'Then why bring them here? Why not let them live out their lives in the jungle where they made their homes?'

'Because it is mine. These worlds are mine and will be mine alone. I am the river. I am the life.'

'What does that mean?'

'These worlds are mine, Beli. I need your kind to sustain them. That is all.'

'That is all? Fuck you!'

'Scream all you want, that is what they all do here.' The horror grips her, and the Sentinel spells it out. 'That is what you have to look forward to, Beli. Screaming in the dark.'

'No.' Akila clutches a crystal to keep from fainting. It cracks under her weight and falls away, smashing into thousands of sparkling fragments. A skull, split in two down the middle, gazes up at her from the shattered stump. Akila picks up a stone pendant from among the glittering wreckage and studies the carvings. Her eyes well up with tears because it is true. This is her fate. To die alone in this cave in the heart of the planet. Buried alive with no one to hear her cries. No one to know her resting place. This is where the Beli escape – for there is no escape for the Beli.

She runs to the black water and dives in, dashing her face on the rock underneath. Trembling in shock, she waits on her knees, blood pouring from her nose and eyebrow, staring into the gloom as the lights fade into nothing. And then all that is left is the glowing red of the blood vessels in her eyelids. Shut tight, squeezing so hard she can see stars, she sobs.

She is grabbed by the back of her neck and dragged into the water. They emerge out of a circular pool ten feet wide, walled in by massive roots, and she is carried to the top. Akila finds herself at the tree and the Sentinel waits, blade in hand. Time to die, again. The Sentinel comes to her, saying, 'What is this quest for escape? Do you really think that if you had found a way back to your world, I could not seek you out and bring you back? Do you think–' Akila snorts out some blood from her nostril, frothing red bubbles on her upper lip.

'Blah, blah, blah.'

HE PICKED up the plate of food and handled it tenderly. He could see that she was trying. The plate was a trap, but it was a gesture in her own way. She had hunted with bait all her life, and did not know how else to get his attention. The sterile beam of a flashlight lit him, and she timidly emerged from behind a tree. He squinted into the light and she moved the beam from his face. She wore a short dress that hung barely mid-thigh. Absurdly, she had pantyhose on. They stood there a while in the strangely quiet night and then a cricket chirped twenty feet away.

'Come home,' she said, in a low, hesitant voice.

Seeing her again, his body was drawn to hers with a magnetism he battled to resist. He knew he should just ignore her and go back up to the platform. All he needed was some more time. Just give me some space to work things out, he thought, but he knew to say it, or to say anything at all, would be to invite an exchange which would in all probability escalate to another fight and he did not want that. But he did not want to relent either. Some more time.

'Come home, Shy,' she said sweetly and he replied, 'Not yet.'

He turned to climb up to the platform.

'Please,' she said desperately. He took the first peg step up the side of the trunk. She stepped forward and spoke with a quivering voice. 'I'm not going back without you.'

'I'm not coming tonight.'

'Then I'm staying.'

'No, you're not.'

She flung the torch to the ground and it bounced on the grass and fell, shining up at her.

'I'm staying,' she whimpered.

He stepped back down, but spoke without facing her. 'You're going back now.'

'I'm not going anywhere.'

He turned around, his face a grim mask hiding the cheerful man she loved, and it took her aback for a moment to see such rage written on his face, directed at her. Through clenched jaws, he breathed, 'Go.'

'No.'

Her face melted under his glare. This was a first, and she did not know how to respond to him when he was this way. She hid her confusion with embarrassment, at lowering her walls and letting herself be seen as so weak. She hesitated and moved back a step, wondering whether she should go after all. Maybe this was a bad idea.

'Just go back,' he said, adding, 'please.'

'I'm staying,' she asserted.

She looked at him with pleading eyes and he glared back, and suddenly in a fit of frustration he chucked the plate and its contents into the darkness. She flinched, her brow wrinkled with despair because when he looked back at her, she saw his eyes rimmed with tears.

'I'm not going back. I'm staying here with you,' she said.

'Just leave me alone.'

'No,' she sobbed.

'Please, just go. I need some more time, Akila.' Her sob caught in her throat at the sound of his voice uttering her name.

'Why can't you understand? Why can't you do this?'

'I'm not leaving.'

'Then stay!' he yelled back. 'Stay, man, stay! Damn it! Fuck!'

She waited, head bowed, a toe anxiously digging the ground.

'I'm staying,' she sobbed.

'Then stay, goddammit,' he yelled again, a tear rolling down his cheek at last. The frustration built up in his chest like an unbearable weight. 'But you're not coming up there with me.'

She could not confront his tear-smeared face, his body trembling with hatred for her. 'I'll sleep down here,' she answered in a whisper, her hands clasped in front, fiddling nervously. Tears streamed down her red cheeks.

It upset him all the more to see her like this. 'No, you will not!' he shouted, turning her with a shove, but she wouldn't go. He watched her shoulders from behind as she sobbed silently. The back of her skirt had ridden up when he pushed her and he grimly regarded her legs, the pantyhose clumsily pulled over her panties. Three rips ran down the sides of the nylon legs. She was barefoot and the material at her feet was dirty and shredded. There was nothing left to say. He breathed heavily, totally spent. As he started his climb up the tree, he said weakly, 'Stay here, go back, do whatever you want.'

THE FATAL blow is a bright crimson with white streaks of fat under the layer of skin. The dead eyes stare at her with that moment of horror frozen forever. Akila holds onto the spear sticking out of the deer's side, looking up at the trees. Her gaze passes through the tree swathed in yellow bell-shaped blossoms. Plucked out of her surroundings, she is in the prison of her mind. She is a pet, kept within the confines of her misery to serve a master who is ruler and god to her life and universe. What sort of life is this? This is no life. It is a series of death sentences scheduled for the remainder of her life.

Akila suddenly stops what she is doing. What is she doing? Her hands are bloody and she is on her knees. Her face is wet with the deer carcass torn open before her and its insides a squashed mess. A trail of intestines is stuck to her forearm and her eyes sting from crying.

She looks down at the mutilated corpse of the deer she is dragging. Where is her spear? Who cares? The world spins about her. She falls to her knees and vomits. Her head feels as light as a balloon and her eyes want to roll backwards.

She leans over the water to wash her face and sees herself

covered in blood. The vision of Macoco at the massacre haunts her. 'Don't look at me!' he hissed. She falls back with a manic scream. The pebbles molest her skin and every breath feels uninvited. This is not living, she repeats to herself. This is not my life. My life was taken from me. It is lost forever.

This is not my life, she tells herself, sitting cross-legged on her bed in her bedroom hut, arms resting limp on either side, watching the bloody wounds on her wrists close in front of her eyes. 'Say you love me,' she whispers. 'Love me.' Her cheeks are dry now, but her eyes tell of tears.

AKILA FLOATS on the surface of the pond. The water giggles in her ears like tinker bells ringing in the empty halls of her mind. Where she should be filled with life, there is rot. The trees around her, every one of them as familiar to her as a family member, are now no more than the bars of her prison.

Cola pushes her to the side of the pond. She has been floating for hours.

THE SEA of stars twinkle in the night mist, and they bob and swirl about, faster and tighter into a whirlpool, off kilter. Akila sits up on the rock unsteadily and thinks the nausea is past until it slams its way up her oesophagus again. It scalds her chest, and vomit pours out of her. She shudders from the purge.

'Dream, damn you, dream! Dream away this nightmare. Why can't I close my eyes and just sink?' she begs herself in tears. She feels so utterly helpless and defeated. She squeezes her eyes shut, mashing the wet evidence of her anguish, gritting her teeth. Sleep! She punches the rock and her knuckles scream in pain, which angers her all the more. Rolling her eyes starward, she claws at her chest, digging into her flesh to punish herself, to cure.

'Fuck you,' she blubbers, hunched over, her shoulders shaking with her sobs. She shakes her head in distress like the old captain who knows his ship has failed him. There is nothing she can do. Akila, the stolen child, Citizen of Fourteen Worlds and the Beli that preserves us all. She pounds her chest and when it makes her cough she clubs the sides of her head with clenched fists, hard enough to make it ring with every blow. She clings on with handfuls of hair. Not tugging but hanging with the weight of her elbows, hunching her even more between her knees. There is no one to comfort her. There never will be. No one to hold her close and tell her everything would be all right. She does not even remember what it feels like. Did her father ever comfort her when she woke up from a nightmare? She thinks he did. She wants to believe that he sat by her, stroking her shoulders and back with his large hand, trying to soothe her fears. But it is like trying to recall details from a dream, and her fists clench tighter, pulling harder at her roots. Her eyes close and her lips move as though she is muttering something.

SHE WRITES in big bold letters on the rock with a blue chalk stick:

To the next Beli,
There is no hope.
Goodbye.
Akila Raina

P.S.: Take care of my salamander, Cola. Love him.

Akila arranges her blade and belt on the rock and stands naked before the pond. Cola comes up to her in the water, snapping. She tilts her head at him lovingly, her tears flowing freely. 'This is your home,' she tells him, 'but it isn't mine. I don't belong here.' Cola snaps in protest. She dives over him and vanishes in a splash. Cola stops snapping and all signs of the splash having vanished, he floats there. Cola the salamander, truly alone for the first time.

THE MORNING was quiet, touched by nothing but a cooing bird or a wayward breeze. He had tossed and turned all night, unable to settle his thoughts because of the thousand voices screaming in his head. When they faded and he felt his eyes close, an image bled through of Akila from the previous night, of her standing with her back to him. The dirty ripped pantyhose, the crumpled skirt, the clumsy fitting at her waist. She had looked so pitiful in that moment, he wished he had lunged forward and taken her into his arms, kissed away the tears from her cheeks and said everything was all right.

Lying face down, he peered through a crack between the planks. There was enough light to see Akila lying curled in a tight ball at the base of the tree. He watched her, his heart scorching a hole in his chest. After a while, she sat up. She wiped her face with her dirty hands, stood up, looking around like an amnesiac, and walked away with short stumbling steps. She never looked up.

He had reduced her to this. The magnificent Akila had begged him. He sat up, nauseous with regret, wondering whether he should have gone back with her. Was anything worth this fight? He wished he could unsee her in that state last night. She had been just as lost as he was, a person in love just like him. And she loved him. He had the most amazing woman in the world – in all the worlds – wanting him, she was the answer to all his prayers. To love someone with all his heart, and be loved in return. To be known and accepted. What right did he have to treat her this way? Even if there had been times when she was unfair to him, why had he hurt her? Shoved her away? She had let him witness her at her lowest just to have him back. He thought of everything she had done to make him feel at home. After all, he had invaded her sacred space. If she needed time alone, he could understand that.

He thought about her waiting the previous day at every meal, trying to show that she was sorry. Trying to make it up to him in the only way she knew how. Even the clothes, he realized suddenly, she had begun wearing them only after he had come. She was somehow trying to match the girls from his past. Trying to show him that this wildling was as sophisticated as they were. Didn't she know that none of that mattered in the least? That she was the light, the rain, the air he needed to live. That without her his world would be incomplete. She was Akila, the wild girl, the girl who raised herself in a jungle on another world. He loved her strengths and her faults. They combined to make the beautiful creature he had pledged to spend the rest of his life with. On nights when he would wake up and see her lying there quietly with lines of tears flowing from her shut eyes, he had sworn that he would do all that he could to make her happy. Show her love to outweigh her sorrow. He knew he had enough love to give her to do that. He may never know all that troubled her, but he was damned certain he would give her reasons to be happy.

SHE IS a spectre of ash. The whites of her eyes flash amidst the grey, searching. Her limping mind has brought her here, to a vision of her insides where the very ground tears and bleeds fire. Through a geyser of sparks touching the tormented skies she sees the titan she has been waiting for. But her eyes show no flicker of fear when it spots her and starts its charge. With every step, the stones at her feet clatter and her knees wobble from fasting for days. She sighs and her tired eyelids droop with the comfort that the end is near. Let the Sentinel try to bring her back from whatever is left, because she has made up her mind to end it here in ten seconds, and nothing can stop it now. The rock giant storms towards the naked woman with great unsteady strides, as volcanoes crumple within themselves and the ground twists and rents to give birth to flaming gashes. It smashes through the side of a cliff, plunging onto all fours, not pausing for a beat. Then at last it extends its arms and leaps at her with its crushing mass. She watches it come in that brief moment of awe before the ground dissolves about her and she can feel no more.

Consciousness is pain. Horrendous pain, like her body is being crushed in a vice, bones ground into dust. It is hot as hell. This *is* hell. Sweat drips off her twisted body, her left collarbone and arm crushed and mangled. Both her legs have bones protruding from her skin. A slow death, then. Somehow she has escaped, only to die an agonizing death. Kill me, you fucking piece of shit! Kill me!

'Stop it!' she screams, while her body convulses. Blood pours out of her mouth. It tastes rotten and comes out thick and black. She can hardly breathe through the pain. She squeezes her eyes shut and tries to clench her right fist. She realizes then that both her fists are clenched and she raises her left arm, as impossibly as a rock floating in the air. There are no breaks, no gashes. It is as it was. Her neck moves, her collarbone fixed.

She can feel her toes wiggling. She has healed. She sits up with awkward relief, shaking her head and laughing at the joke that is her life. And then she stops. She is here to die and yet, here she is, sitting up and trying to pluck the stone poking her butt out of the way. 'Where did that giant go?' she wonders aloud.

'I haven't gone anywhere.'

With a shriek, she discovers that she is seated in a gigantic palm. The titan lies on his side, his body curled around her. A face many times her height gazes at her with gentle molten eyes. The massive eyelids blink abruptly, startling her to her feet and propelling her body backwards. She twists her ankle badly and stumbles off the palm into a chasm. Barely over the edge and the gust of rising hot air hits her, singeing the fine hair on her arms and legs to wisps in the wind. Her whole body bakes as she falls into the canyon towards the blistering light below. Then, with a smack, she hits rock. Her breath, hoarse and hard in the sucking heat, tears at the parched lining of her throat and lungs. Her face is a bloody mess with a smashed left cheek. She shakes, surrounded by the grumbling hiss of the hot air dancing in the haze about her while she is preserved by a giant hand.

'Help us,' a voice beckons over the deafening crackle of rock burning rock, and she gazes up into the surprisingly yearning face of stone. A face she has had nightmares of for the past decade. His lips move and she hears him say to her, 'We have been trapped here for so long. Connect.'

SHE WAS still standing by the pond when he arrived. Still in that pitiful pantyhose and the short grass-stained dress, staring blankly off to the far side. The sinews on her back flexed when she heard him. 'I shouldn't have treated you that way last night,' he said. She turned to face him uncertainly as he approached her. He fell to his knees and hugged her hips, crushing his face into her abdomen and sobbing. She looked at him and the anguish on her face was replaced by a warm welcoming smile. She knew they had a lot to sift through, but they had come through it. She placed her hand on his head, caressing his hair with her thumb, choosing to forget all else for a few moments.

THEY LAY in bed, slivers of light cutting across their backs and faces. Looking sidelong into each other's eyes, noticing things for the first time. The things they had pushed away sparkled again like newly discovered gems. The spots on her face that he knew like stars on a navigator's chart. All the little marks on his face that she adored. The blemish in his eye, the dimple in his cheek.

THEY FISHED on a boulder in the centre of a modest lake as dusk settled. They would have to start back far home soon. Macoco yawned his massive jaws and flexed his wings, politely ignoring them from the shore. 'What the – I almost forgot!' Shyam cried out all at once, and wedged his fishing rod in a nook in the rock. He reached into his shorts pocket and pulled out a thick black thread.

'What is it?' she asked, feigning suspicion. 'Happy birthday, my lovely,' he said, holding out his open palm with her present. She took the locket and thread with excited fingers. She examined the features, weather-worn over the years since she had flung it into the jungle in heartbreak. He was thrilled to have caught her by surprise.

'It's a stone I picked up in the jungle a few weeks ago. I kept it because I remembered what you had said about your favourite dream. It's uncanny, isn't it, how much the stone looks like a dolphin, without the tail, of course.' Akila held it for a moment longer, then she leaned forward and kissed him. As he made the knot behind her neck, she watched the ripples in the water. A bird flew over and its reflection stretched and danced, transformed into familiar shapes from her mind, fleeting in the reflected sky. Afterwards, they made slow love on the boulder. The float on Akila's unattended fishing rod bobbed under the water with a fish on the line.

SEATED CROSS-LEGGED atop the folded knee of the living hillside that moved and spoke, she feels the relief of not keeping her guard up constantly. There is nothing she can do if he wishes to harm her. 'What do you think I can do for you?' she asks.

'Are you real?' Lips of rock move with the words. And those eyes, those burning eyes, study her, unblinking.

'Are you?' she asks in return. 'Is this place as real as it feels or is it just the dream diarrhoea of a mad-fucking-mad mind? You tell me, Rockman.'

He does not reply and she can't tell what he is thinking.

'Actually, wait,' she shouts out, to be heard over the lava exploding into blazing flowerpots. She croaks and spits out some ash. Then she clears her throat and tries again. 'Why have you attacked me in the past?'

'When your memories fade and dreams have more substance, and then one day your wish is answered with a manifestation, do you not chase after it? Would you not chase that hope down to the ends of the world seeing that the rest of your kind have gone insane from isolation? They do nothing but wail at the skies for this curse to end.'

'You broke my bones. I could have died.'

'I tried to touch a dream. And I did.'

'A little too hard.'

'A little too hard.'

Akila marvels at the giant. She has ridden on flying dolphins and the chimera she calls the Fenek, swum with giant salamanders and ridden giant bugs and so much more. But never did she imagine she would one day be chatting with a titan. Maybe this is the beginning of a friendship. The giant throws her a warm smile. 'That is my hope.'

'You can read my thoughts?'

'I'm not eavesdropping, if that's what is upsetting you. We are connected on a level far deeper than mere language.'

'That's not right. You can't just–'

'I'm not stealing anything, Akila. I'm not trying to violate your privacy. I can sense you cringing at the thought of it.'

Akila bites her lower lip and snorts at her helplessness.

'Violate my privacy? You are violating me! They're my thoughts! They're all I have! In this place all I have are these thoughts, wild and ill-tempered as they are. They are mine! Mine to have and to know. Mine to hide or decide to show. They are *my* fucking thoughts!' She weeps, trying to pry loose a slate in the titan's rock skin as some small revenge. 'I may have lost my freedom and my life may be the plaything of another, but these thoughts are my secret friends in the dark and I will not lose that sanctuary.' She leans on her arms, despondent.

'I don't take and I don't give, Akila,' the titan says slowly. 'I share just as you have. We are connecting, you and I.'

'I don't want to connect with you! And you have no right to connect with me!'

'We share ourselves with each other.'

'Why should I share myself with you?'

'For the connection.'

Akila scrutinizes him with glassy eyes.

'Why should I trust you? What do you want from me?'

'To connect.'

'All you creatures want is to rip me into little pieces and nibble at me for eternity while I heal and heal and never die! Crush me into a pulp and see me rise from nothing! Fuck! I am not your saviour, you pile of rock! I am stuck here just like you are.'

'I have accepted that there is no escape for us. But as this shell of a world crumbles and rolls us into the deep, all I ask is to connect with you for a while.'

The hard crust on her lips is cracked and it hurts to speak. 'Connect, connect, what are you talking about?' she beseeches the giant.

'You are human. You should know,' he replies.

'I'm human, so what?'

'You're the one with the gift.'

'What the fuck are you talking about?'

'We are all part of nature. You and I, the ground, the trees and the water. But you, as a human, you can connect with everything. While we are limited to communicating thoughts, you can connect deeper. That is your gift. While the rest of nature follows the course of time amidst the network of life, you can behold it.' She does not understand, but is intrigued that she may have untapped powers within her. Perhaps there is more to her than the imprisoned little girl.

'Show me,' she urges.

'See.'

'Show me.'

'We are connected. You can see.'

'All I can see is your stupid face.'

'Then close your eyes and see.'

The titan unfurls his hand beside her to shield her from an explosion. Akila is disappointed at herself for insulting him. There is no need for that. It is just as she has feared for some time now, that she has forgotten how to be with others, and that terrifies her. She does not want to be this thing that prefers loneliness to company. She wants company, to share herself. She wants to experience what another person can give her. The inner self of another. She has not had that since Fin. But that was before she understood, before she knew she should embrace what she had until she lost it. She was so young that the excitement of the new, of realizing she was in love, had intoxicated her and she had been blind to the inner things. She is certain that if they had more time, she would have seen it and felt it. But the past can't be rewritten.

She looks down at her open palms, black with ash, and beyond, at the coarse rock-surface of the giant hand. Connect. Can I feel him? Did he say we're connected already or that he wants to connect? I'm pretty sure he said both, which is confusing. But I want, no, I *need* to see if there's more to my life than being a Beli. What he is saying makes no sense. Maybe he has gone insane in this hellhole. Then what better company for him than me? Show me that I am not alone. If I can connect, and I can find something hidden there … She deliberates and says aloud, 'Show me the way.' She leans forward and puts her right hand on the palm shielding her from the flames. She closes her eyes, desperate for hope.

SHYAM HAD the hog on his shoulders and Akila brought up the rear with two spears and a bow. 'But it doesn't make sense,' Shyam said. 'How can a living creature alter matter on a molecular level to create these worlds, one atop the other?'

'That is what living things do. We alter matter.'

'We do?'

'Think about it, Shy. We eat food and dismantle its molecular structure through digestion into single molecules of glucose, from which we suck out electrons. We breathe air and extract the molecules we need and breathe out the rest. Snakes, newts, jellyfish and some bacteria manufacture toxins on a molecular level that man could never have dreamt up. Bats can engineer sound frequencies. There are bacteria that eat and breathe electricity. The world of science is discovering crazy facts never associated with living things. What makes you think there can't be a creature out there in the universe that can alter the state of quantum particles for its purpose?'

'A creature called God?'

'Wow, that's offensive to a whole bunch of people. Not me, of course.'

They shared a chuckle over their running in-joke. Akila resumed, 'There's no doubt in my mind that it is possible for this creature to exist. It may be an evolutionary step up the ladder or a mutation reacting to an exceptional circumstance. How it got to Earth is another question. Hitched a ride on a meteor or a comet? Or was it brought here by intelligent life? There are theories that life was brought to Earth, naturally or unnaturally. But that's not the question that plagues me.'

'Then what is?'

'All this time, rather than wonder why this creature is here on Earth, I've wanted to know – why is it doing this?' She gestured emphatically at her surroundings.

AN INKY blackness. The rumbling ground and crackling rivers of lava fade into the distance until her hearing is as empty as her sight.

'I can't see anything,' she admits impatiently.

There is no response.

'Are you there? I can't hear you! What's happening?'

'I'm here. Calm down.' The giant's voice reaches into her.

'I'm calm, you motherfucker, I'm calm. What am I supposed to do?'

'You will see something.'

'There's nothing. It's just black. Emptiness.'

'Emptiness is the key. Look for it.'

'What?'

'Don't speak. I'll guide you through it. It's been tens of thousands of years, but I remember the way.'

She is floating in oblivion.

'You will see a point of light.'

She can't see anything.

'It will be like a lone star in a sea of black.'

There. She can see it now.

'See it pulse. You can feel the pulse. You can hear the pulse. Bright and dim, bright and dim. And then it seeps back into the blackness.'

She longs for the point of light to return. Don't leave me here alone.

'Gather yourself.'

'For what?'

'The light.'

A purge of light emanates from the star, swallowing the entire blackness, until she can no longer recall the bleak solitude. There is only the warmth of the light.

'Swim in the light. Feel your body bathing in it. Your

face, your arms, your fingers, your chest, your stomach, your genitals, your thighs, your feet, your toes.'

She can feel her whole body, more than just a sum of its parts. She holds her hand in front of her face but the light is so blinding she can see it through her flesh.

'Now swim to the side. That's right. You can feel your arms and legs propelling you through the light. And then you are outside it. You can see the light for the beam it is, a stream in the blackness. Swim further back. The stream breaks into other streams, and those into more streams.'

The streams form the rough shape of the giant's hand she is touching.

'That's right. This is me. The energy running through my being.'

'I can feel you.'

'I can feel you.'

She swims further back and sees his entire body, lined with the streams, and she realizes she is looking at his central nervous system. But a giant made of rock can't have a central nervous system, can it? He must have something akin to it to feel. His lonely figure is surrounded by blackness.

'Are there no other connections?'

'You see only me?'

'Yes.'

'Then I am right. This is a dead world.'

'You mean there is no network?'

'I couldn't have seen it even if there was one, but I just wanted to feel it, as I used to. To feel a part of something. A part of everything. Connected.'

She can see the swirling vortex of light at his heaving chest, and then the despair he feels drenches her soul.

'I'm sorry,' she sighs.

'My memories have become the seashore of dreams, a little washed away with every passing tide. There was a time when we reached up and caressed whales in the sky, and soothed volcanoes as we were born to do. We roamed the world, and often came to spend time near humans.'

'There were humans here?' she wonders aloud.

'Here? No, this is an alien place. This is our cage.'

'Cage? You are not of this world?'

'We were ripped from our realm and kept in this place, where the planet screams and it does not hear our songs to soothe it. This world is a phantom with no heart. This is our prison of solitude. We are alone here.'

'So, you were taken from my world just as I was?'

'Yes.'

'Why?'

'As punishment.'

'Punishment for what?'

'For loving you. For loving humankind.'

'What was wrong in loving us?'

'Loving nature's gift to life on Earth. Loving Earth's shepherd, its guardian.'

'Punished by who?'

'Punished by the stranger. Don't you know?'

'What stranger?'

'The stranger from the stars.'

'NOW, HOW do I say this?'

'Nicely,' Akila suggested.

'I'm nice.'

'Correction. You can be nice.'

'Hey, I am a nice guy.'

'Ok, nice guy, go ahead. What do you have to say?'

'Your pictures suck.'

She huddled closer with her DSLR, for a tight close-up of his comical sneer, and clicked a stuttering shutter release. Shyam posed on the Mez, overlooking Machu Falls in his swimming trunks and an unbuttoned cotton shirt. He had on a straw hat and leaned over a neglected paperback.

'I blame my model. Such a diva.'

'Suddenly everyone thinks they're the new Helmut Newton or Annie Liebovitz.'

'Shut up and read your book.'

'I'm pretending, my dear. When I pretend, I don't do, I pretend. I'm a professional.'

She rolled her eyes and said, 'Then pretend to shut up and read.'

'Not sure the hat is a good idea. It's going to underexpose my face, you know.'

'I know.'

'And you've compensated for that?'

'I'm taking 3-shot HDRs so I can pick it up in post.'

'HDR for a portrait?'

She scowled at him with a disdainful hand perched on her hip. He pouted, relenting. 'Yeah, okay mein fraulien, shut up and read.'

Akila clicked more shots and backed away to fiddle with some settings. Busy navigating the buttons, she offhandedly suggested, 'Now let's try some without the hat.'

He threw off the hat and thrust his tongue out at the winking lens.

THE MONKEYS sit quietly, high up in the branches, their golden fur glistening in the afternoon sun. Akila sits among them, lounging back on a series of branches that suit the purpose perfectly. Shadows sway over her naked bronzed skin, and a monkey adorns her arm like a pagan idol. A couple groom one another on her splayed thigh. They are so little she barely notices them on her. Their large green eyes are restless and ever watchful.

* * *

'I LONG for blue. The blue of the sky. The blue of the ocean. When I think of my home, blue is what comes to mind. You call her Earth. But in my mind, as the centuries crept into millennia, and millennia into epochs, I have always known her as the Blue.'

'So have I,' says Akila, standing on his shoulder and holding onto his neck as the giant strolls across the devastated landscape.

'What is your name?' she asks him.

'Name?'

'Don't you have one?'

'My name.' He stops walking and stares blankly into the distance.

'You called me by mine, which is Akila. What do I call you?'

'My name?'

She can sense the anguish growing within him. The shock of having forgotten.

'There was a name,' he mumbles. 'I was called that, a label my own. Given to me by others, but one that I loved the same as a limb. It became a part of me. It sheltered me from being forgotten by others, and yet, I have lost it with time. I did not know how delicate a thing it is, a name. One that survives only when others think of you.'

He remains still for a minute or two, head bowed in contemplation, until at last he speaks. 'I'm sorry, Akila. It has left me.'

He resumes walking as he speaks. 'Give me one. One that has meaning for you. What does your name mean?'

'Akila means wisdom, but it also means the Universe.'

'A name like that. One that will give me spirit as I learn to cherish it.'

'Can you give me some time to think about it?'

'I have time.'

'Aren't we travelling far?'

'I suppose it would be far for you.'

Akila nods, realizing that it must be a brief stroll for a titan.

'You are sure there is water there? Hard to imagine any surviving in this world.'

'Water is precious. Water is life. The stranger couldn't have made these worlds without it.'

'I want to know more about that. I want to know how a creature managed to create these many worlds upon each other. I don't understand how that is possible.'

'Then try to understand.'

She laughs. 'You make it sound easy.'

'You have the tools. Curiosity, the ability to think and an imagination. What other tools do you need?'

It has gotten cooler with the rivers of lava and screaming volcanoes behind them. The ground is black and rough, cracked in the heat of an ancient time, and up ahead, she can see the circular dark pool of water he had described.

'Why isn't this place burning and breaking?' she asks.

'The stranger had its nest here when we first arrived. It

lived in a tree with spreading roots at the centre of this water.'

'I've seen the tree. There is one on every world.'

'Not here. We were so enraged at the imprisonment, we ripped it out and crushed it into pieces. Then it came again and we did the same, and it has stayed away since.'

'It is somewhere on this world. That I'm fucking sure of.'

The giant reaches the water, surveys the eerie pool in disgust.

'How will I find you again?' she asks him, affectionately touching his neck.

'I will be here,' he answers.

'You don't have to wait in this horrid place.'

'Knowing the water will bring you back, it is no longer horrid. You make it beautiful.'

Akila takes an elegant swan-dive off his shoulder.

* * *

THE BRANCHES about her are filled with the golden monkeys, idling in the shade. From her gold-draped throne she casts a piercing stare at a swaying branch. There is a pink-gowned flower with flowing petals. But she does not see the flower, only the idea forming in her mind. I must stop seeing this as an imprisonment. I am no helpless hostage. These worlds don't have power over me. I have power over them. These worlds belong to me. And if they don't know it yet, I'll give them the news. This mad world deserves a mad queen.

* * *

AKILA CLINGS onto the side of the vast circular pool, looking about for her titan. She finds him waiting as he had promised.

Kneeling, sitting back on his feet with a straight back, attentively observing the pool. She does not know whether she should disturb his repose. The fire in his eyes ignites and his shoulders suddenly stir. Akila holds up a hand, bellowing, 'I'm sorry I took a couple of days to come back.'

'Two days is a hair's breadth to the body of time I have waited for one like you, Akila. I can't remember the last time I felt so alive. Every time my eyes closed and I sank into a dream, I feared this was the dream and I was waking from it. I stared at the water that had swallowed you out of existence and I saw no life. Only dreams vanish like you did.'

'You don't know what a Beli is, do you?'

'Beli? Sacrifice?'

'Yes.'

'What about a sacrifice?'

'I am the Beli.'

'I don't understand.'

'Before I tell you my story, tell me yours.'

'But first my name. Tell me my name.'

Her sun-baked granite eyes twinkle and she announces, 'Sholay.'

* * *

AKILA RESTS her eyes and lays her head back upon the branch. The monkeys begin to fuss in the tree. Then they stop their twittering and tentatively gather around Akila. They scramble over her, and soon become a restless golden mass covering her body. The leaves of the tree chime like bells in the wind and the monkeys stop stirring, curling into furry balls that purr in a united hum of peaceful ecstasy. Akila is lost among the beams of light lining the branches of the tree. She senses the life force flowing within it and flowing into it. The moisture in the soil being absorbed, the pores on its bark drinking it in, the roots stretching, growing, reaching out. The hair-like tendrils digging into the soil, exploring. The life force issuing out. The moisture bubbling within the tree, flowing up the trunk, meeting the leaves and being absorbed as energy. The oxygen seeping out of the leaves into the atmosphere like an exhalation.

She discovered on her very first connection that this world too lacks a life force, though it harbours plentiful life. It is flooding with life. And they are all connected. The ants that crawl down the trunk, threading through the jungle along the highways only they can sense. The maggots in the carcass. The lipids on stems. Life, connected. She can feel it.

The ecstasy washes over Akila, through every nerve fibre in her being, filling her up. Filling every void. She is riding it. The power of it. She feels the power. The power of life surging like a rushing river. Inhaling, eating, shitting, killing, dying, exhaling, climbing, sleeping, running, hunting, hiding, crawling, growing, drinking, swimming, pissing, birthing, waiting, blinking, digging. Fuck! The rush of it!

AKILA SAT on his chest, palms touching him, as Sholay lay supine with arms outstretched. They were serenely connected until his glowing eyes shot open and he struggled for breath. Akila tried to calm him. 'What is it? What's wrong?'

He lifted her up in his palm and sat up, holding her in front of his face so he could see into hers. He said softly, 'You know.'

'Know what?' she asked.

'Or you suspect.'

She fell silent.

'Why didn't you just tell me, Akila?'

'I had to be sure.'

'I felt your child. The seed growing inside you.'

She smiled wearily, nodding.

'You should not connect as much, I don't know what effects it may have on the development of the child at this stage.'

'Oh.' She considered what he said.

'Can I ask you something?' he ventured, altering his tone.

'Sure.'

'It's something I have no right asking.'

'Ask, Sholay.'

'My confirmation,' he said slowly. 'Was it the one you were seeking?'

AKILA STANDS up in the mud. The slime hangs off her in dozens of elastic threads stretching to the surface of the brownish-grey muck. The T-shirt sticks to her skin and the stuff oozes off her shoulders. She is thigh-deep in it, and the stink. It is all she can sense. So thick she can taste the stink. Repellently sweet and sour with an aftertaste swirling at the back of her tongue. What world is this? White webs like cotton candy cover large stretches of the lake, strands strung between dwarfing gnarled trees. Snorting loudly, two hairy beasts burst out of the webbing and flounder across the muck in front of her. One stops and stares at her with its tiny recessed eyes, the snout twitching, the fur thick in clumps with the grime. A boar? They are not tusked like the pictures she has seen in her Britannica books. The ground beneath her feet is a layer of sticky gel, squishing between her toes. Her foot slips and she adjusts to right herself. The wild hog dashes away with a squeal, splashing the muck and churning up things from the bottom. Bits of white and yellow plastic show with English lettering on them.

Earth. She's back on Earth. She had thought it was barred to her, but somehow, here she is again. But where is 'here'? It is hot. This is not the Nilgiris. This is far away from school. From everything she is familiar with. Wading through the filth, she reaches the muddy shore and finds a path in the tall grass that runs past two domed structures showing their age. She travels down the path through the forest with no sign of people anywhere. Then she spots what looks like the back of a sign and a dirt road running towards a larger archaic structure. Bathed in slime, she slops her way to the other side of the board. It says 'Mehrauli Archaeological Park' in peeling white lettering, in English and Hindi. Where the fuck is Mehrauli? Already feeling the effects of nausea, she cannot tell whether it is from her usual Earth-sickness that limits her time here or the sewage she has climbed out of. What the hell is she doing here? She wants to explore further, but her head is spinning with a dull, throbbing sensation.

She starts back towards the garbage when the sound of laughter stops her in her tracks. It has been so long since she heard another human laugh. It is a group walking up the road towards the sign. They sound like young people gaily chatting away. She desperately wants to see them but her body compels her to return to the lake. Strangely, the headache has eased now, though the nausea has gotten worse. It is the fucking garbage. She must have swallowed some of it when she splashed through and she cannot delay any more. Running like a mad woman, she leaps into the lake of filth.

THE SALT water stings her eyes as the wave crashes over her, rolling her in the sandy surf. Kneeling in the powder she feels the water receding and she crawls towards the beach on her hands and knees, letting her stomach purge itself when required. The next wave barely brushes her and yet she collapses onto her side. The spasms in her abdomen are incredibly painful. She vomits some more until there is nothing left to come out, and then she vomits bile. Successive waves wash the vomit away and the beach is flawless once again. Returning to Earth after an intermission was not as magical as she had hoped it would be.

The smell and taste of garbage still haunt her mouth. She crawls into the oncoming wave and savagely blows out her nose in the saline water. Sand coats the inside of her mouth and throat and makes her gag. But the stink has gone. She worms her way up the beach and lies where the most adamant waves can only kiss her toes.

Earth. She cannot wait to go back. Pulling the stained T-shirt off, she throws it to one side in despair. Why did things have to change? She had longed to see the Principal's bungalow again. It was her closest connection to her father even though he no longer lived there, but now she appears to be tied to this place called Mehrauli. A dirty, filthy place. What kind of park do they dump garbage in? She sits up, glad she did not pollute her pond with it. Here, it will be lost in the waves. She needs to try again. She longs to see other humans. Hear them laugh. Eavesdrop on conversations. Be an invisible member of their groups as she had been for many years before. She will wait for a day, she decides, and try again, hopefully entering through a less toxic route.

AKILA LOOKS about in the heavy rain, knee-deep on a flooded street packed with traffic. Car horns blare ceaselessly as engines growl and choke in the water. At least this is clean rainwater,

Akila consoles herself, before spotting the open manhole spewing out a brown river. Is she still in Mehrauli? She shields her eyes, searching the beating rain for a clue. A street sign is covered over with posters, mug shots of grinning men in Nehru caps with bright yellow writing at the top and bottom. Hindi posters mean she is in North India. It has been eleven years since she spoke in Hindi and though it was the closest thing she had to a mother-tongue, none of it is coming to her now.

A bus stands in the traffic that has begun to slither forward, one hard-earned inch at a time. The battered front fender is barely hanging on and the dents across its side show evidence of the dog-eat-dog world of rash driving it survives in. The faded green paint shows 'Stage Carriage' in yellow and after it she reads 'Delhi Transport Corporation'.

Delhi! Somehow her focal point on Earth has shifted from Ooty in the south to Delhi in the north, a discrepancy of almost three thousand kilometres. What could have triggered the change, and why now? What connection does she have with Delhi? None, as far as she knows, except for the time she had come here when she was six or seven, and spent a month's vacation at her Bua's house in a place called New Friends Colony. The name had stayed with her because of her utter disappointment at not making any new friends during her stay. Delhi kids were foul-mouthed jerks, she recalled. In her first week she had thought 'behenchod' was a traditional Delhi greeting among boys her age.

She laughs to herself, the rain trickling down her face, at her father's reaction to her use of it. The other kids, of course, knew better than to use it in front of adults and she had gotten a few whacks on the bum and legs that day, perplexed as to why. It was not until a couple of years later, when she was in boarding school, that her best friend Monica from Amritsar told her it meant 'sister-fucker'. Boarding schools are great centres of research and learning where curse words are concerned and she was always a quick study.

Thinking about that holiday in Delhi a decade-and-a-half ago, her heart grows flush with a new hope that perhaps she is here in Delhi because of her father. That must be her connection. She can see her father again! Akila spins about frantically, looking for help to get started. She wants to run to him, ten miles or more, however far she has to. But she does not know the way. And invisible to this world, she cannot ask for directions.

AKILA SPLASHED down in a stream. She picked up her spear and hunting bow, and arrows from the tree where they waited for her return. She chewed on her bottom lip and looked around the jungle in a daze. Her eyes studied the shadows for any recognizable silhouette but she could not steady her nerves enough to concentrate. With a muffled cry she hurled the spear blindly, feeling the satisfaction of hearing it thud into wood. As she gazed down at her stomach, a warm smile dampened by sadness shone upon her downcast face. She rubbed her abdomen with adolescent naivety, a drop of water hanging on the end of her nose.

SHE ROLLS out of a puddle, bruising her body on the dirt path. She has gotten used to the pain of splash-throughs over the years. But the stench here is another matter. She is in the centre of a path lined with a bristly short hedge on one side and a narrow concrete trench on the other. A fissure in the trench is spilling water, leading to the immense puddle she is sitting in. That is the stink rotting the inside of her nostrils and burning its way down her throat. The pungent vinegary stench of concentrated urine and whatever else. At the trench, she peers into the swiftly flowing whisky-brown stream.

Holding up her arms to avoid them sticking to her sides, she does the mummy shamble to a long rubber hose spread across the adjacent lawn. She pours it over her head for five whole minutes before she is content. A domed monument looms discreetly among the trees. Another park then, she muses, or the same one? Though something feels different. She is standing in wet grass as she has done on many worlds but here it is not just the unyielding hardness of the ground with the mat of soft, crunchy grass squishing audibly as she shifts her stance. She gets down on her hands and knees, crawling around, letting her fingers spread and push through the grass to the ground underneath. It is not enough. She rushes to the makeshift cricket pitch and sits, legs folded, upon the naked ground. The wind picks up, and she takes in a great breath of it. The dry summer leaves rustle about her with apprehension. Her eyelids droop without instruction and she gives in to her hunger.

She feels the connection looming. I am the shepherd. All thought ceases as her roots dig deep into the wellspring of energy within the dry soil. The invigorating honey sweetness of it flows through her veins, the struggle with the horseradish burning in her nostrils, her hair follicles tingling. This is not ecstasy. This is what no single word or even a torrent of them could articulate.

The earth is drawing her in and she is pulling the earth within her. Deep inside her. You are a part of me. Penetrate the very core of me. Take me as I swallow all that you are. The heat of it flows inside her, filling her, mixing into her. Dripping out of her. Her body quakes and the universe somersaults with the chaotic introduction of something she cannot yet contain. She comes out of her trance, gasping for air as the wind again tickles the trees.

Three stray dogs have cuddled up against her legs. They remind her of her German Shepherd in his alpha male posture as he strutted beside her father on his early morning strolls. Scrupulously dressed, his tall, lanky frame leaning against the gate as he waved to her.

Her father! She needs to focus on finding him, wherever he is. She scrambles to her feet. I must not get distracted. There is enough time for connecting later, though it feels amazing. She wants to lie on the ground and grind her hips into the soil, to feel that rapture once more. Her mind tries to recount it but it cannot replay what it felt only a minute before. All that remains are the descriptions in her memory and the hunger of her nerve endings pleading that she taste it again.

The image of her father at the gate flashes in her mind and she moves her feet to keep them from connecting and sucking her inward. A human voice sounds nearby and she hunts it out from behind a large tree. A man in his thirties in formal attire is talking on a cellphone, a briefcase nestled on his lap. She had seen the gadgets years ago, before she was barred from Earth. 'No, not yet,' the man drawls into the phone. 'We're still finishing the project, so I'll only be leaving for home in an hour or so. I'll call you when I'm on my way, Madhu. Okay? Yeah. Ok then, chalo.' He sticks his tongue out at the phone and sits back with an open Wilbur Smith paperback. A cellphone, Akila muses, bending closer to its illuminated green screen. I'll need modern stuff like this if I'm going to find my father. My travel time and range are limited, so I'll need whatever it takes.

'I MAY be a little late,' she called out as she left the pond.

'Why?'

'I'm going to go get some pokurus.' Shyam stood looking from the doorway of the hut above. He stretched, speaking through his yawn. 'Oh, wow! That's a treat! I'll come with you. I feel bad about not coming out hunting the last few days. It's this damn knot in my shoulder ... it's been painful as fuck, but I feel much better today.'

'Naah, rest it today as well, so it'll heal fully. No point aggravating it. Doctor's orders, beta.'

Shyam offered her a left-handed salute with a smile. 'Looking forward to the pokurus, memsahib!'

She headed off into the jungle with a wave, jogging most of the way, her breath steady. The pokuru tree greeted her with bountiful branches of the prickly bright-orange fruit, hanging like Christmas ornaments.

In five minutes the two bags on the ground were full. She touched the tree trunk with both hands and the guilt she felt at connecting, ever since Sholay had cautioned her against it, vanished in a starburst of ecstasy. The rush of energy was invigorating and she drank it in, hunting for more. It was not a fraction of what she used to get on Earth, but it would have to do. She sought out the ant nest high in the branches, the birds pecking the highest fruits, the maggots in a damp hollow. She felt them, she felt the burning force of life, and she touched the flames licking at her senses.

A LARGE leather handbag, a backpack and a laptop bag are huddled together to one side. Their contents are neatly arranged in little families across the Mez. A laptop with its charger and a mouse, with a rolled up cable. A bunch of writable CDs and a portable hand disk with its adapter cable. Two cell phones with one charging cable. A couple of novels. A hefty academic book with assorted acronyms on the brightly coloured cover. Pens. Some notebooks and other miscellaneous items. Akila squats on a rock, going through a booklet. The spilled contents of a plastic folder litter the pebbles beside her. What looks like an extension for a telephone cable, a couple of discs including the Windows Installation DVD and a pile of manuals. She opens the manual and trouble-shooter guide for Windows to the table of contents and runs down the daunting list.

THE STONE steps are uneven and she has to be mindful of them as she makes her way up. The walls of the medieval step reservoir rise up four storeys, with a narrow ledge running along at each level. Thankfully they are filled with rainwater to a level or so because even the very idea of splashing down in the garbage lake makes her stomach turn. The street outside is lined by short-stacked buildings on one side and the name Mehrauli shows up again. Why Mehrauli? A couple of times she has been in a Green Park residential colony but it is usually back here. She is trying to make sense of it since it cannot be random. She follows the road to the right, deep in thought.

Mehrauli is a locality in south Delhi, so why here, if her father is in New Friends Colony with his sister, in another part of the city? It is crowded, dusty as hell, strewn with garbage, and it stinks, but she loves being among people again, the more the merrier. However, she cannot picture her erudite, clean to-the-point-of-mild-OCD father having a place here.

Maybe there is more to Mehrauli than she has seen so far. The prospect of exploring excites her no end. She comes out onto a busy junction with honking cars and autorickshaws. A large domed Mughal structure squats across the street, its walls strewn with idling oafs and monkeys enjoying a chaotic traffic jam. Three city buses are trying to make the severe turn, exiting and entering the ill-positioned Mehrauli bus station without yielding an inch either way. With every step Akila feels the energy coursing through the ground, pulsing and surging with light. Although she can sense the onset of nausea and a headache, her rush rises to a sensational high. So many people! A beehive of energy, all busy with their lives. Riding the high, she is prepared to practice her new hobby and go tech-picking.

TWO PILES of IT magazines act as her footrest. Three laptops lie on the rock beside her and another whirs on her lap with her keen eyes focused on the screen. She manoeuvres the mouse with deft flicks of her wrist on a magazine. 'I bet the apartment building I got this one from has some wireless networks. I've read so much about the Internet and what I can do on it. There's even a website which shows satellite images of anywhere in the world. And everyone is connected by now, so I'm sure Papa is too. His address must be online. I'll find him, Cola.'

Cola's head floats on the surface nearby, grown considerably larger. Akila chews her bottom lip as her eyes strain on the pixels. The vivid image on the screen is of a muscular man inserting his engorged penis in the vagina of a woman lying spread-eagled, her lips open in orgasmic bliss. The image flips to another pornographic still, a close-up of a pretty Japanese girl beaming into the lens with her face caked in semen and a penis resting on her cheek. Akila's left leg moves off the magazines while her hand moves between her thighs.

TWO MOTHS and a bee dance to the hum of a tubelight above her. The concrete floor of the garage is coarse with dirt and Akila hunches against the wall with her laptop connected to the power outlet. She searches for available wireless networks in the building, finding two, of which one does not have password protection. She punches the air in victory. The web browser opens to a search engine set as its default page and she claps with excitement. She is no tribesman witnessing technology for the first time. She has read the manuals, the books, the magazines and she has done her research. More than the basics. She has the anticipation of an astronaut before her first spaceflight.

The first thing she types into the search bar is her father's name. Seeing it there with the blinking cursor urging her on, she is filled with hope. He is somewhere in Mehrauli and I will find him. The mouse arrow clicks the search button and the results are unveiled a couple of seconds later.

They are underwhelming at best, since most of the results are based on either his first or last name, resulting in a totally arbitrary list. She should have realized that her father would not be tech-savvy. He is probably struggling with his email account. It is 2005, and all this incredible technology at her fingertips cannot help her find the person who means the most to her.

The Internet is our attempt to recreate what nature once gifted us, she thought. Although now lost or forgotten, it still rules us, this need to feel connected with others, and even beyond, to feel connected to everything. Scouring down the second page of search results, she finds a newspaper article mentioning the appointment of a new headmaster. She opens the link because there is no doubt in her mind that it is her father. She needs to prove to herself that he has not passed away. A lonely old man tortured over the loss of his daughter in a horrible tragedy, the grief eating away at him until he dies. But this is proof he is well and keeping busy at what he was best at, taking care of an entire school of children. The article is brief, simply stating that Mr Raina is the newly appointed headmaster of an all boys' school in Darjeeling. And that is far away.

THE WIND rushed downstream, over Picchu Falls, and stroked the pond. A bird cooed in the jungle and another answered with a distant call. Akila lay on the Mez, her ribcage rising and falling softly. Shyam spied on her through the bushes. He gently pushed through them and stood by the pond. Her skin wore the amber rays of the sun and his eyes roamed over her splayed legs, her hair dancing on the rock with the cool and loving wind.

'What's wrong?' he asked. His voice came out louder than he had intended, but she did not startle. Of course she would not. She had probably heard him watching all along.

He sat next to her and caressed the rock as though it was her, just an inch away from where she lay. He touched her arm and her eyes slid open. Her lips softened into a smile and a tear lost itself in her hair. He did not have to ask and she did not have to explain. He sensed it, the change in her.

AKILA PERFORMS routine maintenance on the huts. She stretches cords for the rope bridge between trees.

SHOLAY IS on his back, hands behind his head, and Akila lies sprawled on his chest, snoring loudly.

SHE SITS on her bed, back to the wall, laptop on her thighs, opening a variety of programmes from the menu to explore how they function. The empty husks of half a dozen jamblis litter the ruffled bed sheet. A bowl of unfinished salad balances on the edge of the bed in the sunlight streaming in through the doorway.

AKILA LIES on the floor, bathed in the moonlight, her legs stretched. Her head lies listlessly to the side, eyes gazing at the moon shining like a headlight on high beam. She blinks awake even though she was never asleep, thinking about something, but she cannot remember what. A thought carried away in the breeze. Her fingers are tucked between her thighs for warmth and she draws them out to examine the little finger of her left hand that had been against her labia. It is wet. Was she masturbating without even realizing it? She grins to herself and shrugs it off. Capturing the wetness between two fingers, she draws it to her nose and sniffs it. Then she licks it, lets it play on her tongue for a second before being lost in the saliva.

She sits up, admitting that this is what insomnia – no, lazy insomnia – does to people. She is hungry for something she cannot articulate. Something to get inside her that she needs but her body feels lethargic from deprivation. She is not bored, though something is not right. She is not right. Why the sudden panic? What does she hunger for, she asks herself. No, not for food. Suddenly she has the compulsion to purge herself of the contents of her stomach. She wants to be empty so she can consume all that she can have and hold and carry within her.

And then she knows, and she cannot think of anything else.

She climbs down to the pond and vanishes. She rolls out of a puddle at the corner of an open lot walled in by buildings on three sides with cars parked in two rows. Akila does not care where she has splashed down. She crawls, searching like the starved, across the tarred street to a shoulder-high wall. She scales it into an empty plot overgrown with flowering bushes and weeds. This is it. She drops to her knees and touches the ground. Give me what I need, I am the shepherd. Come, I want to feel your warmth inside me. Her grated palms taste the Earth like tongues and she can feel it surging, a bolt shooting into her with the energy she craves. The lush cushions of yearning, accepting and being accepted. Every pore on her body dilates, every follicle stands on end, every nerve ending hums with the tremulous touch of life and the living. She swims through the bounding sensations, feeling a humble, all-consuming truth for a moment before it slips away, leaving only a transcription behind. The universe is finite, but its nature is infinite, measureless to the human race, and everything connected.

SQUATTING AT Machu Falls at the end of the pond, Akila wet her toothbrush and applied a dab of toothpaste to it. She dipped it in the water again and put it in her mouth, eyes still bleary from sleep. The brush scrubbed the paste into a froth. She pulled it out and paused for a second as a mild sense of nausea swam up her gullet, latching onto the back of her throat. She spat out the paste in disgust but the taste lingered and she retched, though nothing came out from her empty stomach. A quick handful of water vigorously rinsed out her mouth. Shyam came up from behind with his toothbrush sticking out and squatted behind her, rubbing her back to comfort her.

ALL AT once the jungle was empty. The doe she was stalking had vanished and the birds had fallen silent. Akila relieved the bow-string and stepped out of her hiding spot, scanning the wilderness in no great hurry, for only one thing she knew could achieve this. An insectoid. Instead, she caught sight of a deer peering back at her. In a single movement she stepped forward and retracted the arrow to her eye, and let it fly. The animal dropped without a noise.

Akila waded through the foliage of large arrow-head leaves, senses on the alert. The jungle was too quiet for her not to be wary, and she expected trouble. The leaves covered them like umbrellas when she knelt by the fallen deer and examined the arrow stuck in its side. A clumsy shot, and it was a wonder the animal had died from it as quickly as it did. Sometimes impulsive, half-aimed shots were not neat. She pulled at the arrow. But it was caught on something inside.

Her ears pricked at movement among the bushes and listened for more. It had stopped. She lifted her head slowly between the large leaves and saw nothing. In the jungle, patience is all. She waited like that, watching and listening for two whole minutes, and only then did she return to the deer. The arrow was stuck firmly and she did not want to carry it back that way. After all, she was no amateur showing off a trophy. Real hunters don't need trophies. They hunt to live. The skin, the flesh, the bones, the horns, none of it is wasted.

She cut in with her blade and frowned at the lack of resistance in the flesh. There was something wrong here. She made a longer slit, arching it back around the arrow into a wide 'U' and followed it with a slit dissecting the bowl of the 'U' straight to the arrow. She meticulously peeled back the two flaps of skin, and even in the dim light she could see there was something different about the organs. With an elbow she nudged aside the leaf hiding the sun. The light flashed on the innards and Akila jerked away, falling back on her butt, staring at the bloody mess as the leaves swayed violently, giving momentary glimpses of the horror. Soaked in the pasty blood, there lay the coiled corpse of a fawn with the arrow stuck firmly in its head. Akila awoke with a start and sat up in bed, her throat dry and parched. Beside her, Shyam slept soundly.

THE FISH was almost ready, wrapped in aromatic leaves and skewered over smoking coals. Akila could not stand to eat deer anymore. The smell of it cooking turned her stomach. Shyam was about to pick the skewers off the heat when he lost sight of Akila. He found her bent over at the lake. 'What is it?' he called out to her.

'The smell,' she blubbered back, retching. 'The smell!'

Shyam quickly tossed the skewers on the ground and covered them with dirt. Macoco watched them from the shade of a large golden-shower tree, his ears raised in concern.

'That's deer and fish off the menu then for a good while,' Shyam informed Akila, patting the soil off his hands.

'Yeah, sorry about that.'

'No worries,' he said cheerily, 'That still leaves eggs, hog, lizard, birds, fruits and vegetables.'

Akila wiped her mouth with her wet hand, pensively gazing at her reflection.

SHE IS excited by the sheer number of people in this new place. The noise, the chatter, the beauty and the novelty of being in a crowd. She has had enough of solitude, which has become an ugly word to her. It is a disease that infects and eats at your insides. If only I could be touched by them, feel the shoulders nudging past, have someone respond to a query or give me a helping hand if I should happen to stumble. That hand that holds me. I will love that hand. Smooth or coarse, ugly or beautiful, I won't care for it will be the hand that holds me.

The crowd is bustling on a wide causeway stretching more than five hundred feet, flanked by buildings on either side. It meets a T-point, arriving at the primary causeway. The midday sun hits the rows of peddling hawkers along the centre, and the bottom two stories of the buildings packed with computer hardware stores swarm in the shadows. This is Nehru Place, the electronics hub of Delhi, and Akila is spoilt for choice.

A NARROW sidewalk with sweaty people pushing past in either direction, while some attend to piles of paperbacks and clog the sidewalk further: Akila loves it. An entire side of the main street in Daryaganj is lined with second-hand booksellers. Akila is tempted to dive into the piles of books and kick about à la Scrooge McDuck. Horns blare as vehicles grumble along from the traffic junction. The syrupy pace is owing to a high instance of city buses heading to the Old Delhi bus terminal.

Akila takes a much-needed break in a narrow alley interrupting the sidewalk, hoarding two plastic bags packed with books at her feet. The smell of the fresh bhaturas and richly flavoured chhola is intoxicating. A cool breeze wafts through the shaded alley as she soaks in the sounds and smells. Freshly cooked pav vada, body odours, leaking drains, farts and rotting vegetables. The sight of couples holding hands, smiling faces, a fist-fight suddenly breaking out and people streaking white walls with blood-red paan. She closes her eyes to the cacophony of humanity after a decade with an unchanging playlist of jungle quiet.

When she opens her eyes again, there is a black dog standing next to her. It stares ahead a thousand yards through cars and bikes and rails and people and buildings. The fur at its neck is wet and stuck in clumps around a tight collar of steel wire that is biting into its raw flesh. A five-inch long plastic cord is all that remains of a leash. He blinks wearily and the bulges of fur and pink flesh roll to accommodate the movement when he looks up at her, revealing the right eye as bloody remains crushed into coils of soggy onion skin. He has escaped his captivity with nowhere to go.

Akila's eyes fill with tears and she kneels by him. She caresses his neck, gazing with pity and love into that dead stare. See me, she pleads. Feel me. People cross the alley entrance and she moves away from the noise and sits against the dingy wall. She waves to him to come to her, before remembering that he cannot see her. Come to me, you beautiful, beautiful thing. Come and taste kindness. Those meant to protect and be your shepherds have shown you nothing but cruelty, but now come to me. Come to my gentle touch you, poor, sweet one.

The dog is still staring up at where she had been standing and she rests her head against the wall, forlorn. Her palm on the floor can feel the Earth, and she can feel him. His head turns slowly and looks towards her. She knows he does not see her there, but he walks shakily up the alley. For a moment she thinks he is going to walk past, but he turns in front of her. He limps forward and buckles to the ground between her legs. Then, very gently, so tenderly it bites her soul, he lays his head against her thigh. You never got any love in your life, and yet you're so willing to give it and to trust.

She runs her fingertips over the space where his head lies, wishing he could feel it. But he can, she is connected to him. She can feel him, his searing force. She loves him and she knows he can feel it. She feels the wetness on her fingers and looks down at the red trails on her skin. She can feel his wet snout against her thigh. She lowers her hand and lets her fingers run through the fur, the scab-ridden flesh. How is it possible that she is touching him?

A sound beckons from the alley entrance. A man has broken away from the crowd and stands there gulping down his mango drink from a plastic bottle. When it is empty, he slips it into his carry-bag. Something catches his eyes and he looks into the alley, at the dog lying asleep in the lap of a beggar woman. Akila is struck by a familiarity she did not expect. He disappears into the river of people again. She wants to follow him to solve the mystery but what she wants can wait. She touches the dog's neck lovingly. With her next stroke, she is taken completely by surprise: her hand passes right through him. Then she is struck by the void, the hollow, the sudden absence, the extinguishing of his light. There is a metallic taste in her mouth as she sits there in shock. She had been connected to him as he died. She knows he felt loved in his final moments, and that is some consolation. She rises from his empty frame and moves deeper into the alley, forgetting the two bags of books she had picked out as a multitude of questions rush at her. How did she come to touch the dog? Who was the man, and did he see her? Moments after he left she could not touch the dog anymore, is there a connection? Will she ever see him again?

SHE WAS walking back home, her arms full of fruit, her fingertips still sticky with sap. She stopped walking, swayed and fell hard on her knees with the fruit rolling everywhere. She grabbed her blade and held the point to her abdomen. The blade was steady, but her wet eyes were not. Again, the problem was she could not decide.

HIS GAZE. The lack of hope. The gouged flesh. Then the trust, laying his head on her. Akila cannot shake the images from her mind. The diminution that is death, from vibrant, volatile energy to mere sparks of the matter you are composed of. The cruelty the dog had probably suffered all his life enrages her. Being treated unfairly as a hapless victim in a vicious game. She realizes she is describing herself. Whether it is being abducted as a child and used as a sacrifice in a cruel ritual every three years or being held by the insectoids in order to be used by them to spread to other worlds. Or being tortured by the Sawa for a crime she had nothing to do with. That poor dog, she thinks, tears flowing for one who was the receiver of so much hatred and apathy. I am glad I found you, even if we could be connected for only a minute. I'm glad I felt you flowing with life.

She gazes up at the clear amber sky through the shimmering mist of the waterfall after its thousand-foot descent. A pristine rainbow hangs in the haze like a blessing. She is sitting against the base of the table-top mountain where she had found Macoco all those years ago and she hopes with all her heart that he is alive somewhere in this world. She longs to hold him again. To sing to him. She has since learnt from her reading that he was afflicted by the mast, the release of testosterone in young bull elephants that drives them mad, wreaking indiscriminate violence on anyone or anything around them. I've been to this world twice before, she thinks, once to steal away an innocent egg and then to return the mad adult. You are my responsibility and it's time to go now.

Akila gets up and wades through the knee-deep water along the fringe of the spray, and in a moment she dives forward and splashes through. The trees shudder under a thunderous call as something large shambles closer through the jungle.

THE SAME apartment building she always appears near. What is her connection to this place? It sits on a sloping lane and she follows the road, past a teen riding a scooter with his giggling mate on the back. A few feet past the building she finds the car park she had crawled through one night and the empty overgrown lot where she had connected. She comes back around to the front and knows that she has found the focal point. The man she had seen at the Daryaganj book market strolls out of the building's green gate. This is no coincidence. In a city of twenty million. He does not look much older than her. What makes him different or special? She comes up ten feet behind him and follows along.

Dusk settles to twilight over the network of narrow lanes skirting Mehrauli at the edge of the wooded park. This feels different. It is almost like the people they are passing are giving her dirty looks. Is that old woman shrieking to her husband in Hindi and pointing at her legs? Akila has a T-shirt and panties on. She has walked the Delhi streets a few times naked and not felt as naked as she does now.

She slaps a mosquito biting her thigh. A few people around her react to the sound. Even the man she is following glances back but carries on. They can see her. What? They can see her! This man. It is him; there is no doubt in her mind now, though a thousand others rear their heads. She has made trips to Earth for more than eleven years and in all that time, nobody has been able to see or hear her. She passes the medieval step-well from her earlier visit and freezes in her tracks. She has been on

Earth now for fifteen minutes and there is no hint of nausea. Who is this impossible man making this possible?

SHE CLIMBS out of the fountain in the square at Anupam market in Saket. No more splashing down naked or in her underwear. It was something she had taken for granted and now she misses the freedom, in her wet jeans and spaghetti top. The bright side is that she can finally show off the clothes she has been amassing over the years to more than just her mirror. The place is buzzing with people. Youngsters at the fresh juice stalls, the tandoori restaurants, the Lebanese roll place, the McDonalds, loitering in front of the cinema complex with its tall blue facade and golden stars. Life, she exclaims with excitement.

But that is not why she is here. Where is he? That mysterious guy with the cropped hair? There is something so very familiar about his forehead, nose and chin but she cannot place him. As the thought flutters in her head, she spots him and rushes in his direction. People move aside as she skirts past, revelling in the sensations of elbows and hips, and shoves. She waits near him, staring eagerly at this stranger with a broad smile writ upon her damp face. He is busy chatting with an attractive girl at the cigarette stall. He lights the girl's Gold Flake and then his, taking in the first draught with a hoarse cough. He leads her through the crowd, into the entrance of a bar in a side alley.

Akila feels awkward now, wondering whether she should follow him in there. She's never been in a bar before. She regards the first-floor windows, through which she can see tables with flashing lights bouncing off the walls. There he is again, taking a seat at a window table. Akila watches the couple chat and sip their drinks as people walk through the invisible girl.

AKILA WALKS ten feet behind the mysterious man in Vasant Vihar's Priya Market on a busy weekend night. He is walking hand in hand with the same girl as before. She takes out a cigarette and he lights it for her.

A PACK of cigarettes lies cracked open beside the pond. The short white stick with the orange butt sits uneasily between her lips and she snaps the plastic lighter into flame. The cigarette slips and she tries to catch it mid-air. It has vanished. She frantically looks about until she realizes it has been hanging from her bottom lip the whole time. She pouts at Cola, mumbling, 'Nobody's perfect.' Then she lights it and draws in a deep breath to give the flame life like she's seen others do. The smoke drowns her lungs. The coughing that ensues is painful. What the fuck! Why do people smoke? Shit! She's not going to give up. She lights it again and coughs, but this time she breathes in tentatively. The taste is awful, the sensation of it scratching her throat and lungs, even worse. The next cigarette is easier and the one after goes smoothly and soon she is posing, her wrist bent like the fashionistas in the movies and magazines. The midsection of the stick idles between two fingers and the style is just oozing off her. Yeah, baby, this is it. And before she knows it, she has huffed up the entire packet in record time.

It does not take long for the overdose to enact its sadistic revenge. Her stomach cramps in distress and the nausea humps her cranium. The taste in her mouth is repulsive. Nothing seems to get it out. Not that she is tempted to put anything in her mouth ever again, the state she is in. Three long sessions of vomiting, and two thereafter of painful heaving. The ache is still there. Fuck! She cannot even stand the sight of the empty cigarette packet.

AKILA FOLLOWS the mysterious man through the green gate into his apartment building. A security guard sits up in his chair and is about to question her, but she awkwardly points after the man she is following and the guard slouches back down in his chair, murmuring naughty thoughts to himself. Checking her out as she passes, he scowls at her neck, making her suddenly conscious of the scar. She shields it with a frown, ashamed at being found out for the slave that she is. Her target enters the cramped lift, closing the rickety shutters. She takes the staircase zigzagging up the centre shaft of the building. The lift stops at the third floor and she reaches just in time to see the door of apartment 3C shut and latch.

She retraces her steps down the staircase to the garage, already beginning to feel the nausea of Earth travel at this distance from him. She needs to figure out what is going on here between her and this chap. He certainly does not seem to be aware of her existence and he shows no signs of anything peculiar himself, or any obvious relation to the Sentinel. Just an ordinary guy for all appearances. The napping security guard scratches his crotch in his sleep as Akila comes up to the noticeboard displaying the list of residents.

3C. Shyam B.

She rushes back to the splash through zone, running the name through her head. A relative? A classmate? A schoolmate? The name does not fit any face from her past. She sees the water and almost trips while trying to avoid a cat running across her path. She hates cats. The cat! The boy in the hospital! He was a year her junior. Could it be him? That's right, he had told her his name. She would never forget a single detail of her last night on Earth as a normal girl. Shyam. The boy's name was Shyam. The boy is now a man living in Delhi. Of all people, why someone she knows so little? Shyam.

SHE LAY back in the shade, reading, with her head and shoulders propped up against a rock. Shyam came out of the jungle with a small hog and some fruit in a backpack. He set them on the pebbles, stretched his back and looked around at the serene scene he called home. Akila could sense him watching her for a good long while from where he stood. The next moment, she felt his breath against her stomach and lifted the paperback to see that he had knelt on the ground and was leaning towards her. His face was so close to the bump on her stomach, his nose nudged her skin. At first she could not understand whether he was being horny, and the thought of it made her wet in anticipation. He started raining little kisses all over her abdomen and belly, and then she understood, gripping the book so hard it almost tore apart. His show of love was sincere and she knew how much it meant for him to accept this and that was what choked her right there. What could she do?

The hog was smooth with the fur singed off, and the skin glazed in coconut milk over the spit. They sat that night and nibbled on the crispy skin and chewed the tender flesh soaked in flavour. They sang as they did on some nights and when they were full of food and tired of karaoke videos on the laptop, they sat in the crackling firelight with glasses of jambli juice. Akila shifted to Shyam's lap and leaned back on his chest. They gazed emptily into the sparks rising to dance in the starry sky. He nuzzled the back of her ear and kissed her along her jawline. She felt his breath and knew what was coming. Soon he would attempt to sing one of his favourite songs. Peter Sarstedt's *'I want to look inside your head'* or Cliff Richards' *'Next time'* or some other sappy number. He could not hold a note and he was tone deaf at best but had a way of making the songs his own.

He moved the glass to his left hand and let his right slide down her body, the fingers teasing the side of her breast as he whispered the song. It was Paul Anka's *'You're having my baby'* and his voice cracked regularly until there was no melody to speak of. It meant more than a studio recording ever could. She closed her eyes to hold back the tears. He heard her sniffle and snuggled closer, kissing the side of her face.

A SMALL rock lies beside the hole, its dirt-covered belly upturned to the sky. Akila reaches inside the pit and removes a cloth pouch. She undoes the knot and takes out a curved shard of red from Macoco's eggshell. It looks as pristine as the day she rescued him. She takes out a larger piece and brings it closer to take in his scent. All traces of him are long gone and she knows it because she was the one who washed it clean before hiding it under the rock to preserve it.

AKILA SITS near a howling group of boisterous youngsters, watching Shyam with his girlfriend on the other side of the amphitheatre embraced by Ansal Plaza. She sheepishly checks that the tight collar covering her scar is in place.

SHE WATCHES Shyam and the girl come out of PVR Cinemas in Saket, laughing, their empty cups of soda chuckling with crushed ice. The weather is cooler and everyone is wearing light sweaters and jackets. So is Akila.

AKILA IS carrying three bags filled with paperbacks, cutting off the circulation in her fingers. With all the people pushing past, and shoving her forward, and enveloped in the noises of Daryaganj, she can only watch Shyam enviously. He has a carry bag of books of his own and he is seated in a little restaurant the size of a jail cell at the street corner. A fresh plate of chhola bhatura is slid before him. Breaths of vapour escape as he punctures the fresh, bloated bhaturas with his fingers. Akila has tasted them here before, but never as a customer. A freedom she lost a long time ago. She picks the wallet of a passer-by. Now to treat herself to some of that grub.

SHE STANDS defiantly before the Sentinel, naked in all her bronzed glory. The blade hisses through the air and with a thud the body crumples to the leathery floor. The head trundles to a stop. Blood seeps down the thirteen holes into the depths.

AKILA KEEPS up with them, staying close enough to ward off the nausea. Shyam and his girlfriend have just done a circuit of Lajpat Nagar Market and Akila has her hands full with packets of cooking ware, household utilities and clothes she has collected along the way. Shyam and the girl exit the crowded market, cross the busy street and enter the two-wheeler parking section. The girl straddles her Yamaha Enticer and Shyam sits behind, hanging onto her waist. Akila's glee at shopping and the ecstasy of the crowd sizzle into a solemn glumness. She realizes this is all she has. Some stolen goods. Where is the warm body to hold, the body that invites, the body she accepts?

AKILA IS huddled behind a car, wrapped in two blankets over a thick jacket and pyjama bottoms. It's still not enough to keep her warm in this freezing garage open to the elements. An extension cord is connected to the plug socket. Three laptops feed from it. Two are charging and the third has its screen flipped up with two windows open. She has MP3s downloading on two different P2P platforms, eMule and DC++. The speed she is getting from the open Wi-Fi named 'design office' is incredibly fast with download speeds peaking at 18kBps. This is her nightly routine. She leaves the downloads on for the night, returning at dawn to get her stuff before the guy comes to wash the cars.

IT IS not very early in the morning but the sun is still hidden. Akila is at the centre of the pond, hanging onto Cola's large flat-head. His head is a foot-and-a-half wide now. Akila lays her cheek on him and she mumbles a song, low, in a trickling tune composed of the word 'baby' repeated soulfully like a young Nina Simone or Noor Jahan.

AKILA WAITS outside Planet M music shop in South Ex. watching Shyam exit Cafe Morrison late one night with four of his friends. They stagger drunk to the main road and argue with an autorickshaw driver over the fare to Mehrauli. Though he has glanced at her a couple of times in the past, she doubts he is even aware of her existence. The time will come when she can reveal herself to him. It is not now, she tells herself, knowing in her heart there is no real reason for it not to be. This Beli, a survivor in an alien realm, now queen of thirteen worlds, is terrified of him.

AKILA WADES onto the shore with her spear ready and Zorba stuck to her waist. She is determined to find Macoco and take him back if he has survived and does not kill her first. She sticks close to the water, wary of any immediate danger. The jungle is lush with trees a hundred feet tall, but there is no bird song. Only the roar of the waterfall and the river. A pig-like squeal sounds occasionally in the distance, but sounds travel differently in the jungle. It could be just out of sight twenty feet away or a hundred. She has grown up in the jungles of different worlds and she has faced predators big and small, on land, water and air, and the first big lesson she learnt is this – never take your safety for granted. That is what they are counting on.

Akila considers her surroundings, reflecting on the environment the creatures here have to survive and thrive in: high table-top plateaus where giant flying predators roost. You settle on the relatively safer lower ground between the plateaus, thick with trees, because they give cover against being spotted from above. However, having witnessed Macoco's skills in the jungle back home, she knows this is not much of a deterrent. Evolution is not a decision. It delivers various sets of tools and when the best adapted survive, nature hones those tools.

She looks up at the saffron expanse, at the breath-taking spectacle of a flock of dark specks, hundreds strong, stretching like a dark wing. The Feneks truly rule these skies. She returns to her train of thought on evolution, but it has skipped over the prelude and jumped to a question she should have asked herself from the very beginning. It concerns that first rule she holds in such high esteem. Never take your safety for granted, she repeats. What makes her think it is safer to be close to the water?

She swirls to regard her new frontline and triggers the attack. Her knuckles tense on the spear shaft as the water swells and explodes, shooting the gaping jaws of a monster at her head. In a split-second reflex she knocks it off its path through the air with a swing of the spear. Its elongated body crashes into the sand and Akila backs away instantly to give herself some distance. There is not much time as the creature recovers quickly, rapping its twenty sets of centipede legs on the ground. It is almost twenty-five feet long with sectioned translucent armour like a shrimp. Fifteen black balls for eyes, of varying sizes, populate its head and long, dagger-like teeth fill its snapping jaws.

She cannot outrun it. How long it can stay out of the water, she does not know. Still, she has to move further from the water to test that strategy until she can develop another. The creature circles about her and she is careful to face its head at all times. She is aware of the circles getting tighter, cutting the distance between predator and prey. She must figure out how to turn the tables and become the predator. That first blow to knock it away has told her a lot, mainly that she'll have a tough time piercing the armour with her spear. There aren't many weak points she can see. The belly looks unprotected and maybe under the head, but how can she get it to lie on its back? Judging the closing gap between them, she swings the spear at her shoulders, round her waist, and swipes it behind her in a large arc, lopping two legs off at the joints. The top segments are still moving on phantom limbs as the creature staggers back a little, before resuming to circle, this time the other way. A simple strategy, but it is disorienting enough for Akila to recalibrate.

All this while, she has been moving them closer to the jungle line. She cannot be sure whether she, or it, will be more suited to the jungle terrain. Without any warning, she shoots the spear out in a jab, catching the creature in the face. Three of the round black eyes come off. Its body gathers in a coil to pounce. This will be difficult to out-manoeuvre since she cannot make a run for it and she'll have to face the full brunt of its strength and body weight. She will have to chance a dodge but there is no way to predict the speed of the impending strike.

The jungle behind her shudders as branches fracture and

whole trees come asunder. A shape ploughs out of the shadows, raising sand and dead leaves in a hail of fury. The shrimp creature recoils violently and tries to make for the water. Its forked tail is caught in the jaws of a mighty Fenek fifty feet tall and Akila's heart pounds with exhilaration. She knew he would come. He rips the creature in two with a terrible heave and rips off the armour. Akila can hardly wait to get him home. She lets him enjoy his victory meal, so thrilled she starts grinning foolishly, admiring his might. He flings the shrimp head into the river and swings about to confront her, eyes ablaze and jaws wet with entrails.

'Macoco,' she blurts, and then she knows what she should have done the moment he had ensnared the creature. She should have run. The thunderous Fenek call dries her mouth with dread. She should have run. This is not Macoco.

THE BUMP on her belly was pronounced but she was not heavily pregnant yet. Nothing had changed in their everyday routines. She would still feel queasy every morning when she brushed her teeth and sometimes a smell she had no problem with before would suddenly seem objectionable, like his aftershave or the flowers they had by their bedside. She even avoided the part of the jungle where the flower grew, to elude the scent. Shyam sat at the edge of the pool, watching her prepare her weapons, careful to keep his limbs out of the water and away from Cola. She had them laid out over a rock as she sharpened the blades and made any necessary repairs. She did this twice a week, regardless of whether she felt it was required, and that went for Shyam's tools as well. She said it emptied her mind and relaxed her.

The light from the pond danced upon her face, catching the glint in her eyes, the delicate upturn of her nose, the rude arrogance of her lips, the chin that demanded. Her hair formed little ringlets at her shoulders. Her back was smooth and her athletic breasts had grown fuller, and her nipples and areolas had grown noticeably darker. I love this person, he thought. She has given me everything she can, and she is giving me more. He still felt horrible at the mere thought of the big fight months earlier. He knew he had to remind himself of it to truly appreciate what he had and to never push her away again.

THEY STALKED a tribe of small birds, strutting around with their furry Kiwi bodies pecking at the ground. Akila signalled for a halt with a raised finger. Waiting behind her, Shyam could not see the birds, only hear them clucking drowsily. She gestured to him to move out of the way and swung the spooled nets, once, twice, and with the third she hauled them overhead. The net spread out with its weighed edges and caught five birds, sending the rest into the underbrush in a flutter. Akila ran forward, signalling to Shyam to keep an eye out for predators. She folded the netting methodically and let two of the birds go, keeping only three. She bound their feet and hooked them onto a stick.

Akila was in a particularly good mood that day and wanted to cook the birds herself, using a recipe she had not tried yet. It involved preparing them in the oven while Shyam rinsed their clothes at Machu Falls. He would occasionally watch her gaily hopping between her open recipe and the stove, and then to the clay oven she had built years before he had come. She hummed a tune, performing graceful pirouettes in her short-shorts and apron bulging with her pregnant belly. He ran her name through his mind, buttered with love and rich with joy. Akila.

IT IS so familiar. She finds her footing among roots and shrubs, wading through bushes and low-hanging branches that whip across her face and chest as she flees through a jungle. She is a fool to have even imagined running into Macoco after all these years. What did she expect? This is a world of Feneks and Macoco would not be waiting for her like a dog waits for its master to come home from a trip. Though she knows that is exactly what she had hoped for. To find him longing to come home with her. To have it as it once was. The magic of those days haunts her in moments of loneliness, weighed down all the more by her memories of him.

She twists, she turns, seeking the thickest patch of jungle. But the thicker it gets, the darker it is. And she has soon lost all sense of direction. Her only guide is the crashing about of the Fenek in pursuit of her. The trees get thicker with hanging vines criss-crossing the air and it is perfect. Just what she was looking for. Now to find a place to hide and wait it out. Although her spear is useless against a beast this size, until it gets in the way she'll hold onto it. She swings around a tree trunk with her heart racing, glancing back at the Fenek snared in the web of vines. They aren't enough to contain him and the trees with trunks five feet wide blast to the ground, kicking up their dirty roots. It has slowed the beast and she makes the most of it.

There is light ahead, which must mean a clearing, and a clearing could mean a river or a stream, and her way home. She pushes on, her breathing tearing at the inside of her throat, tasting the disappointment of not finding her dear Macoco.

Her hopes of being reunited with him have been nothing but a childish fantasy, although she believes he is alive somewhere in this world. She hopes that he has found happiness, but the despair of retreating to her solitude tightens her chest. Fleeing the Fenek is part sham, she admits, because being a Beli, she cannot die. What she is truly running from is pain. That she cannot escape. Being ripped limb from limb and feeling the jaws crush and dice her flesh and bones. The agony of it, and then the extended torture of restoration. She dashes into the clearing onto a flat bed of sand that stretches a little over five hundred feet past a river swerving to the jungle on the far side. But there is no escape here.

The river is lined with the hunched forms of a murder of Feneks cooling themselves with swigs of water. Her pulse is throbbing. None of them seems to have noticed her yet. They are a few dozen, about thirty feet tall, some even larger. Others are still arriving, flapping for a soft landing further up and down the river. There is one chance in a million that she can slink unnoticed between the two nearest ones and splash through.

The hitch in that option is the Fenek chasing her. She can hear it coming and there is no time to slink. Stealth is now a luxury she cannot afford. She will have to compromise on it for speed and a bucketful of hope. Her mind runs the possible routes back into the jungle in case things go belly-up. The sand is dampening her footsteps as she sprints but it also hinders her grip and she knows her speed is reduced by half.

The fifty-footer comes barging through into the clearing, leaving a trail of destruction behind him. Akila is about to reach the Feneks at the river, when the sound of the intruder alerts them. They shuffle about, whipping their furry tails to intimidate the challenger. Akila comes face-to-face with a Fenek sizing her up with its enormous eyes. It approaches, making her shift backwards, until others notice her presence amidst the agitation.

The Feneks form a line to oppose the larger outsider and she is stuck in the middle of their face-off. It is open ground with nowhere to run. I'm not much of a meal, she thinks, but this is not about eating her, it never was. It is about dominance in one's own territory. Will the fifty-footer let this unrelated murder have his prize in his domain?

She knows that animals are unpredictable in confrontations and you can never be certain when they might strike or bow down. She cannot base her plan on their unpredictability. However, her own unpredictability is her best weapon. She suddenly rushes at the lone Fenek, setting it off in a charge towards her. She skids in the sand as she turns tack and dashes towards the murder on the other side. The ceasefire is long gone and she has what she needs: chaos.

Neither side quite knows whether they are charging her or the opponent, and some among the murder hesitate in the confusion. She senses the fifty-footer coming up behind her and slides to the side in a cloud of sand, leaving the Fenek to skid past her with a shrill bay, tumbling into the opposing line. Short barks and ear-splitting calls ring out from the struggling mass of limbs and heads clawing and biting blindly at one another.

The river is Akila's only chance. She bolts into the wrestling mess, jumping onto a tail and running up it. It bucks as its owner rolls off the mound and she leaps onto a spotted shoulder. Two Feneks collide from either side, snapping her spear but sparing her. A gaping mouth comes at her with a muffled roar. She weaves and jumps awkwardly, aiming for an upturned belly. The mass of Feneks tumble into the river. Damn it! She must not stop moving. There are fifty more feet of tangled Feneks between her and the water, and she runs, slipping and sliding down an unfurled wing. She leaps across a gulf. The fifty-footer's head thrusts out from below and its jaws snap three feet below her legs. She lands on a neck and bounces, falls onto a back, slides onto a tail and hangs on as it whips about. Flung through the air into the face of a Fenek that knocks her off, she bounds up the wet upturned belly, wary of its legs kicking in the air. This is turning into a mad mud-fight. Akila comes off a Fenek's shoulder and falls ten feet to the sand. She has to steal out of this lunacy and back into the jungle unnoticed. She can get to the river elsewhere.

But the horde of Feneks behind her break in two and the lone bull comes hollering out of the tangle, lunging free of gripping claws and teeth, trying to get at her. Akila brandishes Zorba, a puny piece of metal against the predator snapping its enormous jaws and heaving on its belly. It wriggles forward, its forearms come free and it tears itself out of the reach of the others. It rights itself on shaky limbs, the victor having bested a dozen younger Feneks all at once, in its quest for her. A prize barely five-and-a-half feet tall. The fifty-footer stands up on its hind legs and blusters in triumph so the heavens can recognize his might.

As though in reply, the wind picks up the sand around her and a cloud casts its shadow. The other Feneks stop their screeching and tussling in diffidence. Did she just chance upon the mightiest Fenek of all that can beckon the sky to answer its call? She looks away, unwilling to watch the blow that will tear her to shreds. Hanging above her is no cloud, but a leviathan worthy of the title. A true monster of a Fenek. It is the Alpha of the murder this fifty-footer has intruded upon. He does not roar to answer the loner's challenge, but stares him down with infinite fortitude.

The newcomer lunges at Akila with a lightning strike of flashing teeth and Akila winces in expectation. The sand shifts with a minor tremor of movement but there is no impact. She opens her eyes and finds herself beneath the belly of the giant alpha, its forearms like great pillars on either side. The limp corpse of the fifty-footer dangles by the neck from the alpha's jaws. It shakes it to make certain and then releases it. With a thump, the dead Fenek's head hits the wet sand. The alpha gathers himself up to his seventy-five foot stature before her in all his majesty. He needs no roar to claim his might. The gathered Feneks, covered in mud, face the alpha with their heads cowered. Akila cannot escape now as there is nowhere to go. Not now, having found her Macoco.

HE WAS shaken out of his sleep. The dream plunged into irretrievable depths and he squinted at the dawn breaking through the bedroom doorway. Akila tugged his arm, humming a tune, completing it with the words, 'Good morning, Mary Sunshine.' He followed her, clumsily tripping through his yawn. On the Mez, she presented him with a glass of warm jambli water and after it, they went through their yoga routine.

Coming out of the sleeping child pose at the end, Shyam admired her figure, with her stomach large now, and said, 'It's already the seventh month! Can you believe it? Not much time left!' She laughed and went to the fruit platter she had prepared for their post-yoga breakfast. She somberly ate a piece of fruit, looking through the wicker baskets for something. When she could not find it, she spun about and caught Shyam in her icy glare. In that venomous tone he hadn't being subjected to in a long while, she asked, 'Where are the eggs?'

He was taken aback for a moment and stuttered, 'Are we out?'

'Why would I ask where the eggs are, if we weren't out of eggs?'

'I'll go and get them now.'

'That'll be too late for breakfast.'

'I'm sorry, it slipped my mind.'

'Can I depend on you for these things?'

'Of course you can.'

'These are little things, aren't they? Why does it take so much effort for you to do them?'

'I forgot the eggs, I understand, I'll get them.'

'It isn't just the eggs I'm talking about here, Shyam. The question is, can I depend on you?'

This was frustrating, to be subjected to her reproach as though he were mentally challenged.

'You can depend on me,' he yelled back.

'Don't yell at me.'

'Then don't talk down to me like I'm an idiot.'

She shook her head bitterly, biting at her bottom lip, brow knit as though she might burst into tears at any moment. He caught her grimace and regretted raising his voice. He reached out to her, but she was already turning away. Two steps and she had dived into the pool, leaving him gaping at the rippling water like a fool.

AKILA REMAINS on the sandy banks. The other Feneks have all gone and a hundred feet away, the corpse of the fallen fifty-footer is infested with a number of the large shrimp monsters from the river, wriggling into the flesh. Her face is wet with tears. The world is empty of all else but Macoco before her, crouching his giant form close to the ground and resting his chin on the sand barely five feet from her. He takes in her scent, his wings outstretched, shuddering at the ends. Akila reaches out to touch his nose, but he cringes and moves backwards. His big eyes focus on her feet while staying out of her reach. The serpentine streaks in the sand show the path they have taken with her attempting to touch him for an hour, always resulting in him shrinking away. The mighty alpha is terrified of her.

Akila crumples onto her knees. 'What is it, Macoco? Why won't you speak to me? Why won't you let me touch you?' She wipes her snot with a sandy forearm and tries to catch her breath. She implores, 'Do you want me to go? Is that it? You don't want me here? You want me to go?'

He remains still and silent, watching her feet. Akila's body is a shaking wreck. Shaking from the sheer joy of finding Macoco. Of seeing him after years of convincing herself that there was no real hope. His markings have changed – the spots have become denser and three thick stripes run down his back. And yet, everything about him is deeply familiar.

It is a physical pain in her chest, a twist of an artery or a fizzling out of the oxygen in the blood. The receptor of all the love she knows how to give does not want her to touch him. She is drawn to him, but at the same time, she wants to show she respects his wishes. Was it not the *mast* as she had suspected then that drove him wild? Was it hate for her? Had she driven him to the savage state that she had witnessed? She, the wild child, raised alone in an alien world, did she even know how to love? She has read thousands of books, but what does she understand of the mechanics of emotions? Nothing really. She wants to believe he loved her, but would she recognize that feeling?

Is what she remembers of her father's love real or by now just a description of a feeling from a long-faded memory? She has forgotten his face, no matter how hard she tries to map his long dark mask with the cropped moustache, the determined lips, the stubborn cheekbones. They're not real. They weren't pieced together from her childhood but a photograph she remembers sitting on a table in their living room. Him smiling gently into the camera, carrying her as a six-year-old, pointing away cheerfully. This is her father. What is she to Macoco then? A ghost from his childhood, haunting him?

His eyes … he doesn't even want to look at my face. He is shaking with fear. No, what's the word? Dread. He wants me to go away. He wants this emanation of his nightmares to leave his adulthood. Akila painfully claws at her thighs, punishing herself. It is intolerable to look at him anymore and she knows it is time for her to go. Without a glance back at him, eavesdropping on his breath alone, she goes to the water.

'You hate me,' a faltering voice protests. She stumbles at the sound. Her knees weaken at the familiar voice she thought she would never hear again.

'Macoco?'

'You hate me,' his voice whispers.

'Hate you?'

'Because of what I did.'

'Macoco–'

His eyes come up to hers for the first time.

'I saw blood. So much death. I remember it. I remember doing it.'

Akila bites her bottom lip to keep from interrupting. She knows he wants to say this, he needs to.

'I tried to hurt you. I tried to kill you. All I saw was blood. All I felt was moving forward, to kill.'

She cannot hold back, watching him drown in his boiling torment. 'No, it wasn't your fault. You couldn't control it. I know that.'

'Then why did you abandon me here?'

'WHAT DO you do when I'm not here?' Akila asks Sholay, sauntering thoughtfully along his chest, looking around at the desolate landscape that surrounds them. The horizon is lined with the orange glow of tumultuous earth.

'I wait.'

The very first thing he does when she climbs out of the water is to pick her up. He cannot bear her not touching him for the duration. She understands this loneliness. This yearning.

'Wait? What do you do while waiting?'

'I sleep.'

'The whole time? Isn't it tiresome just to lie here waiting for me?'

'Until you came, the last time I slept was before my kind were imprisoned here. That was a long time ago.'

'Oh.'

'I close my eyes and I breathe. And soon I'm dreaming of another lifetime, a blink in time long ago. I cannot access my memories, but they have access to me.'

SHYAM STRIKES the white cue ball that barely kisses a red solid and stops ineffectually. Three of his guy friends are gathered around the pool table making sounds of derision at his poor turn. Shyam shrugs comically and retreats to a stool with his perspiring beer mug. Sitting on the wet stool, he sips his beer and watches his friends chat, his brow furrowed quizzically. Akila watches from the far end, wondering what he is thinking. He seems changed, or is this something about him that she is noticing for the first time? There is so much to see in Delhi, in India, anywhere in the world. Why is he in a dingy hall cramped with pool tables lined too close together in a back alley in Vasant Vihar?

HE CARRIES a large soft drink as he comes out of the back exit of PVR Cinemas with a stream of people. It is 12.30 a.m. and the market square is deserted. The only shops open are those of the cigarette wallahs and they are surrounded by the fresh batch of moviegoers coming out of the halls. Little beggar kids, three, four and five years old, beg for change and their leftovers of popcorn and sodas. A little one grabs Shyam's half-full cup and speeds away. Shyam appears to be more disappointed than upset. Whether he is disappointed with the child, the drink or himself, Akila cannot tell.

AKILA WATCHES him push his way through the rough crowd at the Sunday book market. She has made this a regular trip to stock up on paperbacks, since he comes here anyway. He does not chat with anyone, never brings friends. The booksellers are familiar with him but he merely offers a polite 'thank you' with every purchase. When he has his chhola bhatura, he seems to tune out the world and focus solely on the metal plate with its steaming contents.

SHE CANNOT stand the monotony of his routine. He is on his evening walk in the Mehrauli park near his apartment. He does not chat with his fellow walkers. In his puffy shorts and ancient T-shirt, socks with worn elastic gathered at his ankles, he does his rounds staring at the ground before him. One time he looks up at her sitting on the bench as he passes. He squints directly at her for a full three seconds and then back to the ground. No recognition. No pause. No reaction. For a moment Akila wonders whether the T-shirt she chose for today lacks pizzazz, but she does not think that is the problem because she has forgotten to wear anything. Luckily she is not close enough to Shyam to be seen by others. But he can see her, so why didn't he react to her nudity? Perhaps his mind could not accept that a naked woman could sit on the park bench in broad daylight. Or perhaps his mind is not open to seeing anything in the world around him.

WITH THE downloads set for the night in the garage, Akila goes up the steps to Shyam's floor. She approaches his door and tries to peek in through the window for any sign of how he lives. It is the one place forbidden to her. She cannot sneak in when he is home like she has done with so many other flats because unlike everybody else on the planet, he can see her. Why has he cut himself off from people? He spends most days in there, making a few trips to the design office in Green Park. He barely goes out in the evenings and then only for the odd movie or to place an order for food that he brings home and eats. The girlfriend is no longer involved. Akila wonders what happened to cause their break up. Is that what drove him into his shell? She does not know him well enough to decide this; perhaps he has always been withdrawn.

Whatever it is, it bugs her to no end. She continues up the stairs to the roof with its stunning view of the city sprawled beyond the dark belt of the parks. He has all this and just sits in his room. He could be out there, meeting people, touching, kissing, and yet he chooses to be a recluse.

'THAT IS unpardonable!' she shouts over the wind as she and Macoco bank into a berg of cloud.

'He has everything! He can do anything! He can travel the world! He can talk to anyone! He can – he can do everything I cannot do and he does none of it. Motherfucker!'

She tries to calm herself. Behind them the entire murder of Feneks follow in meticulous formation.

'It's like looking out of my prison bars at a free man. I see his freedom just as clearly as I see the bars because I'm inside. He doesn't see either. Freedom is wasted on those who don't appreciate its worth.'

She grows quiet then, letting the wind baptize her. This is their embrace. Together again, they relive their favourite memories of sailing together through the clouds. After a while Macoco breaks the silence. 'Do you want me to come back with you?'

She wants to scream 'yes' and point to the nearest lake and say, 'That's the way home, Macoco. Come and stay with me forever.' But she knows she cannot be selfish, no matter how much she tells herself she deserves to be a little selfish. No. She will not steal him from his life like she was stolen from hers. He will choose his own path, a choice I was never given. 'Only when you want to come back.'

Through her thighs and palms she connects with him, and he laughs with the happiness it gives him to feel her love again. Spreading his wings out far to catch the air, he hovers in place.

SHYAM STOOD there waiting for five minutes, measuring time with his breaths. He did not know what to do. He was not angry, he was not even upset. He was lost. Like a concussed man he sat by the water. Sadness poured out of his eyes and he sat waiting, not realizing his right hand hung close to the water. Cola slid over from the far side of the pool, the shadow of his gargantuan form swivelling beneath the surface. He reached the unsuspecting hand, lifted his snout out of the water and nudged Shyam's fingers. Shyam gazed at Cola's dark face, those two button eyes looking up at him, and he saw at once another who felt his pain, of being abandoned, by Akila. They would both wait, as they always did for her. He caressed Cola's head, showing his gratitude for the kindness shown him.

SHOLAY KNELT and laid down his open hand for Akila. Akila was in tears as he brought her up to his face and softly asked, 'What is the matter?'

She shook her head and looked away to the glowing horizon, where chaos reigned and the world's blood ran molten. 'Everything's going to change,' she said grimly, running her hands over her pregnant belly. The baby was moving around a lot.

'Talk to him,' Sholay urged.

THE DOWNLOAD speed is clocking in at around 30kBps on her torrents. She has a bunch of freshly burnt DVD-Rs with porn, movies and TV shows, and a formidable list of downloads lined up for the night. Her nightly cybersex session with five of her usual seven guys is done. It is no longer a challenge to type these guys to orgasm anymore. One, five or seven men, the thrill is certainly gone. For all any of them know, she could be an aged cabbage. Mere cybersex has not done it for her from the third week on, but there is still something about being connected with them online that keeps her going. Them 'spewing their loads' in all corners of the world is some acknowledgement of her existence.

She gets up and stretches her arms with a low moan. The security guard is fast asleep in his cot, wrapped head to foot in layers of blankets, and yet his snores reverberate through the garage. Akila has on a thick down-jacket and sweatpants and fluffy woollen socks. She is not very fond of the cold. This time of the year it gets cool in her jungle but it requires no more than a thin sweater at night and in the early mornings.

On the roof of the apartment building, she perches on the marble bench at the railing, looking out at a hazy Delhi. Only the nearest lights of the Jain Mandir sparkle through; the rest of the city with its twenty million-plus inhabitants is lost to the fog. She feels like a dog, tethered to this man she knew for two hours when she was ten and he was nine.

At the very thought of him her face scrunches with revulsion and fury. She has tried eavesdropping on his psychotherapy sessions to no avail, making it all the more frustrating that she cannot discover his secrets. Whether he has enough of a life to have any secrets worth discovering are another matter entirely. She hates him with a ferocity usually reserved for a tyrannical father or elder brother or husband dictating one's movements.

In these dark, foggy nights when the stars and city are drowned in blackness, she feels a tangy dread in the pit of her stomach. There is no escape. Someday, she will be sent to the crystal cave when her time as Beli comes to an end. The cave with no mouth.

'HE'S HAPPY,' she says, closing her book with a sigh and sitting up on the Mez. 'Our Macoco, Cola. Even now I can't believe it's the same little guy hatched from that egg the size of a coconut.

You should see him now, I wish I could take you there.' Cola peers at her with his button eyes. He is larger than her now.

SHE LIES prone on Sholay's face, pressing her cheek to his. 'Tell me what you dreamt about this time,' she whispers.

'I cried when I awoke and found myself here.'

'Tell me.'

'I dreamt I was walking along the ocean shore with my feet in the water. I was balancing on the serrated line of beach and waves, playing with my time. Time well spent I think, for it brought me joy then, and did again yesterday. It is good to play.'

ARMS AKIMBO, Akila stands with her back to the edge of the Mez, admiring her achievement. And what an achievement it is. She has built a home single-handedly and not just a shack of sticks and a patchwork roof. A system of suspended rope bridges and ladders connects the two large trees and the multi-story structures of huts. It has been a long time in the making and now it is complete. There will always be upgrades, and a few more items of furniture must be procured, but there is no rush. The sense of satisfaction makes her flush. I will not just survive, I will not surrender to the role of a prostate slave. I will prosper, rise to be queen. And this queen needs no king. She is no man's better half. She is whole all by herself, and she will build her palace with her own blood and sweat. You alien scum, this is what I can do. This is achievement, and I'm only just starting.

SHE IS amazed by the deer's sneakiness. The green coat makes it nearly impossible to spot in the jungle, though the series of twisted mushroom-capped horns along the ridge of the neck give the males away. She has chased the deer down a narrow hidden gully she never knew existed and it has now become more about the chase than satiating her hunger. She has come too far to give up and find another prey. The deer enters a trickling stream and follows it down the rocky slope. Her arrow misses him and snaps into shards on the rocks. With movements this unpredictable, even her experienced hand is tested.

This part of the jungle does not look familiar at all. The hunt has led her to the far side of the field of roots whereas she usually finds prey much closer to home. A wall of branches and leaves of a fallen tree bars the way across the stream. The deer flits through a gap and Akila rushes to it and peers into the leafy corridor. It is the ideal hangout for venomous snakes, and she is not keen to encounter any. Regardless, she crawls through, taking note of every step. A flutter of movement causes the branches to twitch, drizzling dew onto her back. She waits for a moment before continuing onward. Her hand slips on the wet branch she is crossing, and she falls through the leaves into shallow water. A submerged rock knocks her elbow badly, leaving it aching.

Water trickles over her face as she notices something out of the ordinary.

Something man-made.

She swirls some water inside her mouth to rinse away the salty taste of sweat lining her lips and spits it out. She is standing in a shallow basin flooded knee-high, with a modest wooded island in the centre capped with a stone structure. From its sides grow dwarfish trees with roots creeping into holes. No wonder she never spotted it from above on her reconnaissance expeditions with Macoco. It is ancient, whatever it is, she thinks, wading closer through the slow-flowing water. The shape of it looks familiar as she hikes onto the island and studies the structure at close quarters. There is no mistaking the pyramid-like conical Mandala reaching almost twenty feet high.

What is a temple doing here? Hindu, Jain, Buddhist or Tao, she cannot tell because there are no carvings to adorn the surface. The stones have been beaten flat to sit neatly. It is admirable work, for it must have been done with stone implements – by now she knows that no other Beli has managed to go back to Earth.

She's had it relatively easy, she muses, moving around to the entrance on the other side. A curtain of fine vines veils the gloom of the man-made cave within. Nothing is discernible from the outside, so she removes the torch from her belt and shines the light inside, exposing the charred black walls. A faint shower falls outside and she decides to wait it out in the temple. The clouds look emaciated, it should not be too long. Shining the torch on the walls for any writing, she spots a stain at the centre of the ceiling.

It is an image. The LED glow reveals a ghostly black silhouette of a hand framed by a dithering white halo of paint. She reaches her hand up to it, aligning her palm with the ancient one. Hers is smaller, and she guesses that the other must belong to a man. She takes her hand away and some of the black comes away on her skin. Upset with herself for disturbing a relic, she checks to see whether the palm outline remains intact. The light shows some rounded symbols beneath the black. She dabs at it and the symbols in white, the length of a word, become clearer, though she has no idea what they mean. She takes out her small 4MP digital camera and snaps a shot of it.

She does not yet know what the symbols say, but the message is clear: you are not the first Beli to have the determination and willpower to build something single-handedly in this place, but they have all succumbed to the will of the Sentinel. What edge have you got over the others? Then she knows that her edge is Shyam. Her jaw-muscles flex as she stares into the face of an insectoid leering in through the vines.

'It's time,' the voice tells her.

Akila wears defiance before the Sentinel, watching it strut towards her with long, supple strides. Fifteen years, and yet she knows so little about it. 'You are almost spent as a Beli,' it declares. Her mind empties of her self-assuredness, and she is once again that little girl standing here for the very first time, unsure of her fate. She grows terrified. Not the cave. Hang me, execute me, have wild animals tear me apart, but not the cave. The blade sings through the air and she sleeps.

WHEN AKILA discovered it was ancient Tamil, she emailed the JPEG to a professor in Chennai. Her eyes are locked on his reply open before her, resting on the two short words within quotes:

Dear Miss Akila,

Thank you very much for contacting me. The picture you sent was very interesting. It is indeed an ancient Tamil script, probably 2000 years old. They've excavated shards of pottery in the Egyptian port of Quseir-Al-Qadine in the same form of ancient Tamil Brahmi script. May I ask where you found this inscription? The context would help me provide you with a more accurate meaning, though a literal translation of it would be:

'Kill it'

AKILA SCALED the crest of a boulder and stood atop it, bow in one hand, a large bird hanging by its legs in the other. Her matted locks were tied, with a single ringlet dangling free over her brow. Below the torn shirt concealing her breasts, the protruding belly denoted her final month of pregnancy. Squinting under the afternoon sun, she surveyed the jungle before her. Shyam climbed up behind her, hauling a bag of fruits and vegetables on his shoulder.

They adjourned to a ragged, fallen tree when Akila's calves began to cramp. It had happened time and again, and the pain could be intense. Shyam helped her down onto the emerald moss that covered everything. He piled their things on one side and had her lie on her side. She sipped from the water bottle with a sigh and asked, 'What is that taste in the water?'

'Don't like it?'

'I like it, just wondering what it is.'

'Kumber. Figured you named it that because it tasted like cucumber, and so I thought a slice of it in the water may be refreshing on a hot day.'

'Nice.'

Shyam grinned with delight and propped up her foot on his leg. He massaged the base and moved up her ankles to her calves.

'Can you do a bit more on the ankles?'

'Sure.'

The sun was lower, the shadows longer, the air cooler, the birdsong sweeter. Shyam spooned Akila, her head on his left arm, her hand in his, while he stroked her stomach with the other. His thrusts were measured and they moved in unison with every stroke. He kissed her from her shoulder to her neck.

THIS IS Macoco's world, Akila reminds herself, admiring the slanting rays and shades of tangerine dusk. She is at the cliff she had leapt off when she was still a child. His Feneks regard her like royalty and she bubbles with excitement, then feels distressed with the sour taste of parting as she leaves. It reminds her of the last time she left Fin. She has not thought about him in so long. The new loss takes the place of the last, but you never really get over it. And to forget is to lose them entirely. She wakes from her reverie when she senses movement behind her. For such a monument of a creature, Macoco has the deftness of a panther. The talents of a predator are engraved in his genes and have served him well. He lies on his belly beside her, his chin resting on his reptilian hands, peering out at the tranquil landscape. A Fenek's low call issues behind them and Akila turns to see what is happening. The younger Feneks are huddled together and chattering. 'Now they will start to fight,' Macoco tells her.

'Aren't you going to stop them?'

'No.'

'Why?'

'Because it is necessary.'

'What if one of them gets killed?'

'The Alpha is not chosen, he earns his place.'

'But you're the Alpha.'

Macoco watches the shadows grow longer and the light turn golden with melancholy.

'I'm ready to go, Akila.'

Akila understands, but she must ask, 'Are you sure?'

'I have seen my younglings grow to have younglings of their own. I have lived as Alpha long enough and I have had my life here. Now I want to live the life with you that was taken away.'

Akila leans her body against the side of his face, hugging him, baptizing him afresh with her tears.

THE MEDIEVAL Shamshi Talab reservoir in Mehrauli lies still in its murky serenity. The water surface swells and bursts like a bubble as Macoco shoots straight up into the blue. With Akila on his back, they zip through the Delhi sky. The Qutab Minar watchfully points at them like a finger.

AKILA PATS Macoco on the chest and announces, 'I'm going hunting. You guys do this.' She enters the jungle, leaving him behind at the pond. Cola's dark form hovers a foot below the surface, the little button eyes watching Macoco warily as he settles down in the cozy plot by the pond Akila has cleared for his arrival.

The mighty Fenek leans over his mangled reflection dancing upon the surface and recalls looking down all these years ago, drops of blood from his chin spreading in the water. A large dark shape comes thrusting out of the water and two massive jaws snap inches from Macoco's nose as he pulls away in time. Cola falls back into the pond with a loud splash. Akila almost comes out of hiding to reproach Cola for his behaviour, but she represses the impulse and stays put. Cola's head is now at the surface, boldly facing Macoco. His head alone is more than four feet wide.

'I deserve that,' Macoco says, keeping a safe distance. 'But you know I had no control over what I was doing. It was the madness that hits every male Fenek at the onset of adulthood. I wish I could have known somehow that it would happen and flown far away where I couldn't have hurt anyone. But the beast took hold of me that day and I paid the price, didn't I? I was gone.'

They stare at each other for so long that Akila fears it must be a prelude to more violence. Then Macoco leans closer and says so softly she can hardly hear the words, 'I remember, Cola.' He sighs. 'I was exiled to another world, I could do nothing for her when she had her troubles. But you, you spoke to me, so why haven't you said a word to her in all these years?'

Akila stares at them through the leaves in utter disbelief.

SHYAM HAD gotten up early today and gone off to do some chores. Akila lay in bed, feeling wonderfully cozy as the morning chill came rolling in through the doorway, tickling her toes. She, tired of lying on her left side and holding her belly, rolled onto her right and stared at the wall instead. Any day now, she thought. A mother. She had never thought she would get the opportunity, but it would be any day now. She was thirty-one years old, no longer a jungle sprite. Shyam pretended not to notice her few strands of white, but she knew they were there. At least she had a chance to experience carrying a life inside her before her time was up. In truth, they were one life still. Soon they would split in two, like the first single-celled organisms, carrying on the legacy a few billion years running. They would come for her then and she did not yet know what to tell Shyam. She had known all along it would not last, but she had to try. Didn't she?

'I am the Beli,' she whispered softly. Nothing more. She looked over her shoulder towards the creaking wood where Shyam stood in the doorway, unable to speak. She saw the fear clinging to him and recognized it without the words. She manoeuvred herself to her feet and went to the doorway, where she followed Shyam's quivering finger to the insectoid standing tall by the pond.

Dear Shyam,

That's terrible! You are such a kind and sensitive person. I can't believe anyone would hate you. She just isn't the one if she couldn't see how special you are. What happened between you two?

Taking in the sun,

Francesca

ON HER laptop, Akila cuts a blonde girl from a picture and transplants it onto an image of a snow-covered lane. She alters the girl's hair to a dark brown and touches it up a bit to cover up her manipulation. She adds the final image to a Facebook profile she has created for the fictional Francesca Lori.

The next night she goes through Shyam's Facebook friends list, examining the smiling faces, the posts of exciting travels, and successes in university and at work. The fictional Francesca Lori has amassed forty-five friends, though she created her to try and get some insight into Shyam's mind. She needs to learn his secrets.

Dear Francesca,

I wish I was with you in Canada right now, away from everything that is familiar to me here. The air is thick with dust and smoke. I want to get out of my apartment and breathe clean air again, but clean air requires a long drive out of the city.

It wasn't her fault, you know. I knew even then that I

was at fault, but when the relationship began, I would not have guessed it about myself, that I, a person who used to dream of love and finding the one, would at the very first sign of commitment look around for an emergency exit. I'm a solitary kind of guy. I enjoy isolation because it gives me the space to do my work and lets me think.

As the relationship developed I found myself longing for it more and more. She wanted to spend every waking minute with me. Please don't get me wrong, I cared for her deeply. It is the closest I've ever been to what I understand as love, but I cannot function like that. I loved to be held in my sleep, have her arm in mine while we walked, but give me a few hours to do my work. Go and do your thing while I do mine. We'll meet later this evening and be together. No, it would not do. Still, as much as I want to blame her for being unreasonable, I know I was cowardly. I know it had nothing to do with all that bullshit.

The truth is, there was an incident when the condom broke and I came inside her. My world turned upside down the moment I pulled my dick out of her and saw the torn latex clumped around the base. I had always wanted to be a father, for as long as I can remember, but at that moment I saw my life coming to an end. The baby would ruin all my plans, my carefully laid plans for my life. All that I had to achieve to make my existence meaningful. A baby meant I would be stuck with her. She's beautiful and sweet, but she wasn't the one. I knew it at that moment. Even as she tried to console me, I knew I could not live with her, a life without solitude ever again and that my life, the life I had dreamt of having, was going up in smoke. She told me not to worry, that she'd take the morning-after pill, and the relief I felt right then, it made me ashamed of myself. Everything I had ever wanted existed right there in that moment. A woman who cared for me deeply and a child, and I cast it all aside with the cowardly choice to retreat into my apartment.

She took the pill and later, when she took the pee test, it came out negative. Of course she didn't care about the way I had behaved, she still adored me, and yet I hated myself. She deserved better, though she didn't want better. She wanted me, but I wasn't ready for her. She gave me a red T-shirt with a silly picture of an elephant's butt with a band-aid. I treasure that silly shirt because it reminds me of the life I could have had with someone who loved me. I know now I'll never be ready to have a child, but I hope, Francesca, that the next time I find someone who loves me, I will embrace her and not let go.

Much love,
Shyam

Akila crushes an empty juice carton in disgust, her eyes damp with resentment for this wimp who lives his life like opportunities come down a conveyor belt, while she has had to hang on to everything she holds dear as hard as she can because she knows there will not be a second chance. She fights for her very survival, and he hides in his room, living life away through work, TV shows and video games. How is that fair?

'YOU ARE nearly spent, Beli,' the Sentinel says, as they stand under the hot noon sun. 'Enjoy the three years you have because the next sacrifice will be your last.' And then. She knows what awaits her. The cavern, the black. She looks up at the blazing amethyst sky to escape it and the life in her eyes fades. The head rolls off the bloody stump and a moment later her body crumples to the ground.

AKILA CAME back from the exchange with the insectoid and took Shyam aside. Unsettled from his first encounter, he hugged her close, whispering, 'What does it want?'

She looked him in the eye, and took a breath before answering. 'Me.'

'The sacrifice?'

She nodded.

'But that'll kill the baby.'

Akila's gaze did not waver even as she thought, me too, you dear fool. My loving fool.

'We can't let them do this,' he pressed.

'There's nothing we can do to stop them.'

'We can kill this one and splash through to another world.'

'We won't be able to kill it, and they will chase us down wherever we go.'

'Ask them for some more time,' he pleaded.

'Don't you think I've tried?' She cannot close her eyes without hearing her shrieks in the darkness.

'Tell them they can come for you once the baby is born.'

'I tried.'

'It'll be any day now.'

'I told it. It doesn't care.'

'They don't care that you're carrying a child inside you?'

'Not when the fate of thirteen worlds depends on me being sacrificed today.'

'I'll tell them then.'

She pulled out from the hug to confront him, saying, 'What will you tell them that I didn't?' She could see him thinking hard for anything within his powers and her gaze saddened, loving him all the more then, sensing the distress in him as he searched for any possibility, avoiding the one. She kissed him lightly on his lips and stroked his cheeks. He was still searching as she drew away. Until desperately, he held her forearm and pulled her back, shouting, 'I'll go.'

She looked at him with surprise. 'What are you saying?'

'Let me be sacrificed instead.'

'I can't let you do that to yourself.'

'What choice do we have, Kili, there's a baby inside you.' For the baby, she reminded herself, her eyes welling up with tears. 'Our baby. It's me or the baby,' he said, tearing up as well.

A RESTLESS Macoco waits on the roof of India Habitat Centre. Akila sits at the edge with her eyes locked on an entrance on the ground floor. She bolts to her feet when she spots Shyam coming out the door. He could be the key to my freedom.

'THERE MUST be a way,' she heaves.

'You said you'd looked for a way before and found where it led, and it certainly wasn't home,' Sholay replies.

Akila clenches her fist tighter. 'There is no way to kill the Sentinel. At least, I can't think of any with the insectoids right there protecting it. And there is the question whether it can be killed at all. If it is connected to the fourteen worlds, can it be killed by something like a knife on one world or will I have to kill it on every world?'

'This man on the other side you are bound to. You are right, he must be the key.'

'No Beli before me has been able to cross to Earth like I have. There is some bond between Shyam and me, strong enough to defy the barrier between Earth and the thirteen realms and if it is that strong, maybe it can pull me through completely to the other side.'

Sholay listens pensively, considering her points.

'What is it?' she asks, finally noticing his gloom.

'If you go, I will be lost again.'

'There will be another Beli.'

'There have been countless others before you, but none like you.'

'If I stay, I'm dead in less than three years. There is no choice, Sholay. It is either escape or death, don't you see?'

'I do. But I can't help my heart from grieving your absence.'

'I'm with you now, I'm connected with you.'

Sholay sighs. 'Soon you too will be a dream.'

ALAKNANDA MARKET is crowded as usual with the Diwali mob collecting Akilas and lights, and rangoli colours at the makeshift stands. Akila buys a pack of colours and a dozen Akilas as she keeps a watchful eye on Shyam, who has just come out of a narrow entrance between shops after his weekly psychoanalysis session.

She waits until he starts walking, then manoeuvres to cross paths with him, nudging shoulders as she does so. They stumble, arms and hands touching, and muttering an absent-minded apology, he continues on his way. She expected more, even possibly a fireworks display as the subjects of the intense bond across parallel planes met for the first time. Perhaps the molecules would wobble and spark, and the earth quake a bit, but there was none of that. His skin felt like the touch of any other and she wonders what she can try next.

THE ROCKS along the pond are scrawled with colourful patterns and geometric designs. Akila adds the last touches to the Mez and stretches her back after being hunched over for the labour. She is pleased with herself. Practice from past Diwalis has honed her rangoli skills and she celebrates with a panoramic picture of the pond on her smartphone. She dives into the water to freshen up, and senses Cola swimming with her. Learning that he can talk but chooses not to talk to her has upset her a great deal and she feels a certain grudge towards him because she does not know what she has done to offend him. She tries to be jolly but she knows it is forced. He's still the same Cola. He has not changed. Only what I know about him has, and I wish I did not know it, she thinks. It hurts that right now they could be talking, like she does with Macoco.

SHYAM IS seated on the marble bench on his rooftop, watching the Delhi skyline explode in dazzling colours as explosions crackle across Mehrauli village. If this was not a festival, it could be mistaken for a war zone. Macoco could not handle the noise. Shaking and whimpering, Akila had to take him back home.

She sits on the higher roof overlooking Shyam, amidst the crowd of TV dishes gawking at the south-west sky. If he were to turn around and looked closely, he would see her. But he does not turn. As the crackers burst to ward off evil and the lights spark up the darkness, the two of them are quiet spectators feeling the approaching chill of winter. He leaves at around 10 p.m. and she is there a while longer. Then, when she too cannot take any more of the gunpowder smoke suffocating Delhi, she climbs the large rubber water tanks on the roof, uncovers the top and drops into the cool water.

She splashes through into the pond and something grips her wrist tightly. She tries to see what has her as she wrestles to break free, but her body is hauled out and lands hard on the pebbles. A dark shape looms over her and she recognizes the silhouette of an insectoid against the bright moonlight. It is not yet time for the last sacrifice – there are almost two years left. She hears a whine, and in the moonlight she can see Macoco's body being held down by four insectoids latched onto him, their vicious mandibles pumping him with venom. Disabling her mighty Macoco so easily. The insectoid comes up to her, a limb clasps her wrist and wrenches the dagger out of her grip. Then the dreaded voice comes through it in a menacing hiss of clicks. 'Did you think I would not discover your forays?'

SHE HOPED it would work, if only to buy some more time. She was not sure. She hadn't been sure for a while. Akila and Shyam stood together on the field of roots with the insectoid waiting some feet away. She kissed Shyam long and hard, tasting his tears.

'I don't know,' he mumbled. 'Will it make me the Beli from here on?'

She held his hand tightly. 'I lived it for twenty years. Now it is your turn, so we can raise our child.'

'I know! But I can't do it.'

'Tell me now,' she said slowly. 'Will you, or will you not do this?' She placed his hand on her belly. 'It is your choice,' she said, 'and it has consequences. I will not make your decision for you.'

He looked away to the treeline, yearning to be back in time a day. Before this nightmare began. You have two choices, he told himself. One is the right one. The other is the wrong one. The choices were unambiguous. One was hard, and the other harder. He had to decide which was which, and he knew the choice would define the kind of man he was. Because the consequences defined the difficulty. One had dire consequences for him alone, while the other had consequences for himself, the woman he loved, and his child.

'I'll do it,' he thought, and a second later realized that he had spoken the words aloud.

'I knew you would,' she said, softly kissing the corner of his mouth. She knew it must have been a terrible struggle inside him, but he had chosen. And she saw hope.

'Let's go,' he announced, but Akila held him back.

'I'll go first. This isn't a done deal. I don't even know whether the Sentinel will go for it. I'll try. You wait here.'

'Are you sure?' he asked nervously.

AKILA IS in darkness. It feels like she is stuck hip-deep in concrete and she cannot push herself out, no matter how hard she tries. She cannot feel her legs or the warmth of the urine emptying out of her bladder. Her skin crawls, every pore uneasy because she knows the fate that awaits her. She imagines it must be around sunrise back home, picturing it vividly in her mind. The sky has cracked with the first rays of dawn. The clouds are turning hues, teased by the blushing shadows. The air is cool and still. The ground is wet with morning dew. The shifting shadows play under the trees. Then there is light streaming in from behind her and in the reflections cast on the crystal stalks she sees the glowing insectoids gather in a semicircle behind her and wait. The Sentinel emerges from the rippling black water. He stands three feet before her and pronounces, 'Stay calm.'

Akila's breathing accelerates and her heart beats harder. Her frantic palms push at the ground.

'There is no escape. Stay calm,' the voice hums.

But she cannot stop, her mind is a blur of nothingness. She is a fly caught by its wings. She is a fish gripped by the tail. There is that reflex to flee, no matter the direction, no matter the chances. Flee if you can. She pushes with all her might and then she can feel herself lifting away easily. No, it is her hands sinking to the wrist and the ground hardens again. She stares up wide-eyed at the Sentinel, teeth biting down so hard her jaws ache.

'Shall I tell you why I had you brought here?' The voice is smooth and calming, bouncing off the walls and crystals with a curious harmonic resonance. She yields and listens, even if she can anticipate what he has to say.

'Your purpose is to be the Beli every three years. Be the sacrifice that holds these realms together. My realms. Beyond that you have no rights, and no identity. You are the Beli, and you are necessary, for as long as you can be. When you are no longer equal to the sacrifice, you are no longer the Beli. No longer necessary. Then you become a mere trespasser.'

He waits for a moment, and tells her, 'This is where I send trespassers. I showed it to you once, some years ago, and I urged you then to accept your role. There is no escape.'

She cannot shake away the images of all-consuming darkness from her mind. She wants to puke out her insides, to pour out her problems and wake up with her nightmare forgotten.

'Almost spent, with barely one sacrifice left in you, you are not worth keeping with all your treachery.'

'I'm sorry.' The words spring out of her throat. 'Please, I'm sorry. I'll never go there again. I'll be good. Please, not yet. A little more time. One more sacrifice. That's all I ask.'

'Then tell me how you travel to Earth.'

'The boy,' she blurts out, eager to please and be done with this. 'I wasn't alone during the first sacrifice. I was with a boy named Shyam. And somehow we've become connected, his world to me. It's not something I asked for, but it happened. I didn't know I was doing anything wrong.'

'Some truth and then a lie.'

'It's the truth! I don't know how it works! It just does!'

'Why do you follow him?'

She gapes up at him, wondering how he knows. The Sentinel settles on the ground before her so they are more or less face-to-face. The lights of the insectoids go out until only one remains, dimly skirting the gloom.

'It has been a while since you thought of Fin, hasn't it?'

Her world spins. Was he always watching? How? Can he read her thoughts?

'Why were you following this Shyam? What were you seeking from watching him?'

'Please.' She shakes her head like a maniac. 'I meant no disrespect. I just wanted a way out! I won't do it again. I won't, I won't. I won't go anywhere. Please, please give me more time!'

'I want more than that.'

She does not know what he means.

'I want more than your promises. I want more than your discipline. As a Beli you are easily replaceable.'

She racks her brain. What is he suggesting? A replacement? Yes!

'Take him! When my time comes, take him. Use him as a Beli.'

'He's too old, why would I take him when I can get younger and fresher stock?'

'Think about it. He is powerful enough to bridge the two of us between worlds, defying your rules. He is the Beli you seek.'

'Interesting, but you only offer a recommendation?'

The light goes out completely. She wants to tear her body in two, rip out her arms and wriggle like a worm to the water, and escape. And even if she only smashes her face into the rock like the last time, she will not mind. She would rather smash her head into a pulp than live an hour in this place in the darkness. Has it been only a minute, or five, or ten? There is nothing to see, nothing to hear, she cannot move. Has time stood still? Is she trapped in a bubble outside this universe? There is nothing. Even her thoughts lend a metallic bitterness to her tongue. Her spirit is drowning.

'What do you want?' she screeches in despair. 'Just tell me what you want!' The echoes bouncing back and forth are no consolation. 'What do you want me to do? Just tell me! What do you want? Tell me something. It doesn't matter what I have to do.'

Then she said aloud, 'I'll get him for you.'

'You'll bring him to me.' A voice at last. She must hold onto it.

'Yes, yes! I'll bring him! You'll have him willingly for the initiation, I promise! Please let me go.'

'What if I want more?'

'More? Yes, yes, anything you want.'

'What will you give me if I promise you your freedom?'

Akila is thunderstruck.

'Your complete freedom.'

'My complete freedom? What do you mean?'

'I will return you to your world.'

Akila searches the blackness for a clue to whether he is being sarcastic.

'But I want more,' he repeats.

'What more can I give?'

'Not just you. The two of you together. Give me an offspring.'

'What?' she stammers, comically repeating the question like a tick.

'Separately you two make adequate Beli, but a child produced from this union could give me what I need.'

'You want me to give you my child, to make it the Beli?'

'You can have many more later when you are free, back on your world. What does one offspring you'll never even know, from a man you detest, matter to you? For a lifetime of freedom?'

'I can't give up my child,' she asserts feebly.

There is no reply. The same turmoil from the last silent spell envelops her, only with far more ferocity.

'Can I?' she asks. She is alone here. They are gone. This is her death then. She is living her nightmare. Her chest is constricted. The claustrophobia is smothering. She wants to shatter the bones that are holding her helpless.

The drool drips from her lip. Has it been an hour or half a day? There is no will left in her. The prospect of being like this for two or three days more, or even a week, chills her to the marrow of her bones. She is certain she will go mad. A conscious madness. There is no time from here on. A drowning in emptiness. She rocks her head from side to side, opening her mouth to the blackness, wailing until her neck aches to the point of breaking. Save me.

'A small sacrifice, to earn the rest of your life.' The voice sounds like an island in the sea of misery. Hungrily grasping it, she answers, 'Anything.'

'This is the escape you seek.'

She knows it is true.

'I'll give you anything.'

4

THE SKY RIPPLED AND *a hand plunged towards him, fingers unfurled, reaching out. Find me. Pluck me from this life and free me of my responsibilities. Take me to a place where I am whole, and not lacking. Give me new air, where the old failed to give me spirit. I need help to climb out of my fate. Show me the other side of the sky. Show me a home where I can be me.*

The hand groped about, clawing at nothing. Do you need my help? Do you need to come to my side? I can try pulling you through.

His hand came up before his face and he looked at it as though for the first time. Is this my hand? The hand that will show me the way? There was no hair on it and the skin was red. His fingers moved, but he did not feel them move. His thumb twitched and he smiled. He had done that.

A shadow played on his hand and he looked up. The seeking hand was still there. I didn't forget you. Take it, he said, take my hand. At the pace of sand sinking in water his hand rose, a twisted form obeying him for no payment or promise. He unfurled his fingers and reached out. The hand from above struck them and came back searching hungrily for that touch again. It found him and plunged down further to take a firm grip of his wrist. That's right, he said, pull yourself out and come to me. The hand tugged and he felt himself rising. Rising out of the wet womb.

THE OPEN air hit his face like a brick of ice and he saw figures and shapes, serpents upon serpents. He screamed and fought the hands pulling him out of the water and onto hardness. But there was no scream, there was burning. His body convulsed and he felt something fight its way out of his throat. He lurched and a torrent of liquid sputtered out. His head spun, the serpents danced, writhing and sliding over scales. The ringing in his ears was like a thousand little bells pealing, and then he heard a voice crying, 'Shyam! Shyam, say something!' And he knew at once. He looked up, ready to confront her, but there was no need. An insectoid held her firmly by the neck and he saw the relief on her face to see him responding and waking up. A second insectoid came shuffling down the wall of roots towards him, those pinprick black spots on the bulbous eyes trained upon him.

5

SHYAM STOOD ON THE leathery ground before the tree for the first time, having only seen it from afar. Although that wasn't really true, for he had stood here more than half a dozen times and experienced the sacrifice, Akila's memories burnt into his brain by the water of the tree. He was no mere voyeur, having felt the tingles in a sharp ring around his neck when the blade sliced through and the darkness fell. The Akila from the present stood a few feet away to his side, her hands securely on her belly while the insectoids stood in rows on either flank. Shyam still felt a bit giddy. His clothes seemed intact for the most part, but his skin was the dark red of fired clay. He gazed at Akila, troubled by her silence. He reached out to her, but the clicking from the insectoids advised him against it.

'How long was I in there?' he asked.

'Two or three minutes,' she replied.

'Can't be,' he said, shaking his head to knock out the frazzle. Akila did not respond.

'I know, Akila,' he said, throwing a cherishing glance at her stomach. The bargaining chip for her freedom still slept soundly in there.

She looked at him, confused. 'What do you know?'

The insectoids froze and out of the shadows a figure emerged into the morning sun. The Sentinel, Shyam thought.

'Everything,' he mumbled quickly. Akila regarded him quizzically. The man standing there was somehow different from the one she had left behind a quarter of an hour ago. Regardless, his presence complicated matters. Not her negotiation as such, but how far she could go in front of him.

'The child is ready,' stated the Sentinel's deep treble.

'But the deal has changed,' Shyam said.

'Shyam,' Akila hissed. 'Let me do the talking.'

'I know the deal was Akila's freedom for our baby.' He pushed on despite her wide-eyed stare, 'But I want to propose an amendment.'

'I have something to propose,' Akila shrieked.

The Sentinel listened, nonplussed by the contention.

'Him,' she yelled, pointing at Shyam, 'for our freedom.'

'You and the baby?' the Sentinel asked.

'Yes. Take him, but let me and my baby go back to Earth.'

'That was not the arrangement.'

'You can change the arrangement.'

'Why should I, when this arrangement only serves you?'

'But you have him! He is powerful, you admitted that yourself, and he will last you two more decades. And then you get another Beli and continue as you have been doing since the – whenever you came to my planet.'

'I don't want him, when I can have the child, the product of a pair connected. Never has there been a bridging between two worlds as there is between the two of you. Your spawn will be a new breed of Beli.'

'You can't have it! You can't have my child!' Sunlight gleamed off the dagger she held to her unborn child.

'You would rather kill the child than give it to me?' the Sentinel drawled.

'I want us to be free! You promised me freedom!'

'You promised me a child.'

'My baby!'

'It is an unequivocal exchange. Your child in exchange for your freedom.'

'No mother would.'

'And you don't have to.'

Akila studied the Sentinel, perplexed, repeating, 'I don't have to?'

'Don't give up your child. It is like you said, no mother would.'

'You'll let us go then?'

'I will kill you and take out the child.'

Akila's glimpse of hope was extinguished and she stood there, a dazed shell.

'Take me,' Shyam urged the Sentinel. Akila was staring at the blade in her hand.

'Silence,' the Sentinel breathed.

'Listen to me! Take me as the sacrifice.'

'You are not necessary anymore.'

'Don't kill her.'

'Neither of you is necessary anymore.'

'But we are! You cannot raise a child! I am the father and she is the mother! If you want the child to be a healthy Beli, we are necessary!'

'The Beli will survive without you.'

'This is no ordinary Beli, you said so yourself. How do you know then?'

The Sentinel considered the proposition.

'Listen to me,' Shyam urged again. 'Take me as the Beli. Let Akila give birth and take care of the baby, until the child is old enough. What harm is there in us taking care of it? When we are no longer necessary, like you said, then you can kill us.'

The Sentinel remained quiet for a few seconds, never looking away from Shyam. Finally it spoke in its disconnected grinding voice. 'You don't understand.' It moved towards him, saying in a measured tone, "The Beli are a means to an end. All I need is the blood for the sacrifice. The sacrifice is necessary.'

The Sentinel stopped at arm's length from him and said, 'First, I will kill you. Then I will cut out the child she is carrying.'

It looked at Akila, standing there, having given up all hope. She dropped the blade with a dull thump on the leathery ground.

'And I will take her life for the last time.'

Akila squeezed her eyes closed. There was no darkness then. Only the silhouette of her father at the open gate, backlit by a brilliant dawn. 'All I've wanted is to be with you once again,' she whispered, and watched him turn, wearing the grin she had inherited.

The Sentinel turned back to face Shyam, its blade showing in its hand, light screaming at the malicious razor's edge. 'Why would I let more than one of you stay, when I despise your kind?' Shyam lowered his eyes, resigned to his fate. An image came to his mind then, of letters written in a language he could not read. And yet he understood.

'I am the river,' the Sentinel called. 'I am the life!'

The image blinked at Shyam, square pixels on a laptop monitor flashing the lonely phrase.

'Kill it.'

Of its own volition, his hand moved to pluck the blade from the Sentinel's hand. It cut the air in a gleaming arc. Followed by the thud of the Sentinel's head at their feet. The insectoids seemed frozen while the Sentinel's body still remained standing. Shyam moved quickly. He collected the fallen head and took Akila by the hand to the edge of the platform overlooking a well among the roots. The insectoids came out of their daze, their antennae stirring. They approached the headless body of the Sentinel to inspect it. One insectoid clicked in a frenzy, regarding the two escapees. Without a moment to lose, Shyam whispered, 'Dive.'

'I know,' she hissed back, eyes bulging from the rush and together, they leapt. The insectoids hesitantly deserted the lifeless corpse of the Sentinel to rush after them.

SHYAM LED Akila out of the stream into the forest, tucking the Sentinel's head under his T-shirt and tying the helm tightly around his waist so it would not fall out. 'Not here,' she screamed. Shyam frantically searched the forest for signs of danger. 'What is it?' he asked, pulling her deeper in through the trees. 'We should stick to the water and dive again, and again, and lose them,' she reproached. They heard splashes behind them from the stream. The insectoids were here. But there was something else, all around them. Shyam did not let her stop, pulling her on harder. She used her free hand to guard her belly and whistled. Shyam thought she had gone insane. 'What're you doing, Akila? They can hear you!'

'We won't survive without their help!'

'What?'

'We won't.'

Shyam could not deal with her craziness in the midst of this, but he knew she was right about finding water again. He should not have left the stream at all, and should have dived to another world at once. He was not sure who was leading whom, or were they just aimlessly fleeing into the forest? Suddenly he saw the bushes tremble as things charged towards them in the underbrush. Something dark and furry came flying out of the nearest shrub, hitting him on his shoulder and knocked him off his feet. He rolled twice and stayed on his back. Akila had to come and pull him up as he lay there staring at the tree tops, frightened beyond belief. Up there, small glowing creatures were flying in from all sides and gathering. 'The faeries,' he murmured, recalling her past. Then he remembered what else lived on this world. Akila was right, they should not have come. He was on his feet like a shot and rushing through the punishing branches with a new ferocity. He saw a glimmer of water through the overhanging shadows and panted, 'Water.'

'We won't make it,' she snapped hoarsely. As he made the hard right, hanging on to Akila, he glanced behind them at the insectoids emerging through the forest with paranormal speed. They were covered with the furry beasts and the first of them crashed into a tree, splintering the trunk. It fought off the jaws that savagely tore at it, beating the ground and the bushes in its manic attempt to free itself of the agony of being eaten alive. The second insectoid came crashing through the branches of the fallen tree, two legs on one side lost. As it struggled beneath the onslaught of the furred horrors, a third insectoid came rushing over the fallen trunk. Shyam caught Akila from falling. She held onto him as they broke through the bushes and lunged into the stream.

A WALL of churning water struck him from behind. He tried to get up, and fell over. His feet were sinking into the unsettled sand. Akila fell over as well but she recovered first and tugged him out in time to have the next wave impotently strike his thigh. The water burst behind them and an insectoid beat its way out of the surf. Shyam and Akila ran through the ankle-deep water, Akila supporting her belly and Shyam keeping the Sentinel's head secure. The insectoid chased after them, hindered by the water and the sand, and with two others following behind. A wave knocked the last one over, and it kicked at the air, wailing in clicks. The insectoid right behind them was getting close and Akila tugged Shyam deeper into the water. He grabbed her and they jumped into the oncoming wave.

THEY CLIMBED out of the cold water, clothes clinging to their bodies, gasping for air. Shyam pulled her back towards the water to dive again, but she resisted and pulled him the other way, onto a hill. The landscape was covered in stones and rocks without a tree in sight. 'What are you doing? There's no water up there,' he yelled, assisting her nonetheless.

'There's something better,' she said, eyes glued to the summit.

'Where are we?' he asked. Halfway through saying it, he saw the whales in the turquoise sky. She did not answer. They ran up the rocks. They heard their pursuers splash through behind them and Akila bellowed with all her might into the sky, 'Fin!'

Shyam saw the three insectoids shake off the water from their bodies, the first among them watching the two humans scampering up the hill. There was no escape. The insectoids could not go up at their usual speed over the uneven rocky terrain, but they were in no rush. They weaved their way forward in unpredictable patterns, like stalking spiders. At the hill's summit, Shyam held on to Akila on the odd-shaped rock that sat there. Under one arm he still held in his shirt the head he had hacked off. Akila threw her head back and screamed again, until her voice cracked and her throat ached. 'Fin!'

The leading insectoid came towards them, screeching. Its clawed hairy arm reached out maliciously to drag her down. A gust of wind made Shyam brace and adjust his footing. When it had passed, he saw the insectoid was no longer there. The remaining two insectoids stopped in their tracks, unable to register the sudden absence of the first. The dark shape of a great hammer ready to fall loomed in the sky. Shyam watched in amazement as the swivelling pod of dolphins came sweeping down in a tsunami, washing away the remaining two insectoids from the rocks. The pod rose into the sky and a small band broke off from the body as the main formation disappeared into the clouds. The band then swung in wide arcs around the two humans standing, trembling atop the hill, their distance closing with surprising speed.

Shyam guessed who it must be. The first love of Akila's life. The love she had never abandoned. They were large, larger than he had thought. Among the four dolphins were two manatee. Akila squirmed out of his embrace and stepped forward to the end of the rock, studying the faces of the dolphins closely. She could not tell Fin apart from the others. He could see she was frustrated, from the way her fingers clutched the hem of her T-shirt.

'Akila.' She heard Fin's voice say her name again after almost fifteen years. An exhalation leapt out of her throat. She wanted to look into his eyes and say, 'Fin'. The dolphins parted and a manatee, twenty feet long and six feet wide, came forward, dwarfing her upon the rock.

'Fin,' she said, and a single tear marked its trail down her right cheek. She looked up at him in amazement and Shyam was dumbfounded. He remembered Fin being a beautifully sleek dolphin, but more than the change in species, it was that he was amorphously different from a manatee. His eyes were not where they were meant to be on either side of the snout. Instead, the snout itself was a face protruding out of the mass of hulking flesh behind. What shocked him most was the almost human aspect looking back at Akila. The flippers hung like stubby arms without fingers. Akila lifted her hand warily to Fin's face and touched his soft skin. 'How?' she asked.

'This is life, Akila. We change.'

'We change,' she repeated softly, considering how his voice was the same and thanking the stars for preserving it.

'You were a dolphin,' she said in a hush.

'When we met I was a dolphin. I didn't start as one, and I won't end as one. Before I became a manatee, I was an orca, and when the time comes I will become a sperm whale and plunge from the depths of the sky to the shallows of space, and someday I will be a blue whale.' He spread out his flippers. 'We are all different, and yet we live the same journey of life.'

'You are still my Fin,' she said, touching his face. His flipper caressed her hand as they gazed at each other with the sad intimacy of lovers deprived of a lifetime of love.

Shyam crept off the rock and wandered down the hill to give them some space. What a marvel it was to hang upside down from the surface of the ocean and look into its hidden depths. For that was how it felt, gazing up at a sky of playful dolphins and roving pods of narwhal amidst two humpbacks. The beings from the thirteen worlds once shared Earth with us humans.

Shyam thought about Sholay. It upset him that Akila had never introduced them. He understood the secrets she had kept to make the plan work, though that did not mean he forgave her for the deception. And yet, why conceal Sholay? And there were other things too. It made his stomach turn, seeing how far his world had altered since he had risen this morning. Looking back at Akila speaking with Fin so intimately, he thought, when the day began my life was perfect. I was with my partner and unborn child. There were no other responsibilities, no bosses or banks or ambitions, only the two that counted. But the moment he was confronted by the insectoid, glowering in the clearing like an ominous monolith, it had become something else. He looked up and was surprised to find that he could make out the stars so early in the day.

'Is this why?' Akila asked Fin, gesturing to his body.

'You could not understand then that the Fin you were so much in love with would change. Would become unrecognizable with time.'

'I never stopped thinking about you.'

'I know,' he said with a melancholic smile, his gaze roving over the valley around the hill. From that height alone one could make out the sprawling designs. The arrangements of rocks depicting frolicking dolphins.

'Don't you see?' he asked softly, and then she knew he was right. It was the dolphin she had fallen in love with. It was there and plain to see, the work of her own hands half a lifetime ago. Her love letters to him, fashioned on full-moon nights. Her eyes streamed with tears and she held them shut to fight back the agony. Shyam saw the designs too from where he stood.

'Did you love me?' she blubbered.

'From the moment we said our first words to each other. And I have never stopped loving you.'

She nestled her forearms around Fin's face and held onto him.

'Akila,' Shyam said tentatively and she pulled herself away from Fin.

'Yeah?' she asked, weakened.

'I'm hungry as hell. Maybe it's all this running, but I need to eat something.'

She nodded, wiping away her tears.

Fin watched her with soft, kind eyes.

'I'm so proud of you,' he said. She bit her lip so she would not cry again.

'You're with child, Akila.'

She looked down at her belly and her face glowed with joy.

'And so is your mate,' he added with delight.

Akila looked up at Fin like he was crazy and then at Shyam, who showed the same confusion. It took them a moment, and then they both looked at the bulge under his T-shirt and said together, 'Oh, that!' Akila laughed. 'That's not a child. It's over, Fin!'

'What is?'

'Our captivity is over! The worlds are free! The Sentinel is dead!'

It was Fin's turn to be confused.

'What do you mean? How?'

'Show him,' she yelled at Shyam with glee. Shyam undid the knot and pulled out the head. The pain was so intense, his whole body went numb for a second and his knees buckled. He folded over, clutching his stomach.

'What happened?' Akila called out. And then he knew the stars were not really there. They showed only in his head as it ached for mercy. Akila scrambled down from the rock to help him. He pulled up his T-shirt to see and Akila shrieked in horror. The dolphins recoiled in alarm at the sight of the Sentinel's head rotted and without shape. A mouth had grown, wide and attached to his stomach. Thin, vein-like, red, blue and green tendrils were strung between the head and his body. He could bear the pain no longer. His back arched as he lurched backward, with Akila catching him just in time. But the stars began to spin and he recognized them. Then there was no more sky or Akila or flying manatee. There was a field of stars. Stars flowing away from him like sparks from a welder as he floated through space on his never-ending journey. A thought came to him and he cherished it. I am the river. I am the life.

6

A VAST CLOUD GLOWS in the infinite. Red and violet and lime yellow, and thick as mucus. At the outer limits the cloud thins to fingers and at the tips there is an energy collating into a point of light. But it is moving, always moving, turning silently in space with the calm of a dream. No, I'm moving, at speeds I cannot comprehend, through veils of liquid gases. Until I am through and stars fill my vision with emptiness between me and any point I can see. Long stretches of nothing.

AKILA SAT atop a milk whale, clutching an unconscious Shyam. She raised a hand to touch Fin's face one last time. It was time to go. They had said their goodbyes with words, but words cannot connect. He felt her deep within, their energies intertwining. He felt her like he had felt no other being before. She felt his joy, but knew she had to go. She drew her hand away with all the strength she could muster.

'I'll end this captivity,' she said, gazing at the lake surface below. 'I'll end this, I promise it.'

Fin did not say a word. He could only watch as she hooked an arm under Shyam's shoulder and stepped off the floating milk whale. With a light splash they vanished. As the whales and dolphins dispersed, Fin remained, watching the water longingly, for a vanished lifetime to return.

'Lovely Akila, read to me...'

AMIDST THE nothingness, a homing light in the distance beckons me closer. Towards the heart of the apple with its silver skin of floating, frozen rock. Closer. I unceremoniously pierce through the outer skin and sail along the plane of the system within. Large rocks bolt past. I can see the light, but its heat does not reach me. Mighty bodies of rock and gas pass me by, but they are not what I seek.

Then I see it, tearing out from the blinding sun, its silhouette ringed in blue. The blue of life. Not cold and despairing, but blooming in radiance. This is the blue I seek. Alone but for a dour companion never leaving her side. The blue crescent grows against the shimmering curtain of space and I peer into its shadow. I welcome it, the darkness that swallows me. At last.

7

SHYAM OPENED HIS EYES dreamily. A large sparkling bear stood over him, licking his face. When it saw that he was awake, it stepped away and Shyam's hand felt for the Sentinel's head on his stomach. It had been the last thing he saw. Before the stars. The head fused to his belly – it was not there anymore. There were no scars or signs of any trauma.

'Where is it?' he asked weakly. Akila entered his field of vision and took his face in her hands. 'Where?' he pressed, trying to sit up. She helped, the worry plain to see upon her face. He realized where he was and the gathered animal spirits around him did not shock or astound him as Akila had expected. Instead, he looked through the Irish elk and the Hokkaido wolves and thylacine, searching the ground for the head that he saw lying on a narrow lush strip some feet away. The fog was thick and he felt claustrophobic after sailing through the galaxy.

'What is it, Shy?' she asked, afraid he was having a seizure or an episode. 'You should rest. Everything is all right now. You're healed. The head can't hurt you anymore.'

'I need the head.'

'Come on, baby, lie down and rest some more.'

'Give me the head, Akila.'

'If this wasn't the wrong time, I'd make a dirty joke,' she whispered, trying to cheer him up.

'There's a way,' he said in a panic.

She rubbed his back to settle him.

'Akila, I almost saw.'

'What did you see?'

'I almost saw where it really is.'

'What are you talking about?'

'The thing – the alien,' he yelled, his voice like stonework. The animal spirits sensed his agitation and took a step back uneasily.

'It isn't dead,' he declared, realizing he was losing it.

'Yes, it is. You cut off its head. You killed it.'

He shook his head, exhausted more in mind than body, and told her, 'The Sentinel is just a transceiver for it to communicate. The creature itself is still alive. Hidden.'

'How do you know this?

'The head,' he asserted, struggling to find the words to articulate his thoughts, 'The head. Please bring it to me.'

'What are you going to do with it?'

'I'm going to connect.'

She stared at him in utter surprise. Those words should not have come out of his mouth, she thought.

Suddenly sitting upright on her knees, she frowned down at him and asked, 'What are you talking about?'

He shot an accusing glare at her through his wet, hanging locks.

'I saw everything – what has happened to you – your whole life. I saw it all.'

'How?' she asked, then pointed at the head. 'Through that?'

'When I fell in the water.'

'That's impossible. You were in there for only three minutes.'

'I don't know how, and I don't know why. But I know a hell of a lot more now than I did before falling in.'

Akila stared into the drifting fog, searching for an explanation she could not find. The animal spirits had faded away, leaving the couple to attend to wounds they could not mend.

'Why didn't you take me to Sholay? Why did you keep him from me?' Shyam felt the words trip off his tongue.

She did not reply at once. When she did, she faced him. 'Because there are some things that are mine. Mine alone. Why must I share everything? Can't I have some things to myself?'

'I gave up everything to come here and be with you.'

'I didn't ask you to come.'

'But that was the plan, wasn't it? To get me here willingly, and this!' He gestured in contempt at her swollen belly.

'It wasn't my plan, any of this!'

'But you went along with it.'

'Look around, man! Does it look like I'm here by invitation? Does it look like I had a choice in anything?'

He knows it is true and he wishes there could have been another way. 'You could have told me why.'

'Then you wouldn't have come.'

'Even after I'd come.'

'Then what would be the point? We'd both be trapped here and I'd be dead at the next sacrifice, and you too.'

'Exactly!' He shook with emotion. 'We're in the same boat here! All I expected was for you to share with me. Share your life as I have shared mine with you. Share the little things and the big things. Share the good and the bad.'

'What I've got, I've killed and died for,' she told him, stroking her belly.

'Then what is the point in keeping it to yourself? Wouldn't you want to share it with someone you love all the more?'

'What do you do when you alone become the keeper of the secret of human existence? Of why we exist at all? Our purpose in the universe?'

'Here's the truth,' he said, nodding as he processed his surging emotions. 'That I learnt it, not from the person I love most in this universe, as I should have, but from a fucking alien. The alien's told me more about you in two minutes than you have in an entire year. That's the fucking truth!'

'It had no fucking right doing that!'

'You're damn right, it didn't! Because you should have done it in the first place. You have a right to your privacy, Akila, but not to a secret that affects me just as much as it does you.'

'Now you know! Now you know the fucking truth!'

'Don't you get it?' He sighed, his shoulders hunched over with exhaustion. 'That's not what I'm upset about! That's not what this is about! It's about you not giving me the greatest gift you could have, and it wouldn't have cost you a rupee. I should have heard it from you. You should have shown me ... it would have meant everything to me for it to have come from you. To have you share it with me.'

Akila seemed just as exhausted as he was. She did not look at him anymore. He could not tell whether it was from remorse or contempt, outrage at having her secrets revealed against her will.

He watched her crawl to the head. She asked, trying not to seem pushy, 'Are you going to connect to it?' She rolled it back to him with a grimace, muttering, 'I'm not touching this thing.' The head came to a stop at his thigh and she sat a few feet away from him.

'Akila ...' he started to speak, but she cut him short, barking, 'Just shut the fuck up and do it.'

Shyam studied the grotesque rotting head gazing up at him. Its face had shrunk and lifted to accommodate the enlarged mouth, lips wide and teeth knotted, wrapped in discoloured tendrils. This would be his first time connecting, and it was with this vile thing. Running Sholay's instructions to Akila through his mind, and Akila's own experience of connecting over the years, he felt he knew what he was doing. He laid his hand on the side of the face, and closed his eyes to concentrate fully.

The darkness. And then the shooting lights of energy. The electric warmth coursing through his nerves. This is our purpose, he thought through the ecstasy, to connect with life. To explore the world with our minds!

Akila watched Shyam's reactions to the connection and felt the intense sensation of a violation. She knew it was not his doing and that he had not asked for it to happen, but the fact remained that he knew everything. All her secrets. He was the face of that violation. Her pain had been the private badge of honour she never revealed to a soul, and now it had been ripped away, the meaning spilt on a dirty floor. She picked up a frog and placed it on her belly. It grumpily ogled back at her. What are you even doing here, she wondered. Are you magical frogs?

A movement near Shyam caught her eye. The tendrils were beginning to wriggle in the grass, slithering like earthworms towards Shyam's thigh. Akila reached out to grab the head, knocking the frog off its perch, just as Shyam came out of the connection and slapped the head away. It rolled to a stop and the wriggling died down entirely, while they both watched it in utter revulsion.

'There is a way I can kill it,' he said, his voice hard.

'How?'

'But its death will destroy these worlds it created, possibly killing everything that lives in them.'

'Is there a good choice?'

He tried to remain firm, but relented, 'I can't kill them.'

'You're saving them.'

'By killing them. By wiping them out of existence.'

She fumbled for an argument. 'They don't exist. Not really.'

'In our realm or theirs, they exist on some level, and who the fuck are you or I to say our existence is more real than theirs?'

She considered this for a while, then shrugged. 'Then you have a choice to make.'

'You make it,' he asserted, adding softly, 'make the choice, and I'll do whatever you say.'

She looked into his eyes, and with a tired chuckle, rasped, 'No. I have enough to bear. It's your choice.'

He looked at a frog near his foot. It hopped to the edge, wiped its eye with its sticky hand, and dove into the water.

'I need to talk to Sholay,' he said at last. Akila considered him suspiciously, and then agreed with a curt nod.

HE CLIMBED out of the large pool, unable to take his eyes off the titan, whose towering form was seated some distance away, with folded legs, like a hill in repose. Sholay's eyes glowed with life as he smiled almost tenderly at the two damp humans before him. He said, 'At last.'

THEY SAT on his right knee, having said their share and awaiting his reply. 'What do you want me to say?' he asked.

'We've told you everything. Tell us, should we kill the alien even if its death would mean the destruction of these worlds?'

'Obviously humans don't remember the time we were there among them,' he said sombrely, 'For more than 50,000 years we have been imprisoned here, plucked from our purposes, marooned on worlds like playthings for its amusement.'

'Billions of living things,' Shyam emphasized.

'Billions of prisoners,' Sholay countered. 'Release us, if you have the key.'

'You don't mind dying?'

'I don't wish it, but I prefer it to this.' He leaned closer. 'Can I help?'

Shyam shook his head. 'I've thought about it, but I can't see how. We can't take you directly to the target because you are too big and going there from the closest lake large enough to accommodate you will warn the alien of our approach, giving it the chance to go into hiding elsewhere.'

8

SHYAM MASSAGED AKILA'S LOWER back beside their pond. 'We'll get one opportunity for this,' she said. He agreed with a low grunt, and massaged her in silence for a while. Macoco lay in the clearing by the pond, anxiously watching Akila. She saw him and grinned. He moaned and gently nudged her shoulders with his snout to comfort her. 'I'll take you home first,' she told him.

'No,' Macoco protested. 'I will help. You need my help here.'

'Everything is going to end, Macoco. There won't be a "here" once we do this. You belong with your family.'

'I am with my family,' he told her defiantly and turned away to sulk.

She fell silent, amused by his immature behaviour. She loved him.

'How do we do this?' Shyam asked, kissing her back and resting his forehead against it for her touch.

'Tell me exactly where it is,' she asked.

'For the last time, you aren't doing this. I'm not trying to be brave or the "guy". If you weren't pregnant I'd let you take the reins by all means.'

She let out a mock laugh.

'I'm serious. But you are pregnant. That water will eat through your skin.'

'You said it's deep.'

'Yeah.'

'Then how are you going to do it?'

'I'm a good swimmer.'

'Not as good as I am.'

'I'm not pregnant. I don't have a fully formed being inside me skin deep.'

She knew he was right. 'But still,' she said stubbornly, 'how can you make it that far? I'm the Beli.'

'We don't know if you still arc, and our baby isn't one. So that's no argument.'

'I'm not arguing,' she said pouting. 'I'm just–'

'I know.' He kissed her again.

Cola's enormous head surfaced and his button eyes stared up at them. 'Me,' he said.

THE ENORMOUS flat head and half the body already lay outside the pond. His dark skin glistened the colour of cola. His head lifted, button eyes gazing at Akila. She stood before him, with Shyam waiting behind her.

'I can't let you do it,' Akila said firmly.

Shyam tried to interject, but she silenced him with a stern look.

'The worlds are ending, Akila,' Cola said to her.

'The worlds are ending.' She tasted the words in her mouth.

'So why do the risks matter?'

'They matter because I care.'

His head rested on the ground, unable to support the weight for too long.

'Your caring alone will not free any one of us.'

'What do you want me to say, Cola?'

'It is a simple plan,' he told her, 'But one that cannot be accomplished without me. You know it, too.'

She did not respond.

'Shyam's skin will dissolve and he will drown in agony long before he reaches the recesses of the roots, where he must be. We have but one chance, Akila.'

A flicker of a smile touched the corners of her lips at hearing his voice shape her name.

'Listen to him,' Shyam blurted out.

She shot him a sidelong glare.

'I will carry him in my mouth and take him there,' Cola said.

'What about you?' she asked, unable to look him in the eyes.

'What about me? I don't matter.'

'You matter,' she insisted, falling upon his slick head and hugging him with outstretched arms.

'This is something I must do.'

SHOLAY STOOD on the deserted plain, the circle of water near him an ominous reminder of the end that would soon approach. He wondered whether there was any point remaining here, or if he should return to the company of his kind, wailing at the swarming heavens thick with churning clouds.

'WE SHOULD let him do this,' Shyam whispered to Akila in the jungle, gilded with portions of moonlight through the trees.

'This is what he wants,' she agreed. 'But I wish he would let Macoco help. He cannot bear to see Cola suffering, and neither can I.'

Shyam rubbed her shoulder to give some comfort. A few feet ahead of them, twigs cracked and the dry leaves on the forest floor rustled as a dark form crawled with great effort through the bushes. He never stopped to rest, a mass shifting in the shadows. His almost human black fingers dug in and heaved the body forward, one herculean step at a time.

HE WOULD not return to the glowing rivers of rock. Sholay had decided he would stay where he had been happiest. Where he had spent time with Akila. If there was any way he could help her, he would have. He wished they had taken him with them. To remain here, alone and ineffectual, was punishing.

At the circle of water, there was no longer any sign of what had once been there. The accursed tree, with its field of roots lurking on the surface, was gone. He had watched as his kind rent and tore at the roots, hysterically throwing the pieces about in the savagery of hate and revenge. But their freedom had not come. A few who had torn at the roots had fallen into the pool as the foundation collapsed beneath them, and he had watched helplessly as they sank into the depths, never to be seen again.

COLA WAS nearing the pool at the field of roots. He stopped to rest, his body trembling with the effort. The sky was turning over to its brighter half with the glow of dawn. Shyam and Akila sat beside Cola, slipping jamblis into his waiting mouth. With her free hand Akila caressed Shyam's knee while he examined the insides of Cola's mouth. It was certainly big enough to hold him if he remained in a foetal position. He refused to think about the one thing that loomed at the back of his mind. His intense claustrophobia.

SHOLAY MOVED closer to the edge of the water. It lay as still as a metal sheet, reflecting the turmoil in the sky. There is a tree, thought Sholay, somewhere on this world. Though we ripped it out, could it have survived? Were Akila and her mate wasting their lives on a mission with no hope of success?

THEY COULD not help Cola down the steep slope. If he slipped, he would crush them both. Akila and Shyam watched from the top as he manoeuvred down the incline, hooking his fingers on tree-roots and rocks. 'Go down to him before he gets to the water,' Akila told Shyam.

'You're right,' Shyam replied, his face a pale mask. She grabbed his wrist before he went over the edge. He looked at her for her next instruction, but she pulled him close and hugged him. She could hear his laboured breaths. He was terrified. She kissed his cheek, the corner of his mouth, his lips, his chin. She cupped his face in her palms and looked into his eyes. 'I'll be waiting for you, Shy,' she whispered, giving him a final, quick, wet kiss. He wanted to be back in bed with her, lying side by side, glazed in sweat on wet bed sheets, studying each other's eyes after a heated love-making session. I love you, he thought, you are my life, chanting it like a mantra in his head. He pulled away from her and began his descent.

THE WATER was cold, colder than anything Sholay had felt since Earth. He dunked his head in the water and saw that there was not much light filtering through below. The walls of the pool ran straight down more than a thousand feet and then ceased, abruptly breaking off into darkness. There was only one chance for him to see what lay beyond. He had to fall in. He would be lost, he knew. He was rock and he would sink to the very bottom. He wondered how far it went. Would he remain trapped below, unable to climb out? None of the others had returned. But if Akila and Shyam were willing to risk everything, why should he not? He leaned forward and slid into the water, realizing how much he had missed it. But there was something different about it. This is not just water, he thought, falling deeper.

COLA KEPT his mouth ajar, inviting Shyam to enter. Shyam looked up at Akila one last time. She was not crying. She was all cried out. He kissed the stone ring she had given him, three times, his eyes fixed on hers. Then he stepped into Cola's mouth and did not waste any time getting used to it. He put on the swimming goggles, lay on his side and curled up so he was fully contained. Already his heart was racing. He had the ring to his lips, his eyes tightly closed. He could sense the light failing as the mouth closed, and soon it was pitch black. The soft, slimy inside of Cola's mouth held him firmly. He could hear Cola's massive heart beating and guessed that they must already be under water now. There was no turning back.

SHOLAY RAN his fingers along the surface of the wall, carved smooth with precision. Where the wall was cut short, he found himself in a larger chamber within. On the far side, he could just make out in the fading light a crooked root sticking out from the recesses. So it had survived after all. As his eyes grew accustomed to the darkness he could define the shape of the tree, hanging upside down from its nest of roots, flourishing as it had done on the surface. What hope was there then, of killing this thing? He doubted for the first time whether salvation was around the corner; he would be trapped in this underwater cavern for the rest of eternity. As his brothers had broken with time and screamed at the skies for release, he had endured. But now he wailed, sinking deeper into the oblivion.

9

DEAD BIRDS AND FOXES and lizards and insects littered his path through the labyrinth of roots. In the water Cola was in his element, even if the lake ate away at his skin. The slimy coating of protection had lasted for only a few minutes. Shyam's directions had been simple enough, and he had listened well. Into the deepest part of the pool, in the heart of the thickest network of roots, directly below where the tree stood, to the stalk connecting into the ground. That was the point Shyam had to reach.

Cola crawled through the narrow gaps, wondering how much deeper it went. It was getting harder to see in the dark. Peering through the tangled mess, he saw no end to it.

Shyam was not sure why he had his eyes closed. Was he afraid of dying? Yes, since he was not sure whether this plan would succeed. He had some things with him in a plastic toilet bag. Those were all the tools he had at his disposal for the mission. It was madness. There was no hope of survival. He tried not to think about the tightness of the space he was cramped inside. The sensation of the walls pushing in. His lungs constricted, like a crushed plastic bottle, unable to inflate. His breaths became short and it felt like no air could enter his lungs. His shoulders wanted to stretch, his bones wanted to burst out of their restrictions. Claustrophobia had crippled him all his life. Not now, he begged. Please, not now. Stretch, he screamed in his head. Open. His hand opened. He shuffled it outward and against Cola's mouth. The surge of the connection with Cola was a burst of life to him. He breathed again.

Cola paused for a second, taken aback by the connection from within. He knew he was almost there as he thrust his way through a tight spot and that was it.

'We're here,' he told Shyam through the connection.

'Can you see anything?'

'There is very little light.'

'I brought some with me.'

Shyam took the LED headlamp out of his toilet bag, keeping it ready.

'When I count to three, open your mouth and let me out.'

'All right.'

'One,' Shyam said, breathing calmly. Now or never.

'Two, three.' He made the count and drew in a deep breath. Just in time, as Cola opened his mouth and the vacuum sent Shyam tumbling outward. He took a moment to orient himself, and then quickly slipped on the headlamp. He turned the dial for the LEDs on his forehead. Thick, interlocking roots were caught in the flood of white light, and he scanned about for the stalk he had clearly seen through his connection with the head.

They were ten feet from the lake floor with its carpet of phosphorescent anemone swaying in the silent current in their hypnotic way. The stalk itself was thinner than the roots, appearing as an innocuous coupler between the tree and the soil. He struck at it with the blade but it hardly made a mark. Three feet lower a bright orange patch stood out, covered with projections resembling mushrooms of varying sizes. At the centre it grew in a pale pinkish hue. The mushroom caps opened and closed as the gills underneath them sucked in water and expelled a warm current. This was the spot, he was certain. He let the toilet bag drop away and focused. The blade he held bounced a streak of light from his headlamp across the stalk.

'Stop.' The Sentinel's voice sounded clearly in the depths, and he knew it was the alien speaking.

Shyam sensed he was being watched but he could not see how. He had only the breath in his lungs to do the deed and he could not waste any more time. He dug ferociously at the pink centre with the end of the blade.

'Please stop,' the voice implored.

The mushrooms came away easier with a swipe of his hand across the surface, bursting into powder at his touch and dissolving. He did not need the blade, he realized, and dug his hand into the orange skin outside the pink centre. He grabbed a handful and tugged it off, and a chunk of flesh came out with it. He looked inside and saw that he was past the outer trunk

'I was wrong to try and kill you. I was wrong to try and take your child.'

The innards of the stalk were now exposed to him as a tightly bound layer of plump tendons. He used the knife to cut through them, and they snapped like rubber bands with every slice.

'I can make things right again. You can live with Akila. You can be happy once more. It does not have to end.'

He was past the tendons now, and into an inner chamber where a thin, inky blue ooze clouded the water.

'I promise, Shyam. I promise. Don't do this.'

Shyam could not decide where to look as he made the final jab. Fuck, this was frustrating. He would have to reach his entire arm in through the opening. He leveraged himself with his free hand and anchored his toes on the stalk. Suddenly a light flashed, followed by a flickering beam that lasted five seconds.

Cola watched in horror as Shyam remained unmoving in the water as though in a trance. The plan was for him to wait for Shyam to get the job done and return with him to the surface. He searched for anything he could do to help, even as he felt parts of his own skin peeling away with every second. Something fell from Shyam, glinting its tail as it spiralled to the bottom among the waving anemone. It was the blade. Cola did not know what had gone wrong.

Shyam saw only the flickering light. He could no longer feel the water singeing his skin or the blade in his hand. He had lost. They had lost. All was lost.

'How can you understand when you cannot even comprehend my existence?' The Sentinel's voice boomed in the strobing light.

'I know you exist, you alien bastard. I'm here to fix that.'

The rate of the flashing decreased until it was only black, and in the emptiness the Sentinel's voice was almost a whisper. 'I have a secret.'

An explosion of stars surrounded him, and he sailed through. Always moving. Never still. Never the same view twice. 'Do you know why I see stars flowing in my dreams?'

Shyam hesitated. 'I've seen your dreams.'

'I showed them to you. Do you know why I see them?'

'The stars?'

'Because they were my home for more than four billion years.'

Shyam could not apprehend such a time frame. How could he? Even the Earth was barely four-and-a-half-billion years old.

'I travelled the galaxy, and do you know what secret I discovered? One that you won't believe, but it is true.'

'What is it?'

'That the planet you call Earth is alone. It is the treasure of the galaxy and this modest wet rock hides away in an unassuming system.'

'Alone?'

'The galaxy with its three hundred billion stars had so much of everything, except for the great accident you call life. Life is Earth's true value. Earth is the jewel, for here alone, somehow there was a conspiracy of variables that struck to conceive the spark.'

'You found Earth by accident?'

'You could say that. The same sort of accident of fate by which your child has found itself inside Akila. I didn't find the Earth. I was here.'

'That can't be.'

'In the beginning, there was my birth.'

Shyam flew over jagged mountain ridges with deep dark measureless pits venting gases, and over great expanses of crashing waves.

'When the oceans and rivers had barely marked time, I was a part of this planet. I was the first to breathe its air and recognize my existence. And you call me alien?'

Shyam was stunned.

'I functioned without purpose. Breathing and feeding on the elements, because I did. Multiplying because it was my nature. The currents and the winds gently carried my spores.'

White feathery flecks drifted in the thick water. Some washed up on rocks, where they were dried by the sun. The wind picked them up and they flew high and far, eventually dropping and sticking under rocks.

'That is when I truly understood the power of life. When I created it.'

Rain fell on the spores. Some were destroyed by the impact and some disappeared into the soil.

'Life will survive by itself. It will endure. But it must be created, or else have its seed planted.'

A point of light jabbed into the atmosphere and marked a white trail to the crust. The ground shifted and bulged. It distended into hills seamed with cracks and burst in a series of vast explosions, throwing up great plumes of smoke and shooting rocks into the sky.

The impact was so massive, the entire landmass around the growing crater swelled and rolled and shattered. Smoke clouds collated like an oil spill spreading at the edge of the vaporized atmosphere as fragments of rock were ejected into space.

'Expelled from Earth's womb into the stars, I felt lost beyond measure. Rolling like a loose blossom in the cosmic winds, I saw I was alone. And I missed my home all the more. Her warm embrace.'

Jupiter passed by and then Saturn. The sun was no more than a bright dot among the peering stars.

'Adrift in the cosmos I discovered the horrible truth of the Earth's solitude. A multitude of stars with a single breath of life. I treasured her even more then, and dreamt among the stars of returning someday. And as I dreamt through cloud nebulae and skirting comets, I began to evolve in my understanding and it dawned on me. I was the first being born with a purpose. And my purpose was glorious. To spread Earth's gift, the gift of life.'

Spores spilled out into space in streaking flakes. Shyam had experienced this before and expected what came next.

'I understood, Shyam. I understood then in the loneliness of space, sowing the seeds of life that I am like a river, the messenger of life. That I am the river. I am the life.'

The stars danced around him as a belt of asteroids cascaded by, rotating dreamily in place. One of them touched another, knocking it lightly off its mark, and a sedate chain reaction commenced with rocks touching rocks, sending them ricocheting in all directions around him. The spores stuck to the asteroids that had been flung out on new voyages.

'And I know that I too changed. I grew into something else as I understood more about the Universe. Whether I matured into what I was meant to be, I do not know, and it will forever remain a mystery.'

There was a vast nebula in neon hues to the left and to the right was the apex of the galaxy. The motion of the spiral arms was itself not noticeable, but the closer they got to the centre, near the dark spot there, he could see some motion. Whether it was a trick of the eye, or a distortion in space, or something at the centre swallowing the stars, he could not tell.

'Then some time ago, I felt I would be home soon. Was it my doing or the cosmic tides bringing me home? I do not know.'

Shyam recognized the images then, of entering the solar system and heading to Earth as he had seen when the head had clung to his stomach. The closer he got to Earth, the more he missed the sea of stars around him. He saw the blue sphere and dove into its shadow. The blackness began to flicker.

'That is when I found the world flooding over with life in the oceans, the land and the air. I wept with joy at the knowledge that only I had, of Earth's role as mother to all life. Now no longer confined to her, but spread throughout the galaxy, to follow whatever paths fate threw at them. That without her, and my mission, the stars would be unthinking rocks and gas.

'I had come home at last, after four billion years. And I found there was no longer any place for me. Not for me, her child back from the stars! I was the first to leave the nest of life and yet I came home a foreigner. I, the river of life, was not welcome back in her embrace.

'Because she had embraced another in my stead. She had

nurtured your evolution and the Earth, the seed of life, became your ward when it should have been mine. The whole world belonged to you. All of life loved you because you could connect with them in a way I never could. A way that did not yet exist when I was born, and was now forever barred to me. Handed over to a species that had not existed for a blink of my lifetime. That could not comprehend how special life truly is.

'How was that right? How was it that I was still lonely, and you had so much? What I knew was this, that I had earned the role of her guardian, earned the love of all life. And if she could not see the wisdom of that, I had to show her. And I did. By punishing you. By ripping away the beings closest and dearest to you. I made thirteen other worlds upon Earth's foundation and supplanted the beings in each.'

'Why?'

'At last a word from you. Do you ask, why?'

'Why these elaborate constructions of worlds and supplanting? Why not just kill them?'

'I create life. I don't destroy it. I took them away because I knew you would be lost without them, and you soon were. Now your kind does not even remember how to connect with life. You have forgotten your role as the guardian and you have lost your place, thinking the Earth belongs to you and you have enslaved her. Why didn't I kill them, you asked? Because they are mine, and mine alone. My roots hold these worlds together and I am no longer alone. Now *I* am connected!'

'Not for much longer.'

But even uttering those words, Shyam wondered whether he could kill the first sentient life on Earth, the first in the galaxy. The one that had spread the seeds of life among the stars. Could he, with one plunge of the knife, wipe out over four billion years of experience and billions of lives on thirteen worlds?

Were the scales balanced with him, Akila and their child on one hand and the rest of those lives on the other? Even his family's existence was not assured. Akila had a plan to escape, but they both knew it was a slim chance.

But did it deserve his compassion? It might be the oldest life form in the galaxy, but it was still a tyrant, with powers evolved beyond his comprehension. It acted not out of a necessity to survive, but out of spite. It robbed the purpose of humankind, and allowed it to devolve into a self-obsessed infestation, gang-raping Earth to sludge. He was not murdering the creature. He was the cure for it. The inoculation for the scourge it had made itself into.

'I can sense your thoughts, human. And I will stop you!'

The strobing light quickened and Shyam felt his vision blur as a humming rang in his ears. Cola felt he had waited long enough and swam out to Shyam. He reached out a hand where the cola-coloured skin had peeled off, exposing festering patches of pink flesh to the scalding water. He held Shyam's shoulder and felt the body jerk. Shyam kicked out and thrashed his arms as though he were drowning. Then he was still again, and Cola thought he had lost him for good. Suddenly Shyam spun about and faced Cola, his face reflecting utter disbelief as he presented his empty hands. The blade was gone. Shyam followed Cola's intimation down to the anemone. He caught a glint of metal from his LEDs among the blissfully waving field. His chest was aching now, and he knew he had only seconds left before blacking out. Already his heart pounded wildly. He pulled himself down along the stalk to the bottom and picked up the blade.

The Sentinel's voice came booming in his head. 'I am the river. I am the life.' Shyam started his way up to the wound he had dug out before being interrupted by the dramatic show-

and-tell. He glimpsed the squirming organ he had exposed and held the knife, ready to plunge it in and tear out the creature's life. He felt like his own chest might implode any moment. The Sentinel's voice resounded. 'I carry these worlds on my shoulders. And you would kill me and let them crumble?'

Shyam clutched the blade tightly in his fist so it would not drop again.

'I am the life!' The Sentinel roared inside his head.

'Then I am the death,' Shyam replied, and thrust in the blade.

10

AKILA STOOD GAZING AT the surface still, waiting for their return. It had been far too long, even for Cola. She blinked and before the movement registered, she stumbled at the edge of the cliff. She thought for a brief moment that she had lost her balance, but then her eardrums almost burst from the explosions around her as the ground quaked, and in the distance, great plumes of dust and earth were thrown into the sky. The ground buckled under her feet. She held onto a tree as a rolling tremor lifted the forest on the far side of the field of roots, and at once she felt a wave of elation run through her body.

Shyam had done it! He had succeeded.

But where were they? The roots began to collapse into the lake and the mound itself was crumbling. She could not see the tree anymore. The water thrashed about wildly. In the midst of it she saw the shape sliding towards the bank. There was no time to lose. She held one arm over her stomach to guard it and rushed down the steep embankment to meet them. Cola lurched out of the water, laying half his body on the shore. Akila was jolted by the sight of him, the large patches of exposed pink flesh. His dark skin hung in strips. She saw him trying to open his mouth and helped him lift his upper jaw. Shyam pulled himself out and rolled on the ground, gasping urgently for air. His skin too was seared to the colour of burnt umber.

Akila felt Cola's jaw go heavy and she could not carry the weight of it alone. It snapped down and his head lay limply to one side.

'No!' she cried. The wind picked up as Macoco's down wash hit them. He landed in the shallows and took in the sight of Akila weeping on Cola's head.

'Akila, we must go,' he yelled through the shrieking of birds and the crashes of falling trees. She stood up at once and took Shyam's arm to lead him into the water towards Macoco who offered an arm for them to climb up. Akila straddled his neck and called out, 'Pick him up.' Macoco observed Cola's lifeless form, half in and half out of the pool that had killed him.

'Akila?' Shyam grabbed her shoulders from behind. 'He's gone. Respect his sacrifice, goddammit!'

'I'm bringing him back!' She leaned forward and said, her tone scathing, 'Pick him up. We're all going.'

Macoco gently lifted Cola's corpse. It was no easy feat, but he managed. The ground shook as he bounded into the sky, his wings thrusting with a passion. He heard Akila say, 'Let's leave this place forever,' and banked to the left to dive headlong into the water.

SHYAM AND Akila were thrown into the air. He had his arms around her already and twisted them about so she landed on him, and rolled to a stop. He recognized the fog instantly.

'I thought we were going home,' Shyam said.

'First we're healing him here. The spirits can do it,' she said, breathing hard. She got up and searched for Macoco, shouting, 'Where is he?' Shyam joined her in the search. It was eerie. There was a sound of approaching thunder, distant yet. Running along the narrow strip of grass, they found

Macoco chest-deep in a pool hardly big enough to fit him. His arm was stuck between his chest and the wall of earth, still holding Cola.

Macoco whimpered with relief when he saw Akila approach. She came up to him and rubbed his arm to comfort her friend.

'I can't move, Akila,' he said in a trembling voice. 'I can feel the ground under me twisting. Help me!' Akila looked to Shyam. He knew there was nothing they could do. This was something they had not foreseen.

'Akila!' Macoco cried out. The thunderous roar drew closer. All three of them looked towards it. The fog gradually began to glow brighter and brighter until a barrage of forest spirits came fleeing in the haze. Shyam braced Akila for the impact but the spirits charged through them. The sound of thunder was coming closer, and then it was upon them. They saw the fog part like a curtain and the ground buckled, throwing them backwards. Akila heard Macoco shout her name as she and Shyam plunged into the water.

SHYAM STOOD up in the shallows, shouting as he cleared his eyes. 'What the fuck was that?' He winced at Akila's pinch on his collarbone. Their eyes locked, and he saw the fear in her eyes. Of a horror experienced.

'Beli!'

He heard the shriek and looked up at the branches populated with misshapen birds. The Sawa, the name echoed in his psyche. They were focused on Akila and him, only tearing their eyes away to look back at the gigantic forest of Paz, towards the approaching thunder. The turbulence of the great trees smashing into each other in the distance induced a wailing lament. 'Beli!' came the screech from a looming Sawa head five feet away. Shyam stood rooted to the spot, transfixed by the piercing eagle eyes as more Sawa approached. Akila held on to his shoulder with one hand, the other on her stomach, and threw them sidelong.

SHYAM COUGHED as the churned sand filled his mouth and nostrils. It whipped his face with a thousand points. His raw skin was sandblasted and he felt it being ground away. 'Not here,' he heard Akila say. 'Why did you bring us here then?' he yelled back and spat out the mouthful of sand that came with it. 'Why the fucking hell would I bring us here? There is no more control in where we go with every splash through.'

'What do we do?'

'This is the worst place to be stuck in if we want to dive in a hurry.'

'Why?'

'The water disappears into the sand in a matter of seconds. Look around you.'

Shyam had been sitting waist deep in water when they had splashed down, but now it had gone.

'Get up!' she yelled. 'We have to keep moving and find another pool right now.'

They began hiking up the sand dune. The ground began to shake and the sand swallowed their feet. They held onto each other and rushed up. The dune was shrinking with the vibration and they were on top soon. The sandstorm increased in fury, rising into a glittering vortex of golden-brown, and amidst it there was a wetness. It was raining.

'There!' he heard her yell. He could not open his eyes. She grabbed his shoulder and they bolted as hard as they could down the other side. The storm howled, and through it they heard the familiar thunder. Shyam strained his eyes to narrow slits just enough to see the wet patch they were charging towards. He let her guide him and was thankful to get wet again.

HIS HEAD had barely come out of the water for breath when he felt Akila tug him up and pull him along at a quick pace. The ground was quaking wildly and as he ran along he splashed his eyes with handfuls of water to wash out the sand. He opened them and immediately spat a curse under his breath, just as the call went up.

'Beli!'

Running into shallower water, they stumbled as the great insectoid spires collapsed around them. Hordes of bugs ran about in a panic until they heard the call, 'Beli!' Then they searched for the anonymous source pointing at the two humans in the river. From the entrance of the mound there was a shriek. It was the Kier, and as his beetle stepped out, he shouted, 'My people! Our world is ending and I give you one last mission to avenge our demise.' He pointed a long polished arm at Akila, a claw aimed directly at her, and screamed with all his might so they could hear, 'Kill the Beli!'

Behind him the rising dust veiled the sun. A great dark shape rose into the sky. Shyam felt no hesitation now. There was only one thing to do. The two of them turned as one, and hand in hand, they jumped in.

FROM THE taste of the water she knew she was in the dry wasteland. It was a relief to not be hunted anymore. They felt the tremor, but it was nowhere as intense as it had been on previous worlds. The crocodiles were huddled in the shade of the boulders. They stepped out to catch their breath. Shyam washed his face again with the tepid water. The sand was everywhere. In his ears, stuck in his nostrils and mouth, tickling his scalp, grinding between his buttocks and chaffing his scrotum. 'Let's get out of here,' he called. 'The thing's done, let's go.' Akila was squinting at the horizon. She said, more to herself than him, 'What is that?'

Shyam peered into the distance. 'A dust storm picking up?'

'No, there are things flying.'

He looked harder and saw the roving shapes. Then, beyond the forms on the ground and the sky, the horizon swelled and buckled.

'Oh shit,' she said, moving backwards into the water. 'Oh fuck.'

'What is it?' Shyam asked fearfully.

'That isn't possible,' she mumbled.

'What is it?'

'It's them!'

'Who?'

'The Sawa and the insectoids.'

'That's impossible.'

She took his wrist and they began to turn to the water. That was when they saw it for the first time. The ground folding and the horizon lifting into the sky. As the escalating surface became perpendicular to the ground, sand and rocks tumbled off its surface. That was the thunder. The worlds were folding in on themselves.

Akila and Shyam did not waste any time leaping into the green water.

SHYAM WAS pulling her back into the water, but Akila resisted, yelling, 'Fin', at the panic-stricken whales and dolphins in the sky. 'There isn't time, Akila. We have to go!'

'But–' She hesitated.

Shyam gripped both her shoulders. He wanted to yell, 'There

isn't time!' But she understood at last and relented. Rocks and boulders tumbled as the hills beyond rose in a sigh that grew into thunder.

THEY FUMBLED out of the freezing water and sped along the black banks of the stream in the snow-covered world. The ice giants were no longer in slumber. They were looking about in wonder at their changing landscape, sensing what was coming. The end of their imprisonment. Then the mountains began to crawl with insectoids and the giants regarded them curiously. The dark specks swept over the white landscape and over them.

SHYAM HELPED Akila out of the circular pool and she looked about for Sholay. He was nowhere to be seen. She began to weep, shaking uncontrollably.

'Akila,' Shyam said, touching her arm.

'I'm losing all of them. They're all gone.' The ground shook in a world accustomed to violence, and through the blizzard of ash they saw great glowing geysers soar into the air as a great chunk of the world began to fold. They had to keep going.

THEY CAME hopping out of the water with the washing wave and ran along it, staring in astonishment at the growing wall of water slapping the sky. They did not miss a step and together, they flopped into the upcoming swell.

THE HUNTERS were nowhere to be seen and they were not missed. Shyam and Akila jogged along the river to catch their breath from all the splashing in and out. The forest lay quiet just as any forest they knew. Then the sky darkened as the world rose to fold in on itself. It was a mesmerizing sight, interrupted suddenly by a Sawa that tore into view and careened towards them all at once, screeching, 'Beli!' It misjudged the turn and its side clipped a tree trunk, sending it flipping wildly at them. Shyam was pushed down by Akila in the nick of time. She gestured to Shyam to look up at the sky. Against the wall of earth and falling trees and crumbling mountains, he saw the white flight of Sawa coming for them. He did not know why, but he crushed Akila's hand against his lips. The warmth in her look returned the sentiment and they hopped into the stream.

THE WATER gurgled in her ears and she shook her head to get it out. Then came the howling. The siren-like call rising and falling from the hills that were alive with song the last time she was here. She clapped her hands over her ears and turned back to the river to dive in. Shyam pulled her onwards instead, for the hills behind them were concealed by a mass of insectoids, and they were at the river, fighting to cross the current. The water was teeming with them, and they were almost upon the pair. Akila and Shyam could only run up the hill, but they knew they could never outpace the insectoids on foot. Their only passage out was the river. Shyam stole a glimpse of them before she urged him on, yelling, 'Never look back!'

The heaving hordes and the rocky embankment were a deadly mixture for the insectoids, and the few that made it stumbled up the slope with missing limbs. The hills howled at a higher pitch. The persistent tremors hindered humans and pursuers alike. Instinct steered Akila's keen eyes over her shoulder to the flight of Sawa hurtling towards them. Through the chaos of the blaring hills, there then came the thunder. Ahead of them the horizon lifted with great eruptions of earth along the fissure. A wave of giddiness swept over them when the ground lifted with it. Akila thought she might go deaf from the noise as her ears rang, and her throat burnt with her hot breath. There was no hope now. Behind them came the insectoids and the Sawa, barring their way, and ahead the world was preparing to collapse on them.

'Don't look back,' she hollered. 'Run! Just run!' She sensed the Sawa's approach and then a dozen shadows overtook hers on the tipping ground. The Sawa's revenge would be upon them any second now. She could not sprint uphill any longer with the load of her belly. Every part of her ached and she yearned to break down and slip away into a dream. The Sawa came overhead, and suddenly Akila's eyes grew large. For a vast shape swept in with wings outspread, a form she could hardly fail to recognize. At a familiar signal, Akila dipped and took Shyam with her. They exchanged wide-eyed looks, panting heavily, unable to speak.

Macoco crashed into the ground, smashing half-a-dozen Sawa beneath him, and rolled over. Clawing the soil, he turned and charged down the incline towards the two humans, to keep the stunned Sawa at bay. They had never seen the likes of an alpha Fenek before.

'Quickly,' Macoco hissed to Akila. The insectoids would be upon them soon and he dreaded their paralytic bites. He swept away the first line, while Shyam followed Akila up his hind leg. As the swarm arrived, he beat his great wings, throwing them about under the current, and lifted off. Though he knocked a couple off his arms and legs, a handful clung on. He felt the pinch of their mandibles and the smarting venom before the numbness.

The folding wall of hills began to lean over. He careened low along the crest of a hill, back towards the river that lay untouched beyond the fold. The Sawa came shrieking at him from his flank. Two were on his shoulder and chest, tearing at his velvet skin with their long talons and beaks. He rolled over in the air in agony, trying to pull them off, banking to the side as they came down the leaning wall, and then he made a last second adjustment. The insectoids in the river scrambled to get out of the way.

MACOCO EXPLODED out of the lake and hung in the air for a moment. Akila realized what was coming. 'Oh shit!' She held Shyam as Macoco rolled to his side to spare his riders. The sand cushioned their fall when they were thrown off. Then they heard the clicking. The jungle was already streaming with the infestation. Macoco tore away the few insectoids clinging onto him by their jaws, crushing a couple, and ripped the Sawa on his shoulder in two. He let out a great roar that pierced the tremors and shook the trees with his anguish. The insectoids were coming at them from all sides, but he crept along on his one good arm.

'Get on,' he wheezed. She saw the distress he was in, but she had no choice. Macoco tried to right himself on unsteady legs. He beat his wings as the insectoids drove through the water, the sand and the jungle. Out of the sky, two dozen snarling Feneks set down and fought back the onslaught. A few insectoids climbed on Macoco, but he still beat his wings to lift off the ground. Around him his former murder were being overcome by the relentless horde as he rose along the sheer face of the plateau. His wings beat the air with laboured strokes and she felt his heart pounding against her thighs as they made the desperate ascent. Below them, she saw the insectoids begin to crawl up the rock face. Their only chance now was the stream atop the plateau.

The ground crumpled, tearing apart the jungle. They barely reached the top. Macoco grabbed the edge. That was as far as he could manage. His wings could barely flap. Two insectoids were on his legs, their jaws dug deep into his flesh. Akila and Shyam climbed onto the rock and tried to help him pull himself up, though they were all aware that it was a pointless effort.

'I can't hold on,' he told her plainly.

'I know,' she said, kneeling by his face and embracing him. Shyam stood to the side, a hand on Macoco's scaly finger. Akila spread open her palms against his skin and closed her tear-drenched eyes. Shyam knew she was about to connect and took his hand away so he would not intrude. This was their moment. She hummed against Macoco's face, and then gently sang, 'I love you pussycat, wo oh oh, you and your pussycat tail, you and your pussycat eyes ...' His claws gouged the rock as his body began to slip and he tried to cling only so he might be with her a moment longer. With his might spent and his limbs useless, he could do no more. 'You and your pussycat nose ...' Her voice cut short when he abruptly dropped away. Shyam had to make sure that she would not fall off as she looked over the edge. Macoco gazed up as he fell along the wall. He reached out an arm and stroked the rock face so when he reached the climbing column of insectoids, his body paved a wide path through them. They rained down after him in their droves and hid his final moments from her view.

'We have to go, Akila, where's the stream?' She shook off her despair and looked around, dazed. 'What?'

'The stream. Where is it?'

'Here,' she said, pushing past him.

They were standing on the damp, empty streambed. Her eyes shot along its path to some boulders that had fallen over its mouth at the rock ledge. She looked back at Shyam, distraught, and he could see her strength drain away, along with all hope of escape. There was the sound of thunder and the plateau trembled. They held one another, looking out over the valley crawling with the dark swarm. All bent on slaying Akila, and they would kill themselves trying. In the distance the surface lifted through the clouds. The ground shook violently and the two moved further from the precipice. Shyam touched Akila's belly and looked into her eyes, and he smiled amidst the noise and destruction. She flashed her trademark grin back at him.

But as the quaking intensified, Shyam's smile faded. The plateau might split apart any moment from the stress. And even as he thought it, the face of the grand plateau across the valley exploded in a great maelstrom of flying rock and jets of water. The cliff burst open and first a head, and then shoulders, emerged out of the wash. Sholay stumbled out and stood tall, surveying the landscape being swept by the tidal wave. A handful of titans came out after him from the gushing breach.

The alarm showed on Sholay's face when at last he saw the sheet of insectoids advancing upon the two humans on top. He nudged the titan beside him without a word. Then he charged towards the plateau and the others followed suit over the flooded jungle. They sprang onto the plateau wall, digging in their feet and fingers, and swept away the insectoids as they climbed. But Shyam and Akila knew that it was too late for any rescue, as the vertical wall of jungle and plateaus came down towards them. Giant fingers rose and ploughed through the rock, followed by Sholay's face. 'What are you still doing here?' A familiar voice demanded.

'The rocks there are blocking the stream,' Akila shouted, so he could hear her over the din of a world ending. He saw the problem at the rock ledge. Two other titans reached the top and stood tall, stretching their arms up. Their fingers skimmed the top of the plateau coming down at them while Sholay knocked away the boulders and dug out rock so the stream would flow once more. But even then, it only came out as a trickle. Sholay stood among the titans, bearing the fold as another arrived on top, crawling with insectoids from the climb.

'Go!' Sholay called out to Akila. She hurried with Shyam to the trickling source. There was not enough water to splash through. They scrambled up the smashed rocks. The plateau on the fold coming down on them had reached the titans' heads despite their best efforts. They braced themselves and eased the plateau onto their shoulders. Locking their joints, they pushed up to resist the plunge. Clambering over the rock, Shyam saw Sholay had dug an opening into the cavern. The source of the stream had been collecting within the rock and when Akila saw it, she looked back at Sholay with hope renewed. He smiled and nodded through the strain of holding back the wall.

Akila waved to Sholay as she took Shyam's hand. They leapt into the dark pool and vanished. The titans could let go at last. They sat down on the plateau, exchanging looks of mirth as the wall descended upon them.

11

IT WAS NOT VERY cold, but being naked and wet, they felt the chill against their skin. Shyam helped Akila out of the Olympic-size swimming pool of the Saket Sports Complex. They were still weary and numb with shock. Without a word between them, they found two bathrobes from the changing room lockers and walked out into the late morning. From among the trees two faeries glowed, watching the couple stroll away hand in hand, and one whispered, 'There goes the Beli, and the destroyer of worlds.'

EPILOGUE

IT WAS A HOT afternoon and the boats were coming in on the sandy stretch of Karamana, Kerala. Thomas watched his father and others work the long wooden craft sideways up the beach, their wet bodies leathery and black from years in the sun. The nine-year-old waited for his friends and watched the sea undulate with its hypnotic rhythm. Then he saw something and called out to his father, 'Acha, Acha!' He stood pointing at the sky, jaw hanging open in amazement. His father carried on with the labour of shimmying the boat up the sloping sand. But Thomas kept pointing, unable to look away from the hazy outline moving against the blue sky. Of a titan treading knee-deep through the ocean.